STRAT!

The Charismatic Life & Times of Tony Stratton Smith

by CHRIS GROOM

STRAT!

STRAT!

The Charismatic Life & Times of Tony Stratton Smith

by CHRIS GROOM

WP
WYMER
PUBLISHING
Bedford, England

First published in Great Britain in 2021
by Wymer Publishing
www.wymerpublishing.co.uk
Tel: 01234 326691
Wymer Publishing is a trading name of Wymer (UK) Ltd

Front cover image © Barry Wentzell
Back cover image © Holly Fogg
Cover design: Chris Groom / 1016 Sarpsborg
Typeset by Andy Bishop / 1016 Sarpsborg
Printed by CMP, Dorset, England.

CONTENTS

FOREWORD

It was that chesty chuckle that let you know Strat was around.

He was a big man, proud, passionate and very particular, determined, often defiantly so, with no time for bullshitters. The football journalist who would turn up a little late – which may just have saved his life, when he missed the Munich air disaster that took out most of his beloved Manchester United.

There were always questions swirling around Strat. Had he worked for MI5 in Brazil? Where had his money come from? Was he going bankrupt? How's he going to make that work? How many racehorses? What was that club he just came out of? Where is he?

Although later in life he lived in racehorse country and then moved abroad, when he was part of our lives he never strayed far from Soho, four office locations within yards of Wardour Street, music at the Marquee and later propping up the bars with all their larger than life characters. The painters, the writers, the gangsters – all the Soho royalty.

He loved football, music, long baths, comedy, impassioned booze-fuelled debates, good writers, live music followed by a drink or two at La Chasse, and then there was the racing. "Beware of sideshows" was one of Strat's oft repeated mantras, but he could never resist them himself. Eve and Gail, long-time collaborators in Strat's universe, would cast their eyes skywards as he enthused about his latest project, but once the course was set he would always find a way to make it happen. But something else always had to give, so we would get used to watching our royalties racing in the 3.15 at Kempton.

But we all loved Strat because time and time again he had gone into battle for us, risking whatever he had. When you were his focus, he would move heaven and earth for you. Any obstacles, he would find the way through – and when he believed, it was enough. It didn't have to be popular, it didn't have to be commercial, it just had to be good.

Peter Gabriel, July 2020

PREFACE

One sunny Friday in June 1983, a young graphic designer/paste-up artist decided to try his luck by knocking on the door of The Famous Charisma Label. Armed with a handful of album sleeves from a couple of independent folk labels, he was looking to pick up some extra freelance work in the music industry and, hopefully, as an unabashed fan of the record label, to meet its mysterious guru, Tony Stratton Smith, into the bargain.

He had seen someone at Rocket Records earlier in the day, but their response was rather blunt and, he thought, a little too judgemental. A second meeting at Sonet Records had been cancelled. As he waited for his 5.30pm appointment at the Charisma offices in Wardour Street, he crossed and uncrossed his legs in some trepidation.

To his everlasting disappointment Tony Stratton Smith was 'sadly unavailable'. Had he known better he'd have taken his portfolio downstairs into the bar of the Marquee Club where the genial boss of Charisma was more than likely having his first drink of the evening with his great friend Jack Barrie, the club's manager. Instead, he was taken upstairs to meet the creative director Pete Jenner. Jenner looked over the limited artwork that was spread out before him and seemed unusually accommodating. "Well, I can see you know how to work within a budget," he said, which the graphic designer took as a compliment.

Given the state of Charisma's bank balance at the time, Pete Jenner's comment was singularly appropriate, though the graphics man had no way of knowing this. Of course, this was a record company that had previously used the likes of Hipgnosis for their album sleeves and were now commissioning brilliant contemporary graphic artists like Barney Bubbles. In reality, he stood about as much chance of getting a commission from Charisma as the proverbial cat in hell.

Still, he loved the label and felt it keenly when he read in 1987 that Tony Stratton Smith had died. Tony was a hero of his and although he never did get to meet him he did the next best thing. He researched his life and wrote a book about him.

The graphic designer was me. I hope you enjoy it.

Chris Groom, October 2020

INTRODUCTION

The *Oxford English Dictionary* defines the adjective avuncular as 'like an uncle', but its modern usage communicates a far more eloquent connotation. To describe someone as avuncular is to portray them as amiable, middle-aged or slightly older, invariably male and perhaps slightly overweight. A liking for alcohol and a predisposition towards nostalgia paint a portrait of an avuncular gentleman as the sort of red-nosed chap you might find occupying his own stool at his local pub, or perhaps his cricket club, dressed in flannels and a blazer, opening a sporting anecdote with the words, 'When I was a boy…'. Without a trace of malice towards anyone, he's a harmless, genial old buffer at home with his place in a world where modern life passes him by, casually dismissed as 'Not really for me, old boy'.

As a general rule 'avuncular' is not found in descriptions of businessmen attracted to the music industry. Managers of rock acts are customarily portrayed as ruthless operators concerned first and foremost with accumulating personal wealth, often at the expense of those whose careers they manage. Similarly, those at the heads of record companies are concerned first and foremost with the balance sheet, and this all too often means commercial prospects outweigh cultural merit. These men – and they are almost always men – are exposed as callous scoundrels, the exact opposite of avuncular.

It is all the more surprising, then, that the award for a lifetime's worth of enterprise and achievement in the business of music, presented annually by *Music Week*, the UK's music industry trade paper, is named after a man for whom the word avuncular might very well have been invented. *Music Week* chose not to call their award The Epstein or The Ertegun, The Blackwell or even The Branson – major figures all and each one a friend or associate of the man whose nickname actually graces the trophy. Instead they called it 'The Strat', in honour of that often overlooked maverick of the music business, Tony Stratton Smith.

A quietly spoken, true English eccentric with something of a rebellious streak, Tony Stratton Smith charmed and blustered his way into the music business during the mid-sixties as the manager of a handful of middling acts. A few years later, when the record labels to which his acts were signed stopped playing by what he believed were the rules, he simply went out and formed his own – The Famous Charisma Label – and set about spinning the record industry on its head. Charisma was an independent label like no other, arguably the most eclectic ever, and it is fair to say that without Strat's total belief and unwavering long-term support there would be no Genesis and no Peter Gabriel and no Phil Collins. A long line of artists owe

Tony a similar debt of gratitude, ranging from the *Monty Python's Flying Circus* team to Malcolm McLaren, Lindisfarne to Sir John Betjeman, from Vivian Stanshall to Julian Lennon.

Anyone fortunate enough to gain access into Strat's personal version of the Mad Hatter's tea party might find themselves mingling not just with musicians and record company alumni, but with the great and good (and not so good) from all walks of life. A former sports journalist, Tony numbered Pelé, Jimmy Greaves and Sir Matt Busby among his friends. As an owner of racehorses, he was instrumental in the success of trainer Jenny Pitman. He drank his way around Soho with Brendan Behan, Betjeman, Jeffrey Bernard and Lucian Freud, all the while regularly rubbing shoulders with a myriad of film directors, politicians and members of the Royal household.

The very idea of an award in his name would have amused Tony no end. Whether or not he cared for such prizes no one knows. What he really cared about were the people, the creativity, about imagination, inspiration and risk, and the sheer joy to be had in bringing all these elements together, lighting the Charisma-pink touch paper and standing back, glass in hand, to watch what might happen when the sparks began to fly.

Company profits were never very high on Tony's agenda. The financial side of the business was simply a means to an end that enabled him to fund the music and mayhem that brought him such enjoyment. Strat was never happier than when the artists he had so carefully nurtured were fulfilling their creative dreams. He was never more delighted than when working with the talents of Peter Gabriel, Alan Hull, Clifford T. Ward, Howard Werth and Peter Hammill – and as he wrote back in 1973, "One day, such happiness should be celebrated with a book".

The idea of a written record of his deeds was obviously on Tony Stratton Smith's mind when he wrote those words for a compilation album released by The Famous Charisma Label to celebrate its first four, for the most part largely successful, years in the music industry. Tony was always looking to the future and no doubt imagined that, as a former journalist, he would be the one to document the history of the company in his own memoirs at some stage. Sadly for us all, that never happened. He was either too busy imagining the next big project, or out enjoying the fruits of the last one, to ever sit still and put pen to paper.

Several of those close to him thought he should be encouraged to write his life story. In fact, Charisma Music Publishing's Jon Crawley even tried to help out with new technology. "I used to buy Strat a Christmas present every year. We would go out for lunch regularly. He would come into my office and say, 'Got any meetings this afternoon, dear boy?' – which actually meant let's go for lunch and that would take out the whole afternoon. So off we went to his usual haunts. We went to the pub first, The Ship in Wardour

Street, had a Guinness or two, and then we would head across the road to the St Moritz for lunch. Strat would sit there and tell these magnificent stories, some of them related to music, but many were not. Obviously there were football and racing stories because he was mad about sport, and some about films and so on.

"So I said to him, 'You know Strat, one of these days you really should write all this down – it would make a fantastic book' and he said, 'Yes, I've been meaning to.' That Christmas I thought, I know what I'll do, I'll buy him a Dictaphone because then he doesn't even have to write it down, every time he has a thought, all he's got to do is press record and talk. So I bought him the latest state-of-the art Dictaphone. I went in to see him to give him his Christmas present and he said, 'Oh Jon, that is really kind, thank you dear boy.' Then he asked, 'It's not too complicated, is it?' and I said, 'No, not at all.' Well, dear old Strat managed to lose it the very same day. He left it in the Marquee Club. So he only had it for a matter of hours and that was it, that was his book up in flames."

When I first met Gail Colson, for many years Tony's steady right hand at The Famous Charisma Label, to seek her help with this project, out of the blue she said, "If only he had written his own bloody book!" Gail was absolutely right. Essentially a very private person, Tony had undertaken so many adventures, met so many fascinating people, witnessed so many landmark events, all of which he kept stored away in the deeper recesses of his brain but sadly never put down on paper. All that remains now are memories, many of them half-remembered fragments from late-night conversations, more often than not curious tales of intrigue and scarcely believable mischief told across a tableful of empty wine bottles.

Did he really take tea with the Queen of Denmark? Was he attacked while tracking down Nazi war criminals in South America? Should he have been on the Manchester United plane that crashed on the way home from Belgrade? Was he working for MI5 or MI6? I can't guarantee to have uncovered all the answers or exploded every myth, but why not take a deep breath, pour yourself a large drink and spend some time in the company of a unique man of the world and one of the most influential people ever to grace the music business.

As one of his oldest friends, the equally remarkable and only slightly less avuncular Vivian Stanshall, would later remark, "Tony Stratton Smith was a gentleman and an adventurer. He was a very rare man."

STRAT!

Chapter 1

The Boy Anthony

"He was quite a serious young man, loved classical music and could often be seen conducting his imaginary orchestra."
Patricia Widdows, one of Tony's many cousins

"She was poor, but she was honest, though she came from 'umble stock,
And her honest heart was beating, underneath her tattered frock.

In the rich man's arms she fluttered, like a bird with broken wing,
But he loved her and he left her, and she hasn't got no ring.

It's the same the whole world over, it's the poor what gets the blame,
It's the rich what gets the pleasure, ain't it all a blooming shame?"
Attributed to Robert Weston and Bert Lee

Billy Bennett's 1930 recording of this popular music hall favourite was not lost on Mollie Smith as she packed her overnight bag at 50, Prince of Wales Lane in the Yardley Wood suburb of Birmingham. Her destination was the Royal Hospital in the All Saints district of Wolverhampton, a hostel for unmarried mothers, through whose doors the heavily pregnant Mollie passed in August of 1933.

A few days later, on the 11th, she gave birth to a boy she named Anthony Mills Smith and when she went to register the birth of her son a month later, the name and occupation of the father were conspicuous by their absence on the birth certificate. It was an inauspicious start to an auspicious life.

Anthony's grandfather, Robert James Smith, was born in 1884 in the Yardley Wood area and, according to the census return of 1891, lived in Slade Lane. In 1909 he married Ruby Henrietta Malin at Christ Church, Yardley, and the couple raised six children; two girls, Ruby Maisie Smith, born 1909, and Mollie Smith, born on December 7, 1910, followed by four boys, Robert in 1913, Ernest in 1914, Henry in 1917 and Alfred in 1919. Their mother, Ruby Henrietta was born at Hidcote Bartrim in Gloucestershire and the Malin family moved up to Birmingham around the turn of the century. By

1901 her parents John and Susannah Malin had settled into a property at Old Farm, Dad's Lane, in the nearby parish of Kings Norton, where her father was employed as a cattleman.

By 1911, Robert Smith was gainfully employed as a wood sawyer at the Pioneer Cabinet Works and was living in Church Road, Yardley Wood, with his wife Ruby and their two daughters, Ruby and Mollie, plus his wife's brother Frederick Malin, a farm labourer. The cabinet works closed down in 1933 and within two years the factory had been completely demolished.

Throughout the thirties and forties, Yardley Wood remained very much a rural village community centred on the church and the public house. By 1925, the Smiths had moved into 50 Prince of Wales Lane, while Mollie lived just around the corner in Yardley Wood Road. At the junction where the two roads met stood the large and imposing Warstock Inn and almost next door to the pub on the Yardley Wood Road side was a small pig farm with nearby open fields that served as a playground for local children.

On the Smith side of the family, Tony's younger cousin Patricia was also born at their grandparent's house, 50 Prince of Wales Lane. "There were four houses in a row," remembers Patricia. "Two houses shared an outside toilet and wash house in the backyard."

Her father Henry, Mollie Smith's younger brother, was a regular at the Warstock, an Ansell's brewery house run by Arthur and Cecilia Whittle. During the sixties, another local boy would use an upstairs room at the Warstock as a rehearsal space for his first band. Their blond bass player, Chris 'Ace' Kefford would go on to form The Move with his friend Roy Wood and in their early days they rehearsed at Kefford's grandmother's house, also in Yardley Wood Road.

If Anthony – or Tony as he came to be known – became something of a free spirit in later life, rootless, boundary-less and with a constant urge to move forward, then his childhood locality may have had a small part to play. The ward boundaries around the Birmingham suburbs shifted and overlapped, making it hard to tell exactly where anyone originally grew up – Warstock, Highter's Heath or Yardley Wood. Many locals talk of one particular spot where the boundaries met and how by stepping one pace in any given direction you found yourself in three different districts, one after the other. Birmingham's own little 'Bermuda triangle' was barely a cricket ball's throw from the Smith household.

Prince of Wales Lane was also home to the Elbief factory, which manufactured the metal frames and clasps for ladies handbags and later turned its machinery to making metal photo frames and mirrors. Before the factory was built, the field on which it stood played host to a visiting funfair. Patricia and her sister would be given a few pennies to go along and have a ride on the swingboats. "I believe Elbief made goods with the trade name of Stratton," recalls Patricia. "An aunt told me that this is why Tony later adopted the name Stratton – but it may be coincidental."

When his mother brought Tony back home from the hospital, they returned to an already crowded house. Mollie Smith had already given birth to a daughter, now three-year-old June Brenda Smith, born on November 2, 1929. According to her birth certificate, her place of birth was 77 Dudley Road, an address used to avoid the embarrassment of stating that this was actually the infirmary of the Birmingham Union Workhouse. The old workhouse site would later become the Dudley Road Hospital.

When she arrived home with June, 19-year-old Mollie was not only unmarried, but unemployed and still living with her parents at 50 Prince of Wales Lane. When the baby Anthony arrived, the social stigma of twice becoming an unmarried mother in thirties Birmingham was no doubt the reason why she reluctantly handed over her son to another member of the family or temporarily placed him in care. As so often occurred in those times, the extended family stepped in to help with childcare and, for a while, both June and Anthony lived with their grandparents at their busy and bustling home. Cousin Patricia remembers that, "Nan's house always seemed to be full of people when I was young."

Patricia Smith (now Widdows) was one of Tony's many cousins and she has fond memories of the Smith family growing up in Yardley Wood. "Mollie was a very beautiful lady who lived just around the corner. She never disclosed who Tony's father was, although I believe he desperately tried to find out in later years, as far as I know without success."

It was rumoured among the Smith family that Tony's biological father was a Birmingham surgeon, but this is part conjecture, although in one interview Tony later hinted that he was brought up by his mother "after the death of his father, a Warwickshire doctor". In 1945, Mollie married a man named Douglas Hughes and, according to his cousin Margaret, Anthony got on reasonably well with his stepfather. For a while, Mollie, Douglas, June and young Anthony all lived together in Yardley Wood Cottage at 1156 Yardley Wood Road.

Day to day life cannot have been easy for the residents of Yardley Wood. Anthony was born barely 15 years after the end of the First World War and Britain was still recovering from the enormous loss of men and resources suffered during the conflict. But if money was always tight for Mollie and her children, they were by no means alone – the rest of the Smith clan, as well as her friends and neighbours, were all tightening their belts. Tony's aunt Kathleen, who married into the Smith family, remembers them all having "not a ha'penny to rub together".

"Tony's formative years are a rather grey area," says Patricia. "As far as I know he was in some sort of care, only appearing back in to the family at about 12 years old. He was quite a serious young man, loved classical music and could often be seen conducting his imaginary orchestra. My sister can remember him taking her to the local cinema to see *Old Mother Riley* so he definitely had a humorous side – as have most of the Smith family. They were always a close-knit unit, my grandmother Ruby was a real star and was loved by everyone – as I recall, they were a rather colourful family."

That appreciation of classical music probably came from spending time at his grandmother's house, not that there was much of an alternative, musically speaking, in the years following the end of the war. Later in life Tony recalled one particular night when he stood outside a sold-out Birmingham Town Hall, straining to catch the sound of Adrian Boult conducting the orchestra within. "When I was a kid, I used to save my pennies to get into concert halls to hear Beethoven and that kind of music," he would recall. "These concerts were the escapism of my generation. In the early post-war there was no sort of pop music – it was all standard ballads, dirge-like melodies."

Tony attended Yardley Wood Junior and Infants school, a two-storey meeting house that was used as a school during the week and as a chapel every Sunday. In later interviews, he would describe his formative years as "not especially enjoyable or stimulating". Patricia's observation that he seemed to disappear for a while could have been due to a period of ill-health. Tony spent a couple of years in hospital due to a calcium deficiency and, like many children in the Birmingham suburbs, was evacuated during the Second World War. Birmingham suffered badly during the blitz. Between August 1940 and April 1943 the city and surrounding area was subject to heavy bombing, the Luftwaffe targeting local factories essential to the war effort; Castle Bromwich and Longbridge specialised in aircraft manufacturing, while Solihull churned out aero engines and many local factories supplied shell casings and small arms.

The Birmingham suburbs continued to develop rapidly throughout the first half of the 20th century, with many more houses, schools and shops springing up to accommodate a growing population. Between 1934 and 1937 the nearby district of Shirley had seen the opening of a Roman Catholic church, an Odeon Cinema, a lido and a new public library. Tony would have made good use of all those amenities and, crucially, from the mid-19th century until 1954, Shirley also had a thriving racecourse, situated roughly where Shirley Golf Club is today, giving Tony easy access to the world of flat racing that would later become a life-long passion.

As a boy, Tony Smith arranged football matches with the local farmer's son and in the summer the boys all played cricket until the sun set. "I remember how awful it was when the light faded," Tony later told Richard Yallop of *The Guardian*. "We would play for hours and hours and when it faded it was gloom. I was a great competitor, but my enthusiasm for it was always appreciably ahead of my skills."

One skill he did attain, however, was writing. To this end he enrolled at Sparkhill Commercial School. "Even at the age of 11 or 12, I wanted to be a journalist, and as Sparkhill taught shorthand and typing, that was where I went," he said. He was 14 when he arrived at Sparkhill for a two-year course.

Student life suited Tony. Documented through his end of term reports, he made the best of it, never finishing out of the top ten in a class of 32 and excelling in English and shorthand. He was obviously focused on his chosen career from the very beginning, working hard in the subjects he felt would benefit a journalist and paying less attention to others – his marks were always well down in maths and book-keeping. By December 1947, he finished top of his form.

During his second year at the school, Tony's shorthand teacher Kathleen R. Dixon also became his form mistress and while his overall marks continued to be very good, other distractions were becoming evident. His report at the end of July 1948 showed he had been absent four times and received six detentions, presumably for his reluctance to attend the book-keeping class, where he scored zero in his term mark. He dropped to seventh in the form, but he scored 97% in Miss Dixon's shorthand class, receiving a certificate for 80 words per minute. In her position as his form mistress, she wrote: "Anthony is very intelligent and progress this term is very satisfactory. I would, however, like him to endeavour to be more steady and reliable in his general behaviour."

Throughout his final term, Tony continued to make progress in those subjects he needed, generally at the expense of book-keeping and, somewhat surprisingly, in French language, which also appears to have been quite low on his list of priorities. Tony seemed to know that even if his overall term mark was low, he could invariably pull out a better result in the final exam. In book-keeping a poor 25% mark over the term magically turned into a very respectable 79% in his exam. Elsewhere, he scored an 83% in English, the same percentage for his typewriting exam, and a massive 97% exam mark in shorthand, which was by now certified at 90 words per minute. Summing up his final term at Sparkhill, Kathleen Dixon remarked: "Anthony is a very intelligent boy and has made very good progress throughout the term. He is keen and interested in all he does, and should do well in a business career." Armed with a briefcase full of highly commendable shorthand and typing certificates, at the tender age of 16 and a bit, he set out on the next part of his journey.

* * *

On leaving Sparkhill, Tony turned down two promising job opportunities, the first with Jack Cotton's property company, the second in articles with a respected firm of architects. Instead he opted for the less glamorous position of "thirty shillings a week copy boy and tea-maker in chief" with the *Evening Despatch*, a now-defunct Birmingham newspaper – "much against my mother's wishes", as he later told the local press. He never regretted his decision to join 'the print' and his first real break came on the *Birmingham Gazette*, where he was employed in the sports department as a racing sub-editor.

"I had great fun working there," he recalled. "I used to nip out and fetch sports editor Jack Littlewood's jellied eels. It suited me really, because I was into cricket – cricket, it still warms me. During the forties and fifties, it was almost a way of life for me." The teenage reporter would take his flask of tea and a pack of sandwiches and sit for hours watching county cricket matches in the sun, enjoying every minute.

When Tony joined the *Birmingham Gazette*, he was not simply joining any old local newspaper but one of the most established and popular regional titles in Britain. Originally founded in 1741 by Thomas Aris, a London stationer who had moved North the previous year, for much of its life the paper was known as *Aris's Birmingham Gazette*, a weekly publication. It quickly absorbed its main local rival, the *Warwick and Staffordshire Gazette*, to become the only newspaper in the town, and changed its name to the *Birmingham Daily Gazette* in 1862 when, as the name suggests, it began to produce its broadsheet on a daily basis. Not too long afterwards it moved to offices in a glorious new home at 160–178 Corporation Street, a striking example of Victorian terracotta architecture, largely the work of the celebrated Scottish-born architect W. H. Ward. For Tony, dressed in his smart new two-piece suit with a pair of sharpened pencils in his top pocket, walking through the huge wide-arched doorway of this imposing Victorian gothic temple for his first day at work must have seemed like entering a magical new world.

Tony never had trouble making new friends, but he really hit it off with George and Jim Thompson, a pair of cricket-mad twins he met during his days as a cub reporter. The Thompson family became firm friends and would remain a grounding connection to his West Midland roots for many years to come. They met for the first time in July 1950 on a coach returning to Birmingham after a minor county's match between Warwickshire and Northamptonshire. "Tony was only 17 years old and still studying shorthand at night school while working as a trainee sports writer/coffee boy with a local newspaper," says George. "We helped him write his match report as this was his first professional cricket match. It was the beginning of a long lasting friendship, of 37 years with unforgettable memories."

Although to the sports-reading public he was known by two pseudonyms, by the early fifties Tony had become reasonably well known to readers of the *Birmingham Sports Argus* and *Gazette*. Most local newspapers published a sports special every Saturday evening, and to differentiate from the regular newspaper they were printed on coloured stock, usually pink or light green. Allied to the *Birmingham Gazette*, the *Sports Argus* was a 'pink-un', and for a long time it was the biggest selling Saturday sports paper in the country. For the *Argus,* Tony covered the Birmingham League and some minor county cricket matches during the summer months under the pseudonym of 'Fieldmouse'. His horse racing coverage, in which he handed out racing tips under the name of 'Fullerton', ran in the *Birmingham Gazette* itself.

"He became a regular and popular visitor to my mother and father's pub The Eagle and Tun in New Canal Street," adds George Thompson. "It was only a stone's throw away from the offices of the Birmingham newspapers. He wasn't quite so popular when my father and his customers found out that this 'Fullerton', who they had been backing and losing money on, was in fact the same confident, young bloke who, at this time in his life, had no real cricket or racing experience, was still only 18 years old and to them was 'Fieldmouse' the young cricket expert."

No one comes into a new job fully formed, and Tony was still listening to and learning from the more experienced journalists around him. At the *Birmingham Gazette*, Dennis Harris was chief cricket correspondent, while the more substantial football coverage was handled by Charles Harrold, Peter Morris, sports editor Jack Littlewood and George Enstone. In particular, Tony held Charles Harrold in high esteem and, a few years later, included him in a list of the journalists he most admired. Harrold later moved on to write for the *Daily Mail*.

By this time Tony had left home, moving out of the family house to live at Moseley with George Thompson's twin brother Jim. "They liked to visit the Moseley Cricket Club and Birmingham Rugby Club, professionally and socially," says George. "The Saturday night dances were quite famous at the rugby club in those days."

Tony's journalistic ambitions and newfound social life were put on hold for two years when he was called up for his National Service. For 15 years after the end of the Second World War, every able-bodied young man over the age of 17 was required to serve his country in one of the armed forces. On the last day of November 1951, Tony swapped his newsdesk suit for the blue serge uniform of the Royal Air Force. On the first day of enlistment, his aptitude tests immediately promoted him from aircraftsman second class (AC2) to aircraftsman first class (AC1). Seven days later, he and his fellow conscripts were at the school of recruit training and in February 1952 he was posted to RAF Henlow in Shefford, Bedfordshire.

After a further month's training, no doubt including plenty of square-bashing, Tony was transferred to the RAF Staff College at Andover in Hampshire, designed to provide training for selected officers for work at the Air Ministry or Group headquarters. For the final nine months of Tony's time there, the college commandant was Walter G. Cheshire, a former Chief Intelligence Officer, who had served with Bomber Command during the war.

Promoted to Leading Aircraftsman in June 1952, Tony was posted to the newly named RAF Pucklechurch in Bristol to join No. 62 Group Combined Reserve Centre. A barrage balloon centre since 1939, it was noted that Pucklechurch "never resounded with the roar of Merlins, but instead there was the quiet hiss of gas, and the sewing of repairs to balloon fabric". A further promotion came in December and Senior Aircraftsman Anthony Mills Smith (3135291) duly served out his remaining year of National Service at No. 62 G.C.R.C. He was discharged on December 24, 1953. Compulsory National Service was gradually phased out between 1957 and December 1960.

On completion of his National Service, Tony was required to fill in form 4304, giving details of his employer and employment. Under the National Service Acts he was still liable to be called up for part-time service as a reservist. The form lists his employer as the Birmingham Gazette and Despatch Limited, Gazette Buildings, Corporation Street, Birmingham. Tony's occupation: journalist, sports department, performing the duties of 'general sports reporting and sub-editing'. The form also shows that he was studying for additional qualifications, the N.A.C. General Proficiency Certificate in Advanced English, Government, Essential Law and Russian language, an odd choice in the light of his failure at French.

Another official duty that Tony performed during 1953 was giving away his sister June at her marriage to Mr Albert Michael Norris. The wedding snaps show 20-year-old Tony proudly escorting June through the lychgate outside Yardley Wood Church. A local lad, Mike Norris had known his bride since they both attended Yardley Wood school together and the pair remained happily married until June's death in 2015.

With his RAF uniform handed back to the quartermaster, Tony pulled his best suit out of the wardrobe and walked right back into 'civvy street' or, to be more precise, the newspaper offices in Corporation Street. Back at the *Birmingham Gazette* in January of 1954, Tony found himself writing alongside a team of exceptional journalists, all of whom would move on to work for the national press. A glance at the sporting back pages during the mid-fifties shows reports and articles from the typewriters of Alan Ridgill, Peter Ingall and Rex Bellamy, as well as our Tony. Ridgill eventually became Northern sports editor at the *Daily Mirror*, Ingall went on to cover football for the *Daily Mirror*, while Rex Bellamy became a leading tennis correspondent, most notably with *The Times*.

It would not be long before Anthony Mills Smith joined his old colleagues in the bigger arena of national print journalism.

STRAT!

Chapter 2

The Sportswriter

"He once showed me his passport, in the days when they were stamped.
It was unbelievable, I think he'd been to every country on Earth.
It was like a child's colouring book."

Alan Hull, Lindisfarne singer-songwriter

Fleet Street beckoned when Tony was just 21. Although he was perfectly happy in local journalism and indifferent about moving to London, his attitude changed when the *News Chronicle* came calling. They'd been monitoring his Birmingham columns and liked his quirky writing style. "They said they wanted me, and wanted my writing," he said, "so I joined. But they didn't allow me to write a word for about a year."

By the end of February 1955, Tony had left the *Gazette* and was heading to Manchester to join the northern offices of the *News Chronicle*, the move eventually leading him south to Fleet Street. "It was only when I came to join the old *News Chronicle*, that I realised I could just possibly be the master of my own destiny."

In the pursuit of controlling his own destiny, Tony left behind all traces of his Brummie accent, a conscious decision to disguise his upbringing. Whether interviewing a South American footballer with only a basic grasp of English, or telephoning late-night copy down a crackly line, Tony decided a cultivated BBC home counties accent would be an asset. By neutralising his background, he felt able to adapt to any given situation, to deal with anyone on their own terms, at their own level. Prince or pauper, Tony treated everyone as an equal and although the move led to a further degree of separation from his family, his cousin Patricia voiced the general family opinion in saying that "when Tony moved to London to pursue his career in journalism, he became our hero".

The *News Chronicle* was a relatively young paper. Launched in 1930 with the merger of the *Daily News* and the *Daily Chronicle*, it was owned by the Cadbury family. Its politics were Liberal but with the party's decline and mounting debts, Laurence Cadbury was forced to sell it to Associated Newspapers, owners of the *Daily Mail*. Associated gave the *Chronicle* two years to improve sales before eventually closing it down in 1960.

But this was in the future in 1955 when Tony arrived and found himself working alongside the great Charles Buchan. A former professional footballer with Sunderland and Arsenal, Buchan had been a journalist since he retired, helped to form the Football Writers' Association and had edited his own magazine, the popular *Charles Buchan's Football Monthly*, since 1951.

Other sports writers around the newsroom included Peter Campling, Crawford White, Captain Heath, John Camkin and Frank Taylor, and joining around the same time was cricket specialist John Arlott. By March, Tony's early previews and match reports were starting to appear in the paper, games at Birmingham, Notts County and Arsenal. Writing under the name Anthony Smith, he had yet to produce the more flamboyant writing style that would become his trademark, but his fondness for an off-beat story made the paper in March when Birmingham, preparing for an FA Cup tie with Manchester City, hit a problem with the colour of their strip. "Both clubs normally play in blue shirts," wrote Tony, "and it was when the strip changes were being discussed that the trouble began – they found that their second strips were an identical red." A toss of the coin decided that City would play in claret and Birmingham in white – so Birmingham manager Arthur White was forced to telephone nearby West Bromwich Albion and Derby County in order to borrow a white strip for the cup tie.

Barely a year before joining the *Chronicle*, Tony had moved across Manchester to write for the northern edition of the *Daily Sketch*, where he would eventually become the youngest sports editor in the paper's history. It was during his time on the *Sketch* that he changed his name to Stratton Smith, ostensibly to avoid confusion with another journalist. "They already had another sports writer called Tony Stevens and the editor thought that a Tony Smith as well would be too much," he said. Some believe that Tony plucked the name Stratton from a branch of the family tree in Worcestershire, although his cousin Patricia disagrees. A keen genealogist, she sees no obvious family connection. Others believe it may have come from the Birmingham company, Stratton Limited, makers of knitting needles, radio receivers and men's jewellery. Either way, opting to add Stratton to his name can't be a mere coincidence.

From that moment onwards he became Tony Stratton Smith, often simply using the by-line 'Stratton Smith' for his newspaper reports. The new name gave him several options; Stratton could became an alternative Christian name – in fact several people still refer to him as 'Stratton' rather than Tony and he would often sign letters and documents as Stratton Smith. Others took it to be a hyphenated surname, suggesting an air of sophistication and breeding that Tony lacked but undoubtedly used to his advantage when the need arose. It also led to a variety of nicknames, in particular 'Stratters' and 'Strat', most commonly used in later years by his associates in the music business.

* * *

Moving to the *Daily Sketch* in 1956, the newly styled Tony Stratton Smith stepped directly into the shoes of the highly-respected S.C. Griffith, a former Sussex wicket keeper and county captain who made his England Test match debut as a makeshift opening batsman, notching up a hard fought 140 against the West Indies in Trinidad in 1948. A man of great charm and tact, he became secretary of the MCC, helping to preserve the traditions of that most British of institutions during a time of huge changes in the game.

One of Tony's first pieces for the *Sketch* sports desk commented on an incident during the MCC's 'A' team in Peshawar, Pakistan, in which alleged poor umpiring led to a bucket of water being thrown over a local umpire. Calling for the introduction of neutral umpires, Tony wrote: "Don't pillory these lads to sentiment. Their lesson has been learned, their apologies made. LET'S STOP YELLING FOR THEIR BLOOD." It was an early example of his use of capitals to make a point.

Tony soon became a regular fixture on the *Sketch*'s back pages. In his mind, football – 'the beautiful game' – needed to be written about in the same way as music and theatre, poetry or literature. So it was that he connected the Tottenham Hotspur captain Danny Blanchflower with the American novelist F. Scott Fitzgerald, and used a quote from the Irish poet W. B. Yeats to introduce a football annual for boys. In his introduction to the *International Football Book No 4*, which he edited in 1962, Tony wrote: "'Culture does not consist in acquiring opinions, but in getting rid of them.' I have a fancy for this saying of Yeats, and football culture does not escape it. English club football, in its organisation and thinking, has found this last two years that it had the strength to reject a great deal which was holding it back."

In similar fashion, while serialising The Spurs Story for the *Daily Express* in April 1961, Tony wrote about Danny Blanchflower: "His attachment at the moment is to the writing of Scott Fitzgerald, the brilliant American who christened the American 'twenties the 'Jazz Age' and only briefly survived the disenchantment of the 'thirties and the depression. This is, perhaps an insight into Blanchflower, and the occasional pain caused him for being what he is – a dreamer. Fitzgerald knew well the power, danger and fatal undertow of illusions – and Blanchflower knows them too."

Football was beginning to overtake cricket in his sporting affections, but Tony was still only too happy to write about his first love, as he did brilliantly during the celebrated Ashes series in 1956. The touring Australian team arrived on April 24 and the next day they took time out from the practice nets to go horse racing on Epsom Downs. Tony tagged along to see if their betting was as keen as their cricket, noting that the off-duty Aussies won only a few shillings on the very last race, thanks mainly to backing their own man, the Australian jockey Scobie Breasley, who came in first on the 9-4 shot Sunningdale.

Weather-wise, the summer of 1956 was almost a complete washout and the first Test didn't get under way until June 7. In his headline for the first match of the series, Tony predicted: "It's our Test, if Lock and Laker get at 'em quickly", and he was proved right. Famously, in the crucial fourth Test, our off spinner Jim Laker virtually bowled out the Aussies on his own, taking 19 out of a possible 20 Australian wickets in the one Test match, a record unlikely to be equalled, let alone beaten. England went on to win the series 2-1, with two matches drawn, and successfully retained The Ashes.

Retaining a keen sense of humour, Tony was not averse to the occasional caustic comment in his cricket column. When the England selectors named Cyril Washbrook, a 41-year-old batsman, in their squad for the Third Test, Stratton Smith wrote: "Blimey, they've named a chaperon…!" Reporting for the *Daily Sketch*, on July 9, he continued: "Washbrook's selection was wrong – his last Test innings in England was against the West Indies six years ago. I wonder if the Aussies have a similar joke up their sleeves? Perhaps they'll invite Sir Donald Bradman to play…"

Back home in Birmingham, George and Jim Thompson were also keenly following the Test series, and to their lasting delight Tony arranged for the Australian team to visit their house for an evening of socialising, with some girls rounded up from a local hairdressing salon. Among the other guests was Sir Leonard Hutton, the former England captain, and Denis Howell, the Minister of Sport. At 11 o'clock there was a knock on the door.

"It was two local policemen who had been sent to close the party down because of the noise and music," says George. "They asked who was in charge and Stratton said that he was, but he would go and get Sir Denis Howell (Minister for Sport) who was with Sir Leonard Hutton and Richie Benaud, the future captain of the Australian cricket team. The two stunned policemen simply said, 'Well, please try to keep the noise down' and then walked quietly away."

Work at the *Daily Sketch* continued apace into 1957 with Tony sharing the football pages alongside Richard Walton, Tony Stevens and James McDermott. Aside from covering the odd First Division match and April's England versus Scotland International, for Tony the first half of 1957 was all about Manchester United and by mid-March, he was avidly following the FA Cup build-up, reporting on United's semi-final win over Birmingham. This game introduced an exciting new talent to the Busby Babes line-up – Bobby Charlton, a young inside-left. Tony wrote: "Private Bobby Charlton has fallen in on soccer's big parade. Slim, brisk, a giant success in this, his first cup game for Manchester United, he is within saluting distance of an

England uniform. I spotted three England selectors along with national team manager Walter Winterbottom, watching United's smooth humiliation of once-so-strong Birmingham on Sheffield Wednesday's ground."

Two days later, United lost what looked to be a relatively simple league match to Bolton Wanderers and when the doubters started to raise their collective voice, Tony leapt to the defence of his beloved Babes. "Boys, lay off!" he wrote in the *Sketch*. "Because Matt Busby's laughing at you and anyone with a tenth of Matt's human understanding is having a giggle, also." He pointed out that every great team needs the occasional wake-up call, and continued, "Success for the Busby Babes isn't yet complete. They're still on a golden path of self-discovery. They've still to know, themselves, just how good they are!"

These were exciting times for the red half of Manchester. With a place in the FA Cup final assured, United were also through to the semi-final of the European Cup and, in April, Tony flew to Spain with the team to cover the first leg against Real Madrid which the home side won comfortably by three goals to one. He also reported on the return leg in Manchester where a 2-2 draw meant Real went through on aggregate, and on the dramatic FA final when United went down 2-1 against Aston Villa after their goalkeeper Ray Wood was stretchered off six minutes into the game.

This single moment, wrote Tony, "killed a great final", adding, "This was madness. The most diabolical, destroying foul I've seen in any Cup Final. This was Wembley drunkenness, the unseeing accident of an over-stiff mixture of atmosphere and occasion. Who didn't feel a rushing moistness to see United's chance of the wonderful League and Cup double they so deserved, eased out on a stretcher, with goalkeeper Ray Wood chillingly still, his face broken and bloody." With no substitutes allowed in those days, midfielder Jackie Blanchflower took over in goal and United effectively held out with ten men until late in the game, when McParland scored Villa's winner.

The following summer Tony reported on the Test series against West Indies in which Yorkshire fast bowler Fred Trueman earned his colours. A colourful character, Trueman did not always endear himself to the cricket establishment, and when he was dropped from a trip to South Africa in 1956 Tony was quick to defend him. "This latest smear on Trueman is unbearable," he argued in the pages of the *Sketch*. "The Yorkshire lad is being pilloried by the cricket overlords, as a permanent example to those who might be tempted to be themselves on tour."

* * *

Sometime between 1956 and 1957, Tony moved down to London, settling into a flat in Putney. Off-duty from his day-job on the sports desk, he could occasionally be found among the crowd that crammed into the dingy basement at 59 Old Compton Street in Soho for coffee, cola and skiffle, a form of music imported from America that lent itself to DIY interpretations by English aficionados. This in turn would lead to their adoption of American rock'n'roll but as a lover of classical music, Tony was not immediately taken with this new fad.

The 2i's was owned by two wrestlers, Australian Paul Lincoln and his partner Ray Hunter, and began life as a hangout for sportsmen, which is what brought Tony through its doors in the first place. "The only experience I had with rock'n'roll, and you couldn't really call it rock'n'roll, was Cliff Richard, Tommy Steele and the old 2i's in Soho, back in the fifties," he later told Michael Wale. "I'll never forget that sweaty, heaving little sewer. They were all Australian cricketers and rugby players, a coffee bar for the sports crowd, a Jack Dempsey's in Soho kind of thing. It didn't work out that way, though, because the cellar was rented out by someone who started putting these bands in, Lonnie Donegan, Tommy Steele, Cliff Richard and a group called The Vipers, with a singer/guitarist called Wally Whyton and Lionel Bart sometimes playing washboard."

Widely acknowledged as the birthplace of British rock'n'roll, the 2i's was not an immediate success, but an impromptu visit from The Vipers Skiffle Group and the hordes of teenagers who accompanied them turned the tide. Songwriter Lionel Bart not only sat in on washboard, but was responsible for painting the already dark cellar walls an even darker shade of black; future record producer Mickie Most could also be found working the cola machine.

"I looked around and I just couldn't believe it," recalled Tony. "My experience had been in sports – out in the wide open spaces – but two or three hundred people compressed themselves in this awful cellar, paying for the privilege of sitting in this sweat-box for three hours. Well, some sort of inaudible sound was coming from the back wall... that's what it seemed like to me."

Aside from a passing interest in The Everly Brothers, the musical landscape of the late fifties left Tony slightly cold. But it was on his way home from the 2i's, on the last train home to his digs in Lytton Grove, Putney, that he came up with his first grand scheme.

* * *

Aware that he would be reporting on the 1958 FIFA World Cup in Sweden that summer, Tony approached Ernest Hecht at Souvenir Press with a view to writing a book about it. "Tony was still at the *Daily Sketch*," recalls Hecht.

"He came to see me in our office in Charlotte Street saying we should do a book on the World Cup in Sweden, a sort of day by day diary. And I said to Tony, that's not a very good idea, it won't work, but why don't we think about doing a book on International Football after the World Cup, and so that's what we did, that's how the *International Football Book Number 1* started."

The series would continue for 35 years. "In those days you couldn't give away material on international football, it was easier to sell a book on Scunthorpe United," says Hecht, laughing. "The first three numbers were quite hard going, but of course it peaked in 1966 – I think we sold something like 75,000 that year. The average before that was 5,000/10,000/15,000 sort of thing. It continued to sell well, though obviously never at the same level as '66, but it always maintained a goodly number because it was the only book of its kind."

The *International Football Book* became a long-running and much-loved publication. Attending the 1958 World Cup himself, Hecht was able to watch Tony's working methods at first hand, although he wasn't always overly impressed by the young journalist. Telephoning a report back from a noisy foreign football stadium was never an easy task at the best of times and Hecht remembers how Tony cut the line dead when others wanted to use it, which hardly endeared him to his peers. But he was not alone in making the occasional mess of it. Brian Scovell, a colleague at the *Daily Sketch*, once sent his match report to the wrong newspaper.

In 1959 Tony edited his first of these football annuals for Souvenir Press, *The International Football Book for Boys* – they would drop the 'for Boys' on subsequent editions – and his introductory paragraphs took the theme of having 'something to say'. Stratton Smith wrote: "From beginning to end it has been fun planning this first *International Football Book*. Fun working with so many people who have something to say, often with an urgency that commands respect, whether or not you and I agree with what is said. 'Something to Say' could almost have been the title of this book. My own enthusiasm for the greatest of all ball games is catholic. No matter 'who' or 'where', if there is a game of soccer I feel compelled to see it."

He went on to highlight the rise of World Soccer and the International game, noting that FIFA currently had 89 countries to its membership, seven more than the United Nations. Tony praised the contributors, from players like Tom Finney, John Charles and Jimmy Delaney, to journalist colleagues Geoffrey Green and David Jack, and stated that, "Every year, football re-creates itself. Events of a few months ago become history. But we have little mind for history in football, because it is a game that is always reaching for tomorrow. Today is never perfect. Here is the marching spirit of a very modern game, and a reason why it catches and clasps the interest of so many millions of people."

When Tony commented that the 'events of a few months ago become history', the vivid memories of one tragic event from the previous year were still very much in his thoughts. Football journalism is not generally known to be a dangerous occupation, but on one viciously cold night in 1958 Tony narrowly escaped involvement in the Munich air disaster, when divine intervention or a simple twist of fate saw him cover a World Cup qualifying match in Wales instead of travelling with Manchester United on their fateful trip to Yugoslavia.

Although he was supposed to appear impartial, Tony was an unashamed admirer of the Busby Babes, in particular the inroads that Matt Busby's team were making into European football. The Babes had successfully fought their way into the quarter finals of the European Cup and had a two-leg match against Red Star Belgrade coming up.

In later years, Tony would tell people that he had actually been chosen to cover the United game against Belgrade, but that fate intervened and he missed the flight. Genesis drummer Phil Collins is one of many who remembers Tony saying that he overslept and missed the plane going out – and in those days, getting on the next flight simply wasn't an option as international connections to Eastern Europe were few and far between. Early on the Monday morning of February 3 the Manchester United party drove to Manchester's Ringway Airport to catch their charter flight to Belgrade. It was a cold and foggy morning and Tony, a notoriously late riser, did not reach the airport in time. As it turned out, the flight was delayed because one of the players had lost his passport but, even so, the British European Airways plane eventually took off without a reporter from the *Daily Sketch* onboard and arrived six hours later in Belgrade, via a stop to refuel in Munich. Above the airport in Belgrade they hit low cloud, poor visibility and snow and it was only after circling a few times that the pilot was able to land safely, the only aircraft that managed to land in Belgrade that day.

Meanwhile, an embarrassed Tony was given another assignment; a shorter trip to Cardiff's Ninian Park to cover Wales versus Israel in a World Cup qualifying match. The following day the *Sketch* ran Tony's glowing review of this game and, tellingly, on the same page a review of Manchester United's draw against Red Star Belgrade, syndicated from Reuters news agency. When Tony failed to take his seat on the plane, no one from the Sketch had been able to replace him at the last minute and though others in the sports department would have given Tony a hard time for his unprofessionalism, that was all too soon forgotten as the terrible events unfolded over the next 24 hours.

On Wednesday, February 5, Manchester United made their way home from Yugoslavia, stopping in Munich to refuel in the early hours of the following morning. The BEA 'Elizabethan' made two attempts to take off, but failed each time due to a boost problem in the port engine. Captain James Thain decided not to abandon the onward journey and stay in Munich overnight, and instead made a third attempt at taking off, but by now snow had caused a layer of slush to form at the end of the runway. The plane hit the slush and slowed dramatically. Unable to lift itself into the air, it overshot the runway, crashing through the perimeter fence and tearing off the port wing on a nearby building. The plane careered into a house and burst into flames. Of the 44 people on board, 20 died in the crash and three more died later in hospital. The Busby Babes lost eight players and three members of the backroom staff. The other fatalities included eight journalists, two supporters and two members of the flight crew.

On the morning of Friday, February 7, the *Daily Sketch* headline announced "WORLD'S NUMBER 1 TEAM IN DISASTER. MANCHESTER UNITED PLAYERS DIE IN AIR CRASH. 26 DEAD." At that stage only three players were known to have survived – Harry Gregg, Bobby Charlton and Bill Foulkes.

The following day's paper carried a major piece by Stratton Smith, headed 'United Will Rise Again'. "Old Trafford today is still and silent," he wrote. "Since yesterday's tragedy it has been the heart of the city – and, like the city, it is hushed with a terrible grief. Hundreds of cables are heaped unopened in the office. A slight, boyish 25-year old wearing a Manchester United blazer is moving swiftly to deal with a dozen dreadful duties. Les Olive is the assistant secretary and until the end of last season the reserve team goalkeeper." He concluded his piece by writing: "Today it is the agony of a nation. Tomorrow, Manchester United will rise again – and with all our hearts we wish it. I loved them all, and I was one among millions. And that love is the future strength of Manchester United."

Tony was soon on his way to Germany, flying out to report first hand from the hospital in Munich. His emotional article on Monday, February 10, began on a personal note: "A million pounds couldn't have taken the place of the smile of recognition Matt Busby gave me tonight, along with a weak wave of the hand. And nothing has thrilled me in years like these words from pretty Dr Charlotte Lehmann, who is ever at his side – I think Mr Busby, touch wood, has passed his crisis." Tony went on to note that Matt had passed the destiny of the club on to Jimmy Murphy, at least for the time being, but when Busby asked Murphy how the rest of the team were, it became apparent that he still hadn't been told. "Murphy struggled for comforting words," wrote Tony, "for neither Matt, nor sports writer Frank Taylor, who lies beside him, are aware of the extent of the tragedy."

Of course, Tony hadn't been the only man to cheat death by covering an alternative football match. Matt Busby's right-hand man and Manchester

United assistant manager Jimmy Murphy was also the manager of the Welsh national team, and he was also at Ninian Park to see Wales beat Israel. Both hugely important games, Murphy had offered to forego his commitment to his country in favour of his club side, but Busby told him that his duty was to Wales on that occasion. On the fateful day, Murphy's place on the plane had been taken by chief coach Bert Whalley, who took the seat next to Busby and was killed instantly in the crash.

A memorial service for the players was held at St Martin-in-the-Fields, London, on February 17, and about a week later a separate memorial to the fallen journalists was held before a packed congregation at St Brides Church in Fleet Street. The readings were given by the England team manager Walter Winterbottom and Geoffrey Green, senior football correspondent with *The Times*, who had also missed the Munich flight in order to cover the Wales/Israel game. Eerily, given the weather conditions that caused the crash, as Green began to address his fellow writers, he glanced up at the tall church windows to see snow starting to fall outside.

The Munich air crash had a profound impact on Tony in more ways than one. Although troubled by the loss of life to players and journalists, he knew he could so easily have been on that flight himself and he felt a sense of guilt that perhaps one of the journalists had died in his place. His friend, Simon G. White, recalls that Tony was shaken to the core when the widow of one of the sports writers blamed him directly for the death of her husband and it was this, White believes, that was directly responsible for Tony leaving the *Daily Sketch*, and subsequently the *Daily Express*, to work as a freelance writer.

The theory that Tony was 'bumped' off the flight in favour of another journalist lacks scrutiny, especially as, given Tony's love of the Busby Babes, it was unlikely he would have taken on the Welsh game voluntarily. However, as there was no one directly representing the *Daily Sketch* on the plane, and certainly Northern sports editor Richard Walton remained in Manchester, it is almost impossible to apportion any blame. Without doubt, any recriminations following Tony's missed flight were soon forgotten at the newspaper and Stratton Smith's highly charged and emotional coverage of the aftermath gained much praise from readers and work colleagues alike. From then on, most of the Manchester United coverage in the *Sketch* came from Tony, particularly his accounts of how the team rallied to reach the FA Cup final that year, swept there on a wave of public support, with just a handful of reserves and crash survivors to patch up the team.

One story that grew out of Tony's near miss was that from that fateful day in February 1958 until his death in 1987, he would never board a flight on which he was actually booked, preferring to arrive late and change planes. However, his friend and music industry colleague Gail Colson – who not only travelled extensively with him, but probably booked many of the flights on his behalf – has a much simpler explanation. "Tony did miss a lot of planes, but that was just because he was never in a hurry, was never very prompt and overslept a lot." The tragedy of the Munich air crash certainly didn't stop Tony from travelling by air in later life, as Lindisfarne's Alan Hull would recall: "He once showed me his passport, in the days when they were stamped. It was unbelievable, I think he'd been to every country on Earth. It was like a child's colouring book!"

Towards the end of 1958, Tony's standing at the *Daily Sketch* had expanded to include a regular feature – the Stratton Smith Soccerscope. One example, in the issue dated Monday, October 6, saw Tony reporting on two international games played in the Emerald Isle over the weekend, with England battling to a 3-3 draw against Northern Ireland on the Saturday, followed by the Republic of Ireland drawing 2-2 with Poland in Dublin on the Sunday. By Monday morning, Tony's copy warranted almost a whole page as "Two big games in Ireland come under the STRATTON SMITH Soccerscope". Tony reviewed both matches in great detail and offered his forthright opinion as to how England should change their team selection to beat the Russians in the next game.

The straight-talking, opinionated style that Stratton Smith was cultivating had earned him the lion's share of the football coverage at *The Sketch*. In November, Tony offered Middlesbrough striker Brian Clough this advice: "Move on, Brian – and stop the slide". Centre forward Clough was struggling to help his Second Division side gain promotion to the top flight, and Tony firmly believed that a move to a bigger club would help all parties concerned, saying as much, apparently to the annoyance of the Football League. In summing up, he wrote: "The Football League, so anxious to probe 'tapping' through the press, need not try to gag me. I'm saying it's a terrible thing to see a player of Clough's class in decline, and bitter, at 23. Gag or not, I say Middlesbrough and Clough should part company."

In May 1959 England flew to America for a short end-of-season tour and Tony was sent out by the *Daily Sketch* to cover the four matches. The first stop was a visit to Rio de Janeiro on May 13 where England lost to Brazil, followed by a trip to Lima four days later where he sat uncomfortably through a 4-1 drubbing by Peru. A week later, the South American part of the tour concluded in the Estadio Olimpico Universitario, where Tony was among a huge crowd of 82,000 crazy Mexican fans whose team narrowly beat England by two goals to one.

With one game to go, Tony flew up to California and booked himself into the Knickerbocker Hotel at 1714 Ivar Avenue, Los Angeles. This grand old place had catered to the cream of the Hollywood film industry, with the names of Laurel & Hardy, the movie director D.W. Griffith, Marilyn Monroe,

Joe DiMaggio and Elvis Presley all to be found in the guest register. Happy in these surroundings, the match at Wrigley Field on May 28 also proved a much happier experience for the England boys who trounced the USA 8-1, including a first International hat-trick for Bobby Charlton.

Back in October 1957, the Central Council of Physical Recreation decided to appoint a small independent committee to examine the state of sport in Great Britain and Tony was among those invited to submit 'evidence' to the committee, alongside the likes of Roger Bannister, Denis Compton, Hugh Gaitskell, Dan Maskell and Walter Winterbottom. The subsequent Wolfenden report on 'Sport & the Community' was published in September 1960 and called for a number of government initiatives, including the establishment of a central 'Sports Development Council'. This went largely ignored until the Labour government of 1964, when Prime Minister Harold Wilson appointed Denis Howell as the first ever Minister for Sport.

While working for the Northern edition of the *Daily Sketch* in Manchester Tony would hold parties at his flat and, as Manchester United and Republic of Ireland full back Noel Cantwell recalls, might have led Bobby Charlton astray. "He (Stratton Smith) would throw these great parties and provide the birds. Bobby was a normal guy, good company, liked a beer. Some evenings, if there were a few birds around, our luck might be in. Bobby would be up there and he'd be as wild as anyone else."

One of Tony's fellow hacks at the *Daily Sketch* was Brian Scovell, then a keen young sports journalist, now one of our most admired football writers. He describes Tony as "a handsome, suave young bachelor... a dilettante and lover of *objet d'art*. He spent more time in nightclubs than at the office and was rarely seen by his colleagues. He had a love affair with Manchester United and particularly Matt Busby. Matt had a number of favourites and Tony was like one of his courtiers. Tony was a connoisseur of good football and at that time United were the best around and he helped build the image of the Busby Babes. When he left journalism, it was a big loss to the game, and in particular United."

According to a close friend and associate Barrington (Bazz) Ward, Tony was absolutely thrilled to be presented with a silver sword by Sir Matt Busby as a mark of their friendship and Tony's close affinity with United. In the early days of the *International Football Book*, publisher Ernest Hecht created the Football Sword of Honour, an award for distinguished service to British and International football, sponsored by Wilkinson Sword, the men's toiletries company. The first of these personalised swords was presented to Matt Busby and announced in the 1964 edition of the annual. Given the added connection of Tony's role as editor for the first 16 of these books, it is quite possible that this was the sword passed on to him by Sir Matt.

Tony's total admiration for Sir Matt Busby never left him. In later years, even though by then he was working in a different creative environment, the good times spent in and around Old Trafford had left a lasting impression. "If you were to ask me who was the biggest influence on me as a manager, I'd say it was a football manager," Tony told one American interviewer, "a chap called Sir Matt Busby, the manager of Manchester United in England, who are famous throughout the game. Matt had incredible success with Manchester United, in fact, I was close to them and him for many years. He was a wonderful man."

By the start of the sixties, Tony felt less comfortable at the *Daily Sketch* and perhaps it was the fallout from the Munich disaster that encouraged him to move on, after which he spent a year at the *Daily Express*. But even in the new surroundings he felt that his writing was restricted. Using a music analogy, Tony later told *Melody Maker* writer Roy Hollingworth: "It was like having to put out a pop single every day; so I got single space, but I was an album man, really."

On the plus side, one player who became a particularly close friend of Tony's during this time was the Chelsea and Tottenham striker Jimmy Greaves. With a nod to Tony's writing style, Greaves remembers that following one particularly indifferent season, Stratton Smith described Chelsea as having been "prolific at both ends". Tony is also reported to have been instrumental in the transfer of Jimmy Greaves from Chelsea to AC Milan in 1961, but while he certainly accompanied the player to Italy for the final meetings, it is doubtful that Tony would have advised his friend to make such an important move against his wishes.

In an interview with Stratton Smith, published two days after the signing, Greaves described the 'cloak and dagger' atmosphere that surrounded the meeting. Both Chelsea and AC Milan agreed that the transfer talks might have been prejudiced by too much advance publicity and consequently, when Greaves boarded his BEA flight to Italy he arrived wearing a borrowed trilby and carrying an umbrella and booked in under the name 'William James'. Travelling with him, Tony was one of only a handful of people on the inside of the deal, and was thus able to report the story from a privileged position.

Standing right beside Jimmy at the very moment the deal was confirmed, Tony scooped the story and it made the front page of the *Daily Express* the following day, Saturday June 3, 1961, with the newspaper headline proclaiming 'Jimmy Greaves signs for Milan – a £40,000 deal'. Stratton Smith's copy continued: "Jimmy Greaves IS going to Milan. The England and Chelsea inside forward today signed a personal contract with the Italian first division club. He is guaranteed at least £40,000 in the next three years. A five-figure part of that will be paid immediately in a lump sum. Greaves will play for Milan on Wednesday in an important friendly match with Botafogo of Brazil."

Such was the significance of the deal to English football, the front-page exclusive with Greaves even pushed Khrushchev and Kennedy out to the sidelines. The Russian leader had just arrived in Vienna for a Summit meeting with US President John F. Kennedy to discuss the uneasy situation in Berlin, but while the *Express* gave Nikita Khrushchev the bigger headline, Stratton Smith's Jimmy Greaves story occupied the more prominent position.

With such a close bond between journalist and striker, it was inevitable that Tony would become a member of the exclusive 'Jimmy Greaves Club'. During his 'exile' in Italy, Greaves looked forward to any visit from the British press and the rare opportunity to enjoy their company over a drink or two. Any sports reporter who made the trip out to Milan automatically qualified as a member and received a special club tie, featuring a map of Italy overlaid with a football and the initials JG. From the *Daily Sketch*, both Tony and Laurie Pignon were recipients, in fine journalistic company with the likes of Brian Glanville, Ian Wooldridge, Bill Holden, Ken Jones and Peter Lorenzo, among others.

It is hard to imagine sports writers getting anywhere as close to players and managers these days and Tony obviously took his journalistic work very seriously, always on the lookout for the next breaking story. He was able to witness some classic football matches during his year at the *Daily Express*. In January 1961, he stood in the pouring rain at Luton to watch Manchester City forward Denis Law put six goals past the Hatters – only for the referee to abandon the match after 70 minutes. In his newspaper report, Tony put the spotlight squarely on the man in the middle. "Referee Ken Tuck was the real hero, not Denis Law – in spite of his six goals," wrote Stratton Smith, with more than a hint of sarcasm. "Law only played in the match; Tuck starred in every laugh-provoking act."

The *Express* already had several big-name sports writers on their team, with journalists like Desmond Hackett, Clive Toye and Mike Langley all covering the football and, once again, Tony found himself having to elbow for position at the paper. He spent time with the England squad during that year and was at Wembley in April to see England score a spectacular win over Scotland by nine goals to three.

Towards the end of August, Tony also reported that Chelsea's young Terry Venables was considering a career in show business. Stratton Smith followed Venables to London's Stork Room, where impresario Al Burnett gave him a trial run in front of a packed house and then offered him £100 a week to appear in his new show 'Extravaganza' at The Pigalle Theatre in Piccadilly. Tony wrote: "The reward for trotting over the polished boards trodden in the past by Sammy Davis and Peggy Lee is about three times Terry's first team pay for pounding the turf at Stamford Bridge. A packed room gave Terry's miming act a big reception and Burnett said, 'He's got the face, the personality and the talent – he'll be tops.' Despite the offer of a show-biz contract ready and waiting, Venables responded by telling Tony, "I like entertaining – like other people like cigarettes – but my football career has to come first. Somehow I don't think Chelsea would care for my doing regular late-night shows."

Still only 27, Tony's sporting dreams had begun to fade. It seemed to him that the daily papers did not want his romantic prose any more. They preferred their own pedestrian tried and trusted formula; get a headline into the introduction, the *Sketch* had told him; get the name into the intro, said the *Express*. As a young writer, Tony had greatly admired the imaginative styles of Neville Cardus, Raymond Robertson-Glasgow and John Macadam, none of whom followed that style.

Towards the end of his year at the *Express*, Tony found himself face to face with a traumatic vision of the future. Macadam, a brilliant poet and art critic before turning his hand to football, had been chief sports columnist at the *Daily Express* during the fifties, but had fallen prey to the hard-drinking culture of Fleet Street and was now often so intoxicated he could barely type his own name. As Tony later told Richard Yallop of *The Guardian*: "The *Express* shoved me into some remote writing area and right opposite me was John Macadam, hero of my boyhood, now subbing greyhound results, kalied and waiting for the 9.20 from Harringay."

Seeing Macadam's sorry state helped convince Stratton Smith that his own future lay elsewhere. Following his final major scoop for the newspaper, the signing of Jimmy Greaves to Turin, the *Daily Express* threw a party in his honour at the London Press Club. Tony used the occasion to tender his resignation.

STRAT!

Chapter 3

The Author

*"We would often go to the track at night – Tony loved the races.
He loved gambling at the races. We spent hours talking to each other and
he was highly intelligent, a very bright guy and a very decent man."*
Eddie Gilbert, fugitive

Having reached the conclusion that his time as a newspaper journalist had run its course, Tony decided to become a freelance writer and, hopefully, an author. "I'd got as far as I could get – I couldn't get much farther than being a football writer for the *Express*," he explained later. "The only other thing you can do, apart from leave, is to grow old in the job. I wasn't that much in love with football. I wanted to write books."

Around the time Tony opted to become self-employed, a family tragedy brought him back to his Midlands roots. On April 20, 1962, his step-father Douglas Hughes was killed in a road accident and, back home at 1156 Yardley Wood Road, his mother Mollie was left the sum of £2,165.00 in her husband's will. While the uncertainty of whether or not Tony actually knew the identity of his real father would remain, he would later tell a close colleague that both his father and his step-father died in accidents on the same stretch of road. It was also reputedly the reason why Tony vowed he would never learn to drive a car.

While his role as editor of the *International Football Book* would provide a regular and much-needed source of income, a second life-changing event came on a working holiday to South America in 1962. In May, Tony left his Chalk Farm flat at 38 Eton Place NW3 and flew down to cover the seventh World Cup in Chile, where from May 30 to June 17, 14 national teams fought for the title, culminating in the defending champions Brazil beating Czechoslovakia 3-1 in the final.

Brazil's Garrincha was among the top scorers and voted the player of the tournament. Tony was particularly taken by Garrincha and Pelé, although the latter was not quite the world beater he would later become, and sought out both players to interview for a book on the tournament. Working as co-editor with Gordon Jeffery and Freidebert Becker, *World Cup '62: The Report From Chile* was published by Souvenir Press later that same year and several other articles from the trip also appeared in that year's *International Football Book No 5*.

One of the many urban myths about Tony is that he wrote the first book on Pelé. According to Ernest Hecht, this probably stems from the articles that Tony wrote for the *International Football Books* during their time together in South America. "After the World Cup in Chile, I was going on to Brazil and Tony was going on somewhere else, possibly Argentina," recalls Hecht. "We had arranged in Chile that we should try and get Pelé to do a serial extra… a series of articles. I negotiated the first part with Pelé's manager and Tony was going to do the writing and, of course, Pelé lived in Santos which is in São Paulo, Brazil."

During that eventful summer in South America, Tony managed to get personal 'at-home' interviews with both Garrincha and Pelé. Plenty had been written about their exploits on the field, but Tony was among the first British journalists to get behind the scenes and talk to them away from the stadiums and training pitches, meeting Garrincha at his modest home in the village of Pau Grande and taking the mountain road from São Paulo down to the port of Santos to interview Pelé. Back home, Souvenir Press published a large chunk of these interviews in the fifth edition of the *International Football Book*, with publisher Ernest Hecht stepping in as co-editor to work on the three large articles written by Stratton Smith himself. Under the heading 'The Innocent Twins', Tony began his exclusive by saying: "Big earners but small spenders, innocent of sophistication, these two young coloured men have led professional soccer back to nature. And in Europe, the old home and former hub of the game, they have the singular distinction of having emancipated the white man. From what? From the expanding mania for tactics and systems which in Europe had long checked the free flow of football artistry like a tourniquet…"

Tony also got to see at first-hand the poverty-stricken areas and the hand-to-mouth lifestyle from which these two superstars, indeed most of the Brazilian national team, had emerged. "Garrincha until recently kept all his money in a sack under his bed. As his little village doesn't bother to employ a policeman, his metropolitan friends had to tell him about possible thieves, and advise him to invest."

Tony learned that on turning 12, Garrincha had pushed a handcart through a textile factory for nine hours a day. He found that he had seven daughters, yet still prayed for a son, keeping a good-luck charm in his bedroom. He learned that success had done absolutely nothing to change Garrincha, who remained extremely modest, "shunning publicity and all things unfamiliar". Apparently, apart from any football injuries, he refused to allow a doctor near himself or his daughters, but continued to depend on the herbal cures of an old woman from his village of Pau Grande whom he had known since he was a boy. A quiet and generous man, as a form of thanksgiving Garrincha had paid off all the debts of his fellow villagers at the general store after Brazil won the 1958 World Cup in Sweden.

At the pretty harbour and sleepy port of Santos, Tony met Edson Arantes do Nascimento – better known to the football world as Pelé. It was a nickname, Tony found out, given to him by his street gang in the town where he grew up, often stealing peanuts to buy his first pair of football boots. While the younger Pelé remained a modest man who lived relatively simply, he had a greater sense of purpose due to his business manager, the "tough, but satin-smooth" Jose Gonzales Ozores. Ozores had money in construction, Brazil's boom business at that time, and had helped Pelé to invest in apartment blocks, sanitary appliances and building materials. The footballer also lodged with the Ozores family, spending many evenings simply watching television with the neighbours' children. Pelé owned property, including the very house in which he was born, but preferred to let them out to poorer families for 'sentimental reasons'. Under the slightly overbearing guidance of his manager, Pelé was certainly making more of his newfound wealth, but disliked the problems that came with such celebrity. "I hate not being able to go out like anybody else, without being recognised," he told Tony. "Sometimes I feel like a veteran, tired and exhausted and then I would like to give up football."

Publisher Ernest Hecht recalls spending leisure time with Tony in Brazil and notes that arranging the interview with Pelé was perhaps not as smooth and easy as Tony made it sound. The cause, perhaps inevitably, was Ozores. "The bastard wouldn't let me near him," Tony told Hecht. "I said, 'That's ridiculous, I paid him 500 dollars for the rights for you to do that' and Tony replied, 'Well he says that was just for him, not for Pelé…' This was the manager who subsequently decamped into the jungle with a lot of Pelé's money, I believe. Eventually Tony managed to wangle his way into the Pelé household via the younger brother, talked to Pelé in the kitchen, and we ran the series. So it did eventually work out."

* * *

Tony was also among the first British journalists to document the growth of football, or rather soccer, in the USA. Having visited American promotor Bill Cox in his Yale Club office just off New York's Park Avenue, Tony returned armed with the facts and figures to show that more youngsters were playing soccer in the United States than were playing baseball and American football combined. Cox had organised a summertime soccer league in New York since 1960 and attendances were steadily rising. His next venture was the organisation of an American Professional League, with clubs in ten major cities, coast to coast. Tony's enquiries revealed that American schools and colleges were not even playing to FIFA rules; that college soccer was played in quarters, not halves; the ball was kicked into play, not thrown in; and they allowed unlimited substitutions. This lack of foresight and attention to detail worried Tony, who wrote: "British and European soccer authorities have done little to help in the States. They are blind to the enormous fillip to the world game a strong United States would give. I urge Sir Stanley Rous and FIFA to set up a permanent commission empowered to report and act on the need for aid in undeveloped soccer areas such as the United States, and so ensure proper and steady growth of the greatest game of them all." He concluded with an impassioned plea to FIFA President Rous: "Is there really nothing we can do to help? I put it to you, Sir Stanley!"

Tony's South American adventure wasn't all about the beautiful game and one encounter during that remarkable summer provided the spark of inspiration that would propel him towards a career in music, as he later told journalist Michael Wale. "When I got to Brazil it just swept me off my feet. I was freelance at the time, so I was more or less master of my own time and the two-week holiday became a nine-month residency on Copacabana beach, busily trying to justify the time I was spending there."

Tony found himself relaxing on the beaches and enjoying the neon nightlife of Rio de Janeiro, Copacabana and Ipanema, where he was introduced to the bossa nova rhythms of Stan Getz and Antônio Carlos Jobim, Gilberto Gil and Tito Puente, music that really fired up his imagination. Tony's guide to these exotic rhythms was new to the city himself and just happened to be a former New York financier who had misappropriated nearly $2million of company funds before fleeing, albeit temporarily, to Brazil.

In a relatively short space of time, Edward M. Gilbert had made and lost a fortune in the American lumber business, and there were questions that needed to be answered. While he took care not to actively broadcast his whereabouts, Eddie Gilbert received plenty of visitors during those first weeks in Brazil and Tony was not the only journalist to track him down. *Life* magazine sent a reporter and a photographer to cover his time in Rio, running a nine-page, photo-heavy feature. There were also visits from his US attorney and *New York Times* journalist Murray Rossant, who actually wrote one of the more sympathetic pieces about him.

Tony arrived unannounced on Eddie Gilbert's doorstep and the pair struck up an instant friendship, with a gentleman's agreement that Stratton Smith would not publish anything without Gilbert's prior approval. After their initial conversations, Tony certainly felt that Gilbert's story warranted a book to tell it properly – quickly offering to write it himself. Gilbert liked the idea, but suspected that Tony also saw it as a deliberate move to get away from sports journalism and into the wider literary arena. The pair got on famously and spent so much time in each other's company that Gilbert suggested Tony move into the spare bedroom in his apartment.

"I don't know how Tony found my address," said Gilbert, "because nobody else could. Somehow he found me and said, 'I'm a reporter from London, England and you may not want to talk to me, but I'd like to write an article about you.' I said fine, be glad to do it. We went and had lunch together. I had very little money, only about $2,500 when I left America. I had just got a little apartment that some guy offered to me at a very low price and I'd been there for about a week. So I said to Tony, you can come and stay with me if you want to, and he said OK. He came back a day or two later and moved in. We spent about three or four months together, all but about one month of my total time there. He left a little before I did, just as I was coming back to the States."

While Gilbert approved the book idea, he did harbour certain doubts about Tony's ability to write it. All he really knew of Stratton Smith's work was that he was a 'soccer hack' – albeit a good one – and more used to a pie and a pint at Old Trafford than smoked salmon and champagne on Wall Street. Without Tony's knowledge, Gilbert wrote to Jack Kerouac, an old schoolfriend, for advice. The author of the cult classic Beat novel *On The Road* wrote back to say that while he had been asked to ghost-write before, he had always refused, that he could only write from his own experiences and encouraged Gilbert to do the same. "Get yourself a tape recorder, have a coupla' drinks first and tell your own story," was Kerouac's sage advice. Gilbert treasured the letter, but never did buy the tape recorder. He simply carried on talking, while Tony continued to take notes. Stratton Smith's work on the biography didn't amount to much – only about 14 pages of typed manuscript – but he did keep a detailed journal of their time together in Rio, which later proved invaluable to Gilbert's eventual biographer Richard Whittingham when he came to write his book *The Boy Wonder Of Wall Street*.

Tony's journal covered their day-to-day existence in Rio, plus conversational notes relating to Gilbert's early life and insightful thoughts on exactly what made him tick, including the following gem: "When he talks about millions (of dollars), it was like a carpenter discussing lathes – they were just tools of his trade, not very important in themselves."

"I got to know him fairly well, although Tony was not the kind of a guy you could get to know that well, but I think we were as good friends as it was possible to be," recalled Gilbert. "He was restricted for money, but he had enough to get along – and we had such a good time together. We sat down and talked by the hour about my life, he would make his notes and then we would go out to nightclubs or see music together. We would often go to the track at night – Tony loved the races. He loved gambling at the races.

We would go to the track and have dinner and watch the racing at least once or twice a week. We spent hours talking to each other and he was highly intelligent, a very bright guy and a very decent man."

Tony was impressed by Gilbert's range of contacts, which included the American writer John Dos Passos, then aged 66 and the author of *Manhattan Transfer* and *The 42nd Parallel*, who lived in Rio at the time. Familiar with his work, Tony was thrilled to be introduced to such a well-known literary figure and the three men dined together several times and spent a long weekend at Angra dos Reis, a small coastal resort about 70 miles to the south west of Rio.

For his part, Tony introduced Eddie Gilbert to Pelé, and while the pair discussed the possibility of a business partnership, Tony decided to widen the project to include Antônio Carlos Jobim. Bossa nova was proving to be popular and already crossing borders – Stratton Smith was certainly a new disciple – and as with Pelé, Tony could see that Jobim could be better promoted in England and the USA. With both men virtually on his doorstep, it was an easy task to approach Jobim's legal team as well, but while Tony was actively pursuing this new project, Eddie Gilbert decided to return to New York to face the music.

Tony flew out to join him there shortly afterwards, albeit briefly, in the hope that they could still finish the proposed biography together and, rumour has it, possibly as a personal favour to Eddie Gilbert. Publisher Ernest Hecht suggests that Tony may not have declared absolutely everything as he walked through American customs. "It would certainly be interesting to know," wondered Hecht, "whether Tony's claim that he went back to New York carrying money or its equivalent sewn into the lining of his suit, to deliver to Eddie's lawyers, was true."

Any further work on the biography was short-lived. Unfortunately Stratton Smith was an unknown quantity as far as the American publishing houses were concerned and there was no joy in attracting one for his book project. As a consequence, Gilbert spoke about the problem to Murray Rossant, one of the few journalists to have treated Eddie's situation with an even hand, and he expressed an interest in taking it on himself, confident that he could attract a publishing deal.

In the event a book about Gilbert was written by Rossant, the head of the financial department of the *New York Times*, who paid Tony for the use of material he'd already researched.

Although none of their joint plans ever really came to fruition, Eddie Gilbert is thankful for the time spent in Stratton Smith's company. "If it wasn't for Tony I don't know what I would have done," he said. "I was desolate. I had been a rich man, the president of a very large company, I was in my thirties and there were very few young people in America who were that successful – but I was absolutely desolate. I thought I would die a bum. And he came into my life at a time when I was ready to commit suicide. Tony saved my life."[1*]

Tony turned his attention back to Antônio Carlos Jobim, agreeing with Gilbert that he would have the rights to Jobim in England and Gilbert in America. Tony attended a show on August 2, 1962, when Jobim, Vinicius de Moraes and guitarist João Gilberto came together on stage to play for the very first time in a small nightclub called Au Bon Gourmet in Copacabana. During the next six weeks, the Jobim-Vinicius-Gilberto trio, together with the band Os Cariocas, played a set that included 'Garota de Ipanema' ('The Girl From Ipanema') and 'Samba do Avião', both bossa nova favourites that would become known the world over. These ground-breaking shows were the only occasions that the three men would perform together. "The whole mood of the show and the music and everything swept me sideways," said Tony. "After the show, I met Jobim and we had a few beers together. I even wrote a line of the English lyrics for 'Single Note Samba', one line that he was stuck on."

The new music that so captured Tony's imagination began on the beaches of Rio de Janeiro among the bohemian mix of artists, students and musicians who gathered on the tropical sands by day and in the lively bar and club scene by night. Mixing traditional Brazilian samba rhythms with light American jazz and Portuguese lyrics, it was a perfect soundtrack to the romantic beach culture and nightlife of Rio at the beginning of the sixties. In the Bar Veloso, Ipanema, two musicians would meet every day to talk, write and watch the world go by. Most days, they admired a beautiful 19-year-old girl who would walk in to buy cigarettes for her mother, often leaving to wolf whistles from the other bar patrons. The girl, Heloísa Eneida Menezes Paes Pinto, inspired the two friends to write about this 'Garota de Ipanema', which became the song that would put bossa nova on the map. The songwriters were Antônio Carlos Jobim, or 'Tom' to his friends, and lyricist Vinícius de Moraes.

Tony may even have passed Heloísa, or Helô as she was known, on her regular trips to the Bar Veloso. He was in exactly the right place at exactly the right time. Jobim was responsible for writing much of the Brazilian bossa nova music that made its way to the US in the early sixties. 'Tom' worked on albums arranged by the great Claus Ogerman, Nelson Riddle and Eumir Deodato, where he sang and played piano and guitar. He recorded albums with Frank Sinatra and other vocalists of note, played piano alongside Stan Getz and João Gilberto and made one album playing guitar under the pen-name of 'Tony Brasil'.

During a business meeting with the influential Brazilian composer,

---

1   * Eddie Gilbert died in 2015, four days before his 93rd birthday.

it was suggested that Tony might become his music publisher in the UK and although it never happened, Tony watched as North America fell in love with Brazilian music. Later in 1962, there was a major concert at Carnegie Hall in New York and in 1964 the jazz musician Stan Getz recorded 'The Girl From Ipanema' with guitarist João Gilberto and his wife Astrud Gilberto on vocals, along with Tom Jobim on piano. The album *Getz/Gilberto* was hugely popular, spending 96 weeks on the US chart, while the Astrud Gilberto single made the top five in the States and became an international hit. Bossa nova had truly arrived.

While Tony's friend Eddie Gilbert served just under three years in prison for financial irregularities, Tony – fired up by the bossa nova and keen now to enter the music industry – flew back to a very cold and wintry London. Within a year he had befriended pop impresario and Beatles manager Brian Epstein.

* * *

Tony Stratton Smith and Brian Epstein met for the first time in Amsterdam in March 1964, when Epstein was in the Netherlands organising a Beatles' European tour for later that year. According to Tony, Epstein asked him to ghost-write his autobiography, but he had to turn it down in order to complete another project, *The Rebel Nun*, a biography of Mother Maria Skobtsova. But like millions of others he was enchanted by The Beatles. "The Beatles were happening. This was exactly what this business needed. They had style, material, everything coming together in one incarnation. Presley had style, but The Beatles were style, plus material. I thought they were terribly exciting, I thought this was really going to happen. I remembered Tom Jobim's advice from a few months before and I thought, this could be it."

It was a coincidence that Tony's own publisher Ernest Hecht has signed Epstein's memoir *A Cellarful Of Noise*. Unfortunately it was a rush job and neither Hecht nor Epstein would wait until Tony was in a position to become the Beatle manager's ghost-writer. "Due to the enormous success of his artists Brian Epstein was proving a hard man to pin down," he says. "It took three months of missed phone calls and re-arranged meetings for Ernest Hecht to lock Brian into a writing and publishing schedule. In the main, Epstein was worried about who should 'ghost-write' his book."

In his 1989 biography of Brian Epstein, former *Melody Maker* editor Ray Coleman recounts what happened next. "At Hecht's expense, Tony flew to see Brian, who was staying in the penthouse suite of the Amsterdam Hilton. Brian received the talkative Tony with his traditional courtesy, and after a day spent avoiding the subject of the book they adjourned to dinner. Stratton Smith, a bon vivant, was impressed. Epstein chose the Black Sheep, the most expensive restaurant in the city and one he knew well from his solo sojourns. He pored over the wine list. Stratton Smith had just returned from Brazil, where the bossa nova rhythms were being launched. Brian was fascinated and the conversation flowed. After they had exchanged ideas for Brian's book, he casually asked Tony when he could begin preparing it. Not for six months, or three at the earliest, he answered. He was writing *The Rebel Nun* at the time. 'Six months?' Brian exploded. He often totally failed to grasp that people might have activities that caused them to give him less than 100 per cent instant attention. Couldn't Tony shelve his current project? The autobiography of Brian Epstein was much more exciting and, he believed, urgent. 'The faster my book is out the better!' Stratton Smith disagreed. Another six months of Brian's life would strengthen the story. He replied stubbornly that he would be happy to write Brian's book, but not until he had finished his current work. Epstein was visibly upset. After dinner, the two men went to a couple of bars that Brian knew in Amsterdam and the business of the biography was left 'open'. Next day, as Tony flew back to London, Epstein phoned Hecht to say that he was not prepared to wait three months, let alone six. He would have to find another writer immediately."

Epstein and Hecht turned instead to Derek Taylor, a journalist with the *Daily Express* who became the Beatles' press officer and, for a short period, Epstein's personal assistant. But Tony's brush with Epstein was something he would take with him for the future. "I learned a great deal from Brian, especially that a manager's role is a creative one. He has to create the situation in which his artists can happen – that requires a lot of skills and disciplines that are quite outside the areas of law and accountancy. I'd like to think that I became one of the few managers who felt that way. Unfortunately very few of them exist now."

* * *

Mother Maria Skobtsova – the 'Rebel Nun' and Martyr of Ravensbrück – was one of the seven martyrs now remembered in the Chapel of the Martyrs at Canterbury Cathedral but precisely how Tony became interested in her remains something of a mystery. He has claimed he was commissioned to write the book – although his publisher disputes this – but what is indisputable is that Tony was greatly moved and inspired by Mother Maria's story. And once Tony got the idea into his head, there was no turning back.

Born in 1891, Elisabeth Yuriseva Pilenko came from the small town of Anapa near the Black Sea, and her many friends and acquaintances included well-known writers, poets, and political thinkers, among them Alexei Tolstoy and Alexander Blok. The first woman to study at the Ecclesiastical Academy at the Alexander Nevsky Monastery, her early interest in social issues led her to become involved in politics, but due to her close association with the Social Revolutionary Party (at one point she even formulated a plan to assassinate Leon Trotsky), she was forced to flee Russia, ending up in Paris by way of Georgia, Yugoslavia and Turkey.

In Paris she lived in abject poverty, surviving on the little money she made by selling trinkets. It was here that she was introduced to the Russian Student Christian Movement (RSCM) and became friends with the Russian intelligentsia – émigrés such as Sergei Bulgakov and Nikolai Berdyaev, and after separating from her second husband in 1932, she was tonsured a nun and took the name Maria (Mary of Egypt). She became friends with Father Lev Gillet and together they ran a community house with a soup kitchen, providing a meeting space where they could minister to refugees, alcoholics and tuberculin patients. Her decision to live a monastic life in the outside world was a conscious one – "I want to create a new form of nun life... a life in the world" – a decision that was enthusiastically supported by Russian Orthodox bishop Metropolitan Evlogy, who wanted her to become "a revolutionary nun". For Maria, the monastic life needed to be an active one.

Mother Maria continued to do everything in her power to ease the pain and suffering of those around her, even under the adverse conditions of the German Occupation in Paris. The danger to her personal safety increased daily, yet she never stopped helping those who needed it most, including many Jews. Eventually, she became involved with the Jewish Resistance in Paris and began hiding Jews in her home. Because she was well known in Paris as a defender of the poor and persecuted, and with her defiant attitude toward the Nazis, it was inevitable that Mother Maria herself was finally arrested and imprisoned in Ravensbrück concentration camp where she died. Yet throughout it all, she remained steadfast, true to her calling, and uncompromising in her love for God and her fellow human beings. Perhaps this quote from Tony's book sums up Maria's raison d'etre: "At the Last Judgement I will not be asked whether I satisfactorily practiced asceticism, nor how many bows I have made before the divine altar. I will be asked whether I fed the hungry, clothed the naked, visited the sick, and the prisoner in his jail. That is all I will be asked."

While Souvenir Press did not commission *The Rebel Nun*, Tony did approach them directly to publish it, though Ernest Hecht still has no idea what motivated him to write such a book. "I always presumed it was his Catholicism," suggested Hecht. "It was his idea entirely, I had never even heard about this Russian nun. It wasn't particularly well written and the subject was rather tenuous, but we did it and it sold reasonably well."

So well, in fact, that *The Rebel Nun* was eventually translated into several languages and various reprints. Tony was extremely proud of his efforts, as he later remarked: "It was a book that I enjoyed writing and that took about six or nine months' work and it was quite a success. I must be the only person in the rock business who has written a book that became a Sisters Book Club choice in America," he said cheerily. "A little piece of me is with every nun in America!"

Whether or not Tony's reason for writing *The Rebel Nun* stemmed from his own religious beliefs is unclear, and even his close friend Jack Barrie was mystified. "I always thought he was agnostic, that he had no interest in religion," he said. "Then another time people would tell me that he was a devout Catholic. The only thing I ever knew about him was that whenever we used to go racing and we got to the place too early, he would often want to go and visit a nearby church, or sometimes we could be driving by somewhere and he would suddenly shout, 'Stop, I just want to look in there.'"

After reporting on a World Cup, writing about the persecution of Mother Maria and researching South American spiritualism, Tony turned to his old friend George Thompson for some much-needed time out, joining him on a cricket tour of Devon. "One night back at the hotel, a game of three card brag was in process and one member of the team had cleaned everyone out – except for Stratton, who stayed on in the game and took back all our losses. He then spent it all in the bar afterwards, such was his generous nature."

Back in the UK, Tony still found work as a freelance sports writer and, in early 1964, he sought an interview with Real Madrid's Alfredo Di Stefano, not just to talk football but to get the full story behind a far stranger, and less beautiful event. Under the headline 'A priceless bird in a different kind of cage', Tony told the bizarre story of how a para-military organisation had kidnapped one of the world's most high-profile footballers during a pre-season tour of Venezuela. In the early hours of a Saturday morning in Caracas, August 1963, Di Stéfano was roughly awakened when a group of men forced their way into room 219 at the Hotel Potomac and, posing as narcotics police, marched the angry 37-year-old player away. Hours later a woman telephoned the hotel, the police, and the leading news agencies with the bombshell that Di Stéfano had been kidnapped.

Despite being in demand for slightly off-the-wall sporting articles like these, Tony still harboured thoughts of a career in the entertainment industry, albeit not as a writer, as outlets for music scribes were few and far between. Besides, Tony was more of a people person, so a complete change of direction was called for, as George Thompson noted: "For the next few years, Stratton would keep disappearing from our lives for long periods as he changed course from sports writing, horse racing, cricket and football, to the music industry. Each time he did reappear, his visit would always bring with it some excitement. Life is all about people – but this time it was about singers and musicians, not cricketers, footballers, racehorses and jockeys, journalists, businessmen and politicians."

With his writing projects completed, Tony turned his attention to Antônio Jobim's original suggestion of a career in music publishing, an idea galvanised by his weekend stay in the Netherlands with Brian Epstein. "Talking to Brian over that weekend got me really fired up about the music business," he said. "Of course, what a bloody wonderful business – it's exciting, it's working with people, it's exercising a bit of judgement, making quick decisions."

Energised by his meeting with Epstein, Tony launched a music publishing company, taking one room on Wardour Street that he shared with a secretary. His baptism was harsh. "For the next year I proceeded to be robbed blind by every out-of-work writer on Denmark Street. Every time they were skint they would come along and flog me a couple of copyrights for £25 each or something. I realised very quickly, that, having gone through a fair bit of money from my savings, that this was no way to do it. I was completely naive about the whole thing. There used to be this thing called The Gioconda Crowd. This was a coffee bar in Denmark Street where all the out-of-work musicians and hustlers and songwriters would sit around, having egg and chips, wondering who they were going to hit next. And I was always the favourite in there. For the first six months they knew they could always rely on me for a healthy advance on a nothing song."

So proud was Tony of his worthless songs that he decided they needed to be made into demos – demonstration records that could be used to interest others in recording them. "I knew a guy at Essex Music called Don Paul and I said I wanted a demo session and could he help me with a few musicians. He said we could have this band that was hanging around his office and so I hired them and paid them off. Next day they came to see me and really laid it on that they were a band and would I manage them? I was quite horrified. I was honest with them and said, 'I seem to have made an awful mess of the last few years managing my own life – it would be rather a strange thing to take responsibility for someone else's.' Anyway, I got involved and the band that emerged in 1965 as Paddy, Klaus & Gibson, did quite well."

Chapter 4

The Learning Curve

"The extraordinary thing is that Strat had this ability to half reveal his gayness, where you would get a brief glimpse through the curtains, so to speak, but then suddenly the curtains would close and you were left wondering which was the real Tony."
Simon White, Marquee Studios

It was no great secret that Tony Stratton Smith was gay and this undoubtedly influenced his approach to the management, image and marketing of several of the artists he took under his wing. Despite his conviction that the music came first and foremost, he understood the importance of projecting the right image and was quite happy to put forward ideas on fashion, sometimes choosing clothes for photo shoots and even suggesting line-up changes if the occasional unfortunate face didn't fit.

No secret it may have been, but in those days homosexuality was still not a subject that was open for discussion. Gay men in the fifties and sixties had far fewer options than there are today when it came to coming out – and most simply chose not to do so. The vast majority were forced to hide their sexuality from everyone except perhaps their closest friends, and many were never able to reveal their true feelings even to their own family. Some men went as far as entering a so-called 'normal' marriage and raising a family in an effort to blend in with the heterosexual world. Such was the lack of information and understanding among their peers, veering from plain ignorance at best to acts of deliberately targeted violence at worst, that many gay men actually felt a sense of shame and never quite came to terms with their situation.

Tony probably fell into the latter category and certainly became very adept at keeping the 'love that dare not speak its name' a carefully guarded secret. The real tragedy for Stratton Smith, and for many men like him, was that he was never able to forge any sort of long-term relationship. None of his closest friends can recall any mention of a regular boyfriend or partner, let alone ever meeting one, and it seems likely that any sexual encounters were restricted to the occasional one-night stand. Rival pop manager Simon Napier-Bell distastefully referred to Tony's lifestyle as having revolved around "fine wine, racehorses and rent boys". If there was a darker side to his private life, Tony was, of course, far too much of a gentleman ever to discuss such things.

Like many gay men during the fifties, if one felt the need to hide their sexuality – and many believe that Tony actively chose to do so – then where better than the male-dominated world of sport. During his days with the press, the football terrace and the cricket pavilion were strictly all-male enclaves, places where Tony could gather his news stories before heading back to the office and join in with the laddish banter and late-night drinking culture of the newsroom. Outwardly, at least, Tony was happy to fit right in and become one of the boys.

The entertainment industry, however, was an entirely different matter. While nowhere near as open as it is today, the environment was far more tolerant and as one musician half-jokingly said, after his first week working in Denmark Street, he thought that being gay was almost compulsory. Yet even in the Soho of the supposedly 'swinging' sixties, attitudes to homosexuality remained firmly entrenched in the last century as far as many were concerned, including unsympathetic members of the police force. Although the law was changed in 1967 – when consenting adults over 21 were exempt from prosecution, providing such encounters were conducted within the privacy of their own homes – as far as the gay community could tell, police harassment was rife and would continue to be so well into the eighties.

For this reason alone, Tony rarely let his private life overlap into his professional world, as his friend Jack Barrie confirmed. "No, normally it didn't. Certainly later on, it didn't appear to interfere with his work at all, but in the earlier days I think it probably did. There was always the point of view that perhaps the way he became involved with Paddy, Klaus & Gibson was because of a physical attraction to one of them and also with one of The Koobas, Keith Ellis. I think Tony was madly in love with him. Generally though, from what I remember, his real penchant had always been for young black youths, which got him into terrible trouble on occasion. He got beaten up quite a few times. I mean, Tony would come in the next day and tell us that he had been mugged and we'd think, oh yeah, right."

Simon G. White, the Director of Marquee Studios, agrees that Tony could occasionally be his own worst enemy. "When it got to that point in the evening where he would always say, 'When you've got to go, you've got to go' and promptly disappeared, he was usually quite pissed, so if he did go and start chatting up the wrong person, it's quite likely that could have happened – but who knows? You can build your own fantasies, but I don't think anybody really knew what Strat was up to – except we all knew that he didn't do much with the ladies."

Nevertheless, by choosing to work in music management Tony was in very good company. As Yardbirds manager Simon Napier-Bell points out, "Most of the best managers were gay..." including himself in his list of the gay and the good, alongside Epstein, Kit Lambert (who co-managed The Who), Robert Stigwood (Cream, Bee Gees), Ken Pitt (David Bowie), Billy Gaff (Rod Stewart), Vic Billings (Dusty Springfield) and the songwriting/management team of Ken Howard and Alan Blaikley. The tradition began with Larry Parnes, the first and most famous pop manager of the fifties, who groomed a stable of singers whose charms were aimed exclusively at teenage girls, much like the Bay City Rollers who were managed by Tam Paton, a notoriously gay libertine.

Napier-Bell noted that Pete Townshend of The Who saw the advantages of having a gay manager in Kit Lambert. As Townshend told him: "Gays were different. They didn't behave like other adults. They were scornful of conventional behaviour. They mixed more easily with young people, and seemed to understand them." Napier-Bell added: "Gay managers seemed to be the best at it. Most of them had got used to playing a two-faced game between the straight world and their own. Jewish managers were also excellent, many of them having played the same double game since they were schoolkids."

Simon White also takes the view that Tony would deliberately muddy the waters, depending on the company he was keeping at the time. "The extraordinary thing is that Strat had this ability to half reveal his gayness, where you would get a brief glimpse through the curtains, so to speak, but then suddenly the curtains would close and you were left wondering which was the real Tony. Because he didn't like the public gaze into his sexuality, he felt that nobody should be able to say what he was or he wasn't.

"Those early days were extremely difficult for a gay man," adds White. "It was still illegal and people were being blackmailed. I knew a lot of people who were being blackmailed. So it was a very nasty and fairly frightening period, but in one sense Tony always kept apart from the gay scene. Obviously he had his bands and a lot of those bands had quite pretty boys in them, but I could never think of any one (of his friends) that I could actually say yes, they go to bed together, unlike Kit Lambert and people like that, who would openly bring their boyfriends into La Chasse. Managers like Brian Epstein, Billy Gaff and Simon Napier-Bell – although Simon played a slightly double game – but with most of them you knew exactly what was going on. Kit Lambert used to buy his boys a pair of boots, so you knew that if a boy turned up at La Chasse in new boots, he was sleeping with Kit Lambert. With Simon Napier-Bell, it was there when he managed The Yardbirds. He used to be very coy about it indeed and although he had a boyfriend a lot of the time, he certainly put it about that he was screwing the ladies as well."

There is a strong suggestion that Tony did have a sexual relationship with at least one woman – the wife of a financial backer during the pre-Charisma days – whereby part of their arrangement was for Tony to sleep with her once a year. Gail Colson, who effectively ran the Charisma office under Tony's control, distinctly remembers arriving for work at his Dean Street flat some mornings, only to find his bedroom door locked and bolted from the inside, whereupon Tony's distant voice would call out, "Oh Gail, can you come back later?" Remarkably, she never saw anyone leave the flat, either male or female. Rumour has it that the cleaner once found a pair of crumpled nylon stockings underneath Tony's bed.

Simon White has his reservations about the rumoured relationship between Tony and the financier's wife. "Well, that is an interesting thought – and certainly something that Strat would be quite happy to demonstrate to Gail Colson. I'm not saying that it's not true or that it didn't happen, but it could also be something that he might want to imply. He would have been quite pleased for Gail to think of him as not just a one-trick pony. So yes, he probably would have liked to keep Gail guessing, particularly working so close to her."

* * *

Paddy, Klaus & Gibson had their origins in Liverpool, the home of The Beatles. Paddy was guitarist Patrick 'Paddy' Chambers, formerly of Faron's Flamingos and The Big Three, who had joined The Dominoes, recently divorced from their singer Kingsize Taylor. Klaus was bassist Klaus Voorman, a graphic designer who had befriended The Beatles during their Hamburg days and never previously played in a band. Drummer Gibson was Gibson Kemp, late of Rory Storm & The Hurricanes and also Kingsize Taylor & The Dominoes. They assembled after a 1964 season in Hamburg, renaming themselves Paddy, Klaus & Gibson before heading south for London, managed by Don Paul who also worked at Essex Music.

Initially tapped for £250 to spend on new equipment, Tony agreed with Don Paul to accept 10% of his 25% management commission. Tony was impressed with the trio after seeing them perform at the chic Pickwick Club in Great Newport Street, just off Charing Cross Road, a place to see and be seen. Michael Caine described the club as the "hub of the so-called swinging sixties" and its regular customers included The Beatles, Terence Stamp and director Harry Saltzman, who offered Caine the lead role in *The Ipcress File* over a meal in the Pickwick with screenwriter Wolf Mankovitz.

Bassist Klaus Voorman remembers his new boss: "Tony was hardly ever without a glass of white wine in his hand. Whenever there was spare time and the pubs opened, we were off. He was the typical English gentleman, very funny, but apart from this I felt he was slightly out of place in the music business. He certainly wasn't the type the rockers or jazzers were usually hanging out with. He was an odd one, an outsider in the biz."

He may have been a stranger in the strange world but Tony worked hard to gain recognition for Paddy, Klaus & Gibson, primarily by entertaining disc jockeys and music writers at the Pickwick while the group were performing there. As he later told the journalist Michael Wale: "I was picking up the tabs for every disc jockey and pressman in the country who thought it was great fun to come down to the Pickwick. The band were good, but it didn't lead to much and when it did, it was in the wrong direction. John Lennon, George Harrison, Paul McCartney and occasionally Ringo Starr came down to the Pickwick fairly regularly and it became pretty clear that one of the attractions for them was the band. At one point they came in about 10 times in 14 days and started to bring Brian Epstein down with them. I got a sinking feeling, because I realised that Epstein wanted to take the band over. But I'll say this for him, he handled it in a very pleasant and nice way."

Don Paul states that whatever Tony might have claimed, it was he who secured Paddy, Klaus & Gibson's residency at the Pickwick and also their first record deal. "I got the group the deal with Pye Records because The Viscounts had been on Pye," he says, "so I knew all the people in the A&R department there, but I didn't produce their records. To be honest, I didn't want to lose my job at Essex Music by suddenly becoming a full-time manager to a band. I didn't really want to do all the donkey-work with Paddy, Klaus & Gibson, so I thought I would handle the artistic side of it and someone else could do the rest. So Stratters got his foot in the door."

Brian Epstein's interest in the group was a double-edged sword. "The band were very flattered... thought it was a dream come true," says Paul. Out of all the attendant Beatles, it was John Lennon who recommended Paddy, Klaus & Gibson and encouraged Epstein to buy out their contract with the group. As Don Paul recalls: "Eventually, Stratters did a deal with Epstein and I got £1,000 – which doesn't sound very much, but in 1965 it was a fair old sum. Tony told me that he'd sold the contract to Eppy for £2,000 – whether he got more than that I don't know – but I was happy to get a thousand and be out of everybody's hair. The band wanted me to leave Essex Music and go with them to NEMS [Epstein's company], but I didn't want to do that. Brian was a lovely guy but he didn't have enough time to spend with them, there were more important people to look after. The first single wasn't a hit and quite soon afterwards they split up."

It was with some reluctance that Tony and Don Paul agreed to the transfer, but Tony felt it was a wrong move. "I don't think it's arrogant to say that I could have done a good job with that band. I had regrets, because I think they should have made it. They weren't a Top 20 band, but they had a marvellous live feel. I think the way I was handling them, building them through the clubs and delaying a record debut was, with hindsight, the best way. With NEMS, record after record came out and they were put on tours where I don't think they really had time to develop."

Tony's judgement proved correct and Klaus Voorman agrees. "Strat didn't want to let us go. I think he had a crush on Gibbo. Brian, on the other hand, had a crush on Paddy. Even though, by this time Brian was quite far out to lunch, we thought he could do something for us. Maybe the move was a mistake, but no blame on anybody. The band wasn't really all that good. We would never have made it."

Paddy, Klaus & Gibson split up in 1966. Chambers later teamed up with Beryl Marsden, one of the best, if less recognised, girl singers to emerge from Liverpool. Gibson Kemp married Astrid Kirchherr, the German photographer best known for her shots of The Beatles during their time in Hamburg, and became an A&R man at Polygram Records. Klaus Voorman revived his Beatles connection, illustrating the cover for *Revolver* in 1966, and later joined John Lennon's Plastic Ono Band.

The split signalled the end of Tony's partnership with Don Paul, as he explained: "I had a bad experience with Tony. He asked me if I would lend him £100, which seems nothing today, but in 1966 it was more like a thousand nowadays. He said, 'I'll give it back to you next week – it's just that I've a bit of a cash flow problem.' Well, the next week came, and the week after that – and this went on for a long, long time. I decided to keep writing to him every week until I got it back. Eventually he paid back the money, but it took nearly a year, so that was it with Stratters and I didn't have any more to do with him."

The loss of Paddy, Klaus & Gibson left Tony at a loose end. His family urged a return to journalism but he was determined to remain in music. "I rather liked it, I liked the atmosphere of it, the way things were done. It suited me – I like a drink and in those days, I liked late nights, hanging around the Flamingo, the Marquee and the Pickwick which didn't close until two or three in the morning."

His next publishing client was Al Stewart who arrived in London in February 1965, looking to join a group but settling for a residency at Bunjies Folk Cellar where he turned into a folk singer almost overnight. Tony arranged for a set of promotional photographs to be taken around London, which portray a clean cut, fresh-faced young man, sporting a sharp suit and winkle-picker shoes.

"Tony Stratton Smith was great, but he didn't ever do much for me," Al Stewart told his biographer Neville Judd. "His attentions always seemed to be elsewhere, shall we say. He was a lot of fun, but as my manager – well, we never seemed to get anywhere. I had a nickname for him, I would call him Stratters Platters!"

Stewart wanted to record a cover version of the Paul Simon song 'Richard Cory' as his first single, but Tony had other ideas and was building interest in one of Stewart's own songs, 'The Elf', partly because Stratton Smith Music owned the publishing. "I'd sat in my bedsit in Lisle Street reading *Lord Of The Rings*," Stewart told Judd. "So I wrote 'The Elf' but I thought it sounded too much like a singalong Mitch Miller thing at the time."

Tony liked the song, no doubt influenced by his own love of J.R.R. Tolkien, and sent Stewart to see Decca record producer and arranger Mike Leander, who helped secure a deal with the label, booking a three-hour session at Sound Techniques in Chelsea where they recorded four songs. As part of the deal, Decca wanted someone to record 'A Pretty Girl Is Like A Melody' (which Stewart hated), to which they added two of Al's songs, 'The Elf' and 'All', a version of the 'Lyke-Wake Dirge' that Stewart had rewritten. Leander also brought 'Turn Into Earth' to the table, written by his friend and Yardbirds bassist, Paul Samwell-Smith, and the session featured Jimmy Page on guitar. In fact Mike Leander never intended to release 'A Pretty Girl...', telling Stewart that a mysterious 'technical fault' made the tapes unusable. Consequently 'The Elf' became the A-side of the single.

Tony hired Tony Hall, Decca's promotions man, to plug the single, convincing Stewart to hand over 1% of the 3% he was getting from Decca in order to cover Hall's services. In addition to various radio plays, Hall fixed an appearance for Stewart to appear on *The Frost Report*, David Frost's late-night television programme. Nevertheless, the record disappeared without trace and after about nine months on Tony's books he and Stewart parted company by mutual consent. "Stratton Smith had said to me that he really couldn't do anything else to push my career along and that I should find a folk manager," he said.

Al Stewart briefly shared accommodation with Paul Simon, then in London and working the folk circuit, and there is evidence to suggest that an opportunity to manage Simon, or at least publish his songs, slipped through Tony's fingers. Tony had asked a new friend, Terry 'The Pill' Slater, to accompany Stewart to gigs, as his wife Eve Slater confirms. "I can remember Terry telling me that he hated going round the folk clubs with Al, as I think either you were not allowed to smoke in them, or it could have been no drinking. One evening, Strat asked Terry to go along to a folk club to listen to an American that had just come over. Terry thought he was quite good, but said to Strat, 'Why on earth do you want another folk singer?' That folk singer was Paul Simon."

When Al Stewart's American flatmate turned up at the office looking for a manager, Tony politely turned the young New Yorker down flat. Tony also lost out on what would have been a potentially lucrative publishing deal when Simon urgently needed cash in hand. He and Stewart tried to offload the publishing rights to Simon's song catalogue for £5,000, a sum well out of Tony's reach. It was a portfolio that even then contained future classics like 'Homeward Bound', 'Kathy's Song' and 'Sounds Of Silence'.

The Al Stewart connection brought another young singer to Tony's attention. Reina James, daughter of the Carry On actor Sid James, was singing with a trio called The Backwater Three and Tony obviously heard something in her voice that encouraged him to put up money for a single. James suspected that Tony was less interested in their brand of American country blues and was looking to find the new Petula Clark – and he had just the song in mind.

"I remember being given the opportunity to make this record," recalls James. "I'm sure Tony was aware that Syd James was my dad and that may have been what moved him into being more helpful towards us. I do know that it was 1965, because I was pregnant with my son. We did it properly in this small studio, the three of us, with me massively pregnant, squeezing into this tiny recording booth. Tony must have known that I was pregnant when he booked the studio. Tony asked me if I could sound a bit more like Petula Clark. You know she had a lot of ghastly vocal tricks when she sang – and I think he wanted me to try to imitate some of those, but I think I messed it up.

"Tony was the most charming man and I just felt desperately sad afterwards that I had made a mess of it, if that's what it was. If I had been part of his stable, I might have ended up doing something. I mean I had another musical life three years later when I made an album, but the chance to have been on Charisma would have been amazing."

It would appear that Tony actively wanted to sign a female singer, and when the chance arose, he found himself a really good one: Beryl Hogg, born in Toxteth, Liverpool, who was barely 15 when she adopted the stage name Beryl Marsden and started singing with local beat groups. After an apprenticeship in Liverpool and Hamburg with various Liverpool bands, she released two singles on Decca, 'I Know' and 'When The Lovelight Starts Shining Thru' His Eyes', neither of which made the charts, not least because she was in Hamburg and unavailable to promote them.

When Marsden's contract with Decca Records ran out, she decamped to London where Tony took her under his managerial wing. "I absolutely adored Tony, I really adored him," she said. "My mum loved him too, because he was quite posh and well-spoken and she liked that, you know. But I was a bit of a rebel, I would always stand up for myself and say I'm not doing that, and Tony, well there were certain things that he didn't understand."

To be fair, Tony was still finding his own feet as a manager but he almost succeeded in establishing Beryl Marsden's name nationally, initially arranging a contract with Columbia, on which she released two more singles under the watchful eye of producer Ivor Raymonde. First up was 'Who You Gonna Hurt?' in October 1965, followed by her cover of Stevie Wonder's 'Music Talk' released two months later. Unfortunately, the spirited Miss Marsden was proving quite a handful for her relatively inexperienced manager. "Yes, Tony and I would sometimes fall out, but not in the way some people think," she recalled. "It felt to me like he was putting others first, so it caused another big row."

It proved to be another short-lived business partnership. "I probably wasn't an easy person to manage," Beryl later admitted.

Tony was forced to agree: "Beryl was a marvellous girl, flawed by a kind of Liverpudlian bloody-mindedness. There is a Liverpool thing and if you're not part of it, it's very difficult to cope with. I had to hire a minder for her and he was the only guy who could actually get some sense out of her. Often, if a gig didn't suit her, she would actually lock herself in her flat so that nobody could get in and she wouldn't come out. Many a time, this minder had to go through a window to get her."

Tony's choice of minder was the colourful Terry 'The Pill' Slater, who had helped him out with Al Stewart and would turn up again and again in the Stratton Smith story.

Tony was persuaded to part company with Beryl Marsden by the Gunnell Brothers, who took over her contract in March 1966 to pair her up with a new band, the Shotgun Express. Rik and John Gunnell were music entrepreneurs and promoters who had enlivened Soho with their Friday and Saturday All-Nighters at the Flamingo Club in Wardour Street, making a star of the young Georgie Fame in the process and subsequently opening a management and booking agency in Gerrard Street. Beryl found herself sharing the vocals with Rod Stewart, fronting a band previously known as Peter B's Looners, which included organist Pete Bardens, Peter Green on guitar, Dave Ambrose on bass and drummer Mick Fleetwood.

Having lost Beryl Marsden to the Gunnell Brothers, Tony did at least manage to keep her band The Krew on his books. They were another Liverpool group that at various times included Howie Casey on sax, ex-Big Six bass player Archie Leggett, drummer Eddie Sparrow, Alan Reeves on keyboards and vocalist Steve Aldo, plus guitarist Paddy Chambers for a short period. The association was not to last, however.

"Tony was a really nice bloke, he found all the band a place to stay in Kilburn, through his friend Alfie Maron who owned the gentleman's tailors next to Tony's office," recalls Howie Casey. "The Krew did a few gigs around London and a short tour of Northern Ireland with the lovely Beryl, but there wasn't enough work to keep us going, so we started doing gigs on our own. Then Tony came up with a job at Courchevel, a ski resort in France, and we were offered other French gigs ending up in Paris, which became our base, and from there we worked all over Europe. Gradually our contact with Tony dwindled and then we heard that he had sold Paddy, Klaus & Gibson to Brian Epstein for a few thousand pounds, the equivalent of a transfer fee, just like in football, which of course was Tony's biggest love."

The beginning of the end for Tony and The Krew happened in much the same way that it had done with Paddy, Klaus & Gibson. The band performed regularly at the Scotch of St. James, a 'showcase' club in Masons Yard, SW1, where you could often find members of The Beatles, The Rolling Stones, The Who, The Animals and Long John Baldry relaxing after hours, and it was here they encountered Lee Hallyday, singer Johnny Hallyday's uncle, who enticed them to Paris and took over their management.

"The Krew were very successful there," says Steve Aldo. "We worked hard in France, we had a really good time there. Lee Hallyday wanted me to stay and get my own band together, but when we came back to London, Strat had moved into Denmark Street and by this time he was more interested in the likes of The Koobas and Beryl Marsden."

Despite Aldo's misgivings, Tony did fix him up with a record deal on Parlophone, the one-off single 'Everybody Has To Cry', with producer David Gooch. The recording was issued in April 1966 with the idea of promoting Steve as a solo performer and the song, chosen by Aldo himself, was written by the relatively obscure blues and soul singer Z.Z. Hill.

Nevertheless, Steve Aldo's time as a Stratton Smith recording artist had run its course. He had an offer of management from Brian Epstein and told Tony he felt it was best they part company. "Strat said, 'Give me a week, Steve, and I'll sort out your contract and give it to you.' Unfortunately, in the meantime somebody had found out about me and Brian, and word somehow got back to Stratton Smith, so Strat called Brian and said he wanted £10,000 for my contract. When Brian told me this, I was furious. Brian told me he'd pay it, but I said, 'No, you bloody well won't pay him.' I went straight back to Stratton Smith and said, 'You can stick your contract up your arse, now I am going back to Liverpool.' So I just came back home."

* * *

Simon White was introduced to Tony through the lively Wardour Street social scene that centred around The Ship and Intrepid Fox pubs, La Chasse, a private members club that catered to the music industry, and the Marquee Club itself. Sometime around 1965, White was training to be a solicitor when a chance encounter with a young band diverted his career path towards rock'n'roll.

In fact, the young band were playing football in the street near where his car was parked in Sussex Gardens. When he cautioned them about kicking the ball into his motor they invited him to their gig that night at the Marquee. That was where he met the club's owner, Harold Pendleton, and through him became involved with Marquee Studios.

Strangely, for someone who spent so much time in and around the Marquee, Tony did not get on too well with Harold Pendleton. The former chartered accountant and jazz fanatic originally set up the Marquee Club in Oxford Street in April 1958, before moving to its spiritual home at 90 Wardour Street in 1964. It was most unlike Tony to ever hold a grudge for very long but, according to Simon White, he never completely forgave Harold Pendleton over a business deal that went astray.

"For a short time Strat occupied one of the rooms of the offices that the Marquee had above the Pizza Express in Carlisle Street," he explains. "He was talking to Harold about going into some sort of partnership or joint venture, because Harold was an accountant and Strat was always a little poor (in both senses of the word) in that respect. However, Harold's strict attitude to the sanctity of the petty cash box caused Strat immense grief and they had a huge row and ended the arrangement shortly afterwards. Privately Strat never really spoke well of Harold afterwards. Of course they still saw each other regularly at the Marquee Club and did business both there and with the National Jazz Festival, although that was usually done through Jack Barrie. But I don't think Harold was ever fully aware of how badly Strat felt about him."

Jack Barrie, who managed La Chasse Club, would go on to become one of Tony's greatest – if not *the* greatest – friend he ever had. He has never forgotten the first time he met Tony, when they were both struggling to find their way in the music business of the mid-sixties. For reasons long ago forgotten Tony had spent the night at Jack Barrie's flat, of which Jack was unaware until the following morning.

"Something clicks when the first time you meet someone they're asleep in your flat, on your settee, the worse for wear from an overindulgence of your Scotch," he recalls. "I can still remember our first conversational exchange."

Barrie: "Do you take milk and sugar in your coffee?"

Stratton Smith: "I prefer brandy in mine. By the way, who are you?"

* * *

The group that benefited, some might say suffered, the most from Tony's fashion advice were The Koobas (originally The Kubas), another Liverpool group. Formed around 1962 by the brothers John and Roy Morris, they started out as a Shadows-style instrumental group called The Midnights and later expanded to include vocalist Roy Montrose. They added Stuart Leatherwood on vocals and lead guitar, and Keith Ellis on bass to become the first Kubas line-up proper. John Morris[2*] subsequently stood down to become their road manager and was replaced by drummer Tony O'Reilly.

The group played a three-week residency at the Star Club in Hamburg during December 1963 and in 1965, under Tony's management, grabbed a place on the bill of The Beatles' final British tour. They may have been part of the Merseybeat scene, but the widely held belief that The Kubas were originally managed by Brian Epstein is one myth that guitarist Roy Morris is keen to dispel.

"It's simply not true, I don't know where that ever came from. Originally we were managed by my brother John, when we were in Liverpool. He managed us until we came down to London, and we first came down in 1963, but it wasn't really happening in the South in '63, so we went back up to Liverpool. Then we came back down to London again in mid-1965, which is when we first met Stratton Smith. He offered us a contract to manage us and I got my brother to come down to work for him. So instead of being our manager, John became part of Stratton Smith's staff.

"Strat was a great guy, always very enthusiastic, but it was still early days and he was learning the trade the same as we all were, I suppose. After signing with Strat we had nowhere to stay in London, so we all ended up living in Strat's flat."

The flat was in Bloomsbury and Steve Aldo of the Krew was also living there part of the time. "There used to be about six of us sleeping on his living room floor," says Morris. "It was a big change for us. We'd never done that one before."

Having lost one band to Epstein, Tony probably wanted to keep the positive connection going by suggesting that Brian had passed a group back to him. Whatever the explanation, Tony took on the mantle of manager, producer and 'occasional lyricist' in 1965. It was at his suggestion that the band changed the spelling of their name from Kubas to Koobas, most likely for 'dubious contractual reasons', according to writer Pete Frame.

Music publisher Mike Berry remembers working with the band: "Tony Stratton Smith wanted a piece of the Mersey Sound. He'd found a group, the Koobas, of which Stu Leatherwood was an integral part. Tony had found them a song called 'Take Me For A Little While', which I was astounded to realise was one of the songs I published. It was only a couple of days before Strat got the cash required to hire a studio in Denmark Street, and away we went. I managed to get it released on Pye Records, and with a bit of help, the record made the lower region of the charts."

Tony was always a great believer in publicity and it was fortuitous

---

2   * Morris later married Clodagh Rodgers and successfully managed her singing career.

for both of them that around this time, the end of 1964, he encountered Nancy Carol Lewis, an American student at Michigan State University and 'campus correspondent' for *Billboard*, America's principal music trade magazine. With the help of the director of *Billboard* Europe, Nancy and her friend Michele Powers Glaze flew to England as freelance journalists to report on the burgeoning London music scene. They based themselves at a cheap hotel in Bayswater and became regulars at the Marquee Club. Nancy also began writing for *Fabulous* magazine, a different animal to the other pop music papers. Priced at one shilling, it was dearer than the competition, but you got more pages for your money, many of which were in colour and printed on better quality paper.

Heavily biased towards Merseybeat, and one Liverpool group in particular, *Fabulous* offered a more personal look at the life of the pop star, with 'at-home' and 'off-stage' fashion features that would appeal to its predominately female readership. As a result, the paper employed more female writers and photographers on its editorial team, at a time when 'the print' was still a male-dominated environment.

A few months into their stay the girls met Jack Barrie, then managing The Boz People, and they all moved into a flat in Hammersmith. Jack had the front bedroom, Nancy and Michele the room behind the kitchen, with the band taking over the living room whenever they were in town. After Michele flew back to the States in October 1965, Nancy stayed on to handle publicity for various acts, her connection with Jack Barrie and the Marquee crowd bringing her to the attention of Tony and subsequently Who co-manager Kit Lambert.

Tony, working out of an office at number 31 Wardour Street, took on Nancy to help brighten up The Koobas image, including the design of 'kooba trews', the flowery stage trousers designed especially for the band. One piece of publicity enthused: "Within a few weeks, the boys had brand new stage gear (surely you've seen those sensation-creating flowered trousers!), an agency contract with Arthur Howes, a recording contract with Pye and needless to say, a fresh burst of enthusiasm and high hopes!"

"The Koobas were a nice little band," Tony told Joe Smith. "They introduced flower-power, in a sense, because they were the first to go on with those awful flowered flared trousers, which were made for us from a little idea by Nancy Lewis. She deserved all the credit on that, she actually made them." Nancy may have come up with the idea, but she has no recollection of acting as seamstress for the band. More likely, those eye-catching trousers were the work of Alfie Maron – a tailor and part-time actor – whose rooms at 31 Wardour Street were directly underneath Tony's office.

Another interesting example of Tony and Nancy's carefully crafted publicity was a story that the Koobas had the backing of a member of the

Royal family. Talking to the national press, Tony would neither confirm nor deny the rumour, telling journalists that a legal clause in their contract prevented him from revealing the name of the other party, who happened to be out of the country at that time. By an amazing coincidence, at the time of the 'Royal rumour' the band had just released their single 'Take Me For A Little While' and were about to go off on tour supporting The Beatles.

The Koobas certainly appreciated the effort that Tony put in to breaking the group. "He was a creative character, very much so," said Roy Morris. "He came up with a few little things like that. And we didn't mind, anything to get in the papers really, that was the whole idea of the flower trousers. They got us plenty of publicity, but if we'd put out a better record we could have done even better. When we were on that tour with The Beatles, Nancy came round at most of the gigs to put the eyeliner on and things like that. Even The Beatles wore stage make-up in those days."

This tour, which turned out to be The Beatles' final jaunt around the UK, took place in December 1965, taking in eight cities over ten days. The main support came from the Moody Blues, but further down the bill were three of the acts associated with Tony – The Koobas, Beryl Marsden and Steve Aldo. The two solo singers were backed on stage by The Paramounts, later to become Procol Harum.

The Beatles tour gave Tony some much needed management credibility, as he later recalled: "Brian again had helped to put me on the map. It was one of those casual, kind gestures which he could often make and which a lot of people forget. In a sense, that tour put me on the map as a manager, because everybody said, 'Who is this guy, this young guy with three acts on the Beatles tour?'"

Tony tried every angle to keep The Koobas in the public eye. Following The Beatles' tour they worked tirelessly; 11 TV shows, several theatre and concert tours both here and abroad, including a storming show at the prestigious La Locomotive club in Paris, and even appearing in the feature film *Money-Go-Round* alongside Sheila White. In an interview with *Record Mirror*'s Peter Jones, Stuart Leatherwood said, "These days a group has got to be prepared to do anything. Our manager Tony Stratton Smith is even fixing with RADA for us to have acting lessons."

Tony personally penned the sleeve notes for The Koobas' one and only album, issued on the Columbia label in 1969, lavishing the boys with praise in prose as flowery as Nancy's trousers. "Experience has washed over them, but time has refreshed, not smothered the innocence of mood and feeling, the cheerfulness of presence, the exciting attack which for me always features The Koobas' performance..." And occasional lyricist? Tony gets a co-writing credit on the track 'Barricades' alongside Keith Ellis and Stuart Leatherwood. After four more singles and the release of their only album, poor record sales finally convinced the Koobas to call it a day, but their bass guitarist, and apparently Tony's personal favourite, Keith Ellis, would turn up again later in the Stratton Smith story.

* * *

Tony's next client was a Hertfordshire group, The Mark Four, initially represented by the Robert Stigwood agency. A raw, powerful and visually exciting act, Tony agreed to work with them on the condition they found a new bass player and he recommended Bob Garner, briefly a Merseybeat and latterly with Tony Sheridan's group. Garner's appointment was accepted by the other members and Tony's next move was to find them a suitable producer. In early 1966 he introduced them to his friend Shel Talmy, the hot independent record producer of the day, who'd already been responsible for hits by The Kinks and The Who.

Like Tony, Talmy was impressed with The Mark Four when the band auditioned for him at Regent Sound Studio in Denmark Street and he wasted no time in signing them to his own record label, Planet. On May 18 they assembled at IBC Studios in Portland Place and recorded their first single for Tony, 'Making Time', a live favourite that featured the distinctive sound of Eddie Phillips using a violin bow on the strings of his electric guitar, something he'd already tried out and a technique Jimmy Page would famously adopt.

Their singer, Kenny Pickett, recalls his first meeting with the new manager. "I was introduced to this chap with a double-barrelled name, a gentle but limp handshake, a public school accent issued from a rather weak mouth; dressed in a crumpled blue suit and just about the most unlikely rock'n'roll manager I could have wished for. Then, his eyes looking into the middle-distance, face intellectually screwed and cheeks shiny, cigarette delicately poised between incredibly delicate fingers like an Oscar Wilde accessory, he would laugh his laugh – and in that split second I think I actually enjoyed getting drunk in the company of the man who had just pocketed our *Ready Steady Go!* fee."

The Mark Four changed their name to The Creation, reputedly found by Kenny Pickett in a book of Russian poetry, although guitarist Eddie Phillips believes Tony was responsible. "He had an idea in his mind of what he wanted to do with the band, both the name and the style."

Hedging his bets, Tony contacted both the Catholic and Anglican churches to enquire whether or not they found a pop group called The Creation offensive. The responses varied wildly, but he carefully turned the whole thing into a useful piece of tabloid press coverage. Lord Charles Hill, Chairman of the Independent Television Authority, claimed the name was blasphemous, prompting Tony to defend his decision in *Melody Maker*: "I chose the name and don't think it irreligious. I have written a religious biography, *The Rebel Nun*, which received favourable reviews from a number of bishops."

Archbishop Michael Ramsey and Cardinal John Heenan both gave their blessing to the new name and, rumour has it, their letter included a footnote from the archbishop adding "The best of luck to the boys."

Shel Talmy, who famously disliked Kit Lambert, states that Tony was one of the few music industry people he could get on with. "The Creation could have been superstars," he says, "but I couldn't hold them together or stop them breaking up. In retrospect, I'm sorry I didn't do a bit more work for Tony, because he was a great character and unusual for a label owner. Strat and I became good friends and we had a lot of enjoyable evenings because he was one of the few people I could speak with about damn near anything. He had a great sense of humour, he was a smart guy and knowledgeable on a lot of subjects, but he would get a bit too drunk from time to time. To be a band manager you have to be an asshole. You have to put yourself on a par with the band, be obnoxious and all that kind of thing. There are exceptions and I think Epstein might have been an exception. The only guy I can think of who was a good band manager that I liked was Tony Stratton Smith."

A couple of months later, The Creation recorded a second single for Planet Records, 'Painter Man'. Possibly inspired by the song title, Pickett had started to include a little modern art during their live performances, encouraging the group's publicist to declare that "our music is red with purple flashes" or vice versa, depending on which press release you read. His action painting was not just confined to painting on canvas; he was just as happy to daub the occasional semi-naked female, should one be available.

When the Talmy-produced single entered the *NME* chart at number 22, journalist Norrie Drummond ran a small piece on the band who "paint as they play" and spoke to Tony, "their energetic young manager", who explained: "They paint because they feel like it, not simply because it's gimmicky. They just paint when they feel moved to. They experiment with the music too. At the moment they're working something out using a violin bow and a potato. But I'm not quite sure what it is."

In later years, Tony would put out a compilation album on his own label and the sleeve notes, probably written by himself, began thus: "One brightening dawn of a summer's day in 1966, The Creation and manager Tony Stratton Smith crept into Great Yarmouth after an overnight haul from Blackpool. Somewhat oddly, they spent the next hour canvassing early-opening garages for every aerosol can of paint they could buy, thereby, and very persuasively, breaking a local Sunday bye-law. That night, on the stage of the ABC, The Creation collared a Walker Brothers audience and made it their own. They introduced their famous 'action-painting' finale, with singer Kenny Pickett making lightning images, then destroying them by fire."

Tony always enjoyed telling the story: "The singer, Kenny Pickett, would have nothing to do during these solos, so we came up with the idea of building a frame, covering it with paper, and introduce 'action painting' with aerosols."

However, what really upset the hall management and the Walker Brothers' entourage, was that at the end of the song, Phillips set fire to the painting, a move that almost got The Creation thrown off the second show. Tony managed to cool things down and the band went on again with the action painting gimmick "... but Eddie got carried away, set fire to it again, and we were forever banned from West Yarmouth!"

* * *

Just a short stagger from the usual Soho drinking dens, at the southern end of Dean Street, across Shaftesbury Avenue towards Chinatown, is a Dutch-themed pub called De Hems. For those in the music business, this was where a place in the charts could allegedly be bought. De Hems was certainly on Tony's radar and he later admitted to arranging, either directly or through a middle-man, for records by artists on his books to be 'assisted' into the charts. Tony was always adamant that the artists themselves had no knowledge of what was happening.

The first was 'Painter Man' by The Creation and Tony claimed he had personally pushed the record to the brink of the Top 20 by 'judicious fixing', laying out a hefty £600 to secure a chart position for the single in October 1966. He decided not to aim any higher, as a) it would have been too expensive and b) because "I have a genuine respect for the Top 20". In his opinion, he had simply "given the kiss of life to a flagging record". In the event 'Painter Man' reached no higher than 35 in the UK charts, though it went on to be a sizeable hit in Europe, comfortably reaching the number three spot in Germany without any outside assistance – even from the manager.

An attempt by Tony to 'assist' a further single by The Creation backfired, the fix detected when an unusually high concentration of sales around the London area aroused suspicion. Tony claimed this was the last time he was involved in chart rigging. In a contemporary newspaper article he criticised the "hit record fixation", which he blamed for a situation where "managers and artists themselves have to pay either to stay in the race or even to come under starters orders. In our world, the golden rule is quite clear – show in the charts or struggle on, getting nowhere. A record's position in the charts controls the degree of interest and promotion a record company puts behind it, makes it easier to earn plugs on radio and television and dictates the number and quality of ballroom bookings a group obtains."

Such was the level of chart tampering, especially in the lower regions where fewer sales were required to claim a decent position, that in 1967 *Melody Maker* editor Jack Hutton announced that the popular Top 50 chart would be reduced to a Top 30 in an attempt to curb fixing. Hutton also drew up a list of people he believed to be involved and forbade his staff writers from dealing with them. Tony's name was on the list. *Melody Maker* journalist Chris Welch found himself fending off calls from a disgruntled Stratton Smith.

"Before we actually met, Strat would ring me up at the *Melody Maker* office quite a lot," says Welch. "Tony already had quite a reputation, but he'd got into a bit of a scrape with chart fixing. There was a big story about chart fixing at the time, where people like Don Arden and other managers were accused with fiddling the charts. Of course everybody had their own charts then, all the music papers ran their own Top 20 and Top 50 and it was fairly easy, as we discovered, to get hold of a list of the charts. People would 'buy' records into the charts by going around the chart return shops and buying up multiple copies. Tony was one of those who were implicated in that and my editor Jack Hutton said, 'You mustn't speak to Tony Stratton Smith or report on any of his bands.' He was effectively blacklisted.

"I knew he was a nice guy and among all the managers he was one of the more pleasant people," continues Welch. "Some of the rock managers could be quite aggressive and tough guys, they were too busy to talk to you. It was either one extreme or the other – you were lucky if you could get to talk to Brian Epstein or Andrew Oldham who could be a bit stroppy, but Strat was always far more approachable. Anyway, he phoned me at the office one day, more or less imploring me to resume writing about his acts. He was saying how it was so very tough in the music business and how he really needed *Melody Maker*'s help. He was just trying to put his case, saying how unfair it was to blacklist him, but it was such a pleasant conversation that I felt quite sorry for him afterwards."

Welch ignored his editor's orders and went to see The Creation at The Flamingo where Kenny Pickett painted on the sheets of paper, splatting paint about and setting fire to it. "No one else was doing this sort of thing – it was called 'auto-destruction' I think – with the possible exception of The Who, but seeing The Creation was great fun, so I gave them a good review."

Nevertheless, it wasn't long before The Creation imploded. "There were four people in the group and two of them hated the other two, they were continually plotting against each other," recalls Tony. "One left because his wife didn't want him to travel abroad, even though that meant making handsome stacks of money which would have insured her security, and that of their family, for some time to come. This is the sort of personal thing you just can't resolve."

Shel Talmy's Planet label was also short-lived but he kept faith with The Creation, producing a handful of their singles after they signed to Polydor Records. Kenny Pickett was the next to go, leaving the group in February 1967, allegedly after he found the rest of the group rehearsing one of his songs without him. For a while he became an in-house songwriter for Shel Talmy and found himself working alongside Tony again, although he struggled to compete with the former journalist.

"And then, comfortable in Shel Talmy's Knightsbridge apartment, Strat once more down on his uppers, long before the Charisma explosion," wrote Pickett. "He on one typewriter, me on another, both of us writing for Shel's dollars. And there the similarity ended. He, prolific and prose perfect, fag in his mouth and typing through one screwed up eye in true Fleet Street hack tradition. His mid-afternoon Scotch and coke dancing on the table as he worked, effortlessly sticking word after word onto the page, while I stumbled and pecked at the typewriter like a hungry chicken. But he was always generous. He would laugh at my humour, pat my back in encouragement and then forget that I existed as he slipped back into his own world of true literature."[3]*

MM writer Chris Welch's perception of Tony as a 'nice guy' is borne out by two instances of his generosity around this time. While still managing The Koobas, Tony encountered jobbing musician Chris Mayfield, down on his luck and sleeping on a bench in Russell Square Gardens, just around the corner from Tony's flat. Generously, Stratton Smith would provide more than just management advice, often bringing out early morning cups of tea and slipping Mayfield the occasional five pound note, until he managed to get his life back on track. Another out-of-work music man to benefit from Tony's kindness was Richard Cole, who had lost his driving licence, never the ideal situation for a would-be road manager. Tony stepped in with a job offer, arguing that although he couldn't drive in the UK, Cole still held an international work permit, and promptly sent him off on a three-week tour of Holland and Germany with The Creation. Cole would eventually become tour manager for Led Zeppelin.

One lesser-known band that briefly came under Tony's tutelage were The Thoughts, another Liverpool group who made their way to London. They had already recorded as the backing band for former Liverbird Tiffany (Irene Green), and guitarist Peter Beckett recalls the move south: "When we moved down to London we were sleeping on park benches and getting together in the pubs at night to play, trying to get a gig here and there. It was pretty rough." They hooked up with Tony and, through his contact with Shel

---

3   * Pickett and co-writer Herbie Flowers would win an Ivor Novello award for co-writing 'Grandad', a UK number one novelty hit for *Dad's Army* actor Clive Dunn.

Talmy, released a debut single on Talmy's Planet Records, the Ray Davies composition 'All Night Stand'.

The Thoughts' biggest gig was opening for The Who at the Savile Theatre on Shaftesbury Avenue where Brian Epstein promoted concerts. This particular concert, in January 1967, was a Sunday at the Savile 'Soundarama' presentation and Tony was given support slots for both The Thoughts and The Koobas, while another band on the bill was the relatively unknown Jimi Hendrix Experience. Epstein and The Beatles all watched Hendrix steal the show and Beckett remembers watching open-mouthed from the wings alongside Roger Daltrey and Pete Townshend, who had the unenviable task of following Jimi onstage.

While he was managing them, The Koobas supported Hendrix on several dates in Europe and in May 1968 Tony found himself on a chartered flight from Heathrow to Zurich as part of a large entourage that included 'his boys', plus band members and roadies for The Move, John Mayall's Bluesbreakers, Eric Burdon and Traffic. They were on their way to play two high-profile concerts at the Hallenstadion organised by 27-year-old local promoter Hans-Ruedi Jaggi, who had already angered the Swiss officials by bringing The Rolling Stones to Zurich the previous year. The 'Monsterkonzert' was to be headlined by Jimi Hendrix, who was flying in direct from New York.

Overall, the first night went without a hitch – apart from one guy who managed to get on stage and snatch John Mayall's cigarette lighter, but even that was returned – but on the second night around 20 kids started to smash up some wooden folding chairs as they were leaving. This was enough for the police to leap into action, aggressively pushing the crowd out of the stadium, rubber truncheons at the ready. In the concert aftermath, the police were heavily criticised for their use of excessive force. As one magazine reported, "The concert was no monster, but the police were."

It was the era of protest. The Parisian student riots of May 1968 inspired the Stones to write 'Street Fighting Man' and Tony gave his own perspective on these troubled times in an interview with *Fusion* magazine in July 1969: "I'm of a different generation… mentally I was prepared for the student unrest, for the rock'n'roll event, because you can't keep the stopper on the bottle all those years without something happening eventually. I was born in the year that Hitler came to power. In fact I did my schooling through the Nazi war. My adolescence was through the rationing and gravest of post-war England and the socialist government was going to create Utopia with two cents in its pocket. A very ascetic world. A very dull one and I'm glad I am coming into the age of general television and the rock and roll thing and exciting things happening in the world. It's much better now than it was. I'd like to have been born into this generation, perhaps that's why I feel so close to both the artists and everything that they are trying to do. Because I recognise that it's got a relevance beyond today's gig."

During 1967 and 1968 the Koobas became a popular attraction in Switzerland where they played all the main clubs – the Atlantis in Basel, the Festhalle in Bern supporting the Small Faces, and the Hallenstadion in Zurich. Their records fared far better over there too, with their version of Cat Stevens' 'The First Cut Is The Deepest' hitting the Swiss charts just before the infamous Monsterkonzert at the end of May 1968. Tony, however, was in such dire financial straits that he talked to Teddy Meier, the promotions manager for EMI Switzerland, about taking over management of The Koobas and, just prior to the band's break-up, Teddy did exactly that. "When Strat gave up their management, I acted as their 'manager' for a short while, without a contract and without money."

There is a very fine line between success and failure and The Koobas are a classic case of so near, yet so far – a good, solid live band dogged by a series of unlucky events. They had filmed a scene for the film *Ferry Cross The Mersey*, playing one of the losing finalists in a battle of the bands competition, but the footage ended up on the cutting room floor. Their version of 'First Cut Is The Deepest' was overshadowed by P.P. Arnold's version, which made the UK charts instead. They recorded their only full-length album in the new psychedelic style, but broke up just as it was released – and with no band on the road to promote it, the record sank without trace.

The Koobas' lack of success was Tony's biggest disappointment, but the experiences, both good and bad, would prove to be crucial, forcing him to take a long, hard look at his relationship with his artists and his own role as manger. In the interview with *Fusion* magazine he admitted: "This group I really poured my heart and money into, because I really thought they had a hot thing." The sum mentioned was $50,000, which seems exaggerated.

"I lost them on The Beatles' tour. This was when they toured around England and were moving on the continent and that sort of thing. The Koobas were doing a lot of festivals in Europe and getting known. They sort of slowly brought me to really look at myself as a manager and them as a group. I realised that they were a constant financial and emotional drain. I was leading myself into tremendous frustrations and also, by continuing the relationship with them, I was keeping a promise to them that I no longer felt they could achieve. I lost a small fortune, but it's true I had a lot of fun out of it and a lot of experience."

Chapter 5

The Nice Manager

"He had vision, compassion, he listened and he bloody well cared."
Legs Larry Smith, Bonzo

In the middle of 1968, a new woman arrived in Tony's life, not romantically of course, or even signed to an artist contract, but someone who could make sense of his wayward impulses and take care of the important details that would always bore him.

Gail Colson was raised in a lively pub in Hampstead, and educated briefly at secretarial college and the Lucy Clayton Charm School. She entered the music business in 1964, working for publicist Jonathan Rowlands and dealing with Tom Jones, Engelbert Humperdinck and Rod Stewart, and from there she became personal assistant to Shel Talmy, later enduring a brief spell working for Tony Secunda, who managed The Move and Procol Harum. It was Talmy's dealings with Tony that brought him and Gail into the same orbit.

"I don't quite know why we hit it off so well, but Tony and I became friends quite quickly," she says. "I would often go to The Ship in Wardour Street, which is where everyone hung out in those days, and we would go to the cinema a lot and go out to dinner together. He had no money at that time, so I would lend him £15 on a Wednesday or Thursday and he'd find it from somewhere and give it back to me as soon as he could. He had a secretary called Sandy Beech, but eventually he had to lay her off because he simply had no money, so I used to do a little work for him on the side, without Shel knowing – although I'm fairly sure that Shel knew."

Gail Colson and Tony Stratton Smith would become heads and tails of the same coin, each reliant on the other: he the impetuous, principled, yet almost childlike impresario; she the sympathetic yet prudent business manager who somehow channelled his reckless integrity into profit.

It was through their new friendship that Gail went on a short tour of the Netherlands with Tony and The Koobas, her first trip abroad with a band. It proved to be an eye-opener for the 20-year-old Colson. They all stayed in a hovel of a hotel in Amsterdam and, being the only female, Gail was given her own room. Unfortunately, whenever she opened the door to her room, a man at the other end of the dingy corridor flashed back at her. Horrified, Gail got one of the band members to take her room while she shared, somewhat uneasily, with the other three. Better the devil you know, she figured.

Tony was in desperate need of some help. He was moving up a gear and about to sign two more management clients, The Nice and The Bonzo Dog Band.

* * *

The Nice – keyboard player Keith Emerson, bass player and vocalist Lee Jackson, guitarist Davey O'List and drummer Brian 'Blinky' Davison – would become Tony's first real success in music, but such was his despair at his string of failures that it almost didn't happen. "I had book contracts and was lined up for a film script. My agent was pleased with me again. He would sit there and say, 'Great, now you've stopped fucking around with music we can do some honest work…'"

Fortuitously, Lee Jackson and The Nice had other ideas. During a chaotic tour of Italy, playing alongside the likes of Pink Floyd, Traffic and The Move, Jackson and Keith Emerson decided they were in need of a change of management. Their record label Immediate was not playing the game with an entirely straight bat, offsetting travel expenses and hotel bills against the band's ever diminishing royalties. Emerson sent a woe-filled telegram back to Jack Barrie at the Marquee asking, somewhat tongue in cheek, if he wanted to manage them. Barrie's response was to point them in the direction of Tony Stratton Smith, with the warning that they could expect reluctance or outright rejection, as Tony was still hurting over the break-up of The Koobas.

Keith Emerson takes up the tale. "At the Speakeasy one night, I was told that Tony was somewhere in the crowd of beautiful people and went on the hunt for him. He was to be found, not surprisingly, at the bar where I introduced myself. 'I know who you are!' he boomed in a most jovial manner, striking me immediately as one of the old school. An Orson Welles lookalike, with a delivery somewhere between Jack Hawkins and Patrick McNee from *The Avengers*. 'I've seen you at the Marquee Club and I must admit I was most impressed – but your marketing is all wrong. The band lacks a central figure, there should be more of an accent on you. If I was managing you…' I managed to interrupt him. 'That's what I've come to ask you,' I said. 'If… I was to manage you,' he continued, ignoring me. 'But I don't think I want to get back into all that again. Bands are nothing but hard work and heartbreak.' Now I really wanted him as our manager and persisted. 'Could we meet as a band and talk more about this?' 'Let me think about it,' said Strat. 'Here is my office number, call me in a couple of weeks.'"

In the meantime, Tony flew out to Switzerland, partly to tie up unfinished business with The Koobas and partly to assess his future. He was still unsure of which path to take when the persistent Lee Jackson called Tony on his return. Somewhat reluctantly, Tony agreed to go and see the band play. It turned out to be a landmark decision and what he heard made up his mind once and for all. "They just slayed me," Tony would tell *Melody Maker*'s Roy Hollingworth. "I became emotionally involved."

During those intervening two weeks, all hell had broken loose after the group burned a Stars & Stripes flag at the Royal Albert Hall during their rendition of 'America' from *West Side Story*. This led to a lifetime ban and potential problems with future tours of the USA but temporarily boosted audiences at UK shows. Perhaps surprisingly, Tony called the band into his office in Wardour Street and took them on, "cementing a bonding, intentionally constructed on so much sand that it could fall apart at any time", said Emerson. "But that's the way Tony wanted it, just a simple letter of agreement was all that was requested. It was a true act of altruism and we had ourselves a manager."

Tony later told journalist Michael Wale they felt they were being neglected. "Frankly, I think they were. At the time I took over, their affairs were in an awful mess, they were £5,000 in debt and in awful trouble. I think I started to become less emotional and more practical about the whole thing. Here was a band worth working with, because if they did break, they would break very big – and that's the way it worked. Everybody was happy, they felt they'd found a good manager and I felt I'd found a good band."

The Nice had originally assembled at Andrew Oldham's behest to back singer P.P. Arnold whose recording of Cat Stevens' 'The First Cut Is The Deepest' pushed The Koobas' recording aside. It was released on Oldham's Immediate label but Oldham didn't see them as a separate act. "Their usefulness to him was as a back-up group," said Tony. "Part of the condition on which they could record was that they find management, which is how I came on the scene.

"When they started, Keith was apt to hide at the back of the stage behind the organ, tuck himself into the shadows. But when The Nice started as a solo act, Keith decided that somebody had to do something... had to be a showman. They thought that people wouldn't just listen to the music. So Keith started all the leaping about, standing on his Hammond organ, cracking whips and sticking knives into the instrument. I don't believe he was into actually throwing knives at that time. I don't think he thought his aim was all that good and he needed more practice. That came later."

With The Nice touring, their recording of 'America' reached number 21 in the UK charts and by this time they had recorded two albums for Immediate, with O'List departing just before the release of the second, *Ars*

Longa Vita Brevis, which included 'America'. O'List wasn't replaced and they opted to continue as a trio.

The burning of the US flag at the Albert Hall displeased the American authorities and prior to their proposed US tour in 1968, Tony and Keith Emerson were summoned to the American Embassy in London. "They had us swear on a stack of bibles that there would be no more flags burnt," Emerson remembers. "Actually, I did do it one more time in America, which horrified Lee Jackson." The composer of *West Side Story*, Leonard Bernstein, was also outraged. Asked for his opinion of The Nice's version of 'America', he stormed, "I utterly loathe what they've done. They've corrupted my work."

Tony recognised the creative dilemma caused by the clamour for instant success with a hit single and the artistic requirements of what was essentially an album-based band, as he told one interviewer: "For The Nice, singles are incredibly difficult. The finest single track The Nice ever recorded was a live version of the Bob Dylan song 'She Belongs To You'. We timed it at over 11 minutes. What's the solution? There's one issue with the double-sided single or there's one trying to evade a bad edit – or there's one to sit back and wait. I think the only answer is to sit back and wait, because if you force the group, if you put pressure on them directly to go into a studio and try to produce a single, I think that's the beginning of the end. You're in the first stage of corrupting what the group is really all about. This is a betrayal. All you can do is to say that I think we need a single, is there anything in the bag? If not, don't worry.

"But we do need it. That's a sort of contradiction in terms, you might say that's a more subtle form of pressure, but it's not. I want the group to always make its own decisions, particularly the artistic – because it's an insult to a group for any manager, however well informed, however much taste he may have, to try to take over their thing. I mean, their thing is theirs, it's not my thing. I'm outside of it – I'm not part of The Bonzo Dog Band or The Nice – our relationship, the link, is a spiritual one."

Tony's description of the relationship with his artists as being largely spiritual should not hide the fact that he not only personally pored over every aspect of the band's welfare but of their live performance too, including the nuts and bolts of equipment issues, not something you would normally associate with the unpractical Mr Stratton Smith.

"I enjoy watching The Nice, The Bonzo Dog Band," he said. "I think this is part of it all, that I never get bored with watching my bands. I sweat before every show when I'm actually there with a band. I get an uptight feeling in the gut. Before the show, I prowl around at the back of the hall. I'm not so worried about the audience reaction, I'm worried about whether it's going to happen – the intangible something – and whether everything, absolutely everything is right on stage. If I'm there, it really twists me inside to hear a bad amp or a bad PA system, or to know that a mic is wobbly – that sort of thing. I'm the least practical and technical person that you could ever meet, but I force myself into an awareness of the technical problems of groups. Because it's part of my job."

Lee Jackson recalls the joys of life on the road with their caring new manager. "Strat travelled with us a lot, all over the place, and there are lots of funny stories about travelling with him. We locked him out of his hotel room in Hamburg once. Keith and I were sharing a room just down the corridor from him and Keith had seen Strat leave his room without fully closing the door. It was just a cheap hotel, and in those days very few hotels had en-suite bathrooms, so Strat was on his way down the corridor in his underpants to use the bathroom. And because he'd left the door slightly ajar, Keith's nipped down and closed it. When he came back, he knocked on our door and said, 'Can I come in, I seem to have been locked out of my room...' and there's Keith and I trying hard to keep a straight face.

"Another time we were in Denmark, and in some of those big European hotels people would leave their shoes outside the door to be polished. We went down this huge long corridor picking up everyone's shoes, staff and guests, mixed them all up and dumped them outside Strat's room. We later heard Strat arguing with the management and he was saying, 'I know nothing about this, but I expect my charges do!' He was very well spoken and if you remember the British actor Jack Hawkins, Strat looked and sounded just like him."

Travelling with Tony was all very well, providing you could actually get him to the airport on time. Road manager for The Nice, Barrington 'Bazz' Ward, was one of many who found that rousing their manager from his slumbers was nigh on impossible. "There was one particular time when we drove back from a gig in Weymouth to meet up with Tony in London so that we could get an early flight out to Belgium. We were all about to fly out to Antwerp and we managed to get to the airport on time, but of course Strat didn't make it, he'd overslept again – and he had the passports. We had to send a cab to collect the passports and drive them back to us."

It was around this time that Tony started to use the newly formed Marquee Martin Agency to book gigs and concert tours for The Nice. John Martin became head of the overall organisation with John Toogood, Chris Barber and Simon White as directors. Toogood – his real name incidentally, not a stage affectation – found himself working closely with Tony, and with The Nice in particular.

"John and I were interested in growing the agency and we thought The Nice would be a fantastic acquisition, but we needed firm management behind it. John and I offered to lend Strat £1,000 for him to kick off the management side and having done that we acquired them for the agency and it became an ongoing arrangement for quite a long time. Once he became their manager, he had much greater access to their business career and he was able to get them out of their contract with Immediate – which meant they were then also available to sign for recording. Now once again, Strat had no real finance to even think about starting a recording company, so he and I used to meet up all the time to discuss things. The end of a typical day for me would be to finish about seven or eight o'clock, after the American telephone calls, and go to meet Strat in La Chasse Club. Almost every single night of the week we'd sit in La Chasse talking about the band, which gigs we should take and which ones we shouldn't. It was a close relationship between manager and agent and we were really looking out for them on a very personal level to make sure everything was done properly."

At the end of 1968, Tony took The Nice to Czechoslovakia and was immediately struck by the effect that a rock band could have on the disaffected youth in a part of the world still troubled by Cold War tensions. As he told *Fusion* magazine the following year: "I went to a Christmas show, the Wenceslas Show with The Nice in Czechoslovakia, which was a very moving experience, to have this theatre built for 1,700, this old imperial theatre crammed with 3,500 young students and Czechs.

"We felt these people really needed it, and if you see for yourself the quality of everyday life in Eastern European countries, it makes you wonder if we haven't got a social duty to do these things. We make no money out of going there. We devoted a whole weekend to doing it but we really enjoyed doing it and felt that we made a much more valuable contact than, say, a routine gig in the north of England. They were begging for the right to record parts of the show because they couldn't get the records, which I, of course, happily did. In fact I gave the Czech national radio permission to tape the whole show and play it whenever they like. I discovered it's already been aired four times."

On their first venture to America, The Nice reportedly made a loss of between $10,000 and $15,000. The performances and critical reaction were generally good, but money was stolen from the band in Boston, club dates were pulled at the last minute and problems with American insurance for the equipment all took their toll on the budget. However, Tony – who during the trip attempted to sign Captain Beefheart – could see only the positive side, as he argued the case with one interviewer. "It's a loss that could also be figured as an investment, of course. It's only a loss if the tour had failed, because then one would have to recover it out of European earnings and forget about coming back to America and recovering it here, at least for some time. You don't expect to make a profit on your first tour of America, so in fact The Nice can view it as a worthwhile investment, and a relatively cheap one, because I know other groups, for example Fleetwood Mac, who lost $15,000 on their second tour."

Over the second weekend in August 1969 the Ninth National Jazz & Blues Festival was held at Plumpton racecourse, near Lewes in East Sussex. Tony had a vested interest in three artists on the bill, starting with Peter Hammill, whose 20-minute solo set opened the Saturday afternoon on the main stage. The Bonzo Dog Doo-Dah Band headlined the afternoon session and towards the end of their set they were joined onstage by a masked drummer who, to the opening bars of 'Pinball Wizard', revealed himself to be Keith Moon. The madcap drummer battered away at Larry Smith's kit during 'Urban Spaceman', 'Breathalyser Baby' and a crazier-than-usual rendition of 'Monster Mash'. Moon and The Who closed the Saturday night session that evening.

The following day Tony nervously waited backstage for the big experiment of the weekend – the collaboration of The Nice with the London Symphony Orchestra. In the event, he need not have worried, as the press happily reported that the "high spot of Sunday night was the merging of the talents of Keith Emerson, the brilliant young organist with The Nice, and Mr Joseph Eger[4]*, the enthusiastic and extremely hip conductor of the New York Philharmonic. In a courageous blow against the huge barriers between pop music and the classics, The Nice played three pieces in conjunction with 41 string and horn players, including members of the LSO."

Record Mirror journalist Lon Goddard reported: "The barriers buckled and a chorus of shouts for more filled the entire festival grounds, but alas – regulations required all music be stopped. Though the demand for an encore was greater than at any point previous, so also was the satisfaction from a brilliant performance and three days of choice music."

The collaboration between rock group and classical orchestra, a musical fusion that could either be exhilarating or fall pitifully short of its target, was something in which Tony was only too pleased for his artists to participate. Whether signing up The Koobas for acting lessons or encouraging The Creation to incorporate action painting during their live gigs, Tony believed that the potential to experiment and blend the creative arts was the most exciting way forward.

"Pop art and all the exciting experiments in painting have, within a matter of 10 to 20 years of their inception in this century, become a part of traditional culture," Tony would tell *Fusion* magazine. "Salvador Dali was once outrageous; Picasso was at one time outrageous. The action painters from America were, within the last few years outrageous. Andy Warhol was outrageous. But these people are rapidly becoming part of the everyday culture. That is why the charts, the hit parade music, does not interest me.

---

4   * Eger would be given his own record release on the Charisma label, the *Classical Heads* album in 1970.

That's another thing entirely, that's over there."

* * *

The story goes that Island Records boss Chris Blackwell once watched with great amusement as Tony led The Nice through an airport terminal, with the band trailing in his wake, "looking like a flock of chicks following their mother hen". On hearing this, Lee Jackson apparently remarked "great, that's gonna be your name from now on... Mother!" Later on, when the band reviewed the sleeve design for their eponymous third studio album on Immediate, Keith Emerson was disappointed with the cover photography, but by then it was too late to make changes for the European market. However, when the American album was released it was not only given a new title – *Everything As Nice As Mother Makes It* in a nod to their munificent manager – but also sported a completely different sleeve.

It is hard to imagine the mild-mannered Stratton Smith getting embroiled in any sort of argument, let alone violence, but part of the remit for any good road manager is to keep both the band and, from time to time, the boss out of trouble. Nice tour manager Bazz Ward recalls an incident in Leytonstone where a young woman with a grievance punched Tony in the face, but Tony generally avoided any form of confrontation at all costs. Surely any problem could be sorted out in a calm, gentlemanly fashion, and preferably over a drink or two. One thing he simply couldn't stand, however, was injustice, especially when it involved one of his artists, and Tony's understandable frustrations with Immediate Records almost led to an altercation with record company boss Andrew Loog Oldham.

During one particularly late night in the Speakeasy, Tony pointed out to Oldham that not only were royalties outstanding from the band's first album *The Thoughts of Emerlist Davjack*, but also, in his opinion, the label was not doing nearly enough to promote the current release, *Ars Longa Vita Brevis*. With his record company on the brink of bankruptcy, Oldham in no mood for pleasantries, and opted instead to threaten Tony with violence. Luckily for Tony, Bazz Ward was on hand to mediate. "When Andrew Oldham squared up to Tony and threatened to do him in the Speak, we managed to jump in and stop it before it all went too far."

Tony was forced to step in and sort out unrest within The Nice over the erratic behaviour of guitarist David O'List. Some believe the problems started after his drink was spiked with LSD by David Crosby on a February trip to Los Angeles, but he was often late for gigs and missed some altogether. Matters came to a head during a concert at Croydon's Fairfield Hall where O'List assaulted Bazz Ward in mid-performance, evidently in the belief that Ward had talked to drummer Davison behind his back. It was the final straw for Emerson, who subsequently called a band meeting with Jackson and Davison to propose that O'List be sacked. All were in agreement, with the onerous task falling to their manager. Immediately after a performance at The Ritz, Bournemouth in October, O'List was officially fired by Tony, in the presence of the rest of the band.

* * *

Around the same time as he took on The Nice in 1968, Tony also became the manager of The Bonzo Dog Doo-Dah Band, taking over the reins from Gerry Bron. The notoriously hard to handle Bonzos were an eccentric group of art students and musicians who mixed music hall and trad jazz with surreal comedy. Irked that the somewhat similar New Vaudeville Band had spent a week at number one in the States with 'Winchester Cathedral', they were desperate to break the American market.

Losing them was more of a relief than a disappointment to Bron, however. "They were becoming quite painful to manage and Tony had obviously said to them that he could do something I couldn't do and crack America wide open for them," he recalled. "So I said, fine, you're welcome to try. It gives me no satisfaction whatsoever, but they never did make it in America. If they'd been more patient and not quite so neurotic about making it overnight in the States, I think they could have become one of the biggest acts of all time."

Once again, potential problems were outweighed by Tony's excitement at their creativity, as he told David Fricke of *Rolling Stone*: "Mentally, the Bonzos were a collection of chaotic talents and they created this incredible thing between them. But they never really thought like a band, they all fought for their individuality. Like Legs Larry Smith always had to have more sequins than anybody else. But that was easy – nobody else liked sequins!"

With the benefit of hindsight, Tony and The Bonzo Dog Doo-Dah Band should have been a match made in heaven. It was Strat's idea to take these English eccentrics on their first visit to the USA in April 1969, and, as vocalist Viv Stanshall recalled, touring with Tony could be an experience in itself. "Strat roughed it with the rest of us, staying in wretched hotels and food. He didn't need to, of course, but he thought it improper if he did not. We lived on a dollar a day: that's a burger and a beer – just. But Strat contrived to introduce me to dry Martinis at the Algonquin, Dorothy Parker, Benchley, Kaufman. We were in New York, for Christ's sake! It would be improper if we did not. Tony Stratton Smith was a gentleman and an adventurer. He was a very rare man."

Indeed. Quite what the majority of yanks made of dear old Vivian

Stanshall and co. is open to debate, although some parts of America totally got it and after one particular Bonzos gig in Boston, Tony was on a definite high. Any reservations he may have had about bringing the band to the USA were allayed by the reaction of the Boston crowd; no wonder he was in such high spirits when he gave a lengthy interview to *Fusion* magazine, Boston's answer to *Rolling Stone*: "America will be marvellous to the Bonzos just as it was marvellous to The Nice. Their minds are working all the time now on reactions to different things. You know, they're Americanising some of their jokes. They're getting into the literature, I suppose you'd say, of the kids' mentality, attitudes. There's a definite literature in the attitudes of the young, in the humour of the young, rather marvellous casual throw-away language of the young here and the Bonzos are going to take to this like a seed to water."

Tony's joy was to be relatively short-lived. The gigs were generally support spots to a variety of mismatched artists and although the Bonzos' performances were largely well-received, record sales didn't reflect the onstage glory and the group went into meltdown on their return to the UK. Tony later concluded: "What they needed – and they got it in England – was steady success. But in America, they didn't get it. The Nice were hard-nosed professionals. The Bonzos did it because they enjoyed doing it. And the minute it started becoming a nightmare, they decided they'd had enough."

Bazz Ward helped out on the American tour. "Tony spent a lot of money on the Bonzos, and personally I don't think they gave him the respect they should have done," he says. "He took them over to New York when nobody else had even heard of the Bonzos." The other essential member of the Bonzos' regular crew was Fred Munt, a long-haired roadie with a thick moustache, known to the band as 'Borneo' for his wild appearance, no-nonsense approach and exceptionally loud voice. Referenced on the track 'The Intro And The Outro', originally recorded in 1967 for the *Gorilla* album, he appears as the bongo-playing Wild Man of Borneo, alongside Princess Anne on sousaphone, Prime Minister Harold Wilson on violin, Roy Rogers on Trigger and, somewhat controversially, Adolf Hitler on vibes. "Fred was tour manager of the Bonzos when I first worked with him, and I found him to be a tower of strength. If Fred and I could survive the Bonzo Dog episode, then we could tackle anything together," said Tony, hinting that life with the Bonzos, in particular their first visit to the USA, was not always a bed of roses.

Bonzo 'Legs' Larry Smith later recalled his former manager and their time together in America with great fondness. "The eloquence of this man, the generosity, the breathlessness – those deep brown eyes, glazed with the tears of helpless, hopeless, hysterical laughter – tears that would run down Wardour Street and then flow up three flights of stairs into the La Chasse most every night. If I recall, we went to the movies twice, once in New York and once in Leicester Square. Bonzo Dog was in New York and Tony spent at least ten minutes convincing Vivian Stanshall and myself that the recently premiered and much acclaimed *Lola Montes* would not wait a second longer and simply had to be seen. It would be a cinematic event extraordinaire, he assured us – and of course we believed him. We duly arrived, following on from the usual liquidous lunch, and flopped into our seats. In minutes, soothed by the air-conditioning (and Lola's lowly voice), the fat boy was asleep – blowing bubbles and gently nodding into his lightweight Panama. Needless to say, the film was appalling and we left him to it. However, the Leicester Square event proved much more rewarding for all of us. The year was 1968 and once again under Tony's suspicious gaze, we marched into a screening of Mel Brook's utterly brilliant movie *The Producers*. It was finally a goosestep in the Reich direction and a film that assuredly changed my life – and I thank the dear boy for that – from the bottom of my jackboots. I thank Tony Stratton Smith for a great many things. He had vision, compassion, he listened and he bloody well cared."

* * *

The Bonzos' American tour may not have gone quite as well as Tony had hoped, but the contacts made at *Fusion* magazine in Boston, particularly with owner and publisher Barry Glovsky and editor Robert Somma, would prove useful. Among the young writers at *Fusion* was Loyd Grossman, a Boston-born music fan who penned reviews for two albums by The Nice and reviewed one of the Bonzos' gigs during his time at the paper.

So impressed was Tony by the set-up at the magazine that he offered to help print and distribute a European edition. Glovsky would ship the complete US page negatives for each issue across to London where Tony arranged for their printing and distribution. "I forget exactly how many issues we did, but it lasted for about a year," said Glovsky. "The man was different from others in that he was a great listener of people, including his bands. Tony was fair and upfront about everything and had no air of self-importance. Whenever he came to the States we would often get together and tell stories about our separate upbringings, which were similar in some ways. I found him very pleasant and accessible and honest. Just a really nice man."

Back home in the Dean Street office, Eve Slater recalls that she and her husband Terry were quickly pressed into action. "Strat came back from a trip to the US and Terry was tasked with selling advertising in the magazine. I found a printer and we had talks with W.H. Smith about the distribution."

Tony had always kept an eye on the careers of the individual Beatles, ever since his friendship with Brian Epstein had helped to ease him into the music business. He greatly admired George Harrison's songs, so much so that he recorded a cassette tape full of observations and questions about Harrison's career and asked a mutual friend, Perry Press, to pass it on. Press, an estate agent who specialised in finding suitable homes for rock stars, had recommended the magnificent Victorian Friar Park at Henley-on-Thames to Harrison and was in the perfect position to deliver the tape.

The cassette was labelled 'Fusion', which gives an insight into Tony's primary motive. Quite possibly, an exclusive interview with George Harrison was intended to be part of his pitch to the magazine's American owners. Perry Press believes it may just have been the journalist in Tony surfacing once more.

"Strat handed me a cassette and asked me to deliver it if the opportunity arose," he said. "The questions were incisive and perceptive, indicating prescient appreciation of George's unique qualities, and I recollect that he adopted his most considered and cultivated tone. My impression was that Strat was genuinely curious about George's musical life apart from The Beatles, though I concede that he might have had an ulterior motive. The cassette failed to reach George because I never happened to have it on me whenever I saw him, and I suspect that I was a bit shy of handing it over and somehow intruding on his privacy."

Even without a Stratton Smith interview with George Harrison, unfortunately for Tony the magazine failed to take off in the UK, but its lack of success was indirectly responsible for a dramatic upturn in the fortunes of the ever-present Terry Slater. His wife Eve recalls: "When *Fusion* didn't happen and there was no other work for Terry to do at Charisma, he joined a guy called Vince Stitt, who put up all the posters for promoters and record labels, but in a very small way. However, because Terry knew everybody at the record companies it was very easy for him to grow the business, which is exactly what happened."

* * *

By August 1969, the new Bonzos' album, *Tadpoles,* was faring well in the UK charts but when the band prepared for another six-week tour of America it would be without Tony's help. The comedy troupe was about to jettison their third manager. As Larry Smith confessed: "We were a pretty impossible band to manage. In the end we cast everybody aside. Eventually, we fired Tony."

Viv Stanshall stepped into the vacant manager's role, but it proved too much for the fragile eccentric. The tour turned into a disaster and the group returned exhausted and frustrated, with the overworked Stanshall suffering panic attacks, Valium addiction and seemingly on the edge of a nervous breakdown.

Tony turned his attention back to The Nice, but it was at this point that Immediate Records declared bankruptcy, owing a massive sum to Emerson and the boys, along with other groups on the label, not least The Small Faces. With a major hit record, but no money to show for it, The Nice were forced into a solid touring schedule to remain solvent.

Tony's growing discontent with Immediate added to the nagging thought that he could do a much better job himself. There was never much love lost between Tony and Immediate boss Andrew Loog Oldham, as he told Joe Smith: "I had a very ambivalent attitude towards Andrew. I don't think anyone could have learned very much from Andrew, he was one on his own. If anything, his career was arrested by a rather childish streak. He had a wilful-child thing that made him very uncomfortable to deal with. If Immediate Records had a businessman, a sense of direction and honest people to execute it, then it would have been a power to this day, because they had ideas. Andrew had enormous flair, but he was irresponsible."

Either way, The Nice were on the verge of disbanding towards the end of 1969, although their decision wasn't officially announced until the following spring. Tony, in his wisdom, had compiled a number of unreleased recordings including the live tapes from the Fillmore East gig that didn't make it onto their third album, as well as a live recording of their most ambitious orchestral project to date, *The Five Bridges Suite*, plus a handful of studio tracks that were close to completion. *Five Bridges* had taken shape on a recent trip to Ireland when The Nice were accompanied by Tony and the members of Yes. The title was supplied by Lee Jackson, bass player and proud Geordie, after the famous bridges that have spanned the River Tyne between Newcastle and Gateshead for generations. The final work was premiered in Newcastle on October 10, 1969, the band performing with a full orchestra conducted by Joseph Eger, while the recorded version was taken from a concert the following week at the Fairfield Hall in Croydon and later released to great success on Charisma.

Andrew Loog Oldham would later accuse Tony of launching The Famous Charisma Label on the back of these, in his view, 'stolen' tapes – referring in particular to the collection of out-takes and alternative recordings from The Nice that Tony would release in 1972 as *Autumn '67 – Spring '68*. In fact, they were languishing at the recording studio and Tony simply bought them, as Gail Colson recalls: "The tapes were left with Olympic Studios in Barnes and the bill had not been paid, so they were holding on to them. We paid the outstanding bill and the tapes were released to us."

According to Oldham, at this time Immediate was like a "wounded animal" and the label was about to go belly up. Given the situation, as manager of The Nice, Tony was simply looking after the interests of his boys. Even Andrew Oldham had the good grace to later concede that had he been in Stratton Smith's position, he would have done precisely the same thing.

Tony always felt that The Nice broke up much too early. "There were nights when they were so good they could move you to tears," he said. "They should have given it a few more years."

Keith Emerson, however, had other plans. With all due respect to Lee Jackson, he had always believed that the weakest link in The Nice was Jackson's vocals, and he even approached Duncan Browne, Immediate's resident singer/songwriter, to become their singer.

Disappointed though he may have been, Tony was nevertheless instrumental in the formation of Emerson's next project, helping to bring in King Crimson bassist Greg Lake when his group played on the same bill as The Nice at the Fillmore West in San Francisco. The personnel in Crimson, led by guitarist Robert Fripp, would always be fluid and as the current band begun to disintegrate, Emerson and Lake clicked during a sound check. "He and I were on stage and he was fumbling through this jazz piece," recalled Greg Lake. "Afterwards we were both conscious of each other's position and I think his manager, Tony Stratton Smith, came over to me and said, 'Can we talk about something personal?' And I said, 'Yeah', because I didn't want to carry on in King Crimson."

This group that would become ELP was rounded out with drummer Carl Palmer, as Emerson later recalled: "At the time, obviously, I was also looking for a drummer and I was asking a lot of people. I asked my manager at the time, and Strat said, 'Carl Palmer is pretty good and he looks pretty as well.' He got me an album and I listened to it, but I wasn't too knocked out by what he played on the album. It was the first Atomic Rooster album. Later we had a jam together and it was really incredible."

Throughout various upheavals, new bands and projects, Keith Emerson retained his admiration for Tony, as he later said: "Tony was a beautiful guy. He was a very reluctant manager, in that his main interests lay in horseracing and things like that, but he was always a very fair man. He was a lot of fun to be around."

* * *

With The Nice disbanding Tony needed another project and, in the autumn of 1969, he branched out into concert promotion. A regular at DJ John Peel's Friday night Midnight Court sessions at the Lyceum Ballroom on The Strand, he liked the venue's plush red and gold décor along with the soft and, more crucially, relatively clean carpets that proved ideal for relaxing on during the early hours to the sounds of Soft Machine, Yes or Family. Tony sensed an opportunity to stage his own shows at the Lyceum on Sunday evenings.

In September 1969, *NME* announced that a year-long series of Sunday evening concerts at the Lyceum would be organised by 'promoter' Tony Stratton Smith. Blind Faith, Led Zeppelin, Humble Pie, The Nice, Fats Domino, Georgie Fame and Procol Harum were among the artists lined up, with several other top acts likely to appear. The series opened on October 5 with Chicken Shack, The Kinks and Van der Graaf Generator, and were scheduled to continue each week, featuring two star attractions plus one up-and-coming band. Tony's shows would begin at 7.30pm and run until 11pm, followed by a disco. Closing time would be flexible and a supper licence was granted for the duration of the series, which it was hoped would extend beyond the planned 52 weeks. An enthusiastic Tony told *NME*: "We plan to create the British equivalent of New York's Fillmore East, with a free and easy atmosphere and a sense of community."

Between October 1969 and January 1970, the Stratton Smith presentations included several artists that were either already under his management or would soon be signed to the new record label he was planning. The Nice, Viv Stanshall and Van der Graaf Generator all appeared more than once, while record producer John Anthony regularly shared the DJ spot with Jeff Dexter and Andy Dunkley. Eve Slater, who had left the Harold Davison Organisation to join Tony and Gail Colson working out of his cramped flat in Dean Street, soon found herself booking the Lyceum concerts. "I don't remember how we decided who to book, but I suppose availability and price were paramount, although I do recall booking Pink Floyd for £750 one time, and we actually lost money. However we did manage to get the Plastic Ono Band – which featured John Lennon, George Harrison, Yoko, Delaney & Bonnie etc."

Tony's Sunday concert on October 12, 1970, featured Led Zeppelin, who apparently received the highest fee paid for a one-off gig in Britain at that time. The fee was undisclosed[5*], and Tony's powers of persuasion were sorely tested by somehow convincing Led Zeppelin's formidable manager Peter Grant, a man who rarely left a gig without his fee, that he would pay up the following day.

Press reports suggest that it was not one of Zeppelin's better performances and it was actually one of the support bands that really caught Tony's ear. After just one hearing, Stratton Smith prised Audience away from their Polydor contract and charmed the group into signing for Charisma within days of appearing on the Lyceum stage.

Aside from the Lyceum box office, tickets for these shows were available through the numerous London branches of Musicland, a chain of record shops owned by Lee Gopthal and run by Alan Firth. Working in one

---

5   * The fee was rumoured to be £1,000.

branch was Steve Weltman, a former tea boy for Brian Epstein at NEMs and fresh from a job at Polydor/Atlantic, and it was through selling so many tickets for those Lyceum shows that he first encountered Tony. Strat appreciated Weltman's youthful enthusiasm and within a year he would find himself employed in the sales and marketing department at B&C/Charisma.

The Slaters both worked on booking and promoting the popular Sunday night Lyceum concerts. Tony found that Terry was a useful man to have on your team and the pair would work together on an ad hoc basis for several years. When Eve and Terry married in September 1968, the photographs at their wedding reception, held at the Revolution Club, show a typically star-studded affair. On either side of the happy couple are friends from the music world – The Who's Keith Moon, Allan Clarke of The Hollies, Lee Jackson from The Nice, Amen Corner's Andy Fairweather Low and Hilton Valentine, lead guitarist with The Animals. Recalling their regular social haunts, Eve confirms that De Hems in Macclesfield Street was where Terry used to meet all the music press every lunchtime, but there is a smile in her voice when she states that "La Chasse was where we all went after work..."

Chapter 6

The Famous Label

"He was a tremendous bluffer. He could write a letter that made it look like he was a millionaire and was offering the greatest deal to someone, when the truth was that we were completely broke and no one had been paid for weeks."

Glen Colson, Charisma PR

While it is fairly easy to put a date on the launch of The Famous Charisma Label – October 1969, when Stratton Smith Productions Ltd was incorporated – the place of birth is less easy to identify. Locations in the running include Tony's flat in Dean Street, The Ship pub on Wardour Street or The Speakeasy Club on Margaret Street, but most agree that the odds-on favourite is La Chasse Club, a private members bar located above a bookies shop at 100 Wardour Street that was patronised by all and sundry from the music world.

La Chasse, managed by Jack Barrie, became Tony Stratton Smith's home from home at the end of the sixties. Opened in May 1967, it was supposedly restricted to members only; one floor up a narrow, winding staircase above Ken Munden Turf Accountant, a few doors along from the unlicensed Marquee Club and, in the other direction, The Ship. Identified from the street by a rectangular illuminated sign that advertised Charrington's beer, it was tiny, smaller than most living rooms, where no more than about 30 people could comfortably fit. Inside was a bar, a few stools and a couple of lumpy couches and on its wall was a collection of framed caricatures of the club's regulars, all drawn by Stuart Leatherwood. Two sash windows looked out on to Wardour Street below and between them was a jukebox, constantly playing, the three favourites 'Sweetness' by Yes, 'Don't Let Me Down' by The Beatles and 'Space Oddity' by David Bowie. Another favourite, oddly, was 'Wigwam', an instrumental that appeared on Bob Dylan's 1970 LP *Self Portrait*.

Music journalist Dan Hedges described it in this picturesque way: "It's up the creaky stairs, a hard knock at the door, and if you've got some reason to be there, you're in. Inside, it's like a shoe box, or the dumpy living room of a particularly uninspiring London flat. After the first ten people, it's standing room only. Dark. Cramped. Thick with cigarette smoke, and the low rumble of the clientele over the crappy stereo. It's people making promises, people making deals, people bullshitting each other stiff about albums that never quite seem to get recorded, and coast-to-coast American tours that never quite seem to get off the ground. There's a couch or two if you're early enough, and a drink at the tiny bar will set you back the equivalent of a small bank loan."

But the real charm of the place was the warm welcome of Jack Barrie, and that customers included pretty much everyone involved in the music business at that time: musicians, managers, promoters, agents, journalists, roadies and club owners, with a few decorous girls – some might call them groupies – thrown in for good measure.

Tony Stratton Smith was more often than not to be found at the far end of the bar, cigarette to hand, nursing a goblet that contained a large vodka and tonic that he and the bar staff referred to as his 'poison'. "Fearful that he might forget something important in the haze of an evening, he would keep notes of conversations, scribbling down ideas and suggestions on the back of a Silk Cut packet," says Glen Colson, Gail's younger brother, who would soon make himself invaluable at Charisma. "I don't recall him ordering a single vodka in all the time I knew him. A peerless bar-room philosopher, he never minded buying three rounds to your one."

* * *

The first Charisma release of any note was Rare Bird's 'Sympathy', which charted in March of 1970, but a more profound motivation for launching the label was to offer a berth to Van der Graaf Generator, Tony's next management client.

Towards the end of 1969 Tony was sharing a Knightsbridge office with the record producer Shel Talmy who, knowing his background in journalism, had employed Tony to write a play for him. Its title was *Dancers And Lovers*. "It was kind of a romantic play on Rudolph Nureyev's defection from Russia and, as I remember, it was a damn good book," says Talmy. "Strat would come over to my office and sit down and write and I paid him. I don't think it was ever published."

Working out of the same building was Mercury Records producer Lou Reizner, who had recently signed the young songwriter Peter Hammill and his group Van der Graaf Generator to the label. One morning Gail Colson, already working in the office as Talmy's secretary, took a call from the group's keyboard player Hugh Banton, who wanted to speak to Tony. He was out, probably still in bed, but Gail arranged an appointment for Banton to come back a couple of days later. At the meeting Tony and Banton listened to an embryonic Van der Graaf Generator demo tape, and when Tony heard

Peter Hammill sing for the first time his eyes lit up. "The voice is a gas!" he exclaimed.

Van der Graaf Generator were unquestionably Tony's favourite among the early artists he signed. Here was a band led by a songwriter of true originality that could really do something worthwhile, he believed. Utterly convinced of their unique talent, all Tony had to do now was to convince everyone else; not an easy task, as he later told David Fricke: "If I've felt any pain at all about my artists, the greatest pain has been Van der Graaf Generator. I truly believe Peter Hammill is one of the best lyric writers in the world. I've also caught on fairly early that he's almost anti-music. Peter almost deliberately, every time he comes close to being accessible, shies away from it instantly and runs off into an impenetrable realm."

As if handling such creative complexities wasn't hard enough, Van der Graaf – at that point a duo of Peter Hammill and Chris Judge Smith – were already signed to Mercury Records, which made Tony's plans to get the newly formed full band into a recording studio slightly tricky. Their first album, *The Aerosol Grey Machine*, was originally intended as a Hammill solo outing, but Tony organised a complicated deal with Mercury whereby they would release the record under the band's name, in return for releasing Peter Hammill from his recording contract. Available only in Germany, it quickly died a death.

Formed at Manchester University in 1967, Van der Graaf Generator were named after an American physicist who invented the electrostatic accelerator, and their line-up, which at Tony's suggestion briefly included Keith Ellis from The Koobas, varied until settling on Hammill, Banton, saxophone player David Jackson, Nick Potter on bass and drummer Guy Evans.

Tony may have been completely sold on Peter Hammill's voice and lyrics, but of all the early Hammill compositions it was the track 'Refugees' that really tugged at his heart. With its themes of separation and loneliness, of home and friendship, Tony loved this song from the moment he heard it, and the melancholy ballad became, and stayed, a firm favourite. In later years, Hammill would introduce the song on stage by reminiscing that, "Strat would often come backstage after a gig, cigar in hand and say, 'Great show, old boy but you really should have played 'Refugees'."

The 'Mike and Susie' name-checked in the lyrics are Hammill's close friends and former flatmates, Mike McLean and the actress Susan Penhaligon. The trio shared a flat for about six months during their student days the song was written about the great sadness Hammill felt when their 'home' broke up and the three friends went their separate ways. As Hammill later wrote, "In this knowledge, the last vestiges of hope lay only in a future Utopia and re-joining of the hands. In the writing, however, the song developed a life of its own (as is always the best way), and the hope becomes much more than that for reunion with my friends. We are all refugees, and there is no home but hope."

'Refugees' became the third single to be issued on the Charisma label, released in April 1970, but it failed to chart, not even in Europe, surprisingly, where even the most progressive of bands could find a sympathetic ear. The track appears on the album *The Least We Can Do Is Wave To Each Other* released in February 1970 and while officially the second album from Van der Graaf Generator, it was their first for Charisma.

The Least We Can Do was recorded quickly, over four days in December 1969 at Trident Studios in St Anne's Court, a narrow alleyway that links Wardour and Dean Streets, with house producer John Anthony on the desk. As with all of his artists, Tony left the band to their own devices in the studio, giving them complete artistic freedom, but unfortunately the final output turned into a game of production ping-pong between two of Tony's friends. To begin with, Tony was unhappy with Anthony's production and asked Shel Talmy to remix it; consequently the first pressing of the album was released with Talmy's mix. Next it was the turn of the band to voice their displeasure and they somehow convinced Charisma to return to the John Anthony mix, the version that has appeared on all subsequent releases.

According to Van der Graaf's David Jackson, Tony's less-than-enthusiastic reaction to the album on hearing the first playback of the master tapes was not entirely his fault. As Jackson recalls, "When we finished *The Least We Can Do...* we played it in Tony Stratton Smith's office, but they had only wired up the left channel on the Revox tape machine. Tony suggested that we ought to remix the album, before one of us said, 'Perhaps you should try listening to it in stereo first.' At that point, Charisma realised we'd made a good album."

The reaction from the music press backed Tony's judgement. *Melody Maker* declared: "This is one of those rare and precious albums which occasionally knock you flat on your back and make you think really hard for once about music. Words like stunning and mesmerising don't tell the half of it." The Charisma press advertisements hailed the album as "an incredible combination of rock, poetry and jazz" and *The Least We Can Do...* managed to slip into the lower regions of the LP Top 50 – no mean feat in a chart dominated by *Abbey Road* and *Bridge Over Troubled Water*.

Signing VdGG was an early indication that Charisma's remit was to offer opportunities to acts whose music might not readily chime with popular taste, but it was nevertheless off to a good start. Peter Hammill would describe the company's management style as "an ethos of benign tolerance". Speaking to *Mojo* contributor Mike Barnes almost 40 years later, he elaborated: "It's not the best thing to be managed and published by your record company, but that's the way it was – and we were given an enormous amount of leeway and encouragement. Strat believed in us and was prepared to see what we were capable of doing. With Charisma, the investment was emotional, as well as financial. And they stuck with us. Not everyone was behind us at the very outset and we didn't make it easy for them, but they gave us the space, we created an audience and it worked out in the end. The flipside to Charisma's benign tolerance is that they didn't know what we were feeling. We were on a raft being buffeted about, without anybody being in control. We were being sent out on tours with more or less a date and the name of a city. Find poster, find club, find promoter, find hotel. Even back in the late sixties, early seventies it was go to a 'phone box on Thursday, find where you are playing on Friday and Saturday, go and do the gigs, drive back to London and just carry on. I used to think, hang on, this is out of control, no one knows what's going on at all."

Tony always loved to indulge in what he referred to as 'cultural cross-pollination' and the introduction of film producer Albert 'Cubby' Broccoli to the music of Van der Graaf Generator ranks high on his list of pulling together the strangest of bedfellows. Broccoli had been a regular visitor to the Pickwick Club in the late sixties and Tony more than likely made his acquaintance there. This subsequent collision of cultures occurred early in 1970 when Van der Graaf were asked to work on the soundtrack of Broccoli's latest film *Eye Witness*, starring Susan George, Mark Lester and Lionel Jeffries.

Peter Hammill told *Disc* magazine, "It's a flashy thriller, very commercial. It's a very horrific film with lots of violent deaths. Because of the style of our music we were asked to do the violent bits. I couldn't really imagine us doing a love theme."

* * *

Even towards the end of the sixties, the role of the pop music manager was still relatively new, but pushing a client towards recording a film soundtrack was an enlightened move. Forming his own record company, however, was even more far-sighted, though there were precedents, most notably Kit Lambert and partner Chris Stamp's Track Records, to which they signed their management clients The Who and, perhaps more famously, Jimi Hendrix.

Of Tony's three management role models – Epstein, Oldham and Lambert – it was the latter whom Tony admired the most. "He had a fine mind, Kit Lambert," he said. "He was an educated man, a man with tremendous interest in all the visual arts, as well as music. He was a very persuasive charmer when he wanted to be and he had the toughest people eating out of his hand. If he'd been able to control himself he would have been the best manager I'd ever met. He could have done it with any good band, not just The Who. In partnership with Chris Stamp, who was the hard edge of the partnership, they were immensely effective. I think Kit was an extraordinary man. I was fond of him to the day he died."[6*]

Wearing his own management hat, Tony was more often than not unimpressed by the treatment dished out to his artists by their various record labels. Van der Graaf, as Hammill has already described, were initially under contract to Mercury Records and were allocated a mere two days to record their entire debut album, *The Aerosol Grey Machine*. "And even then," Tony told *Rolling Stone*'s David Fricke, with a visible display of sarcasm, "they thought they were doing us a favour. It was probably two days that Rod Stewart didn't use."

Among his other charges, Tony felt that United Artists had treated the Bonzos poorly, particularly on their first trip to America. He suffered problems with Decca over Al Stewart's debut single, not to mention Oldham's Immediate Records and their support, or rather the lack of it, for The Nice. It was this complete and utter disillusionment with other record labels that would lead directly to Charisma.

Gail Colson, soon to play as important a role in Charisma as Tony himself, feels Tony's disenchantment with other labels was the incentive he needed. "At one point both The Nice and the Bonzos were touring the States and their labels were next to useless. When The Nice were away on tour, Immediate Records were on answer-phone the whole time and we listened to it and said we could do better, we could do so much better, and eventually we said right, fuck it, let's do it – and we started Charisma."

These motives for launching the label – Tony's disillusionment with other record companies, finding a good home for his beloved Van der Graaf Generator, the inspiration of Lambert and, surely, the realisation that labels made more money than the artists they signed – all coalesced around the same time. But if the La Chasse Club dream was to be realised, then Tony needed the help of someone with practical experience in the nuts and bolts of record manufacture and distribution.

A story emerged later, no doubt perpetuated by Tony himself, that Charisma was forged during a meeting with B&C Records boss Lee Gopthal. Gopthal was a Jamaican-Indian businessman who owned the building in Cambridge Road, London NW6 that was home to Island and Planetone Records. Having worked with Chris Blackwell on Island's mail order business, Gopthal opened his own record store, Musicland, and in 1968 founded Trojan Records to feed the emerging UK interest in ska and reggae. A year later, he founded B&C Records, which stood for 'Beat and Commercial', designed initially as a manufacturing, distribution and

---

6   * Heavily addicted to drugs and alcohol, Kit Lambert died in 1981.

marketing company.

Tony presumably thought that one specific 'light-bulb' moment made better copy for the press but there is the strong possibility that Gopthal funded Charisma in return for their mutually beneficial distribution deal. According to Tony, he'd approached Gopthal to see if B&C might be a potential home for The Nice, as he later told the American radio journalist Joe Smith. "One of the independents I talked to was a company called B&C Records, who were a bit of an afterthought, because in my view they really weren't big enough to cope. But they came up with a counter proposal, saying why don't you start your own label – and what a wonderful thing it would be if The Nice were on your own record label. I spoke to the band and they were supportive of the idea. They were still going to get the same money they would have got from Polydor, which B&C were prepared to fund. Hence the Charisma label was born."

Further funding came from financier André Chudnoff, a Liechtenstein-based businessman and investor who was impressed by the ongoing success of The Nice and introduced to Tony by Johnny Toogood. "His wife was American, and they owned a swish flat in Mayfair," he says. "Now June was interested in the music, whereas André was purely interested in the business side. What I was able to do was to endorse the potential of the bands. You have André on one side, Strat on the other and what André needed was somebody else to endorse The Nice – and the best person to do that was probably me, because I was out there with Strat, promoting and booking them, and I could see how the crowds were beginning to go crazy for them. They were packing places out, starting with the club circuit at places like Mothers in Birmingham and they were breaking all the records, even at the Marquee."

Stratton Smith Productions Limited was incorporated as a limited company in October 1969, its purpose the management of The Famous Charisma Label. No doubt Tony popped open a few bottles in celebration – to properly wet the head of his corporate baby, before the real work began. In an open letter to the music press, he wrote: "Why the need for a new label? In our experience the majors have a continuing problem in as much that they have to reconcile large and often rigid forces to increasingly quick and subtle changes in public taste. The only central truth of the record business is that there is no substitute for talent. We intend never to forget that."

Tony had thought up the name years before, potentially as an alternative for The Remo Four, while another story has him seeing an ornate mirror on the wall of a pub and copying the style of lettering and scrollwork as his template for the original Charisma logo, and the record label with its bold pink and white colour scheme.[7]*

---

7   * The Mad Hatter illustration would replace it later.

Having a record label on paper was one thing, but a management team was needed. Gail Colson automatically became label manager and her brother Glen joined soon afterwards as press officer. Through his association with the Bonzos, Tony brought in tour manager Fred Munt to become Operations Manager, looking after the day-to-day requirements of the acts. Eve Slater left Harold Davidson to join Charisma on the secretarial side, while her husband, Terry 'The Pill' Slater, came in as booking agent. At a slightly later date, Mike de Havilland, who had recently changed his name from Sid Paice when his brother, a photographer, had changed his name to Julian de Havilland, was head-hunted from Tom Jones to be their first promotions manager.

Right from the very beginning, Gail proved an invaluable member of the team, as *Melody Maker* journalist Chris Charlesworth points out: "Gail was supremely well-organised, an absolute sweetheart, absolutely down to earth and business-like. When she hooked up with Strat she became his *consigliore*. She was the money person and made sure that what needed to be done was done. Strat would waft in and out. If it wasn't for Gail, god knows what would have happened to the bloody company. She was fiercely determined and put her foot down. She was incredibly charming as well."

Bazz Ward agrees: "Gail Colson is a very shrewd girl. Her parents owned the Magdala pub up in Hampstead, so she learned a lot from her old man, who was another very smart cookie."

Every good record label needs a good booking agency to keep their artists working hard out on the road. Having used Marquee Martin for a few years, Tony decided that for his new venture, he would turn to Terry King Associates, formerly King's Agency. The company had previously handled artists such as Screaming Lord Sutch and Them and were now working with The Fortunes, Caravan and, more crucially, Rare Bird. "I had such a good relationship with him," says King, "because we had been friends prior to the record company and he knew of my agency. He would ask me for suitable groups and whether I would be interested in representing the groups that he had, or was going to acquire and sign to the new label."

Terry King Associates was also the training ground for Paul Conroy and Chris Briggs, both of whom would become key members of the Charisma family. Conroy became the manager of Charisma's own booking agency and Briggs its second press officer, assisting Glen Colson. The former had met Tony back in his student days. "When I was social secretary at Ewell Technical College, The Nice were the first band I booked," explains Conroy. "We sold all the tickets, I had pockets full of money and this was all so exciting. We had about 1,800 people in the hall. Just after the gig started, there was a banging on the door and it was Strat outside, shouting 'I'm with the band'. He couldn't get in because we'd locked all the doors shut."

Conroy's first job in the music business was as a booking agent for Terry King Associates. "When I started my first day's task, I was given the booking sheets for a number of acts and a National Union of Students book and told to fill them up. I had an interesting collection of bands – The Fortunes, The Foundations, Caravan – most of whom I loved, and also some new acts from Charisma. They were a wild and unruly team, headed by a gentleman who looked like a cross between a headmaster and a priest."

"A good team is vital," said Tony. "We had a combination of experience and bright, young thinking. I wanted to keep it small, so that we could exercise taste and effort without any feeling of pressure. We were prepared to be very patient."

In the long established tradition of running a new business from your own front room, Charisma actually began life at Number 7 Townsend House, 22 Dean Street, Tony's current flat. On any given day, here could be found Gail and Glen Colson, and Eve Slater, with occasional appearances from Margaret Russell, secretary for The Nice, Fred Munt and Terry Slater, booking agent and organiser of the 'Sunday at the Lyceum' concerts.

When The Nice split up in October 1969 Margaret Russell promptly left, as did Suzie O'List, sister of their guitarist Davy, who lasted about two months as receptionist. And, lest we forget, Ken the cleaner. Tony's secretary, Eve Slater, recalls the early days of the label. "There was only Strat's bedroom and two other rooms – Gail and Strat worked in one and I worked in the other. Glen only joined when Gail used to pay him to drive her from her home in Hampstead. Then when he came up to the office, he amused us all so much that he ended up getting a job. Fred Munt didn't work from the Dean Street office, although he was Gail's boyfriend at the time and so was around quite a bit. We were always terribly short of money and I can't tell you how many times the bailiffs rocked up. We had been told that if you personally owned, say, the typewriter, then they also couldn't take away the desk that it was standing on, at least that's what we used to tell them!"

The flat regularly took on the appearance of rush hour at Piccadilly Circus, yet Tony would still insist on his morning bath in which he soaked luxuriously, his record time five hours fully immersed, contemplating what business could be conducted in what was left of the day. Glen Colson remembers the daily routine well: "I would arrive at his office about ten in the morning and make myself useful by delivering things and making coffee. He would rise about 11.30am, head for the bathroom, ordering a coffee on the way, and field telephone calls in the bath. Staff averted their eyes as they passed the phone through the door. The flat was small, but was home to about seven full-time staff who managed, published, booked and mothered Strat's bands. By this time he had four – the Bonzos, Nice, Rare Bird and

Van der Graaf Generator." Initially, Glen Colson was offered the princely sum of £10 per week to drive Tony around town and make tea for everyone, simultaneously learning the duties of record plugger and publicist.

It was not until September 1970 that Tony finally got his flat back and Charisma moved into offices at 87 Brewer Street. It was next door to the Glassblower pub and located over a Soho book store whose stock was of doubtful literary merit. *Monty Python*'s Michael Palin remembers the offices as being "functional, rather than plush, set on three floors above a dirty bookshop. Strat had a tiny office at the top, with two hard wooden benches (giving the little room a rather ecclesiastical feel), a desk, a table, and an interesting selection of moderniana on the walls."

Pity the poor receptionist. The friendly face on the front desk is a thankless position to fill, dealing with all and sundry coming through the doors, particularly in that part of Soho, often subject to abuse over the telephone while informing callers that neither Tony or Gail were available. Suzie O'List was replaced by Angela Hyde-Courtney, who was soon dismissed and left the Brewer Street office under a dark cloud. As Angela remembers: "I came in to work one day and there was no desk – the Monty Pythons had been in and taken all the furniture out of reception for a party. So I hung around waiting for orders and then found out that I had been sacked." Her replacement was Jill Holland, who lasted for at least two years and even survived the move to Old Compton Street, only to succumb to a different type of abuse from within the company – apparently she simply couldn't tolerate Glen Colson's particular line of humour.

The early Charisma Records letterhead listed three company directors, with Marty Machat and R.M. Oppenheimer appearing alongside Stratton Smith's name. New York attorney Machat came onboard at the suggestion of Gail Colson, who had worked with him during her time with Shel Talmy and he was the only real lawyer she knew at the time. His star-studded client list included Leonard Cohen and Phil Spector and he had previously represented Frank Sinatra, James Brown and Sam Cooke. He briefly became a director of Charisma, as well as acting as their legal advisor. Ronnie Oppenheimer was a Sloane Square-based chartered accountant, who briefly joined the company through his association with the Machat family.

"With the label up and running, plenty of hype was needed to keep the ship afloat," says Glen Colson. "Strat would write these fantastic three-page letters to all and sundry, brimming over with the most preposterous claims." It paid off. Tony and his close-knit team may have prepared for patience and the long haul, but as it turned out, The Famous Charisma Label hit all of its targets in the first couple of years.

In fact it was largely Tony's ability to bluff, charm and bluster his way through almost any given situation that helped pave the way for the company's early success. A warm smile, a stiff drink and a certain economy with the truth, tactics learned on the news desks of various newspapers, were all brought to bear in giving his record label the best possible start. As any good journalist will tell you, why let the truth get in the way of a good story.

"He was a tremendous bluffer," says Glen. "He could write a letter that made it look like he was a millionaire and was offering the greatest deal to someone, when the truth was that we were completely broke and no one had been paid for weeks. He had the gift of the gab and could charm the birds off the trees. A lot of his success was due to the fact that he was a fantastic liar. But he didn't lie with malice – he was creative with the truth and he would never give in. He would pull open a drawer and top up with a shot of Jack Daniels, have another fag and just get on with it. I really don't know how he coped. He would have people on one phone about horses, Keith Emerson wanting to split up The Nice on another, Van der Graaf Generator broken down on the motorway and Led Zeppelin at the Lyceum saying they wanted cash before they'd play. Somehow Strat got the cash together, but when he couldn't find the wages for the staff, he just hocked the advance money for another book that he'd written."

Tony never completely gave up the sports journalism, particularly his role as editor of the *International Football Book*, which continued to bring in an additional, and sometimes very necessary, income. Which was probably why, when Tony heard that his mother Mollie was finally moving out of her house in Yardley Wood Road, he decided to give her a call. The purchaser, Robert Cable, moved in to find many unwanted books had been left on the premises. "Some considerable time after moving in, perhaps a year or so, the telephone rang and lo, it was T.S.S. himself. I had inherited the original Hughes phone and number. He asked if I had kept some of his old sports books that Mollie had left in the house, but unfortunately, by then I had given them to a local charity. He expressed his disappointment, but politely apologised for troubling me and rang off."

* * *

On vinyl, the relationship between B&C and Charisma was and remains particularly complex, largely because early single releases on B&C had started to use the CB prefix, which was subsequently continued on all the Charisma records. However, for the very first Charisma single proper, Tony turned to his old friends the Bonzos and released 'Witchi-Tai-To' in December 1969 – or CB116 on the 'pink scroll' label, as vinyl junkies might say. Based on an old Native American Indian chant, it was recorded by Legs Larry Smith assisted by members of the Bonzos, The Who and other associates under the pseudonym of Topo D. Bill, a necessary legal precaution as the Bonzos were still signed to United Artists.

In his interview with David Fricke from *Rolling Stone*, Tony explained: "For this masterpiece of a single, Larry insisted on either 'Witchi-Tai-To' or 'Springtime For Hitler.' We were just closing a deal with a German distributor, so we didn't think 'Springtime For Hitler' would be all that good and went with 'Witchi-Tai-To'." The record was a hit in France, but didn't fare quite so well in Britain despite, or quite possibly because of, being chosen by Tony Blackburn as his record of the week.

Next came Charisma's first LP, the eponymous debut LP from Rare Bird, on December 10. The group was formed by organist and songwriter Graham Stansfield, a classically trained musician who'd worked for five years as a music teacher at a small Catholic school in Putney, and for his pop career adopted the stage name of Graham Field. "We recorded four tracks in a friend's studio in South London, one of which was 'Sympathy', and I made a list of the four groups that I most admired, one of which was Keith Emerson and The Nice," he says. "So I looked up who managed them all and I took the tapes round to all four managers. When I went back later to ask what they thought, two of the managers kicked me out of their office. The other two both said that one of the songs on the tape was one of the best songs they had heard for years and was likely to be a major hit. One was an American guy whose name I can't remember, but his office was about six floors further up the same block from Tony. And he offered us the world but came up with nothing. Tony, however, was completely different. He offered us so much a week to keep us going, rehearsing and preparing for our first album and he also told me that the Radio One DJ Annie Nightingale had heard some of 'Sympathy' and had told him that she thought it would be as big a hit worldwide as 'A Whiter Shade Of Pale'."

It was Tony who inadvertently came up with the group's name when he remarked that Field was a 'rare bird'. "It resonated with us and in the end we just thought, OK, why not use that. We became Rare Bird. The other important thing for me personally was that Stratton Smith came across as a complete gent. I was very innocent and didn't realise that he was gay and how he might have fancied our drummer Mark Ashton, so all that completely passed me by. All I knew was that I was speaking to a gentleman and I felt very safe because I was dealing with a cultured, educated man. I instinctively felt that I was one of a small crowd of people that worked in a certain way and Strat knew that and was on that wavelength."

Rare Bird's drummer Mark Ashton had already bumped into Tony when his previous band Turnstyle, a progressive pop outfit who recorded for Pye Records, had supported The Nice. "Tony was a tall, robust man with a resemblance to the actor Jack Hawkins, very likeable and a real gentleman," he says. "He had a true love for music that was not of the norm and he was a risk taker. We had no idea that he was also starting a label and looking for bands to sign."

In a leap of faith on both sides, Tony not only offered them a management contract, but the group found themselves signing to a label that had yet to release any records. Rare Bird's debut album was recorded at Trident Studios and marked the first collaboration for one of Tony's artists with producer John Anthony.

It was already selling reasonably well on the strength of the band's touring schedule when Tony, partly against the wishes of group leader Graham Field, decided to release the track 'Sympathy' as a single in the second week of December. "Strat had to fight us a bit on that," says Field. "Secretly, I approved of his persistence, but the rest of the guys in Rare Bird, the other three, did not. Because they all wanted to be a heavy group, and heavy groups didn't have singles in those days, they sold albums."

To the amazement of everybody, or perhaps everyone except Tony and Anne Nightingale, the single took off in Europe almost immediately, and flew so fast that the band could barely keep up with its progress. Graham Field has famously written that 'Sympathy' "travelled through the world at such speed, that the band never actually reached a country before it got to number one."

Mark Ashton adds: "We were Strat's first hit record band, with number one singles in France and Italy, although 'Sympathy' was a hit by accident. It barely made the Top 30 in the UK[8]*, but was only released on the continent later in the year after a guy called Steve Rowland recorded a cover version and it went top ten in Holland, so our French label issued our version pretty damn fast."

Following the success of their album and single, Rare Bird went into IBC Studios in Portland Place to record their second LP, *As Your Mind Flies By*. Produced by the band themselves, aided by engineer Brian Stott, it was released in September 1970 and is generally thought to be their best work, featuring the magnificent *Flight*, an epic suite of songs and dramatic instrumental pieces which occupied the whole of side two of the album. Once again the album impressed the critics, with America's *Billboard* magazine placing Rare Bird in their ten best new acts of the year, but strangely *As Your Mind Flies By* failed to chart, either in the UK or in the States.

Tony was well known for accompanying his artists on tour, especially on their early ventures abroad, and Mark Ashton remembers that he travelled with them to a show at the Aragon Ballroom in Chicago in early July. "We blew the place apart," he says. "The kids went crazy and we had rave reviews, but Strat vanished, leaving no contact, he just went off on

---

8   * In the UK 'Sympathy' reached number 27 in the *Record Retailer* charts (and spent two weeks at 24 in *Melody Maker*'s own chart).

some other adventure. It was a crazy thing to do, because if we had stayed in Chicago we could have gained Iowa and then worked the other states."

Graham Field offers a possible explanation for the sudden disappearance of their errant manager. "We found out that the American record company we'd signed with had gone into liquidation. When we turned up at their offices, the bailiffs were already there and taking out the furniture. So I think that Strat went off to try and get a replacement record deal from somebody like WEA. I trusted him to do the right thing and personally I believe he called in to various record companies and tried to get us another deal."

The irony was that however much effort and belief Tony personally put in to a group, their actual business contract did not always stand up to close scrutiny. As the chief songwriter, Graham Field had more reason than most to notice the discrepancy between the massive record sales for 'Sympathy' and the royalty cheques that eventually dropped through his letterbox. "After two years, very sadly I went to see a good solicitor," he says. "He told me 'I'm sorry, but it's pointless working for this contract, because whatever you do they'll just spend your money and so you've got to get out of it and just go and get the name.' So I registered the Rare Bird name and I had to walk out. I did so with the most incredibly heavy heart, because something I really believed in was just being made impossible. What I don't understand is why Tony allowed that position to continue, but maybe he had signed things which he himself could not get out of."

Field often didn't see eye to eye with Gail Colson and when the original Rare Bird line-up disbanded in March 1971, a disappointed Tony told the *Melody Maker*: "British audiences didn't really seem to dig what they were playing – they weren't getting through to them. Whatever international success you get, an artist is never really happy unless he can be successful in his own country."

Graham Field moved on to another label, as did singer/bassist Steve Gould and keyboard player David Kaffinetti who retained the name Rare Bird. Drummer Mark Ashton formed the band Headstone with guitarist Steve Bolton who had just parted company with Atomic Rooster. As Field later acknowledged, "I'm extremely grateful to Strat for existing, because I couldn't have signed with anyone else that I met in the whole business. When I signed with CBS later on... there was no discussion, no guidance, there was nothing – it was like dealing with Marks & Spencer. Whereas with Stratton Smith he would talk about the image of the record, what direction we were going in, all that sort of thing. He absolutely believed in us."

* * *

Living and working around the tightly packed streets of Soho, almost everything the fledgling record company needed was close at hand and when it came to choosing a recording studio, Tony really didn't have to look too far. Trident Studios, set up in 1967 by Norman and Barry Sheffield and utilised by David Bowie, Elton John and Marc Bolan, was among the first UK studios to install a 16-track machine.

Van der Graaf Generator recorded their first two albums there and Charisma became one of Trident's more regular clients, although Simon White, Tony's friend who ran Marquee Studios, recalls being mildly annoyed that Tony favoured Trident over his own set-up in Wardour Street. The early success of producer John Anthony may well have swung Tony's decision.

John Anthony was a serious soul enthusiast, who began his music career working as a DJ in London clubs and by 1968 he was mixing American soul with the early sounds of Pink Floyd and other psychedelic groups. His friendship with Yes – a group whose members were regulars at La Chasse – enabled him to become a producer. Invited to one of the group's early recording dates, he found himself organising the session and subsequently mixing the tapes, which impressed all concerned. During a stint in the promotions office at Mercury Records he encountered Van der Graaf, and he was allowed to produce their album, his first professional credit as a producer.

As well as continuing his work with Van der Graaf, Tony also asked John Anthony to produce the first record by Rare Bird. The success of 'Sympathy' further enhanced Anthony as a producer, which led to him and Trident playing a key role in the Charisma operation. Over the next two years he would work with other signings, including Genesis, Lindisfarne and on solo outings by Peter Hammill. Outside of Charisma, John worked with Al Stewart, Ace and Roxy Music, and notably co-produced Queen's first album with Roy Thomas Baker.

In May 1970 Charisma ran a full-page advertisement in *Time Out* promoting two unusual new albums. Although neither Joseph Eger nor Gordon Turner were rock'n'roll, their music was aimed at the broader interests of the counter-culture. Their LPs, the third and fourth releases on Charisma after Rare Bird and Van der Graf Generator, reflected the more eclectic side of Tony's taste. While Eger's *Classical Heads* offered music, the mind was catered for by *Turner's Meditation: A System Of Meditation By Three-Fold Attunement*. "This system of meditation," ran the sleeve notes, "will lead you, as it has already led many, into a field of delightful and rewarding experience; it will also introduce to you, if that is still necessary, a unique personality in Gordon Turner."

Turner, a founder member of the National Federation of Spiritual Healers, developed a method of three-fold attunement, on which he expounded over a suitably relaxing, and some might say, trippy background.

This unusual recording was produced by Tony's friend Shel Talmy and it can surely be no coincidence that four years later, Gordon Turner's book *A Time To Heal* was published by the Talmy Franklin publishing imprint.

* * *

At the end of its first year, The Famous Charisma Label could boast a UK and European hit single with Rare Bird's 'Sympathy' and a strong-selling album with The Nice's *Five Bridges*. More importantly, the label had released debut LPs from three new signings – Lindisfarne, Audience and Genesis – whose fortunes would flourish in 1971, and signed Jackson Heights and Every Which Way, recently assembled by Lee Jackson and Brian Davison respectively after the break-up of The Nice.

"We had a very interesting first six months," Tony told the journalist Michael Wale. "Thanks to the goodwill of The Nice and a lot of money which I paid them when they split up, I managed to secure the two unreleased Nice albums, which was a nice farewell gesture by the boys, good luck to Charisma sort-of-thing. We had Van der Graaf Generator whose first album had to be one of the best-received albums we've ever done. The sales took our breath away – 15,000 in the first nine months of the label's existence. So in the first year in the UK we had sales at distributive prices of around £117,000."

Bazz Ward recalls how Tony secured the Nice albums from Keith Emerson: "When we recorded the *Five Bridges* album with the full orchestra, we were only getting about £750 for the show and I think it cost nearly £3,000 to do it. So Tony covered the whole amount himself and naturally he wanted it on Charisma. By this time Keith Emerson and the band had split, and there was a lot of, shall we say, 'tension'. Keith wanted the best deal he could get, so Tony said, 'Well I've got the tapes, but you hawk it around whatever record companies you like and I'll give you £200 more than the best offer. It's up to you, but I own the tapes.' Keith did take it round, but of course nobody was interested in it, so it came out on Charisma. Eleven years to the day after it came out, I walked into the Marquee and there was Tony at the bar. He said, 'Hello Bazz, I've got a little gift for you...' and he gave me the gold record for the *Five Bridges* suite.

"He was devastated when they split up," adds Ward. "He tried all sorts to keep them together, and the greatest thing he did, as far as I'm concerned, was letting Keith go to ELP. Tony still had Keith Emerson under contract, but Greg Lake decided that he didn't want Tony Stratton Smith involved, he wanted them to go with E.G. Management. Tony could have held out and said, 'Well I've got you under contract for another year', but Keith was adamant that he wanted to go. So Tony just shook his hand and said well, best of luck, see you around. The only stipulation was that Strat wanted *Five Bridges* on his record label, which he got."

Five Bridges was released in June 1970 and it sold well enough – reaching number two in the UK album charts – to justify a follow-up, *Elegy*, which aimed to show the progressive audience exactly how much was lost when The Nice split up. As its title suggests, *Elegy* was the group's final LP, released in April 1971 with only four tracks, two recorded live in 1969 at the Fillmore East in New York, one Bob Dylan cover version, plus the obligatory crossover classical piece. It continues to divide opinion among hardcore Nice fans; is it the final scrapings from the bottom of an already well-worked barrel or does it contain tantalising examples of the trio's finest work?

One aspect that everyone seems to agree on is the magnificent sleeve, designed by Storm Thorgerson and Aubrey Powell, otherwise known as Hipgnosis. It stands as a testament not only to the imagination and drive of the two designers, but also to Tony's willingness to pursue the creative ideal where lesser label bosses feared to tread. It also helped pave the way for Hipgnosis to become the leading graphic artists in their field.

While by Hipgnosis standards the sleeve for *Five Bridges* was fairly straightforward – a view of a Tyne bridge reflected at an odd angle – the creation of the cover for Elegy is remembered by all concerned as a stressful episode in the Charisma legend. "Keith Emerson phoned us up and said he'd like us to do a cover," recalls Powell, known affectionately as 'Po', of the Hipgnosis team. "So we had to see Tony Stratton Smith and Gail Colson. Gail worked really well as Tony's right hand person. I don't think Tony ever did anything without her approval and she was very forthright, whereas Tony was a charming, affable man, who was probably more interested in what the horses were doing. But Tony could not have been nicer and he was very much of the opinion that artists should be given a lot of freedom and that this didn't only apply to musicians, it applied to us too."

After pleasing everyone with their *Five Bridges* cover, the Hipgnosis duo wanted to shoot a cover for *Elegy* that involved 120 footballs pictured in the Moroccan desert. "Gail said, 'Why can't you shoot this down at Camber Sands?' and we argued that there weren't any decent sand dunes there."

The heated discussions over the album sleeve are etched deep in the memory of Gail Colson. "I can still recall exactly where we were and the arguments between Storm and I, although I really liked him and we got on like a house on fire. My budget was only £75 and he wanted to spend well in excess of £200, which was unbelievably expensive at that time."

Hipgnosis got their way and the Morocco shoot went ahead. "When we delivered the cover to Strat he thought it was the most beautiful thing he'd ever seen," says Po. "From that moment onwards our relationship blossomed.

After that we did a lot of work for Charisma and his other bands. Storm could be difficult, but he could hold his own in any argument or discussion and there was nothing Tony liked better than to engage in some rather highbrow subject and argue Storm into the ground over a pint in the pub just around the corner from Charisma. Tony was very fond of Storm, I can't tell you how well they got on. I know that Strat was gay and Storm wasn't, but he was fond of Storm in an intellectual way. Storm would go to see Strat and about three or four hours later he would come back and I'd ask him where on earth he'd been. Storm would laugh and say, oh, Strat was being a complete asshole and I just had to put him right. But Strat really loved the banter, he thought Storm was completely eccentric – of course, they both were and when you put the two of them together, the results could be quite interesting."

Powell acknowledges the debt that Hipgnosis owed to Charisma and Tony. "That opportunity, the cover for *Elegy*, really did change our fortunes. Every single person who saw that cover said, 'I want something like that, that's exactly the sort of thing I'm after'. Whether it was Jimmy Page or Roger Waters or whoever, everybody was impressed by *Elegy* and that desert image. In terms of the one point in time where people decided they would not accept simply having a group photograph on the front cover and that it should be something more elitist, more interesting, more cerebral, something more surreal or abstract, on their cover, then *Elegy* was the one that sealed our fate."

After *Elegy*, there was one final dip into the Nice vaults in 1973, when Charisma issued a third LP known variously as *Autumn To Spring* or *Autumn 1967 – Spring 1968*. Another compilation, this was the first in the Charisma Perspective series and consisted of alternate studio takes and mixes of material from the group's first two LPs. Once again the cover sported a suitably abstract photograph taken by Storm Thorgerson. Of course, this was purely a marketing exercise aimed squarely at cashing in on the success of Emerson, Lake & Palmer, but the album sold relatively well on the back of Keith Emerson's new supergroup.

Chapter 7

The Mad Hatter

"He was a total shambles by any conventional yardstick, but he had an intuitive feel for what was worthy and noble and artistically valuable."

Pete Frame, rock arborist

With a label boss like Stratton Smith, life at Charisma must have seemed like one big party and Tony felt it entirely appropriate that as a logo it should adopt a reworking of Sir John Tenniel's illustration of The Mad Hatter, first seen in Lewis Carroll's *Alice in Wonderland,* published in 1865.

When the company ended its first financial year in profit, allegedly to the tune of £266.00, the Mad Hatter at the helm decided to host a big Christmas bash for his artists and staff at the Marquee (where else?), on December 9, the same night the recently formed ELP were playing at the Lyceum in the Strand. Of course, no decent party is complete without cake, but it was its absence that caught the headlines, as *Melody Maker* reported, under the headline 'Charisma lose their cake'.

"Charisma's Christmas party at the Marquee last week ended in chaos when the power failed around ten o'clock," ran the story. "Then someone noticed that the lavish Christmas cake, still untouched, was missing, and there were strong rumours that Keith Moon was behind the plot to sabotage the cake. A search party consisting of Charisma's promotion men, Mike Paice and Glen Colson, recovered the cake 'with a few corners knocked off' a few hundred yards up nearby Dean Street. Keith Emerson popped in on his way to the Lyceum where he was appearing, and ten minutes before he was due onstage with Greg Lake and Carl Palmer, he was still at the party. Most of the Charisma bands were present – Genesis, Jackson Heights, Every Which Way and Lindisfarne were all out in force, as were Rare Bird, who received a gold disc for their best-selling single 'Sympathy' from Alan Keen, head of Radio Luxembourg."

As well as throwing a party, Tony celebrated by investing in art, specifically the work of John Bratby, an English painter best remembered for helping to popularise the gritty style of 'kitchen-sink realism'. "Give Strat his due," wrote Pete Frame, best known for his Rock Family Trees, "he was a total shambles by any conventional yardstick, but he had an intuitive feel for what was worthy and noble and artistically valuable. The listening room at Charisma had a great big John Bratby painting on the wall and a desk which had once belonged to J.R.R. Tolkien. There was a framed, handwritten letter from him in the top drawer, confirming that he had written *The Lord Of The Rings* on it. He had a good heart, did Strat, and that's why everyone who worked for him loved the guy."

Throughout the sixties Bratby painted a series of large portraits of celebrities of the day, including Paul McCartney (three canvasses), John Betjeman, David Frost, Billie Whitelaw, Spike Milligan and Richard Attenborough. McCartney subsequently became a collector of the artist's work, as did Tony. Glen Colson recalled: "I remember Strat's Bratby's very well; he had one as big as a door that looked like a drunk had walked into a wall with a bucket of paint."

Ballet was another area of culture that fascinated Tony. Having written an unpublished novel based on Rudolf Nureyev, his interest in the Russian ballet dancer continued when he attempted to get him involved with a classical music recording. Charisma lawyer Tony Seddon, who had taken over from Marty Machat, recalls that this involved the financier André Chudnoff. "I dealt with Chudnoff in connection with a project to make a recording of *The Soldiers Tale* by Stravinsky and with Rudolf Nureyev doing the voice-over," says Seddon. "André was a money man rather than anything else, but he was interested in music and that world. People who had money to invest often wanted to get involved in the entertainment business."

Sadly for Tony, this project never came to fruition as a release on either the B&C or Famous Charisma labels, but the idea was revived in 1977 when a recording of Nureyev in *The Soldiers Tale* eventually made it to vinyl on Argo Records, a subsidiary of Decca. This traditional Russian folk tale featured Glenda Jackson as the narrator, the other speaking roles going to Micheál MacLiammóir as the Devil and Nureyev playing the part of the soldier.

Towards the end of 1970, Tony decided to mark Charisma's first year by launching a two-pronged sales drive in the USA. He confirmed their contract with ABC Records on the West Coast, allowing them to release albums by Rare Bird, Genesis and Van der Graaf Generator on the ABC or Dunhill record labels. The advertising campaign, overseen by ABC president Jay Lasker, was due to start in early January 1971 and would be followed up with promotional tours by the bands in February, March and April. The second phase was to be handled by Mercury Records, who were given the option to release product by The Nice, Jackson Heights and Every Which Way.

Tony appointed Honor Scott as the US representative for Charisma artists, assigned to keep the FM radio stations and underground press fully informed on news from the British label. She was also to liaise with local promoters on the college circuit and her first major project was a five-week, 15-college tour for Rare Bird, Audience and Jackson Heights. Tony himself headed for America to talk to both ABC and Mercury about the promotions. He told *Billboard*: "This is the first time we have made a concerted attack on the US market. It follows the consolidation of our operations in continental Europe through Philips and in the UK through B&C."

B&C, or Beat and Commercial to give Lee Gopthal's outfit their full company name, was the main distributor for Charisma records in the UK, though 'Booze and Corruption' would become a favoured nickname among the Charisma staff. Working alongside Lee Gopthal was Brian Gibbon, an accountant with a thorough working knowledge of the music industry. "B&C was a group in a loose sense," he says, "linked mainly between Tony and Lee Gopthal, because you had B&C, you had Trojan, plus Tony brought in Charisma. Lee was really the leading light in terms of Trojan Records, Lee being a West Indian and at that time all the big reggae artists went through Trojan. B&C was originally set up, not as a label but as a distributor of products, so it would distribute records for Trojan, Charisma and later Mooncrest, but it also had a lot of small Jamaican labels that it would distribute directly to retailers. Lee's offices were in Neasden, where they had a small warehouse and an office facility as well, whereas the Charisma offices were in Old Compton Street, so I would go between the two."

According to Island Records warehouseman Rob Bell, the Beat & Commercial set up at 12 Neasden Lane, NW10, housed in a long rectangular building with its own parking spaces out front. Behind the main entrance was a reception desk with an archaic manual switchboard, where Doreen sat "dexterously switching jack-ended cables", and to the left ran a long corridor with offices either side, the first of which belonged to the B&C team of Lee Gopthal, Jim Flynn, Barry Creasy, Alan Firth and Fred Parsons. Next to these offices was a storeroom-cum-warehouse for Gopthal's Musicland record stores, the last door on the right led to the various offices for Island Records and through them to their own warehouse area.

Steve Weltman brought in Adrian Sear as part of the sales team working out of the B&C offices at Neasden and Sear acknowledged the importance of Gopthal's Musicland chain of record shops, which kept London supplied with the latest imports, as well as home grown releases. "At one time the Musicland shops were the biggest chain of record stores in London and the shop at 44 Berwick Street was the biggest.[9]* It was an incredibly busy shop, as you can imagine Soho in the early seventies was massive for music, and they started the Trojan label in this country on the back of those stores. They realised there was such a huge market for reggae

---

9   * In 1968 Elton John worked briefly behind the counter in the Berwick Street shop.

that wasn't being exploited over here and they gradually transformed from being the retailer into the record company by forming Trojan and B&C."

The B&C/Charisma sales and promotions team, which included Steve Weltman, Lloyd Beiny and Des McKeogh, became regular visitors to the Nellie Dean, a popular Soho pub which just happened to be located opposite Carlisle Street and a pizza restaurant above which lived Barrie Wentzell, *Melody Maker*'s regular photographer whose flatmate was *MM* writer Roy Hollingworth. Here was another spot where, on any given lunchtime or early evening, you could find various combinations of Charisma staff and musicians, journalists and hangers-on, all rubbing shoulders with the Soho locals over a pint of bitter. It was, to paraphrase Lindisfarne's chief writer Alan Hull, the perfect place to find the yes-men with their suggestions, well-wishers with their lies. At the nucleus of these impromptu gatherings would be Tony, glass in hand, eyes streaming with laughter and the smoke from an ever-present cigarette, never happier than when surrounded by this company.

Named after a song written in 1905, there was a touch of the music hall about the Nellie Dean and this may have edged Tony towards the world of the theatrical angels, starting with a new West End stage musical entitled *Lie Down, I Think I Love You*. Produced in collaboration with Daniel Rees, the top billing was shared between Ray Brooks and Vanessa Miles as Tom and Anna, the slightly more sensible couple in a household of student/hippie types. Intended as a British version of *Hair*, the wafer-thin storyline included a plan to put a bomb on top of Broadcasting House, and there was plenty of nudity, sex, drugs and probably a bit of rock'n'roll in the Ceredig Davies score. Also among the hippie cast were Antonia Ellis and Tim Curry, whose next major role would be as Frank N Furter in the original *Rocky Horror Show*, three years later. At one point, Pan's People dancer Louise Clarke was lined up to appear, but it would seem she managed to dodge the bullet; even director John Gorrie walked out of the show during rehearsals, demanding that his name be removed from all literature and publicity. The show opened at the Novello Theatre in The Strand on October 14, 1970, and closed after just 13 performances.

Talking to Brian Mulligan of *Record & Tape Retailer*, Tony admitted: "In the first year we made a lot of mistakes – some through kindness, some through my own stupidity. [The musical] was truly an expensive mistake – a solid five figure one."**

Several artists made just the one fleeting appearance on The Famous Charisma Label, one of which was American guitarist Leigh Stephens, a founder member of Blue Cheer, a hard rocking power trio whose debut album on Philips contained a heavy version of Eddie Cochran's 'Summertime Blues'. Stephens moved to London and became part of a close circle of friends that

---

** Tony admitted losing £50,000 on the show.

included Keith Emerson and his wife Elinor, Ronnie and Krissy Wood, Perry Press, Kim Gardner and Alvin Lee. He was living on a houseboat moored on the Thames in West London, which would subsequently provide the cover photo for his Charisma album *And A Cast Of Thousands*. According to Perry Press, Stephens was restless for a new project and connecting him with Tony and Charisma seemed an obvious move. It's fair to say that the resultant album, released in August 1971, is not one of Leigh's personal favourites.

"It was an album that should never have been attempted," recalls Stephens. "Too soon after Blue Cheer and with not a lot of direction. I was introduced to Strat by Keith Emerson, who heard a demo I was making and liked it. Strat was a good guy. He treated me very well despite a tape operator at Island Studios screwing up the sound on my album, forcing it to be remixed and going way over budget, after which the tapes were lost."

* * *

They say that as one door closes, another one supposedly opens – and the same can be said of rock bands that disassemble. When The Nice folded, Tony kept faith with two of the individual members, gaining two more names for the Charisma roster with groups formed by both drummer Brian Davison and bass player Lee Jackson. Davison's Every Which Way featured the gravel voice of former Skip Bifferty singer Graham Bell, bassist Alan Cartwright and Geoff Peach on flute and saxophone. On guitar was John Hedley, fresh from the John Lewis Blues Band in Morpeth and highly recommended by both Bell and Cartwright. The group made their Charisma recording debut with a single, 'Go Placidly'/'The Light' followed by an album released in September 1970. Produced by Davison and largely written by Bell, their music was described as a hybrid mixture of 'folk, jazz and progressive rock', with Peach's reeds pushing the sound closer to Steve Winwood's Traffic than anything The Nice ever recorded.

It was to be a short-lived venture, unlike Jackson Heights who recorded one LP for Charisma and three for Vertigo. Lee Jackson swapped his bass for a six string and a more acoustic sound and Tony supplied the band name, after the New York suburb. Tony handed the management role to his friend Johnny Toogood from the Marquee Martin Agency. Jackson recruited his band from among his old Newcastle friends. High on his list were guitarist Charlie Harcourt and his group the Junco Partners, a storming blues outfit originally formed in 1964 who had taken over from The Animals as the house band at Newcastle's celebrated Club A'GoGo.

Charlie Harcourt recalls Jackson's approach: "To begin with, Lee Jackson wanted the Junco Partners to be his backing band after the break-up of The Nice, as we all knew each other from Newcastle, Lee playing in The

Invaders and me with the Juncos. I do remember Charisma's office as a very friendly place, in part due to Strat's p.a. Gail Colson and an ex-Bonzo roadie, Fred Munt. It was quite a crazy place at times too, especially with the Bonzos and then the Monty Python mob hanging around."

King Progress, Jackson Heights' only Charisma LP, was recorded at IBC and Advision Studios in 1970, its gatefold sleeve another Hipgnosis montage. In his liner notes, Tony wrote: "Creativity is the ability to reorganise known factors so that they become novel and fresh. In forming Jackson Heights, Lee Jackson vindicates the theory… If acoustic music is sometimes thought to be the soft white underbelly of rock, then Lee, Charlie, Tommy and Mario give to the figure ribs and muscle. There is an invitation to come close in the music of Jackson Heights, and a promise that delight is not wrought by decibels alone. For Lee to 'go acoustic' is rather like a writer taking up the quill after years on a typewriter, but there are no doubt many who say that for exhibiting style and personality, the quill is the finer instrument."

Despite Tony's enthusiasm, *King Progress* did not sell well and the first incarnation of Jackson Heights lasted barely a year. Charisma did not renew their contract and the group moved across to Vertigo. By December 1973 Lee Jackson's acoustic adventure was over, but his next venture would see him try to recreate a keyboard-led rock trio in the style of The Nice; a move that definitely met with Tony's approval and would bring his old friend Lee back in to the Charisma fold.

Johnny Toogood worked continuously as the manager of Jackson Heights and stayed with Lee Jackson when he formed his next group. However, his time with the Marquee Martin Agency was about to come to an abrupt end that would see him joining Tony at Charisma. "The agency started going in slightly different directions from the path that I would have liked. I took over some of the TV and radio promotion for Charisma, liaising between the various distribution centres, record store brochures – anything that would help to promote the label came under my domain. I used to book the bands on television in Europe to help boost sales – there wasn't very much TV in England that I could do at the time, only *Top Of The Pops,* and the bands that Strat was signing weren't really *Top Of The Pops* material."

* * *

An integral part of the press and publicity kit for any record company is the promotional photograph, and many of the early Charisma press shots feature the label's artists in an idyllic English rural country setting. As often as not Barrie Wentzell was PR man Glen Colson's photographer of choice, and the fact that Wentzell worked primarily for *Melody Maker* was a happy coincidence for all concerned.

"There was a pub we liked up on Hampstead Heath," says Glen, "so we would take the bands up there, often with Barrie in tow, snap them surrounded by trees and greenery and then retire to the pub. Nothing too creative about that, but those photographs still stand up today."

Hampstead Heath not only supplied the green and pleasant backdrop for Wentzell's photography, but was popular for another reason – nearby was the Colson family pub, The Magdala Tavern, where he and Gail had grown up. Still run by their parents Jack and Stella Colson, it became a regular stop for Charisma musicians, Vivian Stanshall in particular. Glen had been working closely with Stanshall since he first joined the label – he even did a spell on drums with the Bonzos – and their frontman struck up a friendship with Colson senior, who had served in the Royal Navy during the Second World War, as had Vivian's grandfather in the First World War. Consequently, Viv Stanshall spent many happy hours swapping old naval stories with Gail and Glen's father over a pint or two.

It was probably Hampstead Heath that formed the backdrop for the only known photograph of another of Tony's early signings. Trevor Billmuss was 'discovered' by John Gee, then manager of the Marquee, who booked him into the club specifically to bring him to Tony's attention, yet Billmuss remains something of a mystery, both in his personal background and the question of exactly why he was signed in the first place. He recorded one album for Charisma and the few who have heard it are often bemused as to why he was thought worthy of studio time. *Family Apology* must be a candidate for the label's smallest seller and neither of the two singles made any impact with the listening public either; or on DJ John Peel, who was given the task of reviewing the 'English Pastures' single in *Disc & Music Echo* in July 1971.

"I first heard Trevor Billmuss at London's Marquee about a year ago," wrote Peel. "At the time he was playing principally to several friends in the front who were overreacting heavily to every in-joke. Later, everyone said, 'Isn't he great, well, isn't he?' I didn't really think he was. With 'English Pastures' I'm in a quandary again. It's a pleasant song, pleasantly sung with a pleasant arrangement. When it had finished playing the first time, I couldn't recall any of it. There are a great many singers who have a greater impact on record and it seems probable that this record will be generally overlooked. There's just nothing very distinguished about it, although there's nothing very undistinguished about it either. On the other hand, the Pig (Peel's wife Sheila) is singing along with it on the second playing, so I may well be wrong. 'It's strange, I don't know if I like it or not,' she says, 'there's something about it.' The B-side reminds me of my initial reaction to Trevor's performance. He made me think then of a sort of groovy Noel Coward. There's something for you to think about."

Paul Conroy pinpoints the marketing of the album as the problem. "Someone played him to Strat and then Strat played him to me and I thought he was brilliant. Billmuss was just a nice little boy, you know, but he was very talented in a folky, Peter Sarstedt-style. It was a great record, the only trouble was that once the record was made, we just didn't know how to sell it. Which happened with quite a few of our records; you'd make them and then find they're impossible to promote because you knew they were never going to get any radio play."

Little has been heard of the elusive Trevor Billmuss since, apart from the news that at some point he moved to America, where he was reported to be "happy as an un-famous man".

More promising was The Liverpool Scene, a rock group with poet Adrian Henri at the helm that recorded for CBS and RCA, but although Tony spent a good deal of time luring them to Charisma they slipped through his grasp. "Tony Stratton Smith from Charisma Records was keeping an eye on what we were doing," says Henri. "I met him and he said, 'You know it was remarkable, because I was going to make a substantial offer to buy you out from your management and record contract, and you would all have done very well out of it,' but I think that morning, or just as he was making up his mind, he opened the newspaper and it said Liverpool Scene Splits. So that was that. My one chance of being a real rock'n'roll star was gone." The Liverpool Scene disbanded in April 1970, but Tony continued to pursue his interest in the group and Charisma released a compilation album, *Recollections,* in 1972.

Even more promising was Graham Bell, singer with Every Which Way via Skip Bifferty whom B&C Records art director Frank Sansom has good reason to remember. Barely three weeks into his new job and still finding his feet within Charisma, he was walking down to the post room under the offices in Soho Square when he heard someone berating the young assistant. "This bloke was giving the young boy a really hard time," says Sansom, "so I went over and told him in no uncertain terms that no one deserved to be spoken to like that and to ease off. He turned his verbal abuse on me instead, so I said, look, I'll apologise to you, if you apologise to the boy. No apology was forthcoming, so I turned and walked away, but the guy followed me, spun me around and put his face right into mine. I knew what was coming, so before he could do anything else, I hit him and left him in a heap on the floor. There were raised eyebrows from the crowd that had gathered. Even the boy looked shocked and said, 'Do you know who that is?' Well, I didn't have a clue. He said, 'That's Graham Bell.' Bell & Arc were one of Charisma's new acts at that time and the label had high hopes for them."

Sansom went to Strat and offered his resignation. "He suggested we discuss it over a drink. We walked across to the Nellie Dean and I told him exactly what had happened and said that if he had to let me go, then I completely understood. To make matters worse, about halfway through our conversation Gail Colson rushed in and said that Fred Munt had just told her what happened – and he was not happy. At that time, Fred was Bell & Arc's manager. Strat assured me that I still had a job, which was a huge vote of confidence for me and he completely difused the situation – he must have spoken to Graham and Fred to calm things down. Bell was known to be a bit of a handful."

As Sansom points out, Bell & Arc were briefly Charisma's blue-eyed boys, fronted by the muscular voice of Graham Bell. Another product of the North East scene, an area that Tony would mine successfully, he handed them over to American producer Bob Johnston to work his magic on their debut album. Apparently when Johnston was first introduced to the band, Tony said, almost apologetically, "Don't be misled by their youthfulness." Johnston took one close look at the group and replied, "Hell, man, their eyes are ten thousand years old!"

Bell & Arc had certainly served an arduous apprenticeship. Guitarist John Turnbull and keyboard player Micky Gallagher first joined forces with Bell in Skip Bifferty while bassist Tommy Duffy cut his teeth in The Sect and drummer John Woods had played with Junco Partners and Jackson Heights. Having already made his Charisma debut with Brian Davison's Every Which Way, Bell re-assembled his old mates, naming them Arc. In 1971 they played the Lyceum in London with The James Gang, supported Boz Scaggs at The Roundhouse and turned in a magnificent performance at the Reading Festival, which reduced Tony to tears and had the *Melody Maker* singing their praises. "Bell has finally found a situation to suit the war-bag full of talent that screws itself out in anguished, raging songs of such mood that you think the guy's going to expire there and then," raved their reviewer. In November they would support The Who on an arena tour that visited the southern states of America.

With The Nice a distant memory and Keith Emerson forging ahead with ELP, Tony offered road manager Bazz Ward the job with Bell & Arc. Rehearsing material for their first – and as it turned out, only – Charisma album, they were sent down to Symonds Yat, a small village in the Forest of Dean which overlooks the Wye Valley. "I would cook breakfast and the band would all wander off to compose songs," recalls Ward. "After dinner, it was off to the pub for the evening and then after that, they just wanted to play all night. I had a recorder to tape the sessions, and then they went to Island Studios in Basing Street, London, and recorded their one and only LP after that."

Unfortunately the album didn't live up to the expectations suggested by the band's storming live performances. On returning to England after The Who tour, Bell promptly fired the rest of the band without bothering to tell Tony, much to his annoyance, as it was he that had helped put Bell & Arc together in the first place. Producer Bob Johnston then took Bell back to the States with him to work on a solo album. "As a postscript to the story," smiled Frank Sansom, smiling, "a couple of years later I was sitting in the bar of the Marquee talking to Strat, when Graham Bell walked in. As he came towards us, Strat said, 'Ahh, Graham, I believe you already know Frank…' and Bell walked straight out again."

* * *

During the early years of any record label, company finances are often on a knife-edge, and Charisma was no different. On several occasions Tony's writing, not least the annual *International Book of Football* which he edited well into the early seventies, supplemented the Charisma coffers, even though the music business was clearly his number one occupation.

"I have sold more books than any of my groups have ever sold albums, put together," Tony confessed in one interview, "but I still find that I get more uptight and concerned and involved in what they are doing than in what I myself am doing, which is good for me, good for my soul. I don't care how many books I've sold. I wait, I never ask, I wait until I'm told or until I check the statement, until someone phones me up and tells me that such and such a book is moving fantastically this year. That's great, but I am happier living for my groups."

Each January Tony would make the pilgrimage to the French Riviera to attend MIDEM – the leading trade marketplace (and major social beano) for the music industry that took place in Cannes. Since 1967, the Marché International du Disque et de l'Édition Musicale had become the place to rub shoulders with hundreds of publishers, producers, agents, managers, lawyers, executives, entrepreneurs and journalists from around the world, all busy networking and negotiating deals while up and coming artists played live in the evenings.

Industry men like Seymour Stein, the head of Sire Records, can recall that the first MIDEM was held in the Martinez Hotel where the rooms and suites were rented out to the exhibitors instead of booths and stands, and where the many hotels, bars and restaurants of Cannes played an equally important role in the relentless round of business deals taking place during the week. It was here that Stein first encountered Tony, in the days when he was still only a music publisher touting business for Stratsongs. According to Stein, "Strat was equally at home holding court in the Carlton or Martinez bars as he was at The Ship, his local in Wardour Street. Later on, it was a privilege to do business with him at Charisma Records, along with Gail Colson and it was through that association that I first met Paul Conroy, who was then managing The Kursaal Flyers, and also Lee Gopthal of B&C Records."

At the annual gathering in 1971, sets from Eric Burdon & War and Elton John entertained the suited and booted music executives. Tony, resplendent in tuxedo and bow-tie, was photographed with Eddie Barclay, French producer of Jacques Brel and Charles Aznavour. This proved to be a bumper year, drawing 5,000 people from 40 countries, including 130 companies from the UK. Planning to release their albums on Charisma in the UK, Tony snapped up master tapes for the German group Birth Control and the Chilean band Atacama. He also arranged a catalogue deal for his Stratsongs copyrights with Japan's Toshiba Music Publishing.

Any graphic for a band called Birth Control opens up a whole range of possibilities to offend – and the designers on both sides of the Channel did their best to oblige. The original illustrated German sleeve depicted a giant baby-eating insect busily digesting infants – under the watchful eye of the Pope, naturally. Many record shops refused to display the cover or, in some cases, to even stock the record at all. Both the British and French releases were issued with redesigned sleeves.

Charisma handed the sleeve design for Birth Control's album over to Hipgnosis – and Storm Thorgerson's solution produced one of the label's most controversial covers. Powell and Thorgerson's concept was to photograph an eel in a water-filled condom, an image that attracted opprobrium in Germany, where the ladies employed putting vinyl into sleeves at the packing house reportedly came out on strike in protest. This was certainly the case at the EMI distribution centre in Hayes, Middlesex, where their staff refused to touch the sleeve or pack the record, leaving Steve Weltman and his sales team no option but to go in and pack it themselves. Of course, the band themselves lapped up the extra publicity and their album was voted the second best record of the year in the German paper *Musik Express*.

Aubrey Powell recalls Tony's reaction when he outlined Storm Thorgerson's plans. "I remember going in to see Tony and Gail and saying, 'We want to put an eel in a contraceptive' – and the look on Gail's face was a picture, oh my God what are you thinking? But by that time I think they probably trusted us enough to know that we could handle it. I went down to Billingsgate Market and bought a bucket full of live eels. I don't know if you've ever tried to force a live eel into a contraceptive… but it's an absolute bloody nightmare. Looking back, it caused a lot of controversy. A lot of covers that we could do in that period, you could never do now, not in a million years. I don't think you could put a contraceptive on an album cover now, it would be unacceptable. But once again, it was largely down to the unbelievable support we received from Charisma. When we finished the cover, I can remember Tony saying, 'It's absolutely brilliant, brilliant...' and there was never any thought that it was actually a Durex with a live eel inside, it became much more than that, just a really striking image."

* * *

To be a successful record plugger takes persistence, the gift of the gab, a little bit of cheek and a touch of the unexpected. Judd Lander has all of these qualities in abundance and has used them to full effect throughout his career, never more so than for his somewhat unorthodox introduction to Charisma Records. Like many others in this story, he first encountered Tony in La Chasse but in his case he was selling suitcases that had been pilfered from Harrods' stockroom where he worked at the time. "I met Gail Colson while trying to sell the dodgy suitcases in their office reception – and Gail has never let me forget this. Fortunately for me, Gail and Tony took me under their wings, and eventually I ended up as promotions manager."

Encountering Eve Slater in Charisma's reception, Lander launched into his suitcase sales patter and Eve went off to check whether anyone in the offices was interested. "I think she collared Gail Colson first. Of course what I really wanted was to get into the music business and I'm sure it was the pure cheek of it that actually got me in. The next thing I know, Gail is asking if I had ever plugged a record before – and I thought this was some factory practice, you know, where you put some plastic back in the hole. Gail said, 'No, we'll give you a record, you go along to Radio One and get the producers and DJs to play it.' I thought, that sounds great, I'll have a go at that – and I think I did it free for a while, it was like early work experience in its way. So that's how I started plugging records, but I didn't really know what I was doing. I'd walk in and ask, 'Why aren't you playing our record?' and they'd say, 'Because we don't like it', and then I'd start to get argumentative with the producers. Somehow it seemed to work in my favour, because they suddenly started to play the bloody records and I think Tony and Gail and everyone saw this and thought, hang on, there's something happening here."

Among the groups whose records Lander promoted were Van der Graaf. "Strat asked me to take the DJ Alan 'Fluff' Freeman to see a Van der Graaf gig in Paris. Fluff had really good taste in music and it was he and John Peel who championed a lot of Charisma's early tracks. So we all flew out to Paris and while we were in the hotel reception I saw Tarzan, the actor Johnny Weissmuller. I said to Fluff, look, it's Johnny Weissmuller – we should get him to do the Tarzan yell. Alan really didn't think he would do it, but I walked over for a chat and said, 'Johnny, look I know it's rude but this is Alan Freeman, a famous DJ from England, and it would be great if we could just use you as the tag for his radio link.' So we took 'Tarzan' outside, round the back of the hotel and there was Alan Freeman with a microphone, with all of Van der Graaf Generator watching on and Johnny in full Tarzan mode doing his best jungle call. When we got back, Fluff used this as the 'sting' whenever he played anything by Van der Graaf or Peter Hammill – and then later it became a regular feature on his radio show."

* * *

As a regular patron at the Marquee, Tony was asked to recommend new artists for the club's weekly programme, and he was often offered Sunday nights for a special 'TSS Presents...' slot. For much of 1970, long queues would form along Wardour Street for 'Marquee Sunday Special Nights', which essentially became a showcase for The Famous Charisma Label with bands like Van der Graaf Generator, Jackson Heights, Lindisfarne, Genesis and Audience.

Audience emerged from the ashes of Lloyd Alexander Real Estate, a semi-professional soul band initially signed to Polydor that was between managers when they came to Tony's attention. According to Barrie Wentzell, who photographed them before they signed with Charisma, things started to go wrong when Polydor used his band shot in negative on the cover. "Not a great start," he says, laughing. Polydor spent money on a new, largely untried and untested group and didn't want to splash out any more, including the necessary promotion for the album, at least until they sorted out their management problems. Hence the urgent round of phone calls that eventually brought them to Tony's attention.

As vocalist Howard Werth remembers, "TSS had to buy out our Polydor contract and as soon as that was complete, we went straight into the studio. Tony only works with bands that he personally likes and he's often carried on with a band that he has believed in, when everybody else was criticising him."

While still with Polydor, Audience had made their debut at London's Marquee Club in February 1969 in the company of the artists known as Gilbert & George. For their act that evening, the avant-garde duo donned smart business suits and bronze face paint, sat across a small table from each other and told increasingly dark and bizarre stories. Also present that night was the feminist writer Germaine Greer, presumably reporting on the event for her column in *Oz* magazine. Art-rock indeed...

Audience bassist Trevor Williams talks fondly about his old boss and those nights at The Marquee. "Strat was a tremendous, massively charismatic man with total belief and a supportive attitude in and towards his artists," he says. "All of us liked him a lot. Oddly enough, one of the many visions I have of him in the past was propping up the bar at the Marquee and bestowing alcohol on anyone who came near him. He was a real one-off. I think Strat's reputation and general open bonhomie made him both an attractive social target as well as someone you would really hope would notice your band. When he took an interest in Audience we couldn't have hoped for a bigger break. Being part of the Charisma stable was massive kudos. Playing at the Marquee Club as part of the Charisma stable was doubly great. Strat was easy to work for. He never got in the way and, if he believed in you, he gave you all the leeway you needed. Judging by the efforts he expended in getting us to sign to his label, he certainly believed in Audience.

For the recording of *Friend's Friend's Friend*, the second Audience album and their first for Charisma, both Gail and Tony recommended Shel Talmy as the producer, but the American was rejected by the band. Despite Talmy's track record of hit singles, they had reservations about his methods. Trevor Williams outlines the problem. "We all met at Olympic Studios for discussions. Shel made it crystal clear that he wasn't interested in the extended improvisations. Given Shel's enthusiasm for high royalty points based on fast-selling, commercial singles, his lack of interest was understandable. But his arrogance got our hackles up from the start. Indifference was the last thing we needed at this stage of our career."

The band were also worried by Talmy's preference for bringing in session musicians, often an unnecessary luxury. "Perhaps we were too idealistic," said Williams, "but we felt a producer's role was to get the best from the existing band and preserve its integrity, rather than put something together with hired hands just to make life easier. But Talmy was a production line man. He knew what made a hit and it was usually something people had heard before and wouldn't be offended to hear again." In the end, Shel Talmy was dismissed and the band produced their album themselves, with the help of engineer Mike Bobak.

Audience singer Howard Werth agrees that Tony's larger than life personality made Charisma a good place for any band to be. "As the name of his record company implied, Stratton Smith was an immensely charismatic personality," Werth later told journalist Sid Smith. "He was immense fun to be around and there was a kind of camaraderie that came from being on the label. We did get on with the acts on Charisma, especially people like Van der Graaf Generator and Lindisfarne. I always remember that Strat came on a European tour with us. There was Audience, Brian Davison's Every Which Way and Lindisfarne, and three roadies. Two of them had one lung each and one of them had one eye. I can remember Strat saying, 'Bloody hell, between the lot of them they've got four lungs, five eyes and no brains! That was a typical Strat remark."

The key album for Audience was their third release, and second for

Charisma, *The House On The Hill*, released in May 1971. Once again Tony and Charisma insisted that a 'name' producer be brought in, and this time Audience happily approved the choice of Gus Dudgeon, who had impressed the band with his reworking of tracks for the 'Indian Summer' maxi-single. Everyone set up camp in Trident Studios, where the band members, Dudgeon and chief engineer Robin Cable recorded new material like 'Jackdaw' and 'You're Not Smiling' as well as one of the better cover versions of Screaming Jay Hawkins' 'I Put A Spell On You' and the instrumental 'Raviole', with string arrangement by Robert Kirby. The album stands as their most complete, credible and cohesive collection of songs, where everything came together, according to Trevor Williams "the result of everyone singing from the same hymn sheet – band, management, record company, artwork and production."

The epic title track was written by Trevor Williams, who brought it to the table of the pre-Audience Lloyd Alexander Real Estate where Howard Werth took it on, with Trevor's blessing, to shape and mould into what would become the group's signature piece. An early version of *The House On The Hill* first appeared on their 1969 debut LP for Polydor, but Werth enlarged the song in 1971. Tony turned once more to Hipgnosis for the cover design and Aubrey Powell recalls how they came up with another truly memorable image, even working to a typically tight Charisma budget.

"Charisma never had any money, so the album covers often had to be done to a tight budget – it was almost a case of you can do what you like, but you've only got £50. I'm not joking. In a way, Charisma and Hipgnosis were very similar in that we both believed that the art should come first and the money comes later. And I think that, particularly in later years, the bigger bands often paid for the support of the smaller bands who couldn't afford our ideas, but we did them anyway… and Charisma was a perfect example."

The strikingly unusual cover for Audiences' *House On The Hill* featured a couple in what appears to be a forties thriller scene, with a hint of Agatha Christie as within the fold-out a butler can be seen dragging away a body. The house, or mansion, belonged to the parents of one of Po's friends and the girl in the picture is model Lindsay Corner, once the girlfriend of Syd Barrett, a Cambridge friend of Storm Thorgerson. "The result is one of my favourite album covers," says Po. "I've got lots of favourite covers and *House On The Hill* is not only a great album, but the cover itself told such a story."

After Audience finally ground to a halt in September 1972, singer and guitarist Howard Werth stayed with the Charisma label for a brace of solo albums. In one of rock's more bizarre 'what-if' stories, he came within a whisker of replacing Jim Morrison in The Doors, thanks primarily to Tony's close friendship with Jac Holzman, the head of Elektra Records in America. Tony explained the situation to *Melody Maker* in February 1973:

"Jac gave the early Audience albums to The Doors and they really liked Howard's singing and writing. Then he called me from the States and asked how Howard would feel about working with The Doors. And he (Werth) was very excited about it." Like all good broadsheets, *Melody Maker* jumped the gun by proclaiming that the British singer was "virtually certain" to succeed Morrison and that the band would fly over to England to seal the deal.

The remaining members of The Doors, Ray Manzarek, Robby Krieger and John Densmore, did set up meetings and rehearsals in London and auditioned several British vocalists, including Kevin Coyne and Jess Roden, as well as Werth who was certainly Jac Holzman's choice and appeared to be the favourite to take over. However, after a couple of weeks, Manzarek decided that The Doors should not continue without Morrison and flew back to America. Krieger and Densmore stayed in London and formed The Butts Band, choosing Jess Roden as their singer.

Howard Werth stayed in touch with Ray Manzarek and later worked with the ex-Doors keyboard player in Hollywood, recording sessions that would later surface on Werth's solo album, *Six Of One And Half A Dozen Of The Other*.

Chapter 8

The Golden Touch:
Genesis & Lindisfarne

"A friendly lion sitting somewhere in a tree house somewhere in Dean Street. He had SS in big letters across his belly, which was full of fish and other alcoholic beverages, and his smile had that Charisma ring of confidence."

Peter Gabriel, singer-songwriter

The pivotal event in Tony Stratton Smith's career as an entrepreneur in the music industry, and one that would eventually consolidate his fortunes and those of his record label, occurred on Tuesday March 24, 1970, in the tiny bar and discotheque above Ronnie Scott's celebrated jazz club on Frith Street. It was one of those fateful collisions of the right people in the right place at the right time that can irrevocably change the lives of those involved for good.

Getting to the venue would not have presented a problem, at least once Tony had been cajoled out of his flat. It was barely a three-minute walk door to door, down Dean Street, first left into Bateman Street and first right down Frith Street to Ronnie's, almost opposite Bar Italia. Even if you ignored Bateman Street and took the next left along Old Compton Street then first left up Frith Street, it was still the same distance – you just passed a different set of pubs along the route. Word about the strange new group playing there that night first reached the Charisma office via Rare Bird, whose keyboard player Graham Field brought in a cassette of the group that had recently supported them in Canterbury. "You must hear this," he said to the Charisma boss. Further encouragement came from record producer John Anthony who'd already seen them at Queen Elizabeth College in Kensington and thought them worthy of Tony's attention.

Tony climbed the stairs to the room above the world-famous jazz club to find that he knew almost the entire audience. Of the handful of people milling about, most were members of his own staff, including Gail and Glen Colson and John Anthony. Still, if the evening didn't work out, the Marquee was only a few minutes' walk away. As it happened he never made it to the Marquee. Before the night was out, Tony had taken the five band members to Ronnie's downstairs room and offered them a contract. Charisma's new signing was called Genesis.

Frontman Peter Gabriel later recalled the difficulty of getting an introduction to Stratton Smith in an interview with Jerry Gilbert for *Sounds* magazine. "There was an awful lot of door to door salesmanship that went on before Strat eventually saw us," he said. "When I tried to get Strat to see us, I was told by his secretary that he wasn't interested. It was Rare Bird and John Anthony who persuaded him to come and see us. And when he did, we took it from there."

Stratton Smith's new signing came together in the historic setting of Charterhouse, a private boarding school situated in the beautiful Surrey countryside just outside Godalming. Towards the end of 1966, members from two of the school's beat groups united in a friend's home recording studio, set up over a garage in Chiswick, to make a demo tape that reached the ears of another Old Carthusian, pop impresario Jonathan King. Prior to becoming A&R man at Decca Records, King had pushed two singles into the charts in 1965, 'Everyone's Gone To the Moon' under his own name and 'It's Good News Week' for Hedgehoppers Anonymous, a one-hit wonder group of RAF servicemen. He was able to offer the as yet un-named band their first recording deal.

In fact, it was King who suggested the name Genesis for Gabriel, guitarist Anthony Phillips, bassist Mike Rutherford, keyboard player Tony Banks and drummer John Silver. They trooped into Regent Sound Studios in Denmark Street in September 1968 and quickly recorded *From Genesis To Revelation* but when Decca eventually released the album in March the following year it sold less than 1,000 copies. Decca also released three singles: the first, the Bee Gee's influenced 'The Silent Sun' was apparently written purely to please King, but as their music became progressively more complex, so King – a believer in three-minute pop hits – lost interest.

Genesis' new style of extended, experimental compositions was completely at odds with King's expectation and although Phillips would credit him with setting the ball rolling, he knew things weren't right when King came to see them play. "He was a bit bemused by the direction in which we had gone and I don't think he really liked what we were doing. We were doing these long, straggly pieces and he was all about the two and a half minute pop song. In the six months that we were experimenting with longer forms, I think we really found something much more original and it was at the end of that six months that Charisma signed us. I'd pretty much got the impression that Tony Stratton Smith signed us for what he heard, which was a sound that was alien to Jonathan King."

Although King later claimed to have been a party to passing the group over to Charisma, the group's road manager Richard Macphail, who

126

was at school with the group at Charterhouse, agrees with Phillips. "There was no handing over," he says. "Jonathan King was completely out of the picture by the time Strat signed us."

Even while they were working on their debut album, the signs were apparent that King and Genesis were not a match made in heaven. "There was that whole thing where King got them to sign a contract that was appalling, but fortunately they were all under 18 so it was null and void," says Macphail. "He has since admitted that he wasn't right for them. He said, 'I'm not good with creative people, it always has to be my thing.' When it came to mix *From Genesis To Revelation*, he threw them all out of the control room and mixed it without them. I remember that Ant [Phillips] was incandescent. He couldn't believe that his great masterwork was taken out of his control. Actually, I have to say that from King's point of view I can completely understand that because even then, as 17-year-olds or whatever, they all had unbelievably strong opinions about everything."

When Tony happened upon them Genesis were in the midst of a series of low-key gigs at Ronnie Scott's. As so often in life, the timing and the place proved to be crucial. Macphail was also present. "Ronnie Scott's were a bit envious of the success of the Marquee round the corner in Wardour Street," he says. "They had this room upstairs which they set up as a rock music venue, imaginatively called 'Upstairs at Ronnie's'. Somehow or other we got a residency there on a Tuesday night and it was a dismal failure as far as we were concerned because nobody came.

"But apart from all the recommendations, the main reason Strat went along to see us at Ronnie Scott's was that it was only around the corner from where he lived. Because Strat never used to go anywhere, unless it was to go to the races at Epsom or Sandown. There's a fictional detective called Nero Wolfe who solves all the crimes from his armchair in an apartment in New York, but of course he has a guy who runs around and does all the difficult stuff for him. Strat was a bit like that, so thank God for Upstairs at Ronnie's because he could see for himself exactly what everyone was going on about. I remember the night Strat came and he liked them straight away, it was instantaneous and enduring. I have to say that he had very good taste, because prior to that, I thought I was the only person who could see that they were going to be the greatest band in the world."

At this point in their evolution Genesis were staying at a cottage at Wotton, just outside Dorking, which belonged to Macphail's parents. "We weren't the kind of band who all went down to the pub, so we were cooped up in this little cottage for the entire winter and only went out for gigs," he says. "Many of these were small college gigs or the classic room above a pub, but we would go around the circuit and every time we returned to a place there would be a few more people. It built slowly, which is significant in the Strat aspect because he really hung in there in a way that no one would nowadays."

Genesis were nice middle-class boys whose families no doubt hoped they would go on to university and become doctors, lawyers or teachers. Macphail likens the period at the cottage to a 1970 equivalent of a gap year, with the underlying suggestion that had Tony not offered them a contract then the five bright sons would follow a more traditional career path. "Everybody just shelved whatever they were doing," says Macphail. "Tony Banks was already at Sussex University and Mike and Peter both had stuff lined up. Peter was going to go to film school. So we left the cottage in Wotton, we all moved up to London and Stratton Smith put us on £10 per week."

Macphail recalls that Tony initially offered the group a wage of £15 each per week but that drummer John Mayhew[10*] indicated they could manage on £10. "The others were all stamping on his foot and growling shut up, John – which is so funny, because John was the poorest of everybody. So anyway, £10 a week it was."

Although Macphail was the nearest thing Genesis had to a manager he never ascended to that role, and when it became clear that Tony would manage the group himself he felt conflicted. "My only issue with the whole set-up was not that I wasn't managing the band, I was doing what I was doing and just sort of made my own scene. But normally the model was that you've got the record company, you've got the band and you've got the manager and there's a dynamic to all that. What we had was Strat on one side as both record company and manager, and us on the other. I can remember raising this at a meeting in the Dean Street office and to be honest with you, I think some of the band were a bit embarrassed that I actually asked Strat what he thought about that."

In the fullness of time, Genesis would see the sense of Macphail's intervention and appoint a separate manager, thus establishing a more conventional business model.

As part of the Charisma family, Genesis acquired the services of booking agent Terry King, and soon went into Trident to record their first Charisma LP, *Trespass*, with John Anthony as producer. Funds were also made available for better equipment. "We were always lagging behind King Crimson, we were so envious that they had the most amazing equipment," says Macphail, "but once we became part of Charisma everything started to come good with our £10 a week. And it did go up to £15 at some point."

Just as everything in the garden was looking rosy, Genesis almost self-destructed when guitarist Anthony Phillips quit, a victim of stage fright. After a band meeting in the back of their van parked behind the Marquee it was decided to carry on with a new guitarist and drummer, and this upheaval

---

10   * Mayhew became Genesis' second drummer in 1969 following the departure of John Silver.

brought Steve Hackett and Phil Collins into a revitalised group.

In August 1970 a classified ad appeared in *Melody Maker*: "Tony Stratton Smith is looking for 12-string guitarist who can also play lead; plus drummer, sensitive to acoustic music..."

As it happened Tony already knew Phil Collins. "I've known Phil since he was 16," he said. "In fact, I must be the first professional in the music business to have heard Phil play drums. I auditioned him in a Boy Scouts hall in South London, when he was with a little band called Freehold. The band asked me to see if I could help them get a few gigs; we had a mutual friend – the mother of someone in the band was a friend of a friend of mine – so I said, alright, I'll go down and this was Phil's little band."

Before joining Genesis Collins was a member of Flaming Youth, a short-lived group put together by songwriters Ken Howard and Alan Blaikley, and a regular at the Marquee. "I was in the Marquee one night, having a drink with the owner Jack Barrie," says Tony, "and Phil found out that I was in there and he came round and said, 'Stratton, I want that job in Genesis.' I said, 'Phil I can't just give you the job, because these guys are for real, and they are going to choose who they can play with. What I will promise you is a very early audition.' So I managed to get him an audition with the band within three or four days. They loved him. I can always remember Tony Banks saying, 'We need somebody a bit hard-nosed in the band, as we do tend to waffle a bit and this guy's a real little pro, a hard-nosed little fellow.' I said, 'You're absolutely right, he really wants to make it.'"

The auditions were held at Peter Gabriel's parents' farm in Chobham. Collins turned up two hours early and listened as two other drummers auditioned. "When it's his turn, he sits down, sets up his kit left handed and of course, he just blew them away," says Macphail.

It took longer to find Steve Hackett and by the time *Trespass* was released in October Genesis on stage was a different group to the one on record. In a press release that accompanied the LP Peter Gabriel waxed lyrical about their new protector, "a friendly lion sitting somewhere in a tree house somewhere in Dean Street. He had SS in big letters across his belly, which was full of fish and other alcoholic beverages, and his smile had that Charisma ring of confidence. We knew at once this was the wise one from whose house had come sugar and spice and all things Nice. After a while he made welcome and told us the secret of the Charisma ring of confidence and how it could be acquired through football, hard work and other artificial stimulants. Soon we were based in the tree house, being delivered as little garden patches all over the country so people could be seen digging us. During this happy period they began to pick the fruits and two veg of their work. Under the guidance of arrowsmith Anthony (ligger turned good friend) they bundled their waffles into Trident Studios and put them in boxes, later to be neatly wrapped and personally handled by Frailgleve and more unlimited. Such is *Trespass* by Genesis and so might we all."

Tony, the 'friendly lion', poured all his energies into pushing the career of his eccentric new signing, but it wasn't until their third album for Charisma that the band finally cracked it. When Richard Macphail played him *Foxtrot* for the first time in September 1972, particularly the magnificent 23-minute opus on side two, he said: "I remember I had to wipe a bloody tear from my eye... and I said, 'Richard, this is the one... this is the one that makes their career.' In that one magic hour of hearing *Foxtrot*, everything that one had believed about, and seen in the band, had come through. And from that point on, in my own heart, there were no doubts anymore."

Yet how different the path of both their careers might have been had Tony not ventured down Frith Street and, wheezing heavily, made his way up the stairs to the room above Ronnie Scott's in the spring of 1970. Charisma press officer Glen Colson is under no illusions about just how low the fortunes of Genesis were at that time. "Actually you couldn't get much lower," he says. "I mean, it was a fucking toilet up there and they were playing to, like, ten people. And that's what you've got to remember – at the time when Strat signed Genesis they really were stone fucking dead."

* * *

The story of Genesis might have taken a different route had it not been for another of Tony's signings in 1970. "The truth is that Lindisfarne were the cash cow," says Richard Macphail. "They were pretty big for a while, but pretty much all the money that Charisma made out of Lindisfarne, Strat, bless him, would plough it back into Genesis and we kept going."

Lindisfarne began life in Newcastle as a rootsy, acoustic blues outfit called Brethren but they changed their style when they were joined by singer and songwriter Alan Hull. Soon touting an impressive set of original songs around the folk clubs of the North East, notably at the Rex Hotel in Whitley Bay where the name 'Alan Hull & Brethren' (or vice versa) appeared regularly on posters, they signed to Charisma in June. Only after their debut album was recorded at Trident did they change their name from Brethren to Lindisfarne, after the Holy Island just off the Northumbrian coastline. Evidently another band called Brethren was already working in America.

The generally accepted story of how Lindisfarne came to be signed by Charisma is that Tony was mightily impressed with Ray Jackson's skill on the harmonica, although the full story is more devious, as Jackson later pointed out. "We were asked to do a gig at the Marquee Club in Wardour Street at the request of Tony Stratton Smith, who was interested in a demo tape sent to him. He wasn't convinced enough to sign us on the strength of the tape, but wanted to see what we were like live before deciding. I remember we drove down the A1 in the van from Newcastle early one Sunday morning and arrived in Soho around late afternoon, before playing.

"However, even after seeing us play live Strat was still not 100% convinced of our potential and had to have his arm twisted by our joint manager, then Joe Robertson, who managed another Newcastle band, called Junco Partners. Playing in the Junco's was guitarist Charlie Harcourt, who was desperately sought after by Nice bassist Lee Jackson to play in his new band, Jackson Heights. Joe Robertson would not release Charlie from his managerial contract to join Jackson Heights unless he signed Brethren into the bargain. To keep Lee happy, Stratton Smith agreed to Joe's demands. Lindisfarne owe their kick start in the business to my one-time writing partner Charlie Harcourt."

Whatever machinations brought Lindisfarne to Charisma, drummer Ray Laidlaw is in no doubt that it was the best day's work the band had ever done.

"Tony was one of a bunch of managers/label owners who lightened up the British music industry in the late sixties and early seventies with their charm, wit and intelligence," he says. "At that time the rock music business was in its infancy and Tony, along with people like Brian Epstein, Kit Lambert and Robert Stigwood, were making up the rules as they went along. Just prior to our first contact with him and Charisma we'd had a recording test for the Air Group of companies owned by George Martin. Although not a recording company as such, I presume they would have made the masters themselves and then leased them to a label. Chris Thomas, who had produced our test session at Abbey Road, got back to us after a few weeks and offered us a deal, but by then Charisma were beckoning. We were also offered a management deal by Chas Chandler[11*] but, again, we preferred the Charisma option. Tony was a charmer. A bit more interesting than your average hustler. The Charisma set-up seemed very homely and non-corporate and appealed to us a lot. From a career point of view we should have had separate management, but at the time the one-stop-shop seemed simpler."

Another link in the chain was Greg Burman who manufactured guitar amplifiers in Newcastle. According to Laidlaw, Lee Jackson asked Greg to supply his band Jackson Heights with a new set of amps. Greg went to London and met with Tony to discuss the new equipment and payment details. During the meeting Tony asked Greg what was going on in Newcastle, and Greg spoke about Brethren in glowing terms and Tony arranged to fly up to Newcastle to watch them at the next available gig. "He saw us at the Mayfair Ballroom, where they watched us play a blinder and we then drove

---

11   * Formerly bassist with The Animals, Chandler discovered and managed Jimi Hendrix and Slade.

him straight back to the airport for his flight home," says Laidlaw. "So... Strat already knew all about us. He agreed to have a listen and gave us a gig knowing exactly what our potential was and subsequently negotiated a not-particularly-favourable deal with Joe and Dave[**] that gave the impression he was doing them a favour. Smart cookie. Having said all that, Strat really loved Alan Hull's writing and the sound the band made. I'm sure he made some tactical mistakes that cost us a few quid, but there's no guarantee that we would have fared any better with other management/labels. He was one of the rock and roll pioneers, was extremely good company, loved life and I'm glad to have spent time with him."

By August 1970, Lindisfarne were eagerly awaiting the release of their first album, *Nicely Out Of Tune*, but Tony already had one eye on the future, as Laidlaw explains: "The months prior to August had seen us lurching between Newcastle and London like a yo-yo. As our new manager, record company owner and guide to the mysteries of the music business, Strat decreed that we needed to be seen about town so that when our first recorded work was available, those at the heart of the scene would know who we were. We would scrape together the cash for fuel, drive to London, play at the Speakeasy, the Pheasantry or the Marquee to a bunch of people who, more often than not, were at the venue for any reason other than listening to music. After the gig we would doss on someone's floor, call in to see Strat for a pep talk and then head back up the A1 to home. We did months of this, once or twice a week, paving the way. I don't know how many big cheeses became familiar with us, but we soon made friends with other musicians, the girls behind the bars and the gentlemen of the press. The first two made the dodgy venues much more bearable and the last category proved to be extremely fortuitous when our records were released."

To round out the Lindisfarne story, Tony gave his own view while talking to *Sounds* in October 1972. "At the time I signed them, different managers were looking after Alan Hull and Brethren, but my real interest was in the group as a whole, with Alan making occasional solo albums. I heard a demo tape with 'We Can Swing Together', 'Road To Kingdom Come' and I think it was 'Turn A Deaf Ear'. I had heard of Alan Hull from folk buffs and always thought of him as a club singer, but I realised on one hearing of the Brethren tape that Ray Jackson could do for the harp what Ian Anderson had done for the flute. I think the one thing that excited me about Lindisfarne was the magic of the songs and the balls of the performance. I love affirmative music – music that affirms life. It was obvious they would have to come to London. Neither of their managers wanted to come down, so they asked me to take them on for management."

Tony arranged a deal where Joe Robertson and Dave Wood received

[**] Joe Robertson and Dave Wood, who'd been managing Brethren in Newcastle.

a sum of money and 5% management over-ride for a period of two years. "I think it worked out pleasantly for both of them," he said. "We put the band on at the Marquee on a Sunday night supporting an American band, Raven, but there were only about 50 people there and the group were pretty miserable. I remember encouraging them by saying that within six months they'd be turning people away from the Marquee because there was no more room. And that's exactly what happened."

Having completed work on Lindisfarne's debut album *Nicely Out Of Tune* at Trident, Charisma signed a distribution deal with Elektra Records in America, and with the small advance on their royalties the band decided to upgrade their means of transport. A visit to a second-hand car dealership in North Shields yielded a black Austin FX3 – a big old oil-burning beast similar to a London taxi cab. Its previous careful owner had been the Newbiggin Co-operative Society, which had employed it as a funeral car. Elektra boss Jac Holzman wanted to push 'Lady Eleanor' as a single and, with American FM radio in mind, insisted the group re-record it on 16-track, so an evening session was booked back at Trident with producer John Anthony on standby. The band were all still living in Newcastle and would normally have taken the train down to London but as they had a gig in Preston the next day, they decided to use the Austin. Before they set off they were kept waiting by Alan Hull, who insisted on signing on the dole before they left the North East and then, after about an hour on the road, the old Austin engine developed an oil leak and their progress was slowed by garage stops to top up. Realising they were going to be late for the session, they stopped at a roadside pub to telephone the studio but, as was their wont, stayed for just one more pint.

Vastly underestimating their journey south, by the time they and their ailing Austin finally pulled into St Anne's Court it was nearly midnight. The band now four hours late for the session, John Anthony's patience had run out long ago and he tore a strip off the young Geordies. The recording eventually finished in the early hours of the following morning and the band grabbed a couple of hours' sleep where they could. The tired musicians prepared for their long drive up to Preston, but not before being hauled into the Charisma office for another almighty telling off, this time from the normally unflappable Tony.

Lindisfarne's Rod Clements recalls that somehow Alan Hull managed to miss Strat's ear-bashing, despite having been the cause, in large part, of their late arrival. "Strat didn't actually lose his temper," says Clements. "He just made it clear that they had been worried, and that this behaviour and studio time wasting simply wasn't on, that they'd invested a lot of faith and money in us, and expected better from us, etc. etc. Our response was, I recall, appropriately sheepish, hangdog, mumbling and shuffling. Afterwards I think Alan got a lot more grief from the rest of us, because as well as the problems with the old funeral car, we hadn't been able to set off until Alan collected his dole money, some of which he spent in the pub."

Incidents like this were soon forgotten and Lindisfarne were quickly introduced to the Charisma lifestyle which revolved around their new manager's drinking haunts, and they were particularly impressed with the Speakeasy, the late-night music industry honey pot on Margaret Street near Oxford Circus.

"Strat was always holding court there," says Ray Laidlaw. "He had his own seat at the end of the Marquee bar, and he also had a regular seat at the bar in the Speakeasy, too. This is Monday to Thursday, and after the Marquee bar closed it was always off to the Speakeasy. Most of us were bachelors at that time, single lads living down in London, so we're out and about all the time. Quite often we'd take a chance to go down the Speakeasy and if Strat was there it was, 'Go on, in you come' and he would get us the first round on his account. Then after that we were on our own."

The Speakeasy was the popular hangout for the great and good of the music industry from 1966 to the late seventies. It was managed by Tony's friend Roy Flynn, the first manager of Yes, and later by Laurie O'Leary, who was a bit too close to the Kray twins for comfort. Known to all as 'The Speak', it offered a restaurant and music room, where bands would play for a pittance in order to catch the eye of the record company executives and music journalists that made up most of the clientele. Eulogised on The Who's *Sell Out* album – 'Speakeasy, drink easy, pull easy', sings Keith Moon between tracks – it was a place where musicians loved to jam, with the likes of Hendrix, Clapton and Ritchie Blackmore sitting in with all and sundry, and entry was strictly limited to members and their guests.

"We played there a few times, but nobody took much notice of the bands, that was the sad thing," says Laidlaw. "There was a glass-walled restaurant that only held maybe about 40 people and it was quite dimly lit. Quite often you could find extremely well known rock stars in there, in a state of daze and confusion. We discovered quite early on that you could go in and order a corn on the cob, which was the cheapest thing on the menu, and then when the waiters weren't around you'd find somebody asleep and all you had to do was ease them aside and get their dinner. We also found loads of money on the floor, because it was very dark, they'd be pissed and pulling cash out of their pockets – we used to find tenners and twenty-pound notes on the floor all the time. It was great, man. There wasn't a night down there that we didn't come out with more money than when we went in."

Melody Maker's Chris Welch was a regular, as were most of the *MM* staff at the time. "It was popular because of the tireless patience of the head waiter and the staff, who didn't seem to mind too much when Keith Moon appeared naked and let off fire extinguishers, or Ginger Baker hurled the odd dinner at some rival who displeased him."

One of Tony's earliest promotional brainwaves was the celebrated Charisma 'six bob' package tour in January and February 1971; nine major concert halls, three bands and all for only six shillings a ticket. The organisation for this particular tour was entrusted to the father and son team of John and Tony Smith (no relation to Stratton Smith) and it was they who suggested that the ticket price should be fixed at a mere six shillings; a value-for-money price that might have meant a loss on the tour, but was specifically designed to encourage larger audiences and thus maximum exposure for his three breaking bands – Genesis, Lindisfarne and Van der Graaf Generator – and give added kudos to the label. Everyone emerged a winner.

Talking to *New Musical Express*, Tony told Roy Carr: "It's all a question of a little thought and good promotion. The basic idea is to present good club bands in nice surroundings at a reasonable price. To be honest, we were prepared to sustain a financial loss, simply because I have great faith in all of these bands. But the response has been so overwhelming that everyone will come out of this, not only with a tidy little sum but with a good reputation. I feel that with ticket prices becoming too expensive, the business was in danger of losing its audience and in future this will have to be carefully watched."

The tour opened at the Lyceum Ballroom in London on January 24 and it is interesting to plot how the three bands fared across the country, albeit through the eyes of the music press. Genesis apparently took the honours in London, while Brighton – the town chosen for a press junket – loved Lindisfarne and greeted the other two with complete apathy. No prizes for guessing who came out on top in Newcastle, and all three groups were given rapturous ovations at Manchester Free Trade Hall.

New Genesis guitarist Steve Hackett recalls the camaraderie on the bus: "We'd be travelling up and down the motorway in a large coach. Genesis would be in the middle with Lindisfarne at the back and Van der Graaf in the front. My abiding memory of the Genesis section is of people doing the *Times* crossword. If you wanted to talk about the meaning of the universe, life and death, you went up front and spoke with David Jackson, Peter Hammill, Guy Evans and Hugh Banton. And if you wanted to have a drink at lunchtime you went to the back, sat down with Lindisfarne and discussed the merits of Guinness versus Newcastle Brown Ale."

Lindisfarne's singer Alan Hull was in complete agreement. "Personally we all got on great and there would always be a huge Lindisfarne contingent in the crowd, singing along with every song. But you could always sense the serious Van der Graaf fans shifting restlessly in their seats, and the Genesis crowd, small though they were, would usually treat our set like an extra-long intermission and go to the bar."

Tony told *Melody Maker*'s Richard Williams that Van der Graaf, and in particular their frontman Peter Hammill, "came of age during that tour, achieving a new peak of confidence and ability in front of big audiences."

Lloyd Beiny, who worked in the promotion department at B&C Records, was the advance man on the tour. His initiative pre-empted the present-day multi-million dollar rock merchandising industry. "If a tour was playing on a Tuesday night in Blackpool I would get there Tuesday morning, go round the shops, put posters up, make sure they had stock of the product and so on," he irecalls. "As the record company paid me so little, I thought there were going to be thousands of people here who are interested in Genesis, Lindisfarne and Van der Graaf Generator and in the back of my car I've got hundreds and hundreds of posters saying Genesis, Lindisfarne and Van der Graaf Generator. I thought, 'Well surely someone might want to buy one for a shilling each.' So at each gig I'd set up a stall in the foyer with the three posters for the three bands and I was making, you know, decent money. I mean I was ripping off the posters from the record company, as you do, but actually the record company would probably be quite pleased about it because those posters were going up in student dorms and so on. So at the end of the night I'd walk away with an extra tenner or however much it was."

It was at the Lyceum where B&C Records head Lee Gopthal, attending the show with his young son, noticed Beiny's stall. "I'm standing there in the foyer of the Lyceum with posters of Genesis, Lindisfarne and Van der Graaf that had been paid for by B&C Records, and the Managing Director of B&C Records walks in with his son and he comes over to me, and I thought, 'Oh my God, this is it, I'm getting the sack, I'm out of the music business forever, it's been fun, you know, bye bye.' And Gopthal strolls up to me and he says, 'Lloyd, Genesis, Lindisfarne, Van der Graaf, how much are these posters?' So I said, 'Well you know Lee, they're going for a shilling each.' He said, 'Give me two Lindisfarnes, a Van der Graaf and four Genesis – is that okay, young Johnny?' So he's buying from me the posters that he has already paid for. Which I thought was a hoot."

The tour was extended for a further eight dates in April, with VdGG appearing at all the additional concerts, but with Bell & Arc replacing either Lindisfarne or Genesis if either had prior commitments. The tour greatly raised the profile for all three bands, but in the short term it was probably Lindisfarne who benefited the most, cementing their reputation as a live act and undoubtedly boosting sales of their soon to be released second album, *Fog On The Tyne*.

Not everyone paid just six shillings. While the Charisma tour was on the road, Britain went decimal on February 15, the day that the currency system dropped pounds sterling. The two halves of the tour straddled decimalisation and the 'six bob tour' is sometimes referred to as the '50p tour' – albeit the equivalent of ten shillings rather than six. Ticket prices on the second leg of the tour ranged from 50 shiny new pence at Croydon's Fairfield Hall, 40 pence at Guildford and Edinburgh, and down to 30 new pence for the return visit to the Manchester Free Trade Hall.

The tour helped raise Charisma's profile in the record industry, adding to the general bonhomie that surrounded the label and its affable proprietor. In June 1971, two singles – 'The Knife' by Genesis and 'Lady Eleanor' from Lindisfarne – landed on the desk of David Hughes, the assistant editor of *Disc & Music Echo*. "Two quite excellent singles from the enterprising little Charisma outfit," he wrote in his review column. "This is a very personal label in that the groups who record for it are also under management to the label's boss. The net result seems to be that much more care is taken over its releases than by many of its rivals."

The cultural gap between Charisma and what passed for pop at the time was immense. While it was probably a trifle optimistic that a dollop of organ-led prog and a folksy ballad inspired by Edgar Allen Poe would make an impact on the charts, both groups, dissimilar as they were, would have looked especially out of place in the BBC's *Top Of The Pops* studio when Middle Of The Road, at number one that month, closed the show with 'Chirpy Chirpy Cheep Cheep', hotly followed by Dawn and 'Knock Three Times'.

Elsewhere, glam was all the rage; a form of rock headed by musicians who paid as much attention to their hairstyles, platform boots and eye make-up as they did to their records. Dressed in their finery, David Bowie, Elton John, T. Rex, Slade and a posse of also-rans were rarely off the covers of the music press but Tony and his staff were having none of it. No one involved with Charisma ever wore a silver jumpsuit for work, rest or play.

Unfazed by such disparities, the label attempted to repeat the success of the 'six bob tour' in Europe, and in June the following year sent all three bands to Paris where Genesis arguably fared the better of the three. In fact, during the first two years of the label's existence, several Charisma acts followed in the footsteps of Rare Bird by making inroads into Europe, with VdGG and Audience topping the Italian charts, and Genesis going top five in Italy and number one in Benelux. Genesis would develop a considerable following in Italy but all three groups drew large audiences to their European concerts, as Tony later pointed out: "The Latins took the bands to their hearts and broadened the economic base of Charisma, whilst we were still trying to establish ourselves in England."

The label's increased prosperity enabled Tony to rent a house in the country. Once the home of Sir Hugh Beaver, who founded the *Guinness Book Of Records*, Luxford House was a 16th-century Grade II listed building near

Crowborough in East Sussex, now owned by Cerise, Beaver's daughter, who became Tony's landlord. Its timbered façade hid a home full of nooks and crannies, low ceilings and comfy, well-used sofas. Soon it would become a home from home for Charisma groups, most notably Genesis, needing to get away from it all to write and rehearse. One of the earliest gatherings there was the reception following Lee Jackson's marriage to Jane McNulty on January 25, 1971, when scores of well-wishers boarded coaches to Luxford after the ceremony at Wandsworth Town Hall, a spectacular demonstration of Tony's generosity to his acts.

Tony's early infatuation with the film business led to him trying to involve Lindisfarne with a film called *Some Kind Of Hero*, the story of a US deserter who comes to England in search of sanctuary. Towards the end of 1971, songwriters Alan Hull and Rod Clements were commissioned to contribute to the soundtrack, resulting in at least two new compositions, including Hull's jaunty 'No Time To Lose', before the pair decided not to participate.

"It was through Strat's many connections in the media," Clements told biographer Dave Ian Hill, "and this American director who lived in London, Marvin Lichtner. Strat got me and Alan a rough draft of the script and we met him at his house in Highgate. Very nice chap, nice house and proper money – seemed like a good thing to be getting into. We did the whole bit – a car to pick us up in the morning, take us to the studio to see the shooting, wined and dined. The film was about a Vietnam draft dodger, which at the time was seen as a cool thing to do – and he comes to this country and falls in love with this girl – they go to Scotland, which is where 'No Time To Lose' came in. [Lichtner] had already taken on 'Road To Kingdom Come' as the theme song because he saw the character in the song as being the character in the film; on the run, or travelling – looking for something. I wrote a song called 'Some Kind Of Hero' for it, which never saw the light of day and didn't deserve to."

At some point during the process, director Marvin Lichtner brought in Paris Rutherford as musical director, a move which didn't go down too well with either Hull or Clements. "I don't know whether the money changed," said Clements, "but it went from us having carte blanche, to us having to go down to his mews cottage and playing him our ideas and he played us his. We were looking at each other and thinking, 'Who is he and where does he fit in?' Obviously Lichtner had roped him in and he was going to be the guy who knocked our music into shape. After an hour at his place, Alan and I made our way home and we looked at each other, and just went 'Nah'."

The film was eventually released in 1972, with up and coming actor Garrick Hagon in the lead role – but without any further input from Tony, Hull and Clements, who sensibly decided to have no further part in either the production credits or the soundtrack.

Somewhere between the recording of the first and second albums, Lindisfarne rather overdid themselves at a Marquee gig best forgotten. With Tony, record producer John Anthony and half of the London music press watching on, they launched their set with a brand new song, a lengthy and most uncharacteristic Zappa-esque rant entitled 'Who's Got The Blues, Huh?'. Tony, in particular, was left speechless by this vitriolic piece of musical experimentation. It was certainly not what he had signed the band for and he left them in little doubt as to his displeasure. The song was quickly dropped from the set list and would never see the inside of a recording studio.

When the time came to record Lindisfarne's second album, Tony's love of 'cultural cross-pollination' led him to doorstep one of America's top producers. Bob Johnston had spent several years at Columbia Records in New York, working with Johnny Cash, Simon & Garfunkel, Leonard Cohen and Bob Dylan. When Tony learned that Johnston had gone freelance he wasted no time in flying across the Atlantic to approach the amiable Texan, dangling the historical property of Luxford House as a carrot to tempt him over to England.

"This guy stood on the front steps of my house in Nashville on a Sunday night," Johnston later told journalist John Robinson. "Tells me he's got a group in England who he wants me to record. He says to me, 'I have a castle in Crowborough. If you record the group, and get them to 99 on the charts, you can come and live in the castle for a month.'

"I said, 'Can I really? What will you give me if I get them a number one?' He said, 'You can stay there a year.' So I went over to England and recorded Lindisfarne for *Fog On The Tyne*..." Johnston paused, relishing the punchline to his story. "They went to number one," he adds triumphantly, "and I moved into the castle."

Johnston's input certainly had the desired effect, pulling together the various musical strands first evident on *Nicely Out Of Tune* into a cohesive whole for Lindisfarne's second album, the first Charisma LP to top the charts. *Fog On The Tyne* was recorded at Trident Studios in the summer of 1971 and released that October. The strong collection of songs included some of Alan Hull's finest work, among them 'Passing Ghosts', 'City Song' and the wistful 'January Song', while the title track would become synonymous with the band and their home town. Bizarrely, when Bob Johnston asked to hear everything the band had for the new album, the iconic title track wasn't offered up for contention. It was only when they threw Alan Hull's whimsical ditty into a live show that Johnston heard it for the first time and insisted it was included.

Aided by a hit single, Rod Clements sprightly 'Meet Me On The Corner', which reached number five, the album soon entered the charts to begin a dizzying 56-week run. It reached the number one spot in March 1972 and stayed there for four more weeks. Lindisfarne's album had to climb over strong opposition to reach the top spot, not least George Harrison's triple set *Concert For Bangladesh*, *Electric Warrior* by T. Rex, then at the height of their popularity, and Neil Young's *Harvest*. *Fog* took over from Paul Simon's second solo album and was replaced four weeks later by Deep Purple's big-selling *Machine Head*.

The album also benefited from an early example of corporate sponsorship, with B&C's Steve Weltman organising a joint promotion with the Scottish & Newcastle brewery. B&C arranged for 25,000 stickers to be printed in the style of the Newcastle Brown bottle label, substituting the regular logo with a picture of the band. The brewery stuck these labels on 15 crates of their beer and bottles were sent out to wet the whistle of appropriate press and radio personnel, with the remainder of the stickers retained for retail outlets and consumer promotions. Prior to the sponsorship deal, Newcastle Brown was hard to find outside of the North East, but by the end of the first year the beer had become the favourite tipple in every student union bar across Britain.

* * *

Now that Tony's little independent label was competing with the big boys, the music press started to take more interest in the portly, smiling man behind the company. *Melody Maker* and its writers, recognising the general air of bonhomie that surrounded all things Charisma, were especially sympathetic to the label's ambience and in their issue dated January 15, 1972, Roy Hollingworth penned a double-spread profile of Tony under the headline 'Rock Mogul'.

The accompanying photograph, taken by the ever-present Barrie Wentzell, shows a delighted Strat seated at his over-flowing desk in Brewer Street, the office walls papered with gig posters, band photos and album sleeves. Hollingworth was close to Charisma both culturally and geographically, a fan of the label's acts and an occupant of the second-floor flat, along with Wentzell, in Carlisle Street almost directly opposite the offices of B&C. It was only a short stagger across Dean Street to the Nellie Dean and other Soho watering holes where Tony might be found nursing his large vodka and tonic.

"Charisma is a family concern and I feel will become even more so," the captain of the ship told Hollingworth. "I obviously have to behave like a businessman to a great extent, because I have to protect the artists, and Charisma. I find that business as such doesn't attract me, and I find it very difficult to concentrate on figures or balance sheets. But I force myself, and I have forced myself to understand business, and to cope with it. And I really feel that business has to be an important part of rock. We have to make sure there is enough money, because without money we cannot do things like experiment and improve. The idea of excellence is always in my mind – I feel it in books, I feel it in art and I feel it in music. Unless a thing is excellent in itself, I find it unattractive."

Chris Blackwell at Island and Chris Wright and Terry Ellis at Chrysalis, all of whom were equally if not more successful than Tony, might have wondered how this upstart, who began his career not in music but as a sportswriter, had managed to engineer for himself a two-page splash in the UK's best-selling weekly music paper. The answer was not just his sociable nature but also his philosophy, which chimed with that of *Melody Maker*'s staff.

"The essential thing to remember about rock is that there are very few precedents, and little criteria to it as a form," he told Hollingworth. "And essentially, it is dominated by young people, made by young people, for young people. And regrettably, they tend to feel that it exists in some sort of limbo, that the way they feel it, is the way it has to be. And I mean, no artist in any other field would possibly feel the same way. They are aware of the discipline that governs their art. This lack of discipline within rock, as an art, encourages an awful amount of self-indulgence in musicians. I grieve at the amount of talent that lies rotting, literally rotting, and always able to justify its own decay. There is NO justification! Whenever I see major talents sitting around chewing the cud, doing nothing, or doing something occasionally, which tends to be below their horizon, I think it is stupid."

Tony used the interview to set out what was essentially a manifesto for Charisma and his personal philosophy with regard to the music industry. "With it being a new thing, it was maybe difficult for businessmen to gel with it, it was out of their experience. In the early days, it was exploited outrageously by opportunists. Some of the stories of management I've heard from the fifties have made my hair curl. Fifty per cent in management fees for some of the early stars! It's incredible. No manager is worth that much, except maybe Tom Parker – and maybe Epstein, because he handled the whole thing brilliantly. But the business has settled down, has matured, the musicians have matured. There is now a tradition in rock. There are new traditions. There are much better types of mind now, it's more of a feeling thing. Although there are still some of those old opportunists around. What I'm really trying to say is that two wrongs don't ever make a right, there shouldn't be a conflict between business and creativity. But there was – up until three years ago, music didn't come into it. The business side was out for all it could get. The Cream opened it all sideways, the Cream made it possible for bands like The Nice. I don't feel there is much conflict left.

"I think the way we do it is working. An artist can see me at any time, I even get problems laid on me in the Speakeasy at 2am. The desk thing is there because, well, I need somewhere to work, just as you need a desk. If I want to be heavy, which is very rarely, but sometimes necessary, then I do pull the desk bit – I have them all sitting round here, and make a speech. Sometimes you've got to do it. A real relationship has got to be one – it sounds corny – one of mutual trust. They have got to believe that you believe in them. I think that is the priority. Because a band will respond much better to suggestions, even though it's something that they may not like. If they really feel you are caring about their future, they will listen. And by golly we care.

"The second thing, and that's why we will never have too many bands, is that you've got to look far beyond business. You've got to be totally involved with the artist, even in his private life. And we are. We look after all their problems, tax problems, drug busts, VD. I think a manager is a critical stance really, you've got to stand by them and see how they develop. Lindisfarne won't mind me saying this, but the first gig they did in London was to 40 people and they died a death. I told them that very night, and I laughed – it's important to be able to laugh as a manager – I told them it wouldn't be long before there was a 'house full' sign up outside this club. And in the months to come, there was. You've got to nurse them through difficult situations.

"I will always travel with my bands on their first trip to America, I know how that place can fuck musicians up. The bands we have now, I not only like them, I respect them. I can't fool myself and I can't fool them. I am an intelligent man, it's no use pretending that I'm just a cheery old yobbo. I think, I react and I respond. I therefore prefer to have bands, who to be with is a pleasure, it's nothing to do with money, or music, on that level. It's to do with people."

It was the recipe for his golden touch.

* * *

With Lindisfarne, Charisma suddenly had a hit-making, big-selling group on their hands and, with their second album doing so well in the UK, it was decided they should try their luck in the USA. To this end Tony sought the advice of Peter Rudge, manager of The Who in all but name and tour manager for The Rolling Stones, who somehow managed to get Lindisfarne the support slot on a US tour with The Kinks in February, the same month that *Fog On The Tyne* occupied the number one spot on the LP charts in the UK.

Tony never missed an opportunity to throw a party in celebration, as Ray Laidlaw remembers. "I think the album was at number one for about four or five weeks and there was a big party when we came back from the States about six weeks later. It was held in a large hotel at the bottom of Tottenham Court Road and we all went along, although I remember I was a bit spaced out at the time. I had just got home from America to find out that my girlfriend had left me. So that particular night I was a bit full of that, but there was a load of people there, it was just a bit of a piss up for the press really, a thank you to all the press and everybody who had helped make it all work."

A more important date in Lindisfarne's diary was the Great Western Festival at Bardney near Lincoln in May. Better known as The Lincoln Festival, the four-day event featured so many Charisma artists that the label decided to produce the 'Charisma Chronicle'. In conjunction with *Disc & Record Mirror,* Steve Weltman organised the printing of a free newspaper supplement and in the days leading up to the festival, he and Des McKeogh personally handed out all 100,000 copies. Tony was suitably impressed.

Among those attending, covering it for *NME*, was Martin Lewis. "Lincoln was a magic festival and Lindisfarne were a mid-afternoon act on the Sunday. 'Meet Me On The Corner' had been a hit, and there would have been some Lindisfarne fans there but the vast majority of the audience are only going to know maybe one or two songs. The expression that they stole the show is often banded around, but at Lincoln it was so clearly the case, because they took an audience that, by and large, had never heard of them and in the space of whatever their set was, maybe 30 or 40 minutes, they won over this huge crowd. The reaction was ecstatic. People were singing along to songs they'd never heard before, but there was just this amazing feeling and when Lindisfarne came off stage, everyone in the press enclosure headed straight towards the backstage area."

Lewis was among them and it was there that he encountered Tony for the first time. "I remember looking at Strat and seeing this grown man, who to me probably seemed like a much older man, and the tears were streaming down his face. Tears of joy. I was so struck by this, because certainly in England you didn't see grown men crying, in fact you didn't see anybody cry, people cried in private. To be crying so unashamedly, Strat was weeping with joy and physical tears were literally streaming down his face. He came towards me, towards everyone within earshot, saying, 'Did you see that, wasn't that amazing, it that fantastic…' and there was this unbelievable high, this man was so incredibly happy and I knew that he was the head of the record company, but that's about all I knew. Up to that point my experience of life was that English people didn't show emotion, nobody I knew showed emotion. Later I could see it more in context, of him signing the band and his pride at their success, but at the time it was just the sheer joy, I think, of seeing somebody so emotional that was the most remarkable thing."

In the modern era acts that top the albums charts often take two or three years before releasing a follow-up but this leisurely work-rate was unheard of in 1972, and in September Charisma released *Dingly Dell*, Lindisfarne's third album. Following *Fog On The Tyne* was always going to be difficult, but the album contained enough good material to send it straight into the album charts at number five, including three of Alan Hull's more political songs, 'Bring Down The Government', 'Poor Old Ireland' and 'All Fall Down', a minor hit as a single. Bob Johnston was once again producing, and Rod Clements was asked about working with the American. "He's a middle-aged Texan dope-freak. He's very funny, he has an amazing colloquial turn of phrase, comes out with these amazing Texan-isms. He is a bit of a slave-driver in the studio, with the engineers and tape operators. He works you hard, but he makes you want to do it – and technically he gets such good sounds from all the instruments."

One element that possibly worked against the record was the cover design, a plain grey textured matt cardboard sleeve, with just the name of the band and the title of the album tucked into the corners. All the necessary information was printed on a separate insert and the album came with a sepia poster, but overall it was a marketing misjudgement – both on the part of the band who suggested it and Charisma's promotional department who let them get away with it. When *Dingly Dell* was released in America by Elektra, its cover was a colourful portrait of the band by photographer Ed Caraeff.

Fraser Kennedy, the promotions rep covering Scotland and the North East, remembers the problems trying to sell Lindisfarne's third album. "It was a nightmare," he recalls. "They had this idea that they weren't going to put their name on the sleeve. There was one particular record shop in Newcastle, J.G. Windows and they were so confident that it was going to fly out, they bought 3,000 copies. They had to pay for them and I'm almost convinced they were stuck with most of them – and Windows was one of the biggest shops in the country at that time. Nobody knew who it was, that was that thing. There was no identity to it and it was one of those arguments, you know, if Led Zeppelin[12]* can get away with it then so can we. Well, no they couldn't – I remember the fights we had about it, there were a lot of arguments."

Alan Hull had emerged as Lindisfarne's leading player but, as a committed socialist – a man of the people – with a young family, he was conflicted by success. "I always remember that Alan Hull used to like a drink

---

12   * Led Zeppelin's fourth album, variously referred to as *Led Zeppelin IV* or *Four Symbols*, did not have a title or their name on the sleeve. It was their biggest seller.

and I think Cracky[13]* dug him out of some dodgy situations a few times and I think Strat did too," adds Kennedy. "I think Alan was going through some dire times, you know, and Strat was always there for him, but Alan never really appreciated it."

Record plugger Judd Lander has reason to recall Hull's good side, drunk or otherwise. "I always enjoyed working with Lindisfarne, they were very funny – although it was while I was working with Lindisfarne that I ended up in hospital. Because of the pressures of the job I suffered from anxiety, although it never ever showed because I was always the comedian. I ended up getting an ulcer and had to go to Barnet General Hospital and while I was at the hospital a lot of people kindly turned up to see me. Alan, God bless his cotton socks, wanted to see me. But he was so drunk they had to keep him out – and all I could hear in the distance was 'Judd man, where are you?' and 'Nurse, I want to see him…'"

Lindisfarne returned to the USA in November 1972, playing major support spots with The Beach Boys and David Bowie on his celebrated Ziggy Stardust tour, supplemented by a clutch of smaller college shows. Rod Clements recalls the band being at a lower ebb than on their first visit to the States, partly due to the long hours travelling with the band members separated in two old station wagons. "The moodiness within the band was beginning to show," says Clements.

After a brief respite at Christmas, they went back out on tour in January 1973, with five dates in Germany followed by a major jaunt to New Zealand, Australia and Japan. Alan Hull had begun to resent the time spent on the road, away from his wife and three small children, not to mention the detrimental effect it was having on his songwriting. Moody and forthright with his bandmates, he also directed his anger at Tony and Charisma. "I just wanted to get home and write songs," he told Lindisfarne biographer Dave Hill. "I can't turn it on like a tap."

In response, Tony wrote a long and detailed memorandum to the band, praising their efforts thus far, summarising the current problems as he saw them and suggesting a possible solution – that Hull should take time out to write and recover his creative muse, with his place in the touring line-up taken by another musician. As it turned out, the band had somebody in mind.

In the meantime, Lindisfarne held it together until after the Japanese dates, although Rod Clements has suggested they all knew it was ending, even before the Australian trip. In much the same way that a football team due for relegation can play at its best in the final few matches of a season, with the pressure now temporarily off, the group enjoyed the Australian tour to the full. In the company of Slade, Status Quo and Caravan, the high jinks on aeroplanes and in hotel rooms with the likes of Francis Rossi and Noddy

---

13   * Graham Jones, Tony's chauffeur.

Holder enabled the Lindisfarne boys to revisit some of the excitement and the sheer fun of touring again.

Then it was on to Japan where, despite being treated to the customary Far East hospitality, they knew the end was in sight. The original Lindisfarne played their final gig in Tokyo on February 14, 1973, and as the Valentine's Day pressures finally came to a head, a massive argument erupted between Hull and guitarist Simon Cowe. Hull wanted Cowe out of the band and as the others came to the guitarist's defence, Hull and Ray Jackson announced they were forming their own group. Cowe responded by announcing his intention to form his own group too. This may have been fatuous school-playground taunts but the bubble had finally burst and the only thing the band could all agree on was that it simply wasn't fun anymore.

Referring back to Tony's rambling memorandum, Lindisfarne took his suggestions on board and knew exactly who to call. Billy Mitchell, a close friend who had been active around the Newcastle music scene caught the next available plane to England but by the time he landed back home in the North East, everything had changed. Lindisfarne had split in two, with Hull and Jackson putting together their own band under the Lindisfarne name, leaving the remaining three, Laidlaw, Clements and Cowe, to form Jack the Lad with Mitchell as lead vocalist.

Given the changing situation, Tony could have thrown everything behind Hull and the new Lindisfarne, but Charisma also put their faith, and a considerable amount of marketing, behind Jack the Lad and were rewarded with three fine studio albums and a willing and extremely popular live band. "To be fair," said Ray Laidlaw, "when the split happened Charisma were very supportive of us for a long time. They didn't need to be. Put it this way, if any other band had split and the main writer had gone off, that's where they would have put their money."

When Jack the Lad handed Charisma their second album *The Old Straight Track* in 1974, Tony came up with an unorthodox method of promoting the new release – a cinema commercial. Certainly it was a different approach to record advertising than the usual full page in *Melody Maker* and definitely more expensive. Running in between the Pathé News, the scratchy advertisement for the local curry house and the main feature, not too many people got to see it, which was a shame, because the album itself was arguably the band's finest work.

After a while, Jack the Lad encountered the problem that beset other acts whose record label, management and booking all fell under the same umbrella. As Billy Mitchell recalls: "It was not only the record company and the management, but it was the agency as well – Paul Conroy was the main booker – so not only were we making records for them and being managed by them, but they were booking our gigs for us as well and that was great for the first couple of years."

"But then we didn't get the sales," adds Ray Laidlaw. "And it had got to a point where they couldn't justify the time, because by then Genesis had brought in a great deal. They were now making Charisma a lot of money and they didn't really have the time to spend on us, we were never really enough. Later on, Strat didn't have so much to do with Jack the Lad. He was still very supportive but he didn't come to all the gigs, probably because it wasn't quite romantic enough for him, it was a little bit more rough and ready. But Charisma were great with us. It was Gail who really used to look after us. In fact, I think Gail actually did the books for us for a while, even when they weren't managing us any more, she just did it in her spare time."

Hanging on to the Lindisfarne name for their new line-up, Alan Hull and Ray Jackson added some Geordie mates, three of whom already had Charisma connections. Guitarist Charlie Harcourt had previously played in Jackson Heights, while keyboard player Kenny Craddock and bassist Tommy Duffy had both worked with Bell & Arc. Somewhat optimistically, they tried to coax Phil Collins into the reconstituted Lindisfarne. Ray Jackson: "We both had known Phil quite well from the 'six bob tour'days and thought we might be able to coax him out of Genesis. Phil was playing in a scratch band at the time. He did this to keep his hand in when Genesis were not on the road.[14*] I'd seen him play with this band at a pub in West Kensington and the music differed a great deal from that of his core group. It was quite jazzy and was of a similar direction to the style Alan and I thought Lindisfarne should go."

Jackson recalls meeting up with Hull and Collins in a restaurant behind the Royal Academy. "It started early in the evening and finished quite late. I remember the meeting being fuelled with some alcohol and by the end of the night we had persuaded Phil that we were the band he should be in. We saw Phil off in a cab and Alan and I were elated as we got in our cab to go home. Alas, the following day we had a call from Phil to say that he had been given a strong lecture by the record company boss, Tony Stratton Smith, when he mentioned his intentions. Strat said he should stay with Genesis. I think Strat was totally against the move, mainly because he did not want two of his most popular bands splitting simultaneously and damaging the record company. His argument must have been pretty persuasive and Phil declined our offer. Our search for a drummer was still on, but what a pity for us that he changed his mind." In the end, Lindisfarne Mark II drafted in drummer Paul Nichols, who had previously worked with Kenny Craddock in Newcastle group The Elcort.

The new look Lindisfarne would record one further album for Charisma, *Roll On Ruby* in 1973, and also a live LP, but more attention was

---

14   * Collins' side project group was called Brand X.

paid to Alan Hull's first solo LP *Pipedream* that came out the same year. Harcourt, who had been working in the US returned to the UK to record with the Mk II Lindisfarne. "I believe the original plan was to tour Alan's *Pipedream* album," he says, "but this got shelved and the next thing I knew I was touring Australia with the Mk II. With an all-Geordie band, it was a bit like 'a busman's holiday'. Unfortunately, the punters mainly wanted to hear the old songs that they knew best and the new material never clicked with them, although later on some people found the two albums from Mk II to be interesting and musically more generous."

Issued in July 1973, Alan Hull's *Pipedream* is a real treasure and now regarded as a classic. A Lindisfarne album in all but name, it offers some of Hull's finest work, including 'United States Of Mind', 'Money Game', 'Country Gentleman's Wife' and 'Numbers (Travelling Band)'. For the cover, Hull was insistent on using a painting by René Magritte with the surrealist title *La Lampe Philosophique*, a striking, slightly disturbing, image of a candle-lit man whose nose disappears into the pipe he is smoking.

Hull first saw the picture staring back at him from the newsprint wrapped around a fish supper from his local chip shop and even referenced it in the song 'Peter Brophy Don't Care' on the *Fog On The Tyne* album. Naturally, Tony loved the idea and happily gave the go-ahead, leaving Gail Colson and the finance team to wrangle with the Magritte estate for its use. Magritte's work is carefully guarded and the publishing rights didn't come cheap; £4,000 is one figure bandied about, or as Gail put it, "It cost us a bloody fortune." Sadly, despite the quality of the songs (and the cover art), *Pipedream* spent only three weeks in the UK album chart, barely creeping into the top 30 before it disappeared.

Most of the personnel recruited to play on Hull's solo project became the basis for Lindisfarne Mk II. The band were still hiring their equipment from Greg Burman in Newcastle and Charlie Harcourt remembers yet another connection to one of Tony's artists. "Some of Lee Jackson's enormous bass rig had been used to compliment the PA we were using in Lindisfarne Mk II. I do believe the rig was left somewhere in Germany, because the road crew refused to lift it anymore."

Always popular live, Lindisfarne Mk II recorded *Roll On Ruby* while still with The Famous Charisma Label and *Happy Daze* after their move to Warner Bros, but neither quite rekindled the magic of the original line-up and, by 1975, the second incarnation had run its course.

Chapter 9

The Fulfilment Of Genesis

*"He never interfered, never even called to ask how it was going.
Tony always left you to do your creative thing. He was very good
about that."*
Paul Whitehead, graphic artist

It might not be cricket, but there is no greater confirmation of an act's potential than when another label tries to steal it from under your nose. Any new band on the brink of success will attract attention from other labels, and Chrysalis boss Chris Wright was sorely tempted to steal Genesis away from Charisma. "Terry Ellis[15]* and I met Genesis in an attempt to lure the group to Chrysalis," he says. "At one point I thought we were close to signing them, but I decided to withdraw because of my friendship with Strat. It seemed unethical to me. This was unusual in the dog-eat-dog world of rock where everybody was trying to steal everybody's artists all the time. Most label owners in my position would have had no compunction about nicking ours, but I just didn't think it was the right thing to do."

Despite the friendship between the bosses at Chrysalis and Charisma, the two labels always kept their artists at a safe distance. Gail Colson adds a little fuel to the fire: "Even if Chris Wright and Terry Ellis had tried to get to Genesis, they could never have done so, as we had a watertight contract. Charisma and Chrysalis were always rivals, which is why I didn't want Tony to sell the company to them when he was considering selling Charisma. I never felt the same rivalry with Virgin or Island, but always with Chrysalis."

It is quite possible that Tony heard all about Wright's piece of rock-group skulduggery and later took out his revenge in the stable yard. "As nice as he was, there was a slight element of the loveable rogue about him," says Wright. "He might have said the same about me, of course, but I think Strat was a little bit more devious than me. He sold me a couple of horses that were completely useless, which was naughty of him. One was called A Trick Of The Tail and named after a Genesis album. On the other hand we went to the yearly sales together and he did recommend that I bought the filly that has been my foundation mare, Crime Of Passion, so I forgive him."

While the rivalry between Charisma and Chrysalis was a fairly even

---

15   * Terry Ellis was Chris Wright's partner in Chrysalis, the company's name derived from 'Chris' and 'Ellis'.

contest, the rivalry between Genesis and Lindisfarne at Charisma could be compared to a variation on Aesop's fable of *The Tortoise And The Hare*. While Lindisfarne sprinted ahead, with hits and sell-outs, Genesis bided their time, edging slowly towards their goal, all the while gaining a reputation as a slightly eccentric bunch of art-rockers, this almost entirely due to the antics of singer Peter Gabriel.

Gabriel cut his hair in ways that suggested his stylist was a match for Tony Stratton Smith in the carousing stakes and, as the group's fortunes accelerated, took to wearing strange costumes that at times left his bandmates aghast. Perhaps more importantly, he prefaced songs on stage with curious monologues, a touch of the macabre blending with the less child-friendly end of Hans Christian Anderson's fairy tales. It all contributed to his slightly other-worldly persona.

"Cynthia Jane stands in her white dress, croquet mallet held menacingly behind her head and smiles; red-jacketed huntsmen halt their steeds at the water's edge, while their prey, a fox-headed woman in a slinky red dress, seeks sanctuary out to sea; a low-flying biplane casts a long shadow across a giant chess board." Charged with illustrating the surrealistic lyrics of both Peter Gabriel and Peter Hammill was Paul Whitehead, the artist and graphic designer behind many of the early Charisma album sleeves. Whitehead was heavily involved in the early days of *Time Out*, the listings magazine that has been keeping Londoners in touch since August 1968.

"I had a show at a gallery in the West End of London and John Anthony saw my work there, so we started talking," says Whitehead. "John said, 'I'm producing this band right now, it might be up your street, you seem to have the same kind of sensibilities.' Which we did. And that led directly to the album sleeve for *Trespass*. I remember being taken to meet the band's manager and he turned out to be a very nice guy. Actually I think I first met Tony in the pub, probably The Ship on Wardour Street, and all I remember was Tony turning to me and saying, 'It's very nice to meet you, so you're going to work with Genesis eh? Well good luck.' And that was it. He never interfered, never even called to ask how it was going. Tony always left you to do your creative thing. He was very good about that."

On the day that Whitehead delivered the artwork for *Foxtrot* to the Charisma offices, Tony organised a small reception with drinks and hors d'oeuvres. "This ritual unveiling of the artwork became the norm. Sometimes the whole band would be there or maybe just Peter Gabriel was there, it varied, but it was always really nice. Tony was never, ever disappointed, it was always, 'Oh, this is really wonderful'. Very complimentary and he never questioned the subject matter, or what you were trying to get at or anything, he just loved it."

Tony may have left Paul Whitehead to his own devices, but the cover art for *Trespass* took a different turn when Peter Gabriel told him about the song he'd written called 'The Knife'. The upshot was that Whitehead would slash his pen and ink watercolour of the King and Queen with the knife seen on the reverse. "Peter was surprised, 'You're really going to slash that beautiful picture?' I told him it wasn't a problem. Once again we organised a little gathering for the ritual slashing and then we photographed the result, which really worked well. Even though it was me trying to make the best of a bad situation, in actual fact it couldn't have been planned any better."

Having secured the perfect drummer in Phil Collins, Genesis took a little longer to find a replacement guitarist. With dates in the diary to fulfil, they performed as a quartet for about six months, with Tony Banks playing some of the guitar parts on a Hohner pianet hooked up to a fuzz box. Once Steve Hackett had replaced Anthony Phillips on guitar, the new look band played shows in Belgium and the UK before taking a break in July 1971 to work on the second album. Stratton Smith insisted they take a complete break by inviting them to Luxford House where they could relax, write and rehearse in the tranquil surroundings of the East Sussex countryside.

The dark 16th-Century vibes surrounding Luxford seem to have influenced Peter Gabriel while developing the bizarre and slightly chilling storyline of 'The Musical Box'. As Gabriel wrote in characteristic sleeve notes for the album: "While Henry Hamilton-Smythe minor (8) was playing croquet with Cynthia Jane De Blaise-William (9), sweet-smiling Cynthia raised her mallet high and gracefully removed Henry's head. Two weeks later, in Henry's nursery, she discovered his treasured musical box. Eagerly she opened it and as 'Old King Cole' began to play, a small spirit-figure appeared. Henry had returned – but not for long, for as he stood in the room his body began ageing rapidly, leaving a child's mind inside. A lifetime's desires surged through him. Unfortunately the attempt to persuade Cynthia Jane to fulfil his romantic desire led his nurse to the nursery to investigate the noise. Instinctively Nanny hurled the musical box at the bearded child, destroying both."

There is a Victorian Gothic atmosphere to this Gabriel classic, quintessentially English with a hint of sexual frustration and repression. Some of the new material, including 'The Musical Box' and 'Twilight Alehouse', had already been road tested in concert, but the time spent at Luxford House also spawned 'Fountain Of Salmacis' and 'Return Of The Giant Hogweed', both fine examples of a band flexing their newfound musical muscle. As well as providing space and inspiration for new material, the cosy, sheltered location of Luxford was equally important in incorporating the two new members, Collins and Hackett, who were still becoming acquainted with the Charterhouse trio. Hackett found the process especially exciting. "We spent an idyllic three months writing and then recording," he reported. "It was a very nice growing period."

By August 1971, Genesis were ready to return to London and decamp to Trident Studios with producer John Anthony and assistant engineer David Hentschel. The new line-up was a far more confident proposition in the recording studio and Anthony succeeded in capturing their clearer, crisper, tougher sound on tape. Once again, the sleeve design featured a surrealistic painting by Paul Whitehead, this time depicting scenes from 'The Musical Box', while the croquet lawn and manor house in the background is based on Coxhill in Chobham, where Gabriel spent much of his childhood.

Nursery Cryme was a definite progression as far as the group were concerned, but, strangely, Stratton Smith was not as enthusiastic about the new record as the music press. He told the band directly that he was unhappy with the recording and, as a result, Charisma didn't put as much promotional muscle behind it as they had with *Trespass*. It was released in November, but took longer to chart here, eventually reaching number 39 in the UK. It's not unreasonable to assume that Charisma were concentrating their energies on Lindisfarne at the time.

Genesis would have to wait a little longer for chart success in Britain, but the European market proved more susceptible to their charms. *Trespass* kick-started the interest towards the end of 1971, becoming the number one album in Belgium. Charisma promptly packed Genesis off to Brussels in January 1972 for a celebratory concert and an appearance on Belgian television. Then, as they arrived back in London, they were told that *Nursery Cryme* was number four in Italy. Tony was absolutely delighted. He already knew that European rock fans appreciated his more progressive, classically oriented groups like The Nice and Rare Bird, and had noted just how the Italians had taken Van der Graaf Generator to their hearts. Success in Europe would be key for Genesis and during the following year they toured solidly to promote the new record, including a return visit to Belgium and a particularly successful first tour of Italy in April 1972.

Preparing the sleeve for *Foxtrot* brought Tony back into contact with the Italian photographer and journalist Armando Gallo. Quite independently, Gallo had asked to photograph Genesis while they rehearsed at an old run-down club called The Inferno, in Plumstead, South London. "My contact with Tony was a good thing," says Gallo, "but I've never really worked for Genesis as their official photographer. People think that I was working for them all those years, but I wasn't. When I did the first photo shoot in Plumstead, February 1972, the band was so good, they were so nice and we really got on well together, so they told Charisma that I'd shot some pictures and Charisma called me up. 'Can we see those pictures? We need some pictures for promotion.' They bought 12 shots out of the roll of 36 and they paid me £20 – I thought, gosh! At the time I was paying £5 a week for rent, so £20 was very fair, I thought. But years later, Gail Colson told me those were the best pictures they ever had and the money she gave me was a steal. But I was green and I was just happy that an English record company was buying my photos."

Armando Gallo would go on to become synonymous with Genesis. His book *Evolution Of A Rock Band*, published in 1978, was the first major retrospective on the group and he has subsequently worked as their photographer on various tours around the world. A far cry from the dingy back room of a disused club in Plumstead.

The *Foxtrot* album also saw the start of a long and productive working relationship between Genesis and publicist Peter Thompson. The PR man already knew Tony quite well and was brought in to replace Keith Altham, who had worked with the band on *Nursery Cryme*. Thompson's credentials included stage and theatre productions, and as Peter Gabriel's stage presentation became more and more theatrical Tony probably saw Thompson as the ideal fit. "Charisma were still a relatively new record label," he says. "I don't think they were even trendy by then, because no one actually knew about them. But it always seemed to me that their main band was Genesis, even though they also had Lindisfarne who were much bigger than Genesis at the time."

In time-honoured fashion Tony took Thompson for a drink and invited him to see one of his bands. "We went to the Sundown in Mile End and 'this band' turned out to be Genesis. I thought they were just fantastic and I told Strat that I would love to be involved with them and that's how it all began. I do remember saying that what I felt Genesis needed was national publicity, because at that time the only press these bands got was in *Melody Maker*, *Sounds*, *NME*, *Disc* and *Record Mirror*. They obviously sold through those publications, but the potential was there to break out and I thought they needed national publicity, in the everyday newspapers and Sundays. I was trying to help them break out more. This went on for a few years, but eventually I told Strat, 'I've got a colour supplement and I think we're going to be the cover story', which was totally amazing. What was even more amazing, although it didn't bother me too much at the time, but the person writing it for the *Observer* was Martin Amis, the son of Kingsley Amis. I think Strat was suitably impressed by that."

* * *

In November 1972, Charisma moved house yet again, this time to the narrow-fronted offices above 70 Old Compton Street, almost directly opposite the site of the old 2i's coffee house where Tony had somewhat ambivalently watched the likes of Cliff Richard and Tommy Steele forging the early British rock'n'roll scene. The move was announced with an amusing advertisement in *Melody Maker* dated November 4: a photograph across the foot of a double page spread showing eight of the company's 11 staff members carrying their chattels down Brewer Street. On the right hand side, Gail Colson carefully locks the old door behind her, while further along the road Tony pretends to answer the disconnected telephone that he is carrying. On the far left, Fred Munt struggles with a huge pile of box files, followed by accounts manager Chris Turner (also known as Alice) buckled under the weight of a chair. Jill Holland carries accounts books and a typewriter, while Paul Conroy, trousers rolled up to his knees, appears to be brandishing a loo brush and toilet roll. The smartly suited Colin Richardson strolls nonchalantly along with what looks to be a framed gold disc tucked under his arm.

Also in the frame is a sex shop window – well, this was Soho in the seventies, and the Brewer Street office was directly above one – and on the wall behind Tony is a large poster for Newcastle Brown Ale, quite appropriate given the success of Lindisfarne. Among the staff members listed in the advertisement is Chris Briggs, who had recently joined the company, but just too late to appear in the photograph.

Briggs is yet another example of a music industry stalwart who started his long career as one of the happy band of folk working for Charisma during the early years of the label. Joining around the time of the move, Briggs found himself writing press biographies in Old Compton Street, partly so that Glen Colson could get to the pub earlier; not that Tony even knew who the new man in the press office was for the first month of his employment. Like many others who got their start working for Tony, Briggs would go on to have an illustrious career in the music business, moving from publicity at Charisma to A&R at Chrysalis, A&M, EMI and Sony Music.

Like Paul Conroy, Briggs was an alumni of Ewell Tech where he helped arrange gigs, and he followed Conroy into a job at Terry King's booking agency. "When I first joined Charisma they were based in Old Compton Street," he says. "Glen was getting busier and he wanted somebody to write the press biogs and arrange the photographs – because Glen's main thing was being out and about, you know, face to face with journalists. What Glen really enjoyed about his job was the old-fashioned blag, he liked to blag a journalist to his face and he was absolutely brilliant at it, he was a complete one-off. So Glen offered me the job at Charisma, and I don't think I even met Strat to begin with. I was smuggled into the building by Glen and maybe sort of rubber-stamped by Gail, but the truth is I don't think Strat even knew that I worked there for quite a while. I have an impression of having worked there for about a month and then Strat clocking me for the first time, with that sense of, 'Does he work here, or is he just visiting?'"

The Charisma press office was a sanctuary for music writers who drifted through and listened to music, not necessarily by Charisma acts. Briggs recalls that Steely Dan's debut LP *Can't Buy A Thrill* was rarely off the office record player and that Glen Colson continually played Stevie Wonder's *Talking Book*, particularly 'Superstition'. "Occasionally we might slip a Charisma album in between. You want to listen to your own artists in order to write the biogs and publicity. My memories are that there were certain artists that came into the office a lot. We would hang out and drank with Alan Hull. Glen was very tight with him and there was a lot of socialising with Lindisfarne generally."

Melody Maker staffers Chris Welch, Roy Hollingworth and Chris Charlesworth all enjoyed a positive relationship with Tony and the Charisma press office, which in turn encouraged them to seek interviews with the artists signed to the label. Welch was a fan of Genesis, Hollingworth loved Van der Graaf and Charlesworth was fond of Lindisfarne with whom he visited Ireland for shows in Belfast and Dublin, sharing a room with Tony. "When I went on tour with the likes of The Who or Led Zep I stayed in luxury hotels but it wasn't like that with Charisma," he says. "They were a bit more down-market. We were in some college dormitory together, and Tony snored quite a bit, kept me awake. When we were in Dublin we all went round the Guinness brewery.

"Charisma made themselves very popular with the music press," adds Charlesworth. "Chris Briggs and Glen Colson were liked by the press because they were always buying us drinks and they were friendly, they were funny. Glen didn't like Genesis much, he would call them rubbish. He preferred the lesser bands. This endeared him to us, because we knew he was sincere and this made a lot of difference to us journalists who were sick and tired of PR's ear-bashing us about dodgy acts, which happened all the time. The acts on Charisma were friendly too, so they got a lot of positive press."

Which makes perfect sense. Tony's 'be nice to everyone and buy them a drink' approach, actively practiced by Colson and Briggs, paid off handsomely with good coverage in *Melody Maker*, *NME* and *Sounds*. "Glen gave me a copy of the *Williams Press Guide*, I mean my training period was quite short and then to begin with I was given the job of doing all the local press mail-outs," recalls Briggs. "I quickly got very organised around biogs and I would have a band biog and a photograph sent out to every local paper. Most of the papers just reprinted exactly what was supplied, so I started to write my press releases more like a short article that they could reprint, so they were a little less cheesy than the usual hype.

"Strat had a 'cream rises to the top' attitude with art and with artists and I think that ran right through Charisma. He encouraged us to try and be creative and innovative about how we drew attention to an artist, without actually ramming it down anyone's throat. If I was taking, say, the editor of *NME* to see a band that Strat had just signed, you didn't stand next to him all night telling him how good they were. In Strat's training, you left him out there to make his own mind up, then went to the bar and got drunk. Which is exactly what we used to do. Glen would never pretend; his whole anti-PR style was 'I'm not pretending to actually like this group, it's a job, I just work for Strat – you're over 18, you're the journalist, you make your own mind up.' Brilliant."

* * *

In an attempt to break the lucrative American market, most managers sent their boys off on gruelling tours across the States, supporting mid-level groups like The Guess Who, Quicksilver Messenger Service or The J. Geils Band. Not so Tony. In December 1972, he booked Genesis straight into a one-night stand at the Philharmonic Hall in New York, taking new Charisma signings String Driven Thing with them.

"We persuaded WNEW music director Scott Muni to let us do it because he'd already been hooked on Genesis from the *Nursery Cryme* album," Tony explained. "He was a great judge of up and coming British stuff and he loved the band. I persuaded Scott they were really professional, had a great show and with some trepidation, and sight unseen, he allowed us to do the 1973 WNEW Christmas show at New York's Philharmonic Hall. Believe me, it was chaos – but it was great fun."

The $16,000 cost of the promotion was funded by Tony and Buddah Records boss Neil Bogart and before arriving in New York there was a warm-up show at a Boston college. At Brandeis University Genesis played to a few dozen kids who kept walking in and out. There were issues with Tony Banks' Mellotron, which was unsuited to US electrics. "Brandeis was a total disaster," recalls Tony. "But it was Genesis's very first gig in the States and it was played to literally a few dozen people."

True to style, Tony pulled a neat PR stunt for the benefit of the American press, as Chris Welch recalls: "On the evening of the concert, a genuine, red-painted London Transport bus was laid on to take the radio men and rock writers from the Hotel Americana to the Philharmonic Hall. Heads turned as the friendly old double-decker lurched along Fifth Avenue, and heads on the top deck ducked as we passed under a dangerously low bridge. But the Red Rover successfully navigated the jammed streets and unloaded us right outside the Philharmonic Hall where fans were already converging, some wearing Davy Crockett hats and clutching bottles."

Photographer Barrie Wentzell was also among those assigned to cover Genesis' debut performance in America, but it was not the most fruitful of commissions. "I was supposed to be taking pictures at the gig, but for some reason they had forgotten to get me a press pass permit. As soon as I get there I started to take pictures and a security guard stops me and I come out with the old cliché, 'No, I'm with the band, I've come all the way from London for this.' It turns out that this guy used to be a policeman in Brixton and we end up chatting – but he still wouldn't let me take any pictures inside the hall. I managed to take a few pictures of the band in Central Park and one outside The Bitter End club in Greenwich Village, but that was about it. I remember coming back and Strat was none too happy. None of those pictures got used for anything at the time, but two of the photographs have been pirated many times since."

The concert wasn't without further problems, as Tony told *Sounds*: "I've never been so nervous before a gig since I've been in the business. But what impressed me was that in spite of the technical hang-ups they got 100% reaction. I felt that if one was ever to take a gamble – and it was an enormous gamble – then it should be done with a group that had a really fine show and was coming to the top of the curve in terms of confidence. I think they were just at the right point in time to do this sort of thing. It was a tremendous challenge for them."

From his excitable reaction, you could almost believe that Tony enjoyed the frisson of danger more than the performance. "Oh, it was fantastic. What a hair-raising show. Leonard Bernstein suddenly decided to call an unarranged rehearsal for the New York Philharmonic Orchestra, so our sound check went by the board until the orchestra had vacated the theatre, which was about 6.00pm. Normally in those days Genesis needed something like two hours to set up, because they had quite complicated gear. We couldn't get into the hall until after 6.00pm, so we had to keep the doors closed for half an hour longer so that the band could have some kind of sound check after they set up. I think they performed brilliantly. But there were a few technical hitches and when they came off stage they were so despondent, even though they'd had a tumultuous reception. They are such perfectionists that because they knew they hadn't given 100% from that stage, America was going to judge them by this. I said, look, America has seen very little like you. Genesis 75% right is better than most bands I know 100% right, so don't worry about it, you can be very proud. Then the doors opened and in came all the agents and the drinks were poured and they finally accepted that they'd had a modest success."

Sounds dubbed it 'the sixteen thousand dollar debut', but the risk apparently worked. In conversation with Chris Welch, Tony was enthusiastic: "It was a gamble coming here for one show, and the group can't believe how much New York loved them. New York audiences have become increasingly tough in the last year, and yet it seemed as if they were willing us to succeed.

It was a really happy audience. With the nature of the group's music, you can't put them half way down a bill on a touring rock show. And the gamble of putting them on straight away at the Philharmonic has paid off."

When Welch tried to get backstage after the gig to talk to the group, the dressing room door was firmly locked. Inside, Tony was doing his diplomatic best to calm the band down and tell them otherwise. Peter Gabriel was the least enthusiastic, disappointed with the sound system and genuinely believing that it had been a poor performance. As the band prepared to fly home, Gabriel complained: "I felt very angry at first that we didn't have a sound check, and although I don't feel as suicidal as I did at first, I wouldn't like to do another gig in those circumstances."

However when the dust had settled, a happy Tony concluded: "I always felt Genesis would become a top band. Any band prepared to work at it will succeed. They just needed confidence and consistency, and happily they achieved both about six months ago."

* * *

In a music world where integrity was often thin on the ground Tony Stratton Smith stood out like a lighthouse on a foggy night. No one ever doubted that his intentions were honourable but at the same time there was something slightly off-key about managing groups that were signed to your own record label. In the normal scheme of things managers negotiated with record labels to realise the best possible deal, the highest royalty they could parlay, while the label's business manager does his best to keep it down. They meet somewhere in the middle but when the manager and the label are one and the same there is a conflict of interest, no matter how principled that manager-cum-label-owner might be.

Perhaps it was because Tony was so confident about the future of Genesis and comfortable with their working relationship that he was happy to hand over the reins of management to his namesake, the tour promoter Tony Smith. Smith's father John had worked in the music business for many years promoting artists such as Duke Ellington, Sarah Vaughan and Stan Kenton. Tony joined the family business as a rock concert promoter, working with his dad on the package tours of the early sixties and handling tours by The Rolling Stones and The Who.

By 1973, the conflict of interest had become untenable and something needed to change, and Stratton Smith understood that. Nevertheless, it would have been an emotional wrench as the close personal attachment to the band that he had nurtured so carefully drifted away. Although Genesis would remain an integral part of the Charisma family, there was an element of disappointment and loss at the gradual distancing between Tony and his

Charterhouse boys.

Opinions differ as to who initiated the break. Tony claimed that he could see the flaws in the situation and chose to let the manager's position go; the band maintain they were actively looking for a new man, while the other Tony Smith insists that while he suggested they employ a different manager, he certainly didn't expect it to be him. However, one point that everyone does seem to agree on is that things came to a head one night in Glasgow when Genesis refused to go on stage because an electric fault in the venue rendered the stage unsafe. Tony Smith – or Smithy as he would become known, perhaps to differentiate him from the other, heavier Tony Smith – still has the poster for the show, at Green's Playhouse on February 16, 1973, on his office wall.

Oddly, this was the start of the first major Genesis tour since the departure of road manager Richard Macphail. It was his replacement, Adrian Selby, who refused to let the band take the stage and Tony Smith, who was promoting the show, was given the unenviable task of informing a theatre full of irate Glaswegians about the situation. Back at the hotel, he told the band exactly what he thought, in no uncertain terms – that such a cancellation was unacceptable and totally avoidable – and that they needed to sort out their management situation and sort it out fast. Party to this impromptu band meeting was publicist Peter Thompson. "Strat wasn't there as far as I can recall," he says. "There was this long meeting at the hotel and the end result was that they were changing managers. At that time Strat was managing the band, but that night they changed one Tony Smith for the other Tony Smith. As much as I did love and still do love Genesis, I could understand that they were ambitious, of course, all people are ambitious when they're young. So I understood why they changed managers, but I could also understand why Strat was upset. I think he was pushed into that move, whether he wanted it or not, and that night in Glasgow was certainly the catalyst."

Although making money had never been the deciding factor for Stratton Smith, the commercial success of Genesis was nevertheless keeping Charisma afloat. "I realised that I wanted to be the manager, but I also wanted to be the record company. I had to make the choice before somebody made the choice for me; whether I was going to continue with the record company, and the record company was already a success. I decided to opt for looking after Genesis from the recording side.

"As the music and presentation became more theatrical, the whole logistics of management had to change. It was no longer enough doing the Kit Lambert kind of thing – good ideas and great press and punishing the radio stations as hard as you could. It was becoming an organisation. It was like having a touring theatre company and manpower increased and that was never to my taste, to be honest. I asked the band and said I would like to quietly fade out and work for them on the record side and we made absolutely the right choice. Tony Smith may not have spotted as much in the industry as I have, but my God, he has organised it beautifully."

The switch didn't happen overnight and it was at least a year after the stormy night in Glasgow that 'Smithy' officially became the manager of Genesis. "That night I sat them down and gave them a good old talking to," he says, "about how they should get themselves better organised – and after that, they asked me if I would manage them.

"I was giving the band lots of advice on tour, but at no time was I thinking manager, no, absolutely not – I was too busy on the bloody tours, doing nearly 300 shows a year. No, I liked them and I liked what they did, and I was purely giving them advice. But I think the truth of the matter is that Peter Gabriel primarily, and also Tony Banks, between Peter and Tony they both realised that they needed someone else, a separate manager. And obviously someone had said this to Strat at some point or other and then I think he saw the inevitable. So it was driven primarily by the band and then later on they asked me to do it.

"The following year I was due to promote another tour with them and they still hadn't found another manager. They said they were still looking and so I said, 'Okay, I'll do it'. Partly because I was getting bored with the tour promotion business, but also by this time Harvey Goldsmith had joined the company, so I said to Harvey, 'Why don't you buy me out of the promotion side, and you can carry on with that?' Which is what happened."

Tony Smith's first priority was to raise Genesis' profile in North America and to this end he booked an extensive US tour during November and December, climaxing with two showcase gigs at the Roxy Club in Los Angeles on December 18 & 19. "They'd broken a bit in Belgium and Italy, but certainly not in America, so probably what I brought to the job was that real focus on getting the rest of the world sorted out, which I don't think Strat would have done," says Smith. "He was a bit of an 'Englishman abroad', and that Englishness didn't always work so well in America. The business attitude there was more hard-nosed and much more focused, plus he had a whole record label to run and everything else, so he couldn't just focus on the band. Whereas my attitude to management was always, it's me and the band against the world. So for the next five years my total focus was on Genesis and nothing else."

Tony Smith formed his own company to handle the band, Hit & Run Management, a suggestion from Peter Gabriel. It was later the name of Genesis' music publishing company.

Everyone was happy with the new arrangement, including the Genesis road crew who had their ups and downs with Tony Stratton Smith. Martyn Day, responsible for setting up the stage backdrop and the lighting rig, operating a 'follow-spot' light and hour upon hour of interminable driving, recalls an unusual parting gift from the Charisma boss. "After one tour was over, Strat invited the road crew to his office," he says. "As a way of saying thank you he gave each of us a personalised and boxed Easter egg. Even though it was the Easter season, it did seem a strange and rather paltry gift after so much hard work. One member of the crew felt so insulted that he threw his egg, box and all, straight into a litter bin in Old Compton Street. It wasn't until we got home and broke open our eggs, that we each discovered £25 tucked inside."[16]*

Informed what he had thrown away, the ungrateful roadie rushed back to the waste bin in Old Compton Street but by then both the egg and the £25 were gone. As Martyn Day says, "I imagine that some old tramp couldn't believe his luck, first finding the chocolate egg and then..." Tony's admiration for the hard-working road crew didn't end there. "We also found our names printed on the back of the *Genesis Live* album," smiles Day. "It wasn't quite the same as having our picture on the front of *Sgt Pepper* but in the annals of prog rock it was a small and appreciated recognition."

Nevertheless, Stratton Smith was not always a favourite with the road crews. One unpleasant story that did the rounds involved a roadie urinating in Tony's supper at the Speakeasy. Perhaps he simply took offence to something that Tony had said, as according to Cathy McKnight, wife of *Zigzag* editor Connor McKnight, Stratton Smith could talk his way into, although not necessarily out of, most situations. "Tony often got by with a great deal of bluff and bluster," she says. "Connor always used to describe Strat as an ace bullshitter. Which he was. I mean he could be a bit of an odd character and I think that in many quarters he was disliked as much as he was liked. I know that Connor certainly didn't like him and he didn't like Connor." Cathy later married Harry, who was the road manager for Lindisfarne for many years. "I'm not sure that all of their roadies were that keen on Strat either," she adds.

Live albums are often used by a record company as a stop-gap option to give an act breathing space between writing and recording new material for their next studio LP. Both Lindisfarne and Genesis had live albums released in 1973 as part of Charisma's budget-priced CLASS series.

Genesis, who had already started work on *Selling England By The Pound*, had to be persuaded by Tony to run with the idea. Two British shows from the *Foxtrot* tour, the Free Trade Hall in Manchester and the De Montfort Hall in Leicester, had already been recorded for the American King Biscuit Flower Hour radio show and Tony managed to get hold of the original unmixed tapes, bringing in John Burns from Island Records to help the band mix and edit the final album.

---

16   * £25 in 1973 would be worth about £300 in 2020.

Tony defended the move, telling Armando Gallo: "Genesis were never keen on the idea of a live album at that stage. Peter for one didn't really want it to come out. I finally convinced them to go for the idea because it came out at a very low price, which meant it could go in the large chain stores like Woolworths, W.H. Smith and Boots on a rather more extensive level. It was an attempt to broaden the audience, and in that sense I think it worked. For a time, *Genesis Live* also topped the sales of *Foxtrot*, and gave the band an opportunity to lay off for a long period. They had been working solidly on the road for two years, and they needed time to write and rehearse for a new album."

The King Biscuit recordings were never actually broadcast on US radio, but a few early radio promotional double albums were pressed up to include the full 23-minute version of 'Supper's Ready', which was not used on the single Charisma disc. Tony's decision was vindicated yet again as, somewhat surprisingly, it became the band's best-selling British album up to that point.

In August 1973, Genesis decamped to Island Studios with producer John Burns to record *Selling England By The Pound*. Largely written since the *Foxtrot* tour, several of the songs reflect the decline of English traditions and culture, this largely due to the growing spread of American influence, and it received mixed reviews from the critics on release. However, the fans' reaction was much more favourable and it reached number three in the UK charts, partly helped by the band going straight back out on tour to promote it. It was further assisted by the single 'I Know What I Like (In Your Wardrobe)', which gave Genesis their first top 30 chart position in February 1974.

'I Know What I Like (In Your Wardrobe)' was one of the first Charisma singles promoted by Judd Lander in his new position as company record plugger. "Genesis were a band that made albums and they didn't really want to do singles, but we convinced them," he recalls. "Gail and everyone said, 'We need a radio cut, we can't get that album track played in full on the radio.' So they actually had an edit made specifically for radio and it got them on the daytime playlist and as a consequence we had a hit. It wasn't a smash hit, but it helped to get them in there."

According to new manager Tony Smith, the single could have fared much better had the band agreed to a certain television appearance. "The single was doing quite well, going up the charts, and they asked if we would do *Top Of The Pops*," he says. "But Peter Gabriel called me up and said, 'No, I don't want to do *Top Of The Pops*, it's too poppy for us.' Consequently, one of my first actions as manager was to call up Strat and tell him that we weren't going to appear on *Top Of The Pops*. There was a huge battle, a huge row and I got really pissed off actually, because the single would probably have gone much higher than it did. I think it was number 27 when they asked us to appear, and maybe it went a little higher, but it didn't go top ten. This was the first time that Strat and I crossed swords, and he obviously thought, 'Who is this jumped-up bloody tour promoter, what is he doing?' In retrospect it was the right thing for the band to do at that time, but the wrong thing to do commercially."

With his customary vision, Tony insisted that the *Selling England* tour should be filmed for a possible cinema showing, but the resulting footage was rejected by the band, who felt it was simply not good enough. The concert film was never officially released.

This was also the first Genesis album sleeve to dispense with the services of Paul Whitehead. It was based on a painting called *The Dream* by Betty Swanwick who at some point in the seventies moved to the village of Tidebrook in Sussex, less than ten miles from Tony's house in Crowborough, and while working on the songs for *Selling England* Peter Gabriel spotted *The Dream* in an exhibition and decided it would be perfect for the cover. Gabriel asked Swanwick to add a lawn mower to her original work and that feature, alongside the man sleeping on the park bench, made the visual connections to the track 'I Know What I Like (In Your Wardrobe)'. When asked to describe her work, Betty said she was "part of a small tradition of English painting that is a bit eccentric, a little odd and a little visionary." She could equally have been describing Tony, Charisma and, for that matter, many of the artists who recorded for the label.

Following a long tour to promote *Selling England* the band took time out to recover. Phil Collins, the workaholic, recharged his batteries by assembling Brand X, and Mike Rutherford teamed up with former bandmate Anthony Phillips to work on a new album. Eventually most of Genesis regrouped to write and develop the music for their next opus, choosing to work at Headley Grange in Surrey, last occupied by Led Zeppelin who had left the house in a bad state of repair and infested by rats.

It wasn't the rats that kept Peter Gabriel away from the early stages of writing and rehearsal. This was due mainly to the problems his wife Jill was having with her first pregnancy, and an approach by William Friedkin, director of *The Exorcist*, about a possible film collaboration. Friedkin had read and enjoyed Gabriel's short story on the sleeve of *Genesis Live* and despite widespread disapproval from the rest of the band, he left to work on some early drafts of a film script at home, thus enabling him to spend more time with his wife. Tony shared the band's concern that this might cause longer-term problems and diplomatically stepped in to persuade Gabriel to finish work on the record. There is also a suggestion that Friedkin had buckled under pressure, not wishing to be known as the man who broke up Genesis.

Although much of the music was already written by Banks, Collins, Rutherford and Hackett, Gabriel insisted on his concept for the record and writing all the lyrics himself, further annoying Mike Rutherford who had another concept in mind. With the writing and rehearsals completed, the album was recorded at Glaspant Manor, Carmarthenshire, Wales using the Island Mobile Studios and producer John Burns. Despite a certain amount of disharmony in the ranks, *The Lamb Lies Down On Broadway* was easily their most ambitious project to date, filling a double album with the story of Rael, a half Puerto Rican punk teenager living in New York City who is forced to live underground while searching for, and ultimately rescuing, his brother John.

Much of what happens in the story was the result of Peter Gabriel's surrealistic dreams, some might say nightmares, and even the name Rael is thought to be a play on Gabriel. Phil Collins has suggested that the entire concept is about split personality, alongside themes of sexual reinvention, alienation and consumerism. Described by the *New York Times* as "the Ulysses of concept albums", Tony managed to neatly sum up the new double album thus – "*The Lamb* is a hymn to the integral innocence of the human spirit, meeting the bacon-slicer of a corrupt society."

The upshot of the dissent within the group was Peter Gabriel's decision to leave, a story that received banner headlines in the music press. Many felt Genesis would be unable to continue without him, but in the event they prospered mightily with Phil Collins stepping out from behind his drum kit to take over as vocalist. Remarkably, he sounded very like Gabriel, an argument that defeated almost 400 other applicants.

Tony voiced his reservations: "I don't think there was a single vote in favour of Phil initially, but that changed within six weeks. As far as the writing went, I took the view – as, I suspect, did other members of the band – that Phil might not be adequate. As regards the singing, I had an extraordinary feeling that we were doing something a tiny bit dishonest, in that Phil's voice sounded so similar to Peter's. I think Phil was a far more skilled actor than anybody had given him credit for, and sitting and playing behind Peter for so long, there was a kind of unconscious wish to do it the way Peter did."

Steve Hackett remembers Tony's reaction on hearing a rough recording of Collins' vocals. "He was wandering by and said, 'God, he sounds just like Pete. Sounds like you've found your vocalist, chaps.' Tony was very good at going in and giving everyone a short sermon and buoying everyone up and then leaving. Everybody thought that Phil had done such a great job on it, that there were no questions from then on."

Tony always doubted that Collins would have become as successful had Gabriel stayed with Genesis but admitted Collins' common touch and robust gift for entertainment made Genesis easier to market. "In the long term, the only thing the band lost was Peter's mind. But I believe that was a very substantial loss, and perhaps made the difference between Genesis being a world heavyweight champion for life and just a very good heavyweight champion.

"I used to joke with Peter Grant, Steve O'Rourke[17*] and Kit Lambert and a few others about this that... if Genesis hadn't split up, in my view, I honestly think I had a band touched by God, in the original band. If Peter Gabriel hadn't left in 1975 to go for a solo career, I would have had the best band in the world. At that time they all believed in each other, the writing was developing hand over fist and they were creating a marvellous atmosphere everywhere they went. They were such nice people that they were making friends everywhere in the business. I mean everybody loved them because they were for real."

Genesis stayed loyal to their label until Stratton Smith sold it to the Virgin empire in the mid-eighties. "Strat was a really important part of our life," says Mike Rutherford. "You'd always come away from a meeting with him feeling that there was hope, after all. He was very much a good viber, which we needed at the time we signed."

17'   * Managers of Led Zeppelin and Pink Floyd respectively.

Chapter 10

The Easy Touch

"Strat used to walk into the Nellie Dean and everybody would say,
'Ahh, it's good old Strat' – whereas we would all be more honest with
him about things, but he didn't always like being told."

Paul Conroy, Charisma booking agent

Tony Stratton Smith was a kindly soul who disliked letting folk down but with so many acts vying to get a record deal with Charisma, one of the disadvantages of being the label boss was the sack-load of poorly recorded cassette tapes that crossed his desk each week.

Tony certainly listened to more than his fair share of dodgy demos, as he explained to *Melody Maker*'s Roy Hollingworth. "We had this load of guys who were hanging around the office. Been hanging around for days wanting me to hear some tapes. They were determined to see me and were also annoying the lads downstairs, so I decided to give them a little time. They had an acetate, actually, and I listened to about four tracks off it. It was obviously an expensive job, but even while I was listening to it they were making excuses, saying this wasn't really where they were at, but we've got to play you something and this is all we've got. They asked me not to judge them by this. After about three tracks I realised it was crap – as far as I was concerned – and we switched it off. So they started again, telling me they'd really made a lot of progress since this was made, they'd really changed. I said, 'Well for God's sake, when did you cut this, when did you lay this down?' One of them just stood there and said, 'Last Sunday'."

Rare Bird, Lindisfarne and Genesis were all success stories, but as intuitive as he often proved to be, Tony didn't get every decision right. Not everyone on Charisma was a winner. One of the least successful bands on the label was Spreadeagle whose lead guitarist, Andy Blackford, takes up the story of how they came to Tony's attention. "We were stuffed. We'd pinned all our hopes on a gig at the Pied Bull, Islington. Our manager had invited Tony Stratton Smith, the four times larger-than-life proprietor of Charisma Records. Amazingly, he turned up. Less amazingly, the power supply failed and we had to play an acoustic set. And we'd never rehearsed one. I can't begin to convey the horror of that evening. It was like the dream where you're in the supermarket wearing only a vest that's just too short to cover your privates. The journey home was even quieter than the gig. I reviewed my options. Traffic wardens could earn up to £40 a week with overtime, and the uniform was free. Two days later, our manager received the call – we had a deal."

Evidently Tony had been impressed by their professional response to adversity. "Knowing what I do now, he was probably more impressed by our bassist's snake hips and shoulder-length blond hair," continues Blackford. "Charisma would buy us a Mercedes van, PA system and back line amplifiers. They would 'pay' us each a 'non-returnable advance' of £15 a week. And crucially, they would finance the production of our first album. We were going to be rich and famous. It was in the bag. We celebrated at The Greyhound in Fulham Palace Road. We watched a band that was much better than ours – but fuck 'em, they didn't have a record deal and we did."

Spreadeagle went on to release one album for Charisma, the Shel Talmy-produced *The Piece Of Paper* in 1972. When it failed, Tony was resigned to its fate. "I think, in a way, you can be proud of certain failures and Spreadeagle are a classic case. When I first saw them, playing in a little bar in East London, I got hooked on two songs. So I signed the band, started to work with them and a year later that's all they had – two good songs."

After Spreadeagle, Andy Blackford didn't completely turn his back on music, moving on to work as a journalist for *Disc* and *Music Week*. He later carved out a successful career in advertising, as the copywriter on various campaigns and he wrote the bouncy jingle for the Um Bongo fruit juice television commercials.

Another of Charisma's commercial failures was Capability Brown, who in 1971 were making a big noise on the live circuit around London, largely due to their impressive vocal harmonies. Taking their name (at Tony's suggestion) from England's most celebrated landscape gardener, they were a tight six-piece in which everyone sang and swapped instruments, the line-up comprising Tony Ferguson, Dave Nevin, Kenny Rowe, Grahame White, Joe Williams and Roger Willis. Lead guitarist Ferguson and bassist Rowe were previously in pop band Harmony Grass, while Rowe had also played with Steve Marriott's Moments.

"We were a progressive rock group that had six lead singers and three lead guitar players," says Ferguson. "We didn't fit with either Genesis or Van der Graaf Generator but Tony managed to convince me otherwise. We met him in the summer of 1971 and were immediately taken with him. He was unlike any record boss we had ever met. Softly spoken, sympathetic and with some great ideas, he was more of an artist than a businessman. He had listened attentively to our music, which showed in his encouragement. He was very seductive. We then met the staff – Paul Conroy, Gail Colson, Fred Munt and many others whose names I've forgotten, and they took over everything – publicity, shows, marketing, press and TV."

When Tony signed Capability Brown they were still developing a style that fused progressive rock with the glorious West Coast harmonies of Crosby, Stills & Nash, as evident on their debut album, the Steve Rowlands-produced *From Scratch,* released in 1972. It's noticeable that the tracks chosen for singles were cover versions, Russ Ballard's 'Liar' and 'Wake Up Little Sister' from Charisma stablemate Alan Hull. They would also cover material by Rare Bird and were one of the first British bands to attempt a Steely Dan song, 'Midnight Cruiser'.

"Tony was unbelievably supportive," adds Ferguson. "In 1972 he requested another album from us, but this time with David Hitchcock in the production chair. Things did not go smoothly and after a week or so the band realised that the relationship was not productive. We were scared to tell Tony, as our position was somewhat tenuous since we weren't exactly selling millions of records, but Tony was professionally sympathetic to our dilemma. Although we didn't have an alternative, he introduced us to the Beatles' house recording engineer, John Mills, who took us into Apple Studios and recorded the whole album, *Voice,* in a couple of weeks. John Mills was brilliant – it was a great call by Tony."

For their second album, *Voice,* released in 1973, the band became even more experimental, notably on the track 'Circumstances', a 20-minute song-cycle that took up the whole of side two in typical prog fashion, and one that many cite as having a big influence on later work by Queen. Always a popular live attraction, Capability Brown never quite found the commercial success that their harmony-drenched music often promised, despite enthusiastic coverage in the British music press and the usual unconditional support of Tony.

"I know that Tony wasn't completely happy with the result," recalls Tony Ferguson. "He was looking for that stand-out track that would spearhead sales, but unfortunately we didn't have it. He met us at the studio towards the end of the record and told us, 'It was great – but not great enough'. It was a bit of a body blow."

Despite the best efforts of Tony and Charisma, in 1974 Capability Brown went their separate ways, with Willis, White and Ferguson briefly joining the pop band Christie before forming Krazy Kat in 1976. "I have nothing but fond memories of Tony Stratton Smith," says Ferguson. "Unlike the majority of industry executives, he was a concerned leader who didn't show favouritism – he spoke the artists' language. The communication and respect that Tony garnered from his artists was special. Not many executives in the industry did that, maybe Ahmet Ertegun, David Geffen or Jimmy Iovine – and the only other indie label that had that same family feeling was Stiff Records, with Dave Robinson."

* * *

In late 1971, when Bell & Arc were in America supporting The Who, Tony travelled with them and one night in Chicago he and Graham Bell visited a club called Rush Up where they encountered Copperhead, an eight-piece jazz-rock outfit from Minnesota, similar in style to early Chicago or Blood, Sweat & Tears. Four of the band made up the brass section, including trombonist Don Lehnhoff, who was previously with Mitch Ryder & The Detroit Wheels, and trumpeter Eddie Shaw who had played bass for The Monks in the sixties. Ever on the lookout for 'anything good of its kind', Tony didn't have anything like them on his label and was seriously considering signing them to Charisma.

Don Lehnhoff remembers that first meeting. "They dropped by the after-hours club that we were playing after their gig. Graham Bell sat in with us and sang a screaming version of 'Summertime' – in fact, I believe it was Graham's enthusiasm for Copperhead that was a factor in Tony's interest." This chance encounter sparked off a whirlwind string of events, with Tony flying the band to London for a ten-day vacation, including lost nights at La Chasse, a Lindisfarne gig and a visit to Luxford House. "The whole experience was surreal," recalls Lehnhoff, "but Tony was an amazing and gracious guy, who I will never forget."

Drummer Bob Anderson takes up the story: "Tony took a liking to me for some reason and invited me for lunch a few times. This, of course, was a pint of Guinness stout, about the consistency of a milkshake. He took the role of mentor and enjoyed answering my queries about the music business, and would be very reassuring with a very gentle Buddha-esque little smile and chuckle. I was just 19 and completely blown away by how fast his plan for Copperhead was unfolding."

Anderson recalls the time they spent at Luxford. "Strat told us wooden beams in the house were from old English sailing ships. There were exotic trees and plants from all over the world and 12 snow-white doves that lived there. [He said] the company plan was to put the full power of the agency behind Genesis, Bell & Arc and Copperhead. They even discussed Copperhead being the opening act on the Stones' next US tour. Tony offered the band to producer Bob Johnston who came to see us and said there would be no problem making us successful. Then began a scenario in which none of the band could understand what the hell was going on."

In the event, all went quiet with Charisma. "It wasn't until three years later," continues Anderson, "when I was touring England and I looked up Tony he explained how Bob Johnston and Capitol had actually broken our management contract with Charisma and literally stolen Copperhead away from them. Mystery solved. After 50 years in the business I can safely say that Tony Stratton Smith was the most amazingly brilliant character I have ever encountered. The day we met, he chuckled and said 'Sorry I'm late, I was having tea with the Queen of Denmark.'"

Another Charisma also-ran was String Driven Thing, a husband-and-wife team of Chris and Pauline Adams, plus percussionist John Mannion. Having built up a local following in Scotland in the late sixties, they released their self-titled debut album in 1970 and expanded the line-up to include bassist Colin Wilson. Early in 1972, Chris Adams travelled to London in the hope of interesting the Strawbs' management with a three-song demo. Flicking through the record company section of the Yellow Pages, he spotted Stratton Smith Enterprises, dialled the number and found himself in conversation with the head of Mooncrest Music, the publishing arm of Charisma. Within a week, Stratton Smith himself was in Glasgow to see the band play a showcase gig at the Burns Howff pub. One week later, String Driven Thing was signed to his label.

John Mannion left around the same time and the group returned to Glasgow to rehearse, with a princely retainer of £20 per week. A month later, they headed back down south to play their first ever live show as a 'signed' band, at a community hall in Tunbridge Wells, quite close to where Tony had his country retreat, followed by an appearance on the bill of the 1972 Reading Festival. It was an audacious move, but it worked and the group set to work on their first album for Charisma, to be titled – like its independent predecessor – *String Driven Thing*.

Recorded with producer Shel Talmy over just two weeks in August 1972, the album received rave reviews in the music press, *Melody Maker* in particular taking the group's side. In typical Charisma style, the album's distinctive gatefold sleeve, designed by Hipgnosis, cost more than the actual recording sessions. The future of the band looked bright; the single 'Circus' was making waves on both sides of the Atlantic and there were plans for the group to join Genesis on their UK and US tours. Unfortunately, in early 1973 Chris Adams was hospitalised with a collapsed lung, which seriously impacted on progress.

Already holding reservations about Tony's managerial nous, Adams tells it thus: "The pattern continued when we were booked as support on the *Foxtrot* tour. Ten days before the start, my lung collapsed, at which point any sensible manager would have pulled us. But not Mother Management[18*]. The posters had been printed, and if it were humanly possible, we would be on stage at the Rainbow for the opening night. Normally it takes three or four weeks to recover from a spontaneous pneumothorax, but against the odds, I managed to make it. Understandably, though, it was one of our poorest

---

18   * Mother Management was the name Tony chose for his management wing.

performances, and the press made a point of saying so."

Although String Driven Thing did play some British dates with Genesis, the all-important American tour never happened. "It was due to a string of such dire management decisions that every band who ever walked through Strat's door eventually ended up disintegrating in one way or another," adds Adams, somewhat churlishly. "There was a pecking order in Charisma. Each signing would be given its shot at fame, but first came a lengthy apprenticeship, supporting the 'bigger bands', often on Charisma national tours. Lindisfarne had jumped the queue, as it were, so after VdGG's demise, Genesis became IT. There were those in the industry, Shel Talmy among them, who regarded them as Strat's folly, but this merely spurred him on, and so they were given the best of stage gear and virtually unlimited time in the studio to complete *Foxtrot*. Strat had given his bands their head in the studio, which meant huge recording bills, but little commercial success. Then along came Lindisfarne, who made a radio-friendly album cheaply and became big overnight."

"Strat's strategy of piggybacking each act on their predecessor's success was excellent, but sadly he left the day-to-day management of the artists to an individual who couldn't have managed a fart after a plate of peas, and no matter how great the general, in the end he lives or dies on the ability of his quartermaster."

While critical of Tony's management techniques, Chris Adams acknowledges that life for a band on the Charisma label was unlike any other. "Despite all the strategic flaws, Strat was an inspirational figure," he says. "In the end, my memories of him are always fond; that breathy whisper of a voice, the twinkling eyes, the wicked laugh. I remember the agency got us a TV gig in Paris and he sent us off in his own private car, a huge Rover, driven by his driver, Cracky, a Welshman with one lung. Cracky enjoyed the finer things in life, so we devoured huge platters of hors d'oeuvres on the way across, and before we returned, he had helped us eat and drink our way through the substantial float and the TV fee. When we got back, empty-handed, Strat just shook his head and chuckled, as though we were his wayward children. And of course, in a way we were, all of us in his Wonderland, with the Mad Hatter himself at the top of the family table."

* * *

The success rate within the record industry – that is the ratio of hits to misses – has always been weighted heavily, probably by at least 20-1, towards the misses, but such is the profit potential of a hit that most labels can withstand a few signings that fail to make the charts. An even more embarrassing pitfall is declining to sign, or otherwise losing, an act that becomes phenomenally successful elsewhere. Decca famously passed on an opportunity to sign The Beatles. They also let go of David Bowie, as did Philips. Charisma's great lost band was Queen, who might have been signed by Tony had fate not dictated otherwise.

In early 1972, Ken Testi was helping Queen gain a foothold in the business, as part manager, part enthusiastic fan. Charisma's Paul Conroy had known Testi since they shared a flat together when he worked as booking agent for the Red Bus Company and was handed an early demo by the then unsigned group. Conroy's first impression was not overly favourable, but he arranged for Testi to meet with Tony to discuss signing them.

Tony liked what he heard and made an opening offer of between £20,000 and £25,000 – plus, according to a somewhat sarcastic remark from producer John Anthony, "a tour of Belgium and a new van". As far as Gail Colson is concerned, the signing of Queen was a done-deal. Paul Conroy had brought them in, she had personally typed up a contract and an announcement was about to be made – as she says, "until John Anthony took them round the corner to the Sheffield Brothers at Trident Studios". Money, of course, never played a major part in Tony's decision making. The only criteria involved, as press officer Chris Briggs points out, was whether or not Tony liked them. "Strat was just a fan, really, and he only ever signed things that he liked. When Paul Conroy tried to get Strat interested in signing Queen, Strat never looked on it as a business decision, he simply asked himself, 'Do I like the group or not, do I like their music?'"

From Queen's point of view, money was a major factor – as it would be throughout their ongoing career – and eventually they decided not to accept Tony's offer, opting instead to use it as leverage with other interested labels. It was a surprisingly brave, some might say arrogant, move for a fledgling band without a record deal. "They were worried they would be identified as the second string on a small label," says Ken Testi. "Queen would have had a lot of personal support from the staff there, but felt resources were limited. It wasn't a bad offer, but it came at a time when some bands' advances had been in telephone numbers. CBS had been paying out monstrous amounts."

Others at Charisma were keen to recommend that Tony take on the new band. Art director Frank Sansom also had a word in the boss' ear. "I received a cassette from Trident Studios and it was Queen," he says. "They really wanted to be on Charisma, so they sent this tape round and the minute I heard it I said, 'Look, we really should put this out.' I begged and begged, but Strat's tongue-in-cheek comment was, 'No, dear boy, we can't have two Queens on this label.' And that was that. Then he said we should put them on Mooncrest[19]*. I said, 'Strat, they don't want to be on bloody Mooncrest, they want to be on The Famous Charisma Label.' He dug in his heels on that one

---

19   *Details on the launch of Mooncrest can be found later in the chapter.

and I really couldn't understand it, but sometimes with Strat you had to know when not to push it."

Paul Conroy was still booking gigs for the band and put them on at Kings College Hospital in Denmark Hill, South London. Ken Testi chose this as another A&R gig and several record labels sent along representatives. Apparently Tony also turned up to see them play that night, even though the group had already effectively turned him down. Unusually for the normally placid Strat, the evening ended in a heated argument. John Anthony felt that Queen could get a better offer, had told them so and pointed them in the direction of Norman Sheffield, his boss at Trident Studios. Following a meeting in the Trident offices at St Anne's Court, the band took on Sheffield as their manager, with all the additional production and recording facilities that the studio had to offer, while simultaneously edging out the enthusiastic and hard-working Ken Testi.

Using Charisma's original, and extremely reasonable, offer as a carrot to dangle in front of the other labels, Norman Sheffield landed a substantial recording contract with EMI and John Anthony was in the frame to produce their debut album. Where once Anthony and Tony had worked so closely together, there were now irreparable differences between the two. Many believed Anthony was the in-house producer at Charisma, but having been usurped by Dave Hitchcock and John Burns during the recording of Genesis' *Foxtrot* and losing out to Bob Johnston on Lindisfarne's second record, this latest unpleasantness over Queen effectively ended their relationship. When asked to comment on his work with Stratton Smith, John Anthony would later say, "I have nothing to say about him that is in any way good."

If Tony was actively on the lookout for a flamboyant glam rock group, another opportunity presented itself in October 1972 when the New York Dolls flew in to London to play a handful of dates, including a prestigious support spot with The Faces at the Wembley Empire Pool. Several English record labels were courting the sexually androgynous band, led by Track, whose label boss Kit Lambert took the group out to dinner immediately after the Wembley show. Virgin and Charisma were also in the frame and Tony seemed particularly keen to sign the Dolls. He made several visits to see their managers Marty Thau and Steve Leber in their hotel suite at the Dorchester, while over at Virgin Richard Branson was sniffing around the managers too. Unfortunately for Tony, Thau and Leber decided that Charisma was an unsuitable home for their glam punk rockers. Tragedy struck barely a week into the Doll's London visit when drummer Billy Murcia died from a drugs overdose, leaving the group to fly back to New York without a record contract – or a drummer.

* * *

By October 1971, Tony was deep in negotiation with Philips Records over a possible merger that would have given the record industry giant a one-third share in Charisma. At that point, Philips Phonographic Industries distributed Charisma product everywhere apart from Britain and North America. However, following a weekend meeting with his co-directors, no doubt over a bottle or three, Tony called a halt to the talks, opting to retain complete independence for the label. "However, we shall be holding further discussions both in London and Baarn, the Netherlands location of Philips HQ, about closer co-operation," he told *Billboard* magazine, keeping his options open.

The following year Tony turned to an old friend now working at Buddah Records for his stateside distribution, a move that would give the *Monty Python's Flying Circus* team a foot in the door of American television. Nancy Lewis, who had originally helped Tony with PR and trousers for The Koobas, proved to be the key contact. During her time in London she had worked for Who managers Kit Lambert and Chris Stamp and returned to the States to set up a New York office for their Track Records. Lewis takes up the story. "In 1972 Strat called me to say that he wanted to get a distribution deal for his label in America. He had this band, Genesis, that he really wanted to launch over here. So I set up a meeting with Neil Bogart, the head of Buddah."

Preferring to work with a relatively small independent company, not unlike his own, Tony empathised with the set-up at Buddah, and the deal was done. *Billboard* magazine reported the news on February 26, 1972: "NEW YORK – Charisma Records UK firm has signed a three year distribution pact with Buddah Records. This marks the first British label picked up by Buddah for distribution in the US. Headed by Tony Stratton Smith, Charisma Records has made constant chart action in the UK and in the European market. 'We have had a going concern here for a while,' remarked Stratton Smith. 'Our affiliation with B&C Records in the UK has helped a great deal, but I must add that our artist roster is quite strong.' Charisma handles *Monty Python's Flying Circus*, a satirical comedy show on the BBC which has received critical acclaim across Europe.[20]* A film by the Flying Circus, *And Now for Something Completely Different,* is being distributed in Canada and is expected to be issued here by April, with a simultaneous record release by the same group."

Buddah head Neil Bogart stated: "I feel that Charisma gives us a most important source of progressive rock artists from the UK. We have firmly established ourselves in the black marketplace with our deals with Custom, Hot Wax and T-Neck. Now this move will firmly entrench us in the progressive rock marketplace."

---

20 * Details of Charisma's relationship with *Monty Python* can be found in Chapter 13.

* * *

When Charisma decided to change the design of their record label from the striking pink, some say magenta, solid background with the white scroll logo and lettering to the suitably English and eccentric Mad Hatter illustration, somewhat surprisingly the job fell to an American, Glen Christensen, then art director at Buddah Records in New York.

"As I remember it, the Buddah Group had two leaders," says Christensen. "Neil Bogart, a record industry maven known as the Bubble Gum King, who was the big ideas man, and Art Kass, who handled the business end of things. Neil wanted a new label design for our releases and as the art director at Buddah, I was given the assignment.

"The idea came to me pretty quickly – 'Who had more Charisma than the Mad Hatter!' became my pitch – so I researched Alice, and designed and created the montage. I signed the piece in ink with just my last name, Christensen, done very fine and small, and tucked just under the tree branches at the extreme lower right hand edge of the drawing. I also designed the black and white logo using just the Mad Hatter with the label name arched over the top."

While Bogart and Kass appreciated the acquisition of the British rock bands, Nancy Lewis championed the Monty Python team in America. "Strat came over and brought a stack of his product to Neil and right at the bottom of this stack were two Python albums which I had not heard. We started talking and Strat said of the TV series, 'I can't imagine it will ever come over here.' So Tony and I decided we should really try to get it organised; there was a whole series sitting there, at Time-Life Television, who had all the BBC rights."

Initially, Time-Life showed absolutely no interest in showing Python to an American audience, considering the humour to be 'too English' for them, added to which the cost of converting the actual tapes from PAL to NTSC format was prohibitive. Nancy, however, had other ideas. "Buddah put out the first album and it was amazing; we started getting response from the FM radio stations, from people who had never, ever seen the visual side of Python," said Lewis. "It was pretty staggering. So we thought, if it works without the visual side, it can't be too British to work with the visual side. There's got to be a market here."

After hearing tracks from the first album, *Another Monty Python Record* on radio, rock fans joined the campaign to get Python on to the small screen and eventually *Monty Python's Flying Circus* aired on US television for the first time in 1974.

Tony apparently sweet-talked Atlantic Records into letting him take office space in the Warner Communications building on West 52nd Street and Nancy Lewis left Buddah to establish the New York Charisma office there. For a while they shared a space with Giorgio Chinaglia, a top Italian footballer who had joined the New York Cosmos football team from Lazio. Later on, they moved down a floor to share an office with The Rolling Stones US management. Whenever Tony visited New York he would often hold court at the bar in Bombay Palace, an Indian restaurant at the foot of the Warner Communications building in the Rockefeller Center – "somewhere that everyone could always find him," says Lewis.

Nancy and Tony had a minor falling out when Tony asked how she saw her career developing, and Nancy replied that one day she would like to manage the company. Tony took her remark to mean she was after his job. Fortunately, Nancy discovered that any falling out with Tony, whether real or imagined, never lasted too long. While working with the Monty Python team on the film set of *The Meaning Of Life*, she met her husband to be, the British actor Simon Jones. By coincidence, Jones already had a connection with the Charisma crowd, having played the part of Joachim in Vivian Stanshall's movie *Sir Henry At Rawlinson End*. When the couple were married in London in 1983, Tony was an honoured guest at their wedding – with Gail Colson as Nancy's matron of honour.

Colin Richardson joined The Famous Charisma Label in 1972, initially to work in the agency, but quickly moved into international management for the label. He had first encountered Tony while working for the Bonzos at Gerry Bron's management company. "I knew Fred Munt, who used to be a roadie for the Bonzos, and one day I took a phone call from Fred asking if he and Tony Stratton Smith could come in and talk about them. It was a swelteringly hot day and Strat, who was pretty overweight, was sweating quite profusely. Fred was a jeans and T-shirt guy, whereas Strat was wearing a jacket and tie, maybe a full suit, but he had his jacket off and was carrying it and I remember his bright red braces, that's what sticks out in my mind."

Richardson was brought in to work at the Charisma booking agency but he soon realised that Paul Conroy and Nigel Kerr didn't need him, so he switched to European record promotion. "Strat was a great guy to work for, he really did have charisma," he says. "Anything good of its kind, that was Strat's attitude and he put out stuff that no one else would dream of releasing. He was proud of the way Charisma worked, as were we all. Genesis and Lindisfarne made the money that he then spent on smaller, worthwhile projects."

* * *

Tony's love of all things literary was widely known and when the original writing desk used by J.R.R. Tolkien came up for sale, his interest was stirred. The desk had been purchased by Tolkien's wife Edith in 1927 and the author himself used it well – writing, typing and illustrating all of *The Hobbit* and drafting large sections of *The Lord Of The Rings* on its leather top. After his wife's death, Tolkien sold the desk at auction in November 1972 with the proceeds going to the Help the Aged Housing Association. The auction took place at Sotheby's in Belgravia and when Lot 116 was called, Tony made sure he was the highest bidder, paying £340 for this piece of famous furniture that sat proudly in his Charisma office for many years, the certificate of provenance tucked safely into one of the eight drawers.

There is a postscript to the Saga of the Desk. After Tony's death in 1987, it was sold at auction by his estate and bought by an English book dealer, who took it to the Antiquarian Book Fair in New York that year. Along with some Tolkien first editions, he placed the desk on display with a sign that read, 'This is the desk on which Tolkien wrote *The Hobbit*.' As luck would have it, the desk was spotted by Mary Ruth Howes, a former student of Wheaton College, which houses The Wade Centre, a repository for the books, manuscripts, letters and other writings of seven notable British authors – Owen Barfield, G.K. Chesterton, C.S. Lewis, George MacDonald, Dorothy L. Sayers, J.R.R. Tolkien, and Charles Williams. Knowing how important this item of furniture would be to The Wade, she gave the dealer the details of this literary research centre and also telephoned The Wade to tell them about the desk. Associate director Marjorie Mead followed the item back to England, negotiated the purchase and the desk now proudly sits in the Marion E. Wade Centre in Wheaton, Illinois – alongside a certain wardrobe once owned by C.S. Lewis.

The desk was just one example of Tony's extraordinary reach. A glance into the more opaque corners of Charisma's output reveals a couple of records by the National Youth Jazz Orchestra, who were recommended to Tony by the writer Derek Jewel. This multifarious nature of the label made working for it a complete delight for press man Chris Briggs, who never knew from one day to the next what was coming his way.

"Strat was so eclectic," he says. "In the course of a couple of weeks I would be taking journalists up to Oxford to review a Genesis tour date and then I'd be ambling around Trident Studios trying to sober up following a night out with Alan Hull, or I'd be round at another London studio not quite knowing why I was there. Often you would be sent round to sit in as the Charisma representative. It was like, 'Oh shit, Albert Finney is in so and so studios today and no one's going, where's Strat?' 'Oh, Chris you'd better get round there.' So you'd be sent round to represent the company without really knowing anything about what was happening. You had to walk in and introduce yourself to someone like Albert Finney and it was totally flying by the seat of your pants, the whole thing.

"The next day you might be dropped off at John Cleese's house because they were doing music press interviews for the Monty Python albums. Cleese had a house in Abbotsbury Road, opposite Holland Park. Strat would say, 'Get a taxi over to Cleese's house, you're babysitting the interviews today.' Maybe Peter Thompson was supposed to do it, but it's actually for *Melody Maker* and Peter didn't really like dealing with music journalists. Then you might find yourself in a meeting with Viv Stanshall, talking about *Sir Henry At Rawlinson End*, not to mention all the new artists that Strat was signing – Audience, Clifford T. Ward, String Driven Thing. An incredible mixture, and all in the same week or month."

Chris Briggs might even have found himself faced with an author whose book Tony wanted to publish. During 1971 the Canadian songwriter and poet Leonard Cohen visited the UK with the intention of setting up a publishing company, using the name Spice Box Books Limited, after his second collection of poetry *The Spice-Box Of Earth*, published in 1961. Cohen had met Tony in August 1970 at a festival in Aix-en-Provence in southern France, where Rare Bird were also on the bill. Charisma Books "resulted from a pleasant idea that Leonard Cohen and I had at a dinner party," said Tony. "As partners in the firm, we plan to cater for only a few writers of quality who have been unable to get their manuscripts into print."

Tony brought in John Mayer to mastermind the project and the first book planned under the new Charisma Books imprint was to be a collection of poetry by the Canadian writer Irving Layton, who had tutored Leonard Cohen at Toronto University. "Layton is one of the most moving poets I've ever read," said Stratton Smith. "I find it appalling that he has not been published yet outside Canada."

Sometime between November 1972 and 1974, however, there appears to have been a falling out between Cohen and Stratton Smith. In London to promote his documentary film *Bird On A Wire* and to encourage sales of Layton's *Collected Poems*, Cohen told *NME*'s Steve Turner that he was no longer playing a creative role in the project, "for reasons that he doesn't care to divulge".

Despite the best intentions of both Tony and Cohen, Irving Layton's collection of poems didn't actually appear as a Charisma book until 1977. In the meantime, several books appeared by artists on Charisma, including *The Mocking Horse* by Alan Hull and *Killers, Angels, Refugees* by Peter Hammill. Pete Frame also put together *The Road To Rock*, a collection of interviews from his influential *Zigzag* magazine, of which Tony would later become the owner.

Cathy McKnight joined the 'family' as head of Charisma Books and stayed loyal to the company for several years. Her initial introduction to

Tony was through Dennis Muirhead, an Australian lawyer who specialised in drug and music cases. Having already worked for an 'avant-garde' publishing house, McKnight's first exposure to her new boss was memorable. "It was a very cold day in February 1973 when I climbed the stairs to the Charisma offices in Old Compton Street," she would write. "The cramped reception room was filled with various characters, most of who quarrelled in a rich mixture of four-letter words about a variety of seemingly disconnected subjects. My arrival was greeted with a mixture of disbelief, bewilderment and hostility. After a tortuous half-hour wait – relieved only by the sudden and unexpected appearance of an old friend, who instantly warned me in no uncertain terms against having anything to do with these people – I was ushered into the great man's office.

"Strat was a large man, of indeterminate age, dressed (almost) impeccably, with twinkly eyes and an odd rumble of a laugh which punctuated his speech at random and often irrelevant intervals. I couldn't categorise him then, or since. After a lengthy preamble, spanning the far-flung points of the literary stratosphere, it slowly dawned on me that I was being selected as the architect of Strat's venture into the literary world. The fact that there was already an incumbent in this job seemed irrelevant, and I was taken on to translate Strat's lost literary loves into paperback form – Charisma books had grandiose beginnings."

McKnight thus embarked on a relationship with a man "whose dominant characteristics seemed to be constantly at odds with themselves; was he a genius or a charlatan, an original thinker or an intellectual con artist of the highest order? Strat was undoubtedly a man of vision, and while those visions so often led him up blind alleys, occasionally those strategies would be gloriously rewarded, his judgement vindicated, and he would cruise forward again, ignoring the diktats by which most people find their lives governed, either in business or socially. This extraordinary jumble of contradictions made him the worst possible person to work for, and yet the few years I did at Charisma remain the most interesting and exciting times of my entire working life, and I revered Strat in the same measure that he infuriated me. I still miss him, and all those wild ideas, presented as if they were the obvious, the only possible approach to any given situation or problem. An unforgettable!"

When McKnight took on this colossal task, no one had even thought to mention that there was already somebody in the position. "I took over from somebody called John [Mayer] and I had practically nothing to do with him. In fact I'm not even sure he knew that I had been offered his job," she says. "We were in Soho Square at that point and I never really spoke to him. It was actually a very difficult situation because apparently he would just sit in his office and drink, although I never actually saw this, but when he finally left there was an empty half bottle of brandy in one of the desk drawers. Then Sarah Radclyffe was brought in as my secretary, she was literally given to me by Strat and Michael Wale, because her father schooled racehorses and they wanted to have an 'in' with him. I was made to sack the girl who was my secretary, about which I was extremely angry, but it turned out for the good in the end."

Most of the output of Charisma/Spice Box Books was published during Cathy McKnight's tenure between 1973 and 1975. Alan Hull's collection of poetry and *No One Waved Goodbye*, a collection of essays on rock casualties edited by Robert Somma, both found their way into print in 1973. Also that year came *Smokestack El Ropo's Bedside Reader*, another counter-culture compilation, this time edited from a regular column that appeared in *Rolling Stone*. As the publicity declared, "a heavy-duty compendium of fables, lore and hot dope tales, from America's only rolling newspaper". This was a somewhat surprising addition, as Tony was defiantly anti-drugs himself, although no doubt it made popular reading for Charisma's core audience.

Another four books appeared in 1974 and followed a similar pattern in content. A collection of poetry from another Charisma songwriter: *Killers, Angels, Refugees* by Peter Hammill; *The Road To Rock: A Zigzag Book Of Interviews*, edited by Pete Frame; *The Autobiography Of A Brown Buffalo* by Oscar Zeta Acosta, a Chicano lawyer who was supposedly the real-life model for Hunter S. Thompson's 'Dr. Gonzo' character; and a further book of poetry, *Tonight We Will Fake Love* by Steve Turner.

Back in 1971, Turner had seen the original announcement in *Melody Maker* that Stratton Smith and Leonard Cohen were joining forces to start a publishing company and had sent in his manuscript, more in hope than expectation. "To be published by Charisma was a fulfilment of my dream to see poetry marketed alongside rock music," wrote Turner years later. "I sent *Tonight We Will Fake Love* to them and, some months later, received a phone call from Stratton Smith accepting me as one of their first authors." Even so, from acceptance to publication it took three years for Turner's book to appear.

No one actually knows why Leonard Cohen distanced himself so quickly from his association with Charisma Books. One possible answer is that he was frustrated that their first project proposal, the poetry collection by his great friend and fellow Canadian Irving Layton, took so long to get into print. Even though things started to click with the arrival of Cathy McKnight, she was never told the reason behind Cohen's disappearance. "As far as I know, he never came to London to meet up with Strat during my time – I was certainly never introduced to him."

With Cohen pulling out so soon, none of his own work was ever published by Charisma/Spice Box Books either. Also surprising is the fact that, for a man with such lofty literary aspirations, Tony didn't publish any writing of his own on what was effectively his imprint.

"He did occasionally come up with some very whimsical ideas, but none of them really came to much," recalls McKnight. "The problem was that Strat knew absolutely nothing about book publishing, which was quite different from pressing records, and I had some real battles with him. For instance, in those days you had to buy the paper well in advance of the publications and I always had to sit down and explain to Strat, and principally to Lee Gopthal, exactly why I needed the money up front to buy all this paper and Lee simply could not get his head around it. There were a lot of practical difficulties, but on the whole it was an amazing experience. I learned a lot myself, although not necessarily about publishing."

* * *

In March 1973, Tony and Lee Gopthal announced the formation of the Mooncrest label – a joint venture between B&C and Charisma that appeared to be nothing more than a new platform for many of the artists already recording for B&C.

The name had already been used by Charisma's publishing arm, when promotions manager Mike de Havilland was given the task of bringing together the music publishing for both Charisma and B&C and set up Mooncrest Music in early 1972, incorporating two other related publishing companies, Brewer Music and Trojan Music. Mooncrest the label was to be run by Tony and Lee Gopthal, with Clive Crawley, Mike de Havilland and B&C directors Jim Flynn and Fred Parsons. The first releases were singles from Nazareth and Libido[21]* and two albums, *Razamanaz* by Nazareth and *Sunny Days* by the Canadian band Lighthouse. The introduction of Mooncrest was designed to phase out the existing B&C and Pegasus record labels, leaving B&C to run purely as a marketing company. As Tony told *Billboard* magazine, "The emphasis will be on quality pop singles as a means of breaking albums."

Nazareth immediately gave the fledgling label a hit single when 'Broken Down Angel' broke into the top ten in April, closely followed by The Hotshots who reached the top five with a ska interpretation of 'Snoopy vs The Red Baron'. The Hotshots were actually Trojan recording artists The Cimarons with B&C's Clive Crawley taking the lead vocal. Both of these records fitted perfectly with Tony's original remit that Mooncrest would be a "quality pop label" working alongside the more progressive acts on Charisma and the reggae artists on Trojan. The label was also used to repackage tracks from the early Pegasus and B&C catalogue,

---

[21]   * Formerly Australian rock band Python Lee Jackson, but now with Dana Gillespie on vocals instead of Rod Stewart.

which included some quality folk material from Steeleye Span and Shirley Collins. When B&C subsequently crashed and burned in 1975, Mooncrest Records was sold on to Saga as part of the overall package and the label name was lost in the process.

Record plugger and harmonica player extraordinaire Judd Lander has good reason to remember Pegasus/Mooncrest artists Nazareth. "As well as plugging the records, I used to end up playing on people's albums and working with Nazareth is where I learned to play the bagpipes. Nazareth couldn't find a piper anywhere, so when I spotted a set of pipes in the Rose Morris shop in Shaftesbury Avenue, I borrowed them. I couldn't play them, but I went into the studio pretending that I could. I was having a real meltdown in the studio, it was the worst fucking din in the world." Lander's handiwork can be heard on the album *Exercises*, initially released on the short-lived B&C subsidiary Pegasus Records in 1972. The label only released about 14 albums before closing the same year, with the majority reissued on Charisma's new Mooncrest imprint in 1973.

Judd Lander's new found skill also helped him to win an unusual bet with the head of Charisma. Streaking was the new phenomenon; everyone seemed to be randomly removing all their clothes and running from A to B, disrupting sporting events and providing the tabloid press with extra column inches and much amusement. One night over a drink in the Nellie Dean, Charisma's out-of-hours office, Lander laid down the gauntlet and Tony, always one for a fun gamble, picked it up. "We called it The Smelly Dean in those days," says Lander. "Somebody had done a streak and everyone was talking about it. I announced that I could do better and we ended up having a bet that I would run from the Nellie Dean, down Dean Street and into Trident Studios in St Anne's Court, all the while playing the bagpipes and totally starkers. The next morning that's exactly what I did, marching naked into Trident where they had my clothes ready, got changed, left the studio and strolled back up to the pub. As I'm walking back, a couple of policemen came by and said, 'You haven't seen a fella with no clothes on, playing the bagpipes?' I said, 'Sergeant, have you been drinking?' and carried on. Walked back into the Nellie Dean to great applause and pocketed about £200 from the bet. Charisma was a mad, lovely, great, eccentric company that set the trend for a lot of the independent record labels. The whole ethos, taking up the fight against the bigger boys, it was the challenge and the adrenaline that made it all work."

The level of drinking in those days was such that Chris Briggs is astounded that any work ever got done at all. "Everyone drank all day in those days," says Briggs. "People would turn up at the office and whatever you were doing, you stopped to go and join them for a drink, that's the world that you lived in back then. It wasn't unusual to be coming back from lunch and just drop in to Warner Bros. to see Derek Taylor[22]* – and then it would be seven o'clock and you'd think, 'Oh shit, I never made it back to work.' Going around Soho with Glen, it was a world where no matter how drunk you were, everyone else appeared to be drunker – or higher. So whatever level of out-of-control-ness you thought you had achieved, you were never anywhere near catching up with those around you. I mean literally everyone drank. So if you went out for a business lunch you were offered a drink when you arrived, you might have a gin and tonic or a vodka and tonic, then you moved on to the white wine, then you had red wine, then you had a brandy to finish and that was just a normal lunch. Some people did that every day of their lives. We seemed to go for lunch with Strat an awful lot and going to lunch with Strat would mean that you'd sit down, get a menu and then you'd suddenly lose Strat for half an hour. Then you would look around and realise that he was over on the other side of the restaurant talking to Francis Bacon. This was usually in Wheeler's, the well-known oyster bar in Old Compton Street, and I just remember sitting there thinking, oh yes, of course, that's the artist Francis Bacon, as though it was the most natural thing in the world."

* * *

Looking to strengthen B&C and Charisma's sales presence in Scotland and the North East, Steve Weltman arranged for an advertisement to appear in *Music Week* magazine seeking to hire a Promotions Representative. As a result, Fraser Kennedy found himself added to Weltman's five-strong field promotion team, one of the first such teams in the record business at that time. This nationwide team was directly responsible for breaking all of the Charisma acts during the early seventies, selling records to retail, handling the local radio, press and TV and attending most, if not all, of the regional concerts.

"One of the things I couldn't believe, was that we never had to put in the sheet for our expenses," says Kennedy. "It was one of those amazing things where you would be out spending money all over the place, claiming it and nobody ever questioned it – and we did that for about two years. It was a terrific time, and a terrific job. My responsibilities were to sell and to promote Charisma, Mooncrest, Trojan and some Island stuff – there was some strange deal that we had with Island Records.

"I always remember being told that Island Records and Trojan Records were buying the same masters from the same people for the same amount of money and it was whoever could get it into the shops first who got the lead. The story was that the money would be put behind a tree in Jamaica

---

22   * Derek Taylor, former PR to The Beatles, had been appointed Head of Special Projects at Warners where his office was as hospitable as Apple's press office where he presided for two memorable years.

and then you'd go away for a bit and when you came back, the master tapes would be there. The money had gone and the tapes were there.

"We forged a great relationship with the dealers, they really liked Charisma, Island and all these small labels. The record shops were mostly independent dealers in those days, so they liked what those labels did. There was a real sense that if a record was on Charisma or Island then people would listen to it. If it was on Pye or Decca, maybe don't bother, but if it was on Charisma then it was definitely cooler."

About a year later, as part of the restructuring and strengthening of their promotional activities, the B&C/Charisma Group created the new position of Head of Promotions. Steve Jukes, who had just been appointed manager of the newly signed Sussex label, took over as head of the promotion department and Kennedy, who had previously been area promotion manager for Scotland and the North East, became overall Field Promotions Manager.

Meanwhile, over in America, in September 1973 Neil Bogart left Buddah Records to start up his own label, Casablanca, which would become home to Kiss and Donna Summer. Art Kass took over as sole president at Buddah. Barely two months later, Tony switched his complete North American distribution from Buddah to Atlantic Records, but Gail Colson believes the move was based solely on business, rather than any personal preferences. "Tony definitely liked Neil Bogart very much and he would have been missed, but I think the answer is most probably that either the contract had expired or was due to run out and Atlantic were offering the better deal."

Ahmet Ertegun, the Chairman of Atlantic Records, was among the most astute record men in the business. Having launched the label with a slew of successful black R&B acts he'd moved into rock, succeeding first with Crosby, Stills & Nash and then the UK bands Led Zeppelin and Yes. He now found himself handling a third British act that would go on to become another huge seller for the label, and the timing couldn't have been better for the Atlantic boss.

"My friend Tony Stratton Smith had told me about a phenomenal group he was recording, called Genesis," Ertegun told *Billboard* in November 1973. "Among the first projects we were to have under the Charisma deal was a new Genesis album, *Selling England By The Pound*, which we released in 1973. On record, the group had a sound like no other. On stage, its visual presentation was stunning and thoroughly original."

Art Kass must have been spitting feathers. Buddah had already started pressing the new Genesis album with their label when the changeover was announced. Buddah publicity director Nancy Lewis concurs with Gail: "I can't imagine that Charisma moved because of Neil's departure. I suspect it was a better offer – and as I recall, Buddah had paid very little for the initial deal."

Tony had already established the Charisma office in New York that was headed by Nancy Lewis, but B&C Finance Director Brian Gibbon has reservations about the success of this particular venture. "The Charisma office in the States was a complete disaster. I got the office funded through a friend at Atlantic Records, because by then Genesis were getting big enough in the States that we actually needed to be on the doorstep of Atlantic – just to make sure they were doing things properly. Then we sent Bob Barnes out there and he became our general manager in the States, which was probably a mistake. He was chosen partly because he was a safe pair of hands, but the problem was that it's such a big market and you've really got to know the market and we didn't. With hindsight it would probably have been better to take on an American guy to run it. It was not that Bob did such a bad job, but it's such a steep learning curve and it simply didn't work. That office was always haemorrhaging money."

The ever-reliable Bob Barnes had been thinking about a move away from the production department since late 1976, when he told Gail Colson, "I'll just stay on for a month, until you get someone else." Eventually, on New Year's Day 1979, Barnes left the familiar surroundings of Wardour Street and went to work in Charisma's New York office – initially alongside Nancy Lewis, who had been the Charisma contact in NYC since June 1977, and her assistant Roz Levy.

For Tony, of course, it was all a matter of priorities. Talking to *Record World* about the practicalities of a small independent record label relocating to New York, Tony was in mischievous mood: "There seems to be a greater sense of order and energy (in NYC), a more business-like approach. And being from England, California seems to be more of a foreign country than New York. For the special situation of a British company, the time difference between England and New York is important. Otherwise, if I were in Los Angeles I would have to call during drinking hours, which is absolutely unthinkable."

* * *

Today, in an era when corporate juggernauts ride roughshod over the artistic tendencies of their signings, and where image is all too often prized higher than talent, it is hard to imagine a time when the smaller independent record labels could compete with, and occasionally beat, the bigger corporations. Yet the late sixties and early seventies was such a time, when labels like Island, Transatlantic, Chrysalis and Charisma regularly stole the cream of the available talent from under the very noses of the big guns like CBS, EMI and MCA. Even the beloved DJ John Peel had a go at running his own label, working with Clive Selwood to form Dandelion, a short-lived company that spawned fine albums from Medicine Head, Bridget St John and Clifford T. Ward.

Writer John Tobler was an early champion of the label, and of Ward in particular. Writing for *Let It Rock* in October 1972 he said, "The Dandelion label, I hereby predict, is about to take off and astonish a lot of people who've dismissed the company as a load of no-hopers." He then went on to praise the likes of Bridget St John, Kevin Coyne and Medicine Head before adding: "Clifford T. Ward is a total newcomer to Dandelion and he's going to be a monster. He writes excellent songs, has a rocking little band with him, and Londoners will have seen his name on fly posters all over the place. When it happens, just remember who told you first."

Obviously sharing Tobler's opinion, Tony quietly enticed Ward away from John Peel's record company, thus ensuring that Tobler's prediction happened on The Famous Charisma Label instead. When it came to running a record label, perhaps John Peel lacked the vision and dogged persistence that enabled Tony to keep Charisma afloat. But timing is everything and quite soon after signing, the former teacher and somewhat reluctant pop star found success, with his delicate love songs 'Gaye' and 'Wherewithal' both making the charts.

Ward recalled how he came to change label: "Clive [Selwood] gave Tony Stratton Smith a pile of Dandelion albums to see if he was interested in any of the artists. Tony picked me out, but he made the wrong decision, as Medicine Head had the hits."

Fortunately, Tony's vision was different and in March 1973 Charisma released the beguiling 'Gaye', giving Ward his first hit single, much to the surprise of the singer himself. "It wasn't one of my favourite songs," said Ward. "It was just a song for the album, but Charisma thought it would make a good single and they released it. There were three girls I knew called Gaye and I suppose they were all part of the Gaye in the song."

Although the decision to sign Ward was based on the strength of that early Dandelion album, Tony was surely beguiled by a song that contained the line: "I've been reading Browning, Keats and William Wordsworth..."

Ward's album *Home Thoughts From Abroad* was completed in February 1973 and released on April 20. Peter Thompson was brought in to work his PR magic on Clifford, homing in on the 'schoolteacher turned pop singer' angle and ensuring that almost every newspaper in the country ran with the story. 'Gaye' spent around 15 weeks in the charts, peaking in July at a respectable number eight. Ward's plaintive ballad was up against stiff competition: David Bowie's 'Life On Mars' and 'Saturday Night's Alright For Fighting' by Elton John, alongside top ten hits for The Osmonds, Mungo Jerry, Slade and, more bizarrely, Peters & Lee. The *Home Thoughts* album fared less well, spending a couple of weeks in the lower reaches of the top

40. In terms of actual records sold, the figures for both were quite high, but such was the healthy state of the industry at the time that any artist needed to sell an enórmous amount of vinyl to break into the top ten. According to Clive Selwood, 'Gaye' also made the top five in Brazil, yet Clifford barely saw a 'cruzeiro novo' from his South American sales.

The North American market proved to be more of a problem, as finance director Brian Gibbon recalls. "Interestingly, we got that one big single away ['Gaye'] but we couldn't release it in America because of the title. I spoke to the record company people – it was Atlantic Records, I think and they said, 'Well, you can just change the title.' Understandably Clifford said, 'I don't want to change the title, it's the name of the bloody song.' They told us it would never get it played there because of the connotations. We had to say, 'Look, he can't change the title because he sings it all the way through the damn song.' It was a ridiculous situation."

That August, Tony hosted a lavish Luxford House party to celebrate the success of his new artist. Ward's personal manager Ken Wright turned up, but Ward failed to appear and sent no apology for his absence. His dislike of socialising and distaste for the attendant fuss and nonsense surrounding a 'hit record' was about to become a potential problem for Charisma.

Ward continued to maintain a low profile. He bought a farmhouse and loved being at home with his family. He felt no desire to spend time away from home. Managing an artist who flatly refused to tour and promote their own work is the kiss of death to most music careers and, certainly, Ward could have fared so much better had he gone out on the road. But Tony kept faith in the man and his writing ability, and Charisma continued to put out his records despite Clifford's complete refusal to appear at a venue somewhere near you. As record producer and later Ward's manager Clive Selwood remarked: "Tony had sunk a lot of money into Genesis, but I knew he had this tenacity. If he believed in an artiste – which is why he would have signed them in the first place – he would stick with them as long as was commercially possible."

Having signed an artist, Tony would often take a back seat in their day-to-day management, but he would occasionally put his journalistic background to good use by helping out with sleeve notes, marketing and advertising. As he told *Music Week*, "It was not unknown for me to do ad layouts on the back of envelopes..."

The press advertising for Charisma records tended to be fairly straightforward, often just a picture of the album sleeve, a succinct headline and a small piece of body copy. One perfect example appeared in *ZigZag* 49, January/February 1975, and made full use of the diversity of artists on the label. Pictured were album covers for Clifford T. Ward's *Escalator* and Peter Hamill's *Nadir's Big Chance* and the headline told the story perfectly.

It simply stated: "You'll hate one of these albums… chances are you'll love the other."

* * *

Another of Tony's more problematical signings was Jo'burg Hawk, a mixed-race band from Sandton in South Africa. Frustrated by police raids on their communal home where black people and white people were banned from living together, their manager somehow persuaded Tony their home was on Charisma. "We wanted to develop the African side of our music, but it was becoming increasingly clear that we could not do it in South Africa," said guitarist Dave Ornellas. "We needed to spread our wings, break the shackles of apartheid and let the music come through."

With the world, and particularly the UK, focused on the injustices of apartheid in South Africa, the people and the media in Britain generally welcomed Jo'burg Hawk with open arms. With Tony and Charisma behind them, they soon found themselves working hard in London, playing three gigs at the Marquee Club, given star billing at the Reading Festival and opening a tour for hard rock trio Budgie. The label released *Africa She Too Can Cry*, a compilation of tracks from their first two records. From struggling to earn a living on the southern tip of Africa, they were now receiving the full rock-star treatment; the deal negotiated by Hawk's manager Geoff Lonstein including flights to the UK and accommodation in a magnificent three-storey house in the comfortable north London suburb of Highgate. "We were treated like real stars, with a fleet of Bentleys at the airport to collect our 16-member party when we landed in London," said Ornellas. "We thought we had arrived."

The reality was somewhat different, however. Despite their fancy house in one of London's smartest neighbourhoods the band was permanently broke, with their manager keeping them on a shoestring budget. Both Ornellas and new guitarist Julian Laxton remember how they had to survive on a meagre hand-out of £1 a day. Yet they proved to be especially popular in Belgium, bizarrely representing that country in the Eurovision song contest and finishing ninth. Hawk also toured Scandinavia at the end of 1973 and went down so well that breaking America was expected to be the next step. Unfortunately, Charisma were excluded from representing the band in the US due to a clause in their contract and the label gradually lost interest. As the gigs dried up and the momentum died down, the band disintegrated and its members flew back to South Africa.

Paul Conroy, with whom the band stayed after moving out of their fancy Highgate lodgings, was witness to their antipathy towards city life. One night one of them got stoned and freaked out, barking at the moon in Conroy's back garden. "The band were all going stir crazy and shouting about wanting the wide open spaces – and [roadie] Ron's answer was to drive them all the way down to Beachy Head and let them out to have a run around down there!"

Tony may have signed Jo'Burg Hawk with the very best of intentions, but not everyone saw it as an unqualified success and certainly not the editorial team at *Zigzag*, who were clearly surprised at the extravagant deal offered to Lonstein. They were quick to take a sly dig at Tony, who only two years before had stepped in to save the magazine from going under. The May 1976 issue contained a half-page commentary under the heading 'Famous Mistakes in Rock History – number two of an occasional series: Tony Stratton Smith journeys to the distant shores of the Zambezi to sign Jo'burg Hawk to Charisma Records.' Next to a vintage line drawing of a group of African warriors, the tongue-in-cheek caption read as follows: Jo'burg manager (dressed up in captured British uniform for the occasion): "Hello dere, Bwana. We wants £25,000 as an advance, 15% artists royalties, minimum guaranteed earnings of £250,000 over de next three years, an' unlimited supplies of ganja." Stratton Smith (sweating heavily in the noon-day sun): "It's a deal. Come along men, let's get back to camp before those bloody porters find where I've hidden the vodka." And just in case Strat took it a little too much to heart, underneath in small print was added: 'Just joking, Tony old chap!'

The signing of Jo'Burg Hawk had not been a complete disaster, by any means, but Paul Conroy knew the frustrations involved in trying to get behind some of Tony's more left-field ideas. "Strat would get these big ideas, he had these visions, and he was the most charming man," recalled Conroy. "He was totally believable and would explain things in such an intellectual way that you simply couldn't argue with him. We would all bitch like hell and say to each other, 'Why are we doing this, why are we doing that', but Strat had such warmth and charm that he could draw you into something. In fact, Gail and Glen were the only two who would actually stand up to him and say, 'Strat, you're fucking mad, why are you even trying that?'"

By his own admission, and particularly in the early days, Tony was guided as much by his heart as by his head and when his more unconventional ideas did work out everyone reaped the rewards, no one minding the extra footslog to make Strat's dreams happen. Conversely, Tony's whims and romantic visions could also confound and frustrate those in the Charisma office, as Glen Colson found out on more than one occasion. "Strat said to me, 'Glen, I want you to take this young man down to the studio...' and it was the young boy that starred in the film *Death In Venice*. Strat had signed him up as a singer and he wanted me to take him over to Trident Studios and record some demos with him."

The beautiful young man in question was Björn Andrésen, a Swedish actor and musician who caused quite a stir when playing 14-year-old Tadzio in the 1971 film adaptation of the Thomas Mann novel. In the film he becomes the object of affection for a dying older man, played by Dirk Bogarde. Four or five years on, Tony was still clearly smitten, too.

"So I took him down to Trident," continues Colson. "I got the mics set up, the engineer was ready and I said to him, 'Alright mate, go for it.' He started to sing 'Her Majesty's a pretty nice girl, but she doesn't have a lot to say,' which was the old Paul McCartney song[23]*. I said, 'OK how about trying one of your own songs' and he replied, 'Oh, that's the only one I know', and so that's all he sang. Strat had flown him over from God knows where to do these demos. But that's exactly the kind of thing Strat would do. It infuriated us all, because we wanted him to sign people like Dr Feelgood."

Tony always kept a close eye on some of his former charges and with Charisma up and running, he got back in touch with Beryl Marsden to ask her to record a single for his new label – a cover version of Bob Dylan's 'All Along The Watchtower'. Beryl was somewhat surprised at Tony's choice of song, but the chance to work with her old boss was too good to resist and she travelled down to Trident Studios in St Anne's Court, nevertheless.

Once again, Glen Colson was given the job of putting the session together, but it wasn't a complete success. "I did produce a session with Beryl at Trident Studios and we used all the regular Charisma musicians, but it was probably my last session as I was somewhat overwhelmed by the experience. God only knows where the tapes are now." Sadly, Beryl's long shot at being a Charisma recording artist fell at the first hurdle. The single was never released.

With any level of fame and celebrity, there will always be someone on hand only too happy to take advantage – and Stratton Smith's good nature could be a prime target. For his part, Tony loved being the centre of attention but while at the epicentre of back-slapping and bonhomie, he was not always able to separate the genuine well-wisher from the hanger-on. Paul Conroy knew the type. "Strat used to walk into the Nellie Dean and everybody would say, 'Ahh, it's good old Strat' – whereas we would all be more honest with him about things, but he didn't always like being told," says Conroy.

"I think he got used to people saying, 'You are marvellous Strat, you're great, good old Strat', and his interests were so wide that he was meeting all sorts of people who just wanted to be part of showbiz or the music business. We could smell them, you know – and he was like that when hiring new staff as well: sometimes you'd wonder if Strat genuinely liked them or whether he just wanted to help people out."

Glen Colson agrees: "We did resent some people, because we classed ourselves as Strat's mates and a couple of times – well quite a few

---

23   * 'Her Majesty', the closing track on The Beatles' *Abbey Road*.

times actually – people would seemingly float into Strat's life and he would recklessly give them carte blanche to do things. We resented that, because Charisma was our life. We'd thrown our lot in with Strat, but we knew that these people were just crawlers and they were rubbing our noses in it."

Others suggest that once anyone got too close to Tony for his own comfort, he would drop them, even those who had been part of the inner circle, Glen Colson included. Glen finally walked out of the Soho Square offices in 1974, after arguing furiously with Tony over Charisma's musical policies. "I think he was only too pleased to shed people that knew a lot about him and instead have people working for him that only knew him by reputation," says Colson. The over-riding problem was, as Paul Conroy succinctly put it, "While Gail was trying to make sense out of the finances, Strat would be giving away the family silver."

For the most part, if he felt he could make a difference, Tony genuinely did his best to offer a helping hand. One person to benefit from Tony's generosity was a young record plugger called Simon Alexander, now better known as the illusionist/magician Simon Drake. A friend of a friend, Tony somehow discovered that Simon was alone during Christmas 1974 and invited him to Luxford. "He sent Cracky to pick me up and drive me down to Luxford, where I spent Christmas with Strat, Cracky and the journalist Michael Wale. Michael spent the entire time in bed as I recall, as he was ill and in considerable pain, I never found out what that was. Strat was always extremely gentlemanly and kind and there was never a hint of any ulterior motive. He was like a very gentle uncle figure towards me."

Simon Drake would crop up again at various key points in Stratton Smith's life, including finding himself the focal point for two of the more bizarre ideas from Tony's vivid imagination.

Working across town at Nat Joseph's Transatlantic Records, Martin Lewis was handling the publicity for Gerry Rafferty, Billy Connolly, Stray and the Pasadena Roof Orchestra. However it was the mountain of publicity generated for the folk rock band Gryphon, often appearing in the most unexpected of places, that really impressed Tony.

"I was really on a roll when Strat first offered me a job," he says. "I was immensely flattered, but I didn't want to take it. He didn't want me to replace Glen Colson or anything like that, in fact he wanted me to work with Glen, which was flattering but I liked my position at Transatlantic. I was total kingpin there, whereas I would be one of several people at Charisma, so I said, 'Thank you Tony, I'm very happy where I am, but let's keep this association going.' Turning the job down actually gave me more power with Strat than I expected, the power of saying 'no'. You simply didn't say no to Strat, I mean why would you not want to work for Charisma, but he took it very nicely. I told him that I'd only just started and I loved Nat Joseph,

I had a really good rapport with him, so Strat said 'OK, I respect that.' He respected my loyalty to Nat and that deepened our friendship – even though I was only young, he knew I was doing a good job.

"I did sometimes wish that Nat could have been as eclectic as Strat, but he was not as passionate about the artists. Nat didn't like to go drinking, whereas I did and so did Strat. He was social, he was gregarious and he loved to tell stories, he was an anecdotist, the life and soul of the party, and I loved all that. Nat had seen enough of the business and the last thing he wanted to do was go down the pub and hang out with the artists. Socially I wanted to be with Strat, so for several years my life was split between Nat and Strat. Nat was my day-job, my wife, and in that sense Strat was my mistress. Because while I loved Nat Joseph, I had much more fun with Strat!"

* * *

Tony's intuitive ear for an off-the-wall hit worked once more in 1974. The Australian folk singer Gary Shearston, who had been recording since the early sixties, arrived in England in 1972 after four years in America where visa problems had prevented him from performing and, consequently, the album he recorded for Warner Bros. went unreleased. On signing with Charisma, some of these tracks were rerecorded in London for his *Dingo* album, but producer Phil Chapman was struggling with Shearston's cover of Cole Porter's 'I Get A Kick Out Of You'.

"When we had finished the album, I couldn't help feeling a sense of unease whenever 'I Get A Kick Out Of You' went through," recalled Chapman. "On the multi-track recording, all the featured instruments played continuously from start to finish, and given Gary's almost-trademark underplayed delivery on what was already a non-dramatic song, the end result was somewhat soporific.

"So, one Saturday morning I went into Olympic studio three determined to do something, anything, to this track. Seven hours later, after stripping it right back and mixing it section by section, I finally ended up with something that I thought was listenable. On Monday morning I played the remix to Hugh Murphy, the producer, and we both agreed it was much better than the existing version, but we still hid it on side two. We were both dumbfounded when Stratton Smith picked 'I Get A Kick Out Of You' as the single."

Tony's intuition proved correct and the single gave Charisma another top ten hit. Gary recorded two albums for the label, but never managed to follow up his single success. Sadly their association didn't end well, much to Tony's chagrin, as Pete Frame recalls: "Gary became disenchanted with Charisma and signed with some high-powered manager. I can't remember his name – but Strat wasn't keen on this guy. The record company/artist relationship went sour and then disintegrated."

Shearston later recorded a version of 'A Whiter Shade Of Pale' for Transatlantic Records, but the single fared little better and failed to trouble the charts. He returned to Australia, where he continued to write and perform, and in 1992 he was ordained as an Anglican minister. He tended to a congregation in New South Wales until his death in 2013.

* * *

After recording the fourth Jackson Heights album, *Bump 'n Grind* for Vertigo Records, bassist Lee Jackson was looking to ring the changes once more and in August 1973 he called up Swiss keyboard wizard Patrick Moraz, inviting him to join. Unwilling to join the ailing Heights, Moraz suggested forming a new band and in a bid to repeat his earlier success with a progressive keyboard-led trio, Jackson brought back former Nice drummer Brian Davison and the new outfit became Refugee. Through his earlier connections with Tony and Lee Jackson, Johnny Toogood completed the continuity by managing the new outfit.

"I went out to Switzerland and found Patrick Moraz," says Toogood. "Lee told me to see if I could get hold of this guy and bring him back. Refugee only made the one record, but it was an amazing album."

Lee Jackson admits to being disappointed with the first Charisma LP he made as Jackson Heights. "The second band were a lot better, but we'd moved on to another label by then. I still remained friendly with Strat though; I used to go to all of Charisma's social events and visited Luxford, many, many times. He would hold these big parties on the lawn. In fact Jackson Heights' first rehearsal was in one of the barns there. However by the time we started Refugee, I think somebody had abused that privilege because Luxford suddenly wasn't available anymore, but Strat paid for us to go into rehearsal at various places in London for about three months, while we were putting the new band together with Patrick Moraz and Brian Davison. That band was hideously complicated, but very good."

As well as naming Jackson Heights, Tony came up with the name Refugee. "We were having one of those long sessions in the Nellie Dean pub and for three hours we'd been at it and nothing was coming out. When Strat arrived, I said, 'I'm off, I've got a date' and so off I went to the Speakeasy. The next morning I got a phone call from Strat and he said, 'It's alright Lee, we've got the name, we're going to call the band Refugee.'"

With Lee and Brian back in the fold, Tony was more than happy to put the new line-up back on his label and they recorded one album for Charisma in March 1974. Although it was a promising debut, the band barely lasted a few months, playing only a handful of gigs before Moraz was headhunted by Yes to replace Rick Wakeman. After one audition, Moraz landed the job. "I had to tell Lee Jackson and Brian Davison the next day," says Moraz, "I told them with tears in my eyes. They were very nice and gracious about it. We still did the three outstanding gigs and they went very well. It really was a sad day for me when I had to tell them."

Around the same time, a strange and tragic event occurred. British Hammond organ maestro Graham Bond, who had been out of the music scene for some time, had heard the rumour that Patrick Moraz was going to quit Refugee for Yes and telephoned the Charisma office to put himself forward as a replacement. Bond, once a brilliant R&B musician, had been troubled for some time with drugs and mental health problems – so perhaps it was understandable that Charisma was less than enthusiastic in their response to his call. A few days later, on May 8, 1974, Bond walked onto the platform at Finsbury Park underground station and jumped in front of a train.

Chapter 11

The Fiasco

"From a creative point of view, Tony was brilliant but occasionally his personal life did impinge on his business acumen, so sometimes we were in a salvage position on certain things, where we all thought, 'Well that's never going to work' – and usually it didn't."
Brian Gibbon, Charisma accountant

Working in the accounts department of a record label can be much the same as working in accounts departments at any large company, a mundane but necessary role in the scheme of things, enlivened only by scraps of information that reveal precisely how many records are selling and how much a rock star is actually earning.

Working in the accounts department at Charisma, however, was a trying task at the best of times. While the cash flow occasionally slowed to barely a trickle, the working day was never dull. "A lot of the time the situation was on a knife-edge," says accountant Peter Mills, who quickly discovered that for all the bluster, for all the press adverts and for all the optimism that gushed from the lips of the company's founder and mouthpiece, all was not always well in the piggy bank.

"When I first joined there was a guy in accounts called Roger Moore and at some stage I think he got a bit miffed that he hadn't been promoted, so he left and I took over from him," says Mills. "During my first few weeks with the company I was just trying to settle in and catch up on some projects that needed sorting out, but the phones were constantly ringing with people wanting to come in. Fortunately Roger was still dealing with the Charisma accounts and he managed to hold them at bay very well, so I learned quite a bit from him."

Mills soon released that the problem arose not just because Tony Stratton Smith often went ahead with projects without considering the financial liability but because of the number of people on the payroll. "I forget how many there were at any one point, but when I started at Charisma we were in Soho Square and we had quite a lot of space, so there must have been about 15 to 20 people employed there – and I think Old Compton Street was the same. So there was quite a big payroll, obviously a lot less than it would be today, but in terms of income it was really quite high and that was obviously the biggest overhead. We were never flush with funds and we were constantly going back to Phonogram and asking for a further advance on UK sales. I can also remember taking a few trips over to New York with Brian Gibbon to try and wheedle money out of Atlantic and people like that, for advances on sales. It was a real struggle."

Such experiences would stand Peter Mills and the rest of the Charisma accounts department in good stead, as the financial pool became even murkier when, by 1975, B&C Records found itself in serious financial trouble, which led to Charisma changing their distribution account to the much larger Phonogram.

With Charisma already distributed in Europe by Phonogram International, this seemed a logical and necessary step to take. "We had to go cap in hand to them to bail us out or we would have gone under as well," admits Gail Colson.

The circumstances surrounding the demise of B&C are mired in confusion, but an article in the October 1976 issue of *Black Music* magazine offered some details and is probably as close as anyone will get to what actually happened. In March 1975, Saga Records was looking to expand and placed an advert in *Music Week* stating their wish to buy a record label as a 'going concern'. Essentially a classical/MOR/budget label, Saga wanted to move into the rock market and although their ad brought no response, Saga's chief accountant Bill Ross suggested that B&C might be willing to sell.

The previous year, Saga had pressed about £20,000 worth of records for the B&C and Trojan labels and it had taken Ross a good six months to reclaim the money. This confirmed in Ross' mind the industry rumour that B&C were in financial trouble and thus ripe for a takeover. Saga boss Marcel Rodd telephoned B&C directors Lee Gopthal and Brian Gibbon and although they weren't prepared to sell the company outright, an arrangement was suggested. For a 10% interest in the company, Saga would loan B&C £150,000, dependent on viewing the audited figures. Bill Ross spent a week in the B&C accounts department and was so worried by his findings that Saga pulled out, but as if to corroborate the trouble they were in, B&C came straight back with an offer to sell the whole company on two conditions – that the offer was not less than £25,000 and that the deal could be concluded within 24 hours.

Wary of this, Saga proposed the formation of two new subsidiary companies, B&C Recordings Limited and Trojan Recordings Limited (retaining the existing board of directors) and that on formation, the assets of the parent companies (stock, recording contracts and masters) should be transferred to them, but none of the liabilities. The new subsidiaries would then be sold immediately to Saga. The plan was agreed and on May 31, 1975, Saga handed over a cheque for just under £30,000. However, instead of using the money to re-float their floundering company, B&C/Trojan simply paid off their overdraft at the bank, dismissed all their staff and applied to be put into voluntary liquidation. What exactly went on between the old company, their auditors and the liquidators remains shrouded in mystery.

Saga subsequently discovered that their purchase was far from the 'extensive rock catalogue' they thought they were getting. Both Nazareth and Steeleye Span's contracts had run out and Charisma had taken the decision to withdraw their distribution agreement and place it elsewhere. Saga also thought they were obtaining the services of key B&C and Trojan staff, but many saw the potential wreck coming and jumped ship.

Adrian Sear was one of those to find themselves on a fast sinking vessel. "I stayed at B&C right until the end," he says, "but the company was already in trouble before that. B&C did have Nazareth who were doing well, and the Trojan records were still selling very well, but what put the final nail in the coffin was Charisma leaving. I don't think Strat actually fell out with Lee Gopthal, simply that he was offered a better deal. Saga were famous for selling very cheap records to supermarkets and in fact they had some amazing albums, they were very good at classical."

Sales Manager Steve Weltman had seen signs that both companies were in danger of overspending, a situation that eventually came to a head when Charisma and B&C asked him to employ a 20–24-strong sales force. "I told them this was crazy and was not affordable," relates Weltman. "TSS said that we had to get the extra people as we were going to sign Pink Floyd. Lee Gopthal said that he was about to get the Buddah and Kama Sutra labels for distribution. I said, 'Let's revisit the sales team idea once those deals are concluded.' They both said I should go ahead and hire the people. I told them it would make both companies go bankrupt, but they still disagreed. I said in that case I would have to resign, but when I got to my office the next day to tell my team, I was told that I had been made a director. I resigned anyway and went off to manage Nazareth for Mountain Management."

Over in the design and marketing department, Frank Sansom also thought his career was finished – yet again. "I arrived back from a luncheon appointment to find a little strip of paper on my desk saying that I had been made redundant. So I was just contemplating what this would actually mean, when Strat walked in and said, 'Don't worry, you're coming to work for Charisma, here's a cheque.' Strat took care of it all and that was when I actually moved across to Charisma full time. With B&C I had been looking after all the labels, Trojan, Mooncrest and Charisma, so I always felt that I had one foot in each camp, but it was good to know that you were wanted to be part of the team, that was really nice of him."

Charisma took on several B&C staff, mainly from the marketing and production departments. As Brian Gibbon recalls, "At that time Charisma itself didn't really have a marketing department, it was more of an A&R label so to speak, plus they still had the agency and there was a small publishing unit as well. Some of those who were doing that work at B&C went under the Charisma banner. Unfortunately, I found myself in the middle of this conflict between Lee and Tony and the B&C staff inherited by Charisma, even though the B&C staff that moved to Charisma were pretty good, I mean nobody else had the experience in their particular fields of marketing and promotion."

The B&C 'fiasco', as it is often referred to, certainly caused a few headaches for Charisma lawyer Tony Seddon. "When I first joined, most of my contractual work had been with B&C and Trojan because they had the bigger turnover, so you would go to see Strat and Lee Gopthal," he recalls. "They were not partners in a legal sense, but they shared offices and staff together. I'm sure they had their differences, but Strat recognised Lee as being a music man and Gopthal certainly had a way to get to the reggae market and discover people. When B&C went bust we had a lot of work to do to make sure that Charisma didn't get dragged down with them. Officially Charisma were always a separate company but because they lived together, so to speak, they shared a lot of expenses, they shared part of the distribution and were often referred to as being part of the same group of companies."

It was a worrying time for all concerned and Gail Colson was in no doubt that Charisma was close to going the same way as their former distribution company. "When B&C went under, Tony and I went cap in hand to Phonogram International and it was actually Phonogram in Holland that bailed us out. I distinctly remember ringing around the studios, the printers, ringing every single person that we dealt with to explain the situation. I was saying that because B&C had gone under we wouldn't be able to pay the bills that month, but we were desperately trying to get the finances. It was, 'You have my word that we will pay, but please, you've got to give us time,' – otherwise we could easily have gone under as well. There were at least a couple of months where we were so close to going under."

Some have suggested that Lee Gopthal blamed Tony for B&C's demise, but according to Gail Colson, Charisma simply wasn't strong enough financially to help him out. While the two companies severed all ties, and Tony and Lee barely spoke to each other in the aftermath, Brian Gibbon takes a slightly different opinion. "I don't think blame is the right word. I think 'support' is the right word, because when B&C went under I believe that Tony could possibly have done more for Lee Gopthal," he says. "Not by bringing Lee into the Charisma fold necessarily, but maybe supporting him a little more – because if it wasn't for B&C in those early years, Charisma would have gone down. So I think their falling-out was a shame and many times I was put in the middle of all that. Between Lee, who effectively employed me in the first place, and Tony and then having to negotiate the severance of a person who actually helped start the business, which is always difficult."

It was no secret that Tony actively shied away from confrontations, even with artists themselves, and then either Gail or Brian Gibbon would have to take control. "From a creative point of view, Tony was brilliant," says Gibbon, "but occasionally his personal life did impinge on his business acumen, so sometimes we were in a salvage position on certain things, where we all thought, 'Well that's never going to work' – and usually it didn't."

Barry McKay, who took over as Lindisfarne's manager, also found quite a few holes in the corporate purse. "Strat had such faith in Genesis," he says, "that the money earned by Lindisfarne, which should have gone to them, actually paid for Genesis while they struggled to make it. This was topped off when the sharks at B&C Records went bust with what remained of Lindisfarne's earnings, which was a very large sum indeed. At one stage Charisma would have gone bust if Lindisfarne had not let them off having to pay royalties when due. When Charisma then made its fortune with Genesis, were Lindisfarne compensated? Of course not! Yet Lindisfarne, being the decent people they always were, attended Strat's memorial service. Of course, everyone liked Strat."

A direct result of B&C's demise was that after two years in Soho Square, in July 1975 Charisma moved back into their old offices at 70 Old Compton Street. Peter Mills became company secretary and Sue Sinclair and Roz Bea came in to help out in the accounts department, while Lisa Bonnichon joined as production assistant to Bob Barnes. Beverley Veal set out to make the tricky position of switchboard operator/receptionist her own. In a series of drastic cuts and changes, Charisma shut down Mother Management, previously handled by Fred Munt who promptly set up his own company with String Driven Thing as his first client. Charisma Books also closed down, forcing Cathy McKnight and Sarah Radclyffe out into the cold, and even the booking agency fell by the wayside, leaving Paul Conroy and Nigel Kerr to move on to pastures new.

* * *

In many respects Tony tripped lightly through these financial shenanigans. If he was troubled by anything at all it was more likely to be his weight, which gained steadily in direct proportion to his success. Mingling, as he did, among the snake-hipped, tight-jeaned, half-starved musicians in his charge, Tony's well-upholstered belly could easily have become the cause for mild amusement, if not savage ribbing. But as anyone on the receiving end of a playground bully will testify, attack is the best form of defence – and a touch of self-deprecation never goes amiss.

There are many examples of Tony's witty response to his comfortable build, often in the sign-off to his personal correspondence. In a letter to Dwight Hansen, an American Van der Graaf fan, he wrote, "Sorry to be so slow in responding, but the summer months are actually our busiest – I haven't been able to look at a beach for months. Never mind, that might have saved me – anything so large and white on a beach will have invited a harpoon!" In another reply to a close friend, Tony suggests that they meet up for a meal and a drink, and concludes by saying, "But no jokes about me getting too fat – I know it, I know it, I know it only too well!"

In person too, he could use his charm to disarm. The very first time he met the composer Jim Parker at a meeting in the Charisma office to discuss a collaboration with the poet John Betjeman, Tony introduced himself by saying, "Hello, I'm Tony – but I'm usually known as Fat Strat."

At one point Tony's weight ballooned to an uncomfortable size, as Lloyd Beiny remembers during a night at La Chasse. "Strat used to get so drunk that he really couldn't function and Cracky, his chauffeur, was always there to make sure that he got home safely and then got to work on time the next morning. But I remember on one occasion, Strat had put on a lot of weight, I mean he was really big, and he simply couldn't bend over and do his shoelaces up. So Cracky was summoned. We're all sitting at the bar in La Chasse, with Cracky sitting patiently over the other side and Tony calls him over, 'Dear boy, would you mind...' – and his role was simply to bend down and tie up Strat's shoelaces."

Tony never learned to drive a car. Even if he had, his love of the drink would have made driving downright dangerous, if not impossible. As far back as January 1972 he had been persuaded to get a car and a driver, as he told *Melody Maker*'s Roy Hollingworth, "So that I could do 'the bit' properly, whatever 'the bit' may be."

It was a rare allusion to the trappings of the successful city businessman. But a man needs to get around town in style, so what marque to choose? It had to be British. Several friends remember his early dalliance with Rover and Wolseley cars, both fine examples of home grown motor manufacturing, with Wolseley Motors Limited largely based in his beloved Birmingham. However, the car that most people associate with Tony was the Bristol; a true English thoroughbred of an automobile, relatively new to the scene having been launched in 1945 as a division of the same Bristol Aeroplane Company that produced the Beaufighter and the Blenheim.

Ian Campbell, part of the racing crowd that included Vera Bampton, Noel Bennett and Simon Christian, worked in the wine and spirits trade, with Berry, Bros & Rudd in St James's Street, which Tony patronised whenever he required an expensive bottle of wine as a gift. He and Tony became firm friends, and he believes Tony was introduced to the Bristol car range by two of his racing friends, Ron and Vera Bampton. As you might expect from the sub-division of an aeroplane manufacturer, their vehicles were built to exacting aircraft standards, using aircraft construction methods and under strict quality control, and the Bristol quickly earned a reputation as among the finest cars in the world. The Bristol 411 was capable of reaching a top speed of 143mph and while speeding was not an option in the tight warren of streets around Soho, it was quite possible on the open roads outside of London. Tony entrusted his big and beautiful beast of a car to driver Cracky, a wild-eyed Welshman and general rock'n'roll roadie.

One of Cracky's earliest gigs was working as the road manager for Geno Washington & The Ram Jam Band. Sometime around 1967, he and fellow roadie Mike Pearson found themselves back home in Wales prior to a gig in Cardiff and Mike stopped by the print shop where he used to work. Among the apprentices was a 15-year-old boy called Keith Allen, who listened to the tales of the two roadies and, lured by the apparent glamour of life on the road – and the expectation of three weeks of sex, drugs and rock'n'roll – ran away from home via the Geno tour van.

In London, Cracky Jones moved into what was effectively a roadies' commune, sharing a large upstairs flat in Oxford & Cambridge Mansions, on the Old Marylebone Road. Most of the incumbents were Welsh and hailed from Llanelli, as did Cracky, and among them was at least one plucky female who, rumour had it, worked as a Bunny Girl at the Playboy Club in Park Lane. Derec Jones remembers Cracky having breathing problems, the result of having only one lung and chain-smoking Turkish cigarettes. The flatmates all frequented a nearby pub that regularly put on drag acts and one night, long after everyone else had gone to bed, Cracky returned from the pub with a posse of punters and drag queens in tow, to give them a guided tour of the flat.

According to American guitarist Brian Goff, during the early seventies Cracky was touring America with Led Zeppelin as a personal roadie to bassist John Paul Jones. Goff first met Cracky in Los Angeles when Zeppelin passed through in 1972 and by the time they hooked up again in London soon afterwards the Welsh roadie was working and driving for Tony. Consequently, the teenage Goff found himself spending time in Tony's company, staying at Luxford, being driven down to Brighton to see Monty Python and introduced to Graham Chapman at the Marquee. Apart from being mesmerised by the old English grandeur of Luxford House, his fondest memory happened in the back seat of the Rover, driven by Cracky, en route to a gig somewhere. "I asked if the window could be rolled up a little," says Goff "and Tony just chuckled and said, 'Oh, you are a delicate flower aren't you!'"

Cracky worked with Van der Graaf Generator and was immortalised on the sleeve of their album *Pawn Hearts* in the cryptic credit 'Nohjnohjcrackycracky' (apparently the band's affectionate catchphrase for their two Welsh roadies), but he was also shared out among the other Charisma bands. During one particularly long and arduous Lindisfarne tour in late 1971, Cracky was drafted in as a replacement for one poor roadie who couldn't stand the pace. The experienced Cracky was made of far sterner stuff and slotted seamlessly into the rigorous life on the road.

Lindisfarne's Ray Laidlaw remembers the Welshman well. "Cracky was a lovely boy. He had a mysterious past and the perceived wisdom was that he had been a sniper in the army. I don't think he had, but we all played up to it and I think he quite liked that. The funny thing with Cracky was that although he set up the road crew, he had asthma, and as soon as he tried to lift anything heavy, he couldn't do it. So he ended up being Strat's driver and then driving us around for a bit, but he was good fun and always a good craic."

In addition to Cracky's driving skills, Glen Colson recalls that the Welshman was employed as Tony's cook, but was prone to the odd culinary mistake. "They were down at Luxford one time and Cracky always fancied himself as a bit of a chef. He found a bottle of wine to use in the gravy and Strat went absolutely fucking berserk when he found out – because this particular bottle was priceless, it must have been worth something like three or four hundred quid and Cracky went and used it to make gravy."

Working as Tony's chauffeur, Cracky's main task was to ferry people around London in the Bristol, at least when he wasn't engaged in "chatting to unorthodox ladies in Soho coffee bars", according to Terence Dackombe, booking agent for GT Moore & The Reggae Guitars. On one memorable occasion Tony sent his car on a long-distance outing to Devon, slightly outside of the regular runs around Soho. Although we can't be certain that Cracky was the driver that day, it would have given him the chance to really open up the Bristol's V8 engine. Tony's cousin Patricia Widdows recalls the story: "Tony's mother Mollie lived to see his success and during the latter part of her life she moved down at Babbacombe in Devon. She was proud of her son, but was never overly impressed by shows of wealth or lifestyle. On this occasion, having forgotten her birthday, Tony sent his chauffeur-driven car all the way down to deliver a large bouquet of flowers to her little cottage. Mollie was not impressed, in fact she was a little embarrassed, but then Mollie lived a quiet life. The family always found the story amusing."

The big old Bristol and narrow country roads were not really compatible; add in a dark night and a country bus and there could only be one outcome, as Bush Telfer, a friend and associate from the Lambourn racing community, remembers. "It was a typical boozy Saturday night – it must have been, because the buses were still running from Newbury through Lambourn – and Cracky was driving back to The George to drop someone off, when he hit a bus. Because these were country roads, they're not wide enough for a bus and a Bristol to pass each other without one or the other pulling right in to the side. Cracky was in a bit of a state when he got back, he knocked on the back door of the pub and I opened it and said, 'Cracky, what's the matter, what's wrong?' He went as white as a sheet and said, 'I've only gone and pranged the Bristol', so I looked outside and there was a big piece of car missing, the full front side of the wing had completely gone. I thought, oh my word, Strat will go berserk, he loved that car. But Strat took it all with a pinch of salt, he was a very calm person, never really got flustered and he simply said, 'Well dear boy, it's just one of those things, and a lot of buses do that, late at night.'"

The loyal Cracky was always on hand to drive Tony to and fro, to collect him from a bar at a moment's notice, place a bet or drop him off at a business meeting. As well as the long hours spent in each other's company, according to accountant Peter Mills, Cracky did pretty well out of his expense account. "Cracky would probably have known more about Strat than anybody. I didn't really see a lot of him, apart from when he came in to collect his expenses. Out came the petty cash box and out went most of the money and that was on a fairly regular basis. I think Strat was a bit like the Queen, he didn't carry any money himself so Cracky held the cash for him, spending this, that and the other and these enormous bills kept coming in."

As well as working with Geno, Zeppelin and various Charisma artists, Cracky eventually found himself attached to Pink Floyd. This followed a major bust-up with Tony, a huge argument that apparently came to a head halfway down a motorway when Tony discovered that Cracky had been dealing drugs with the Lambourn stable lads. It was something that Tony could never tolerate and Cracky was quickly packed off to work as the chauffeur to Floyd manager Steve O'Rourke. Even after crossing such a personal line, Tony would not see his old friend and long-term employee out of work.

Cracky's replacement, at least behind the wheel of the Bristol, was a young man called Tom Hancock who had been working in the same role for Brian Gibbon, with Anton Nicholls subsequently taking over as Brian's chauffeur.

Chapter 12

The Liquorice Allsorts Man

*"Strat had a fantastically enlightened attitude – and remember, this was
an era in which quite a lot of artists got badly turned over. I don't think
Strat was ever the world's best businessman, but generally if anyone at
Charisma didn't get paid, it was purely because Strat himself hadn't been
paid. But his advice about dealing with artists was brilliant
and most of what he said to me in 1972 is still true today."*
Chris Briggs, Charisma PR

*Z*igzag was in trouble. The independent music magazine that became
the inspiration and template to many other British rock mags that
followed was launched in April 1969 and struggled along on a hand-
to-mouth basis for issue after issue, many of which were written and produced
on editor/publisher Pete Frame's kitchen table in the rural surroundings of
his Buckinghamshire cottage. Named after 'Zig Zag Wanderer' a track on
Captain Beefheart's debut album, the magazine featured, interviewed and
shone the spotlight on everyone who was anyone, from superstar to busker,
on both sides of the Atlantic. The line-up of acts they managed to cover was
unique in that all they really had in common was Frame's belief in the merits
of their music.

Tony Stratton Smith was an avid admirer of Frame's magazine. It
was consistently well written by people who passionately loved music and,
even then, strictly about the music they loved. It was an ethos that Tony
could relate to completely. He'd already tried to launch the Boston-based
Fusion magazine in the UK, and when he learned that the Aylesbury-based
version was on the verge of collapse, he offered his help.

Through Strat bailing out *Zigzag*, Pete Frame and his pals were
freed from the financial and administrative burdens that bored them anyway.
As Frame recalls: "He bought *ZigZag* in the autumn of 1972 and the first
Charisma/Spice Box issue was number 26, in November. I was taken on as
editor, but only stayed until issue 30, when Connor McKnight took over. He
subsequently left and Andy Childs became editor – until late 1975, when
Strat decided to relinquish ownership. He handed it back to me, lock, stock
and barrel, together with all the copyrights. Free of charge."

The second editor to work under Tony's stewardship, Andy Childs started to write about music while still at school, putting together his own fanzine *Fat Angel*, largely inspired by *Zigzag* itself and, surprisingly, his English teacher. "Pete Frame had somehow managed to keep *Zigzag* going for about four or five years before Strat got involved. Anyway it was a big financial struggle for Pete and it had got to the point where he needed an injection of money, plus I think he'd burnt himself out a little bit. So Strat, who was always a fan of the magazine, bought it and installed Connor McKnight as editor."

Childs met Connor, Strat and Michael Wale in the Nellie Dean. "That was basically my job interview, drinks in the Nellie Dean, which was very Strat. I told them about what I had done and we all got on very well and then a couple of days later Gail Colson rang up to say, 'If you want to do it, we'd love to have you.' After Gail called, I didn't think twice."

Now connected to, and published by, the Charisma Books offshoot, Charisma gave *Zigzag* office space. "When I first joined," recalls Childs, "the office was at 70 Old Compton Street, above what was then a coffee shop. They sold beans and grounds so the whole place reeked of coffee, it was a lovely smell. You'd go into work in the morning and really smell the coffee. We shared the office with Cathy McKnight, who ran Charisma/Spice Box Books, but she was in the office with us and we both shared a secretary with the record company. Later we all moved into the basement at Soho Square – the B&C /Charisma offices – and we were down in the dungeon next to the post room."

During the period that Charisma/Spice Box published the magazine, *Zigzag* could easily have turned into a soapbox for Charisma artists, but subsequent issues show that this was not the case. Pete Frame confirms why. "Part of my deal with Strat was that he didn't interfere with or influence the content. But I did interviews with Genesis and Bert Jansch, among others, and several Charisma acts were featured – purely because they deserved it. Strat never put any pressure on me (or Connor, or Andy) to push his artists."

Andy Childs agrees. "Strat was always very hands off, he didn't interfere at all. There may have been the occasional nudge, you know, 'Why don't you interview Peter Hammill... or do this and do that.' By which I mean that he was very open to ideas, but he would never come in and bang his fist on the table demanding that we put so and so in the magazine, or on the cover. To his credit he never once did that, and I don't even think Strat got free advertising – which was handled by a chap called Jim Maguire – although I suppose he might have got a reduced rate. The circulation at the time was about 20,000 to 25,000, something like that, which really wasn't very big, so advertising space was quite valuable to us and it was important to get the advertising revenue in, that was what really kept the magazine alive."

To mark the fifth anniversary of *Zigzag* and to raise funds for the magazine, Charisma helped to underwrite a memorable benefit concert. When the core team of *Zigzag* writers, Pete Frame, John Tobler, Andy Childs and Connor McKnight, drew up their wish-list for the concert, the American country-rock artists Mike Nesmith and John Stewart featured highly on it. Tony put the full force of the Charisma agency behind the task and Paul Conroy set to work turning fantasy into reality by taking care of the bookings and work permits, and even managed to hire the Roundhouse in London's Chalk Farm. Country singer-songwriter Mike Nesmith was encouraged to perform at the concert with Tony dangling the additional carrot of the production job on the next album by influential acoustic guitarist Bert Jansch, a legend in folk circles, whom Tony had signed to Charisma in 1974.

The benefit concert took place on April 28, 1974 and was, in the words of Pete Frame, "A day trip to utopia, a celebration of our treasure trove corner of rock culture. It sounds very hippie-dippy (now), but we thought the readers and the musicians were our brothers. We loved them all." Those appearing included three of the magazine's favourite British bands, Chilli Willi & The Red Hot Peppers, Starry Eyed And Laughing and Help Yourself, plus two highly-rated American acts – Michael Nesmith, together with his pedal-steel player Red Rhodes, and John Stewart with his bass player Arnie Moore.

While in England, Nesmith famously got to work with Jansch, but after meeting the Chilli Willi guys at the Roundhouse concert he also worked on five tracks for them, although only two made the final cut on their *Bongos Over Balham* LP. Chilli Willi were signed to Mooncrest Records, the Charisma subsidiary label, and Tony was encouraged to partly fund the Naughty Rhythms tour, along with Pink Floyd manager Steve O'Rourke, who managed Kokomo, and Andrew Lauder from United Artists. The tour was the brainchild of Jake Riviera and based along the lines of the old sixties package tours, an idea that Tony had previously plundered for the Charisma packages of the early seventies. By this time Glen Colson was working with Kokomo and firmly believed that Charisma should have been snapping up bands from the London pub-rock circuit.

As Charisma moved offices all around Soho, so too did the *Zigzag* team. While putting together issue 45, published in September 1974, editor Andy Childs detailed one such move in his Blabber & Smoke column and demonstrated just how close the two companies had become. "If fate takes its course, as I fully expect it to, this will be the last *Zigzag* to emanate from the crumbling offices of Old Compton Street. No, we are not taking over Centre Point, and we're not moving out into the country either, we're just being transferred to the main Charisma building at 37 Soho Square (right opposite the Nellie Dean... a hangout for tramps, cut-throats, press officers, wastrels, record-company executives, lunatics and other VIPs). At the moment, we're the only people left in the building. The Charisma Agency has gone, Hustler (the management company) has gone, the music publisher chappie's vanished. Life at Soho Square will have its advantages, but I think I'm going to miss the close little office community that we had here."

Temporarily freed of the editorial worries that *Zigzag* entailed, Pete Frame actually became a Charisma employee for a few months. "I worked for Charisma as A&R Manager from late '74 until the summer of '75," he says. "But it was a most unsatisfactory period. There was no money to sign new acts. Only the income from Genesis albums was keeping the label afloat, so I went part time, working two or three days' a week. The acts that I liked, and spent time with, were Clifford T. Ward, Gary Shearston, Chris & Pauline Adams (String Driven Thing) and Bert Jansch."

In the end, Frame and the magazine he founded were reunited when Tony, who was apparently unable to find another buyer, simply handed the whole package back to where it came from. Andy Childs recalls what happened. "God bless him, Strat stuck with it for a couple of years, I suppose, and I think anyone else might have looked at it and thought, 'Well, this isn't going anywhere' a lot earlier, but he did stick with it. I think in the end he decided that he would offload it. It had just become a bit of a liability, because he had a staff of maybe four or five of us, which was too many and *Zigzag* wasn't making any money. In fact it was probably losing money, because the circulation wasn't getting any higher and it probably also had something to do with whatever else was going on at Charisma at that time."

Among those approached to buy Zigzag was Elton John, a fan of the magazine, but he declined. "In the end I don't think Strat could sell it, really," says Childs. "But it was still a very magnanimous move to give it all back to Pete. I mean *Zigzag* was Pete Frame really, the whole feel of the magazine, the tone of it, the humour of it and everything – it had always been Pete's magazine."

With Frame back at the helm, the magazine continued to roll. Paul Kendall took over as editor and the magazine was bought by a printer, Graham Andrews, who put in an injection of cash. As the music scene changed, however, so unavoidably did *Zigzag*. The one-time champion of psychedelic rock, blues, folk and country found itself promoting the new punk scene under the editorship of Kris Needs, a protégé of Frame's who also lived in Aylesbury. It continued until early 1986, having published around 140 issues.

When Charisma moved to the larger, brighter offices of Soho Square, press officer Chris Briggs not only found himself in a new working environment, but he also moved into a nearby flat, literally seconds away from work and equally close to Tony's favourite drinking establishments.

"Of course we all lived in pubs like the Nellie Dean, that was like our other office and when we moved to Soho Square, it became even more so," he says. In fact, Briggs took over the spare bedroom in *Melody Maker* photographer Barrie Wentzell's flat that had once been occupied by Roy Hollingworth. It was above the Pizza Express on the corner of Dean and Carlisle Streets, overlooking the door to Charisma's offices. "I could look out of the window and watch out for Strat's Bristol coming into the square. Luckily, Strat was not an early riser and Cracky would pick him up and drive him into work. I'd watch for Cracky and the Bristol to turn in to Carlisle Street and circle the square looking for a parking space, knowing that would give me time to get in to work. My walk to work was simply tumble out of the Pizza Express side door and then stroll across the street."

When Tony bought in to *Zigzag*, Briggs found himself contributing copy to the magazine in addition to his day-to-day tasks. "Strat had me writing for beer money. I was out most nights seeing bands," he told one journalist. Briggs had taken on press work previously handled by Glen Colson and still hankered after a job in A&R. It was a combination of these extra pressures and a fortuitous connection through a *Zigzag* interview that saw his time at Charisma draw to a close.

"I got an interview with Dave Mason, whose PR was Christine Eldridge, who was the press officer at CBS, and her husband was Roy Eldridge who was the press officer at Chrysalis Records. Roy was about to be promoted and Christine told me that her husband needed a press officer. One of the reasons I left Charisma was that it became obvious there was never going to be an A&R department that had any separation from Strat's own taste. There was no long-term future, unless you were happy to be spreading Strat's vision of life and music around – and if not, then you should move on."

Chris Briggs swapped the press office at Charisma for a new position at Chrysalis, where he eventually got a crack at the A&R job he had always craved – signing Generation X as his first act to Chris Wright's punk-friendly label and acting as tour manager for Blondie's UK tour. The experience gained in his first proper job, working alongside Tony, Paul Conroy and Gail and Glen Colson, proved invaluable, as well as enjoyable. "When I first started doing A&R, certain managers would be horrified by the idea that you needed to actually like the music," said Briggs, "because to them it was a business and you were making a business decision. The one thing I was never very good at was to coldly calculate whether or not something would be commercially successful – my decision would always be much more driven by gut-instinct, which is exactly how Strat would do it.

"The more you do this job, the more you learn that being talented is only a tiny part of it. Luck, timing, right time, right place, great manager, all manner of other things are just as important. There are an awful lot of people who don't manage to write that one perfect song. What if Alan Hull hadn't written 'Lady Eleanor'? That was his door-opening song; not necessarily throwaway pop, it still had the personality of the artist, but it was just that little bit more accessible and that's what got people to listen to the rest of their material."

Briggs is one of many who feels indebted to Tony for shaping his thinking and – ultimately – his career in the music business. "What Strat would tell me about how to treat artists and how to get the best out of them, has always stuck with me," he says. "Strat had a fantastically enlightened attitude – and remember, this was an era in which quite a lot of artists got badly turned over. I don't think Strat was ever the world's best businessman, but generally if anyone at Charisma didn't get paid, it was purely because Strat himself hadn't been paid. But his advice about dealing with artists was brilliant and most of what he said to me in 1972 is still true today."

Tony was entering a period where he eased back from his management interests to concentrate purely on the record company side of the business, and he was scathing about the trend for successful groups starting their own labels, among them The Rolling Stones, Led Zeppelin and Deep Purple. "It's just an ego trip," he told the *Melody Maker*'s Chris Welch, with much amusement. "One of the biggest jokes in the business is groups launching their own labels. Half of them don't even want to work on their own careers, and yet they want to take responsibility for a young group's career? It's hard work, you know, very hard."

Tony was less disparaging about Apple, the label launched in 1968 by The Beatles and Rocket Records, which was run by Elton John and his manager John Reid. "The most professional since Apple is Elton John's Rocket label," he said. "They've got first class people. But the joke is that most of them think it's about making records. They don't look back into their own careers and all the people that helped them. They might say 'hello' to them in the Speakeasy, those people that created a situation for them, saying to promoters in Newcastle or Birmingham, 'Give these boys a gig, they are good.' I can remember people turning down Genesis for a support slot. That's what goes on in getting a group going. Sheer bloody leg-work. And they always think it's down to their own genius."

It was during this same interview with Welch, published in *Melody Maker* on February 23, 1974, that Tony announced his decision to give up all personal management. When asked why, he said: "It was a natural decision really. Remember, when we started Charisma we thought we had to have management as a service to give the records a chance, because there was so little good independent management about. We viewed Charisma as a sort of nursery, and it worked brilliantly. I don't think there's any doubt about that. It's had an amazing track record with Genesis, Lindisfarne, Rare Bird, Clifford T. Ward and all the other bands we're now working on."

Tony acknowledged that as bands became more popular they needed independent management, as had occurred with Genesis and Tony Smith. He realised they shouldn't keep all their eggs in the same record company basket, and the problem extended to several of the early Charisma artists. Lindisfarne's Ray Laidlaw and Chris Adams of String Driven Thing have both pointed out the problems inherent in such a system, although both admit that as a caring record label, Tony and Charisma were a hard act to follow.

"The problem is, as bands get bigger, they become more time-consuming," Tony told Welch. "If the record company is making all the decisions, it can sometimes be said that the company is being guided by self-interest, when it comes to persuading people to do gigs in different parts of the world. There has been discontent, but this came about from us trying to split ourselves into too many parts. We're into records and music publishing, management and agency, and back-up services like pluggers and press officers. It's like going through a bacon slicer every week. I've done an awful lot of travelling and I don't get any younger. When you're in Detroit with Genesis, you're wondering if you should be in London with Lindisfarne, or Texas with Graham Bell, and I felt it was impossible for me to give them the amount of involvement that I thought they were worth. When a struggling group starts out they will do what is asked of them. As they get bigger they require something different. It's as if they have grown up and are ready to leave home."

Acknowledging that it was eight years since he began in management with Paddy, Klaus & Gibson, he drew a parallel with horse racing, the Sport of Kings to which he would eventually devote his time. "It's the difference between training a racehorse and being a steward at the track. If you view the record market as the racecourse, for me it's now much less personal than if you were back in the yard with your half dozen horses or so, mucking them out, looking after their problems, ringworm and drugs!" Tony added, chuckling. "But I know enough about management to know that it was beginning not to work. I have to be honest with myself, as I hope I've always been honest with other people, but I know in my gut that management is a total involvement with one or two artists. When you can't give that involvement, then you should get out."

In the same interview Tony outlined exactly what he loved so much about the challenges at Charisma. "I love breaking in new bands. It has been great fun, and in a sense, I hope that doesn't stop. My ambition now is not to become the biggest record company in the world, but merely the best. Not much to ask, is it?

"I do have a gambling streak in me, and I like picking winners.

How far that instinct relates to ego, I don't quite know. But I've never had a vicarious fulfilment out of an artist's success. If it doesn't sound too presumptuous I've always had an intellectual satisfaction out of judging the matter and form of an artist's work, and saying to myself, 'This is good and in certain circumstances, the world will see that it is good'. It doesn't happen all the time, of course! But there is great satisfaction when that happens. The way we work (at Charisma), I motivate the team, and I can only sign an artist whose work I like very much and I can personally get on with. That's very important. There are many artists around who I wouldn't work with if you paid me a fortune, you know? Because I know I'd be extremely unhappy. It's a rough enough business, without more pain and tension than it's worth."

It's been suggested that Vivian Stanshall was among the artists who felt aggrieved that Tony spread his time and effort too thinly, though perhaps his reaction was motivated more by the way his own career had panned out than any perceived lack of support from his old boss. On his 1974 album *Men Opening Umbrellas Ahead*, the former Bonzo Dog frontman took acidic pot-shots at the vagaries of the music business and the people who inhabit it. Aided by his former bandmate Neil Innes and most of Traffic, this album was released by Warner Bros., not Charisma, and according to *Melody Maker* journalist Chris Welch, the character of 'Redeye' (and possibly 'Hawkeye' too) is largely based on Tony. One can certainly see the parallels:

> *"Here comes old Redeye, he's full of drink,*
> *mouthing his mouth off to a load of kids*
> *Saying nothing personal, but he's up the creek*
> *While you're home sleeping, he's down at the Speak (easy now)*
> *Here comes old Hawkeye, see his skilful squint,*
> *his ready intelligence, you see it in print*
> *Flits into Amsterdam, flies back to New York in a comfy first class*
> *compartment…"*

* * *

Bert Jansch arrived at Charisma after Warner Bros.' Reprise label rejected an album he had made with bassist Danny Thompson, another alumni from the folk group Pentangle.

At the time Jansch was being managed temporarily by an accountant named Roger Myres and one night in the Speakeasy, an associate of Myres was talking to an employee of Charisma about Jansch's situation. The following day the news had reached Tony that Jansch was out of contract and Tony promptly set about bringing the eminent guitarist to Charisma. It emerged that Tony had long been an admirer of the Scottish guitarist and within two weeks the deal was signed and sealed. Tony stated: "If ever a man is due his place among the superstars, it is Bert Jansch", and his particular vision for turning Jansch into a superstar centred around teaming him up with a number of top American musicians to add an authentic country feel to Jansch's British folk sensibilities.

Tony's real masterstroke was to hire the former Monkee Mike Nesmith as producer, who in turn brought along the exceptional pedal steel guitarist O.J. 'Red' Rhodes and drummer Danny Lane to help work on Jansch's record. Nesmith and Tony had got on particularly well at the *Zigzag* benefit a few weeks beforehand. In the warm summer sunshine of 1974, all the participants were summoned to meet at Tony's house in the Sussex countryside.

A large part of the album was recorded at Luxford House, where a couple of the ground floor rooms were hastily turned into makeshift studios with cables running out to Ronnie Lane's mobile studio, a gleaming silver 1968 Airstream trailer parked on the drive in the top half of the grounds. It has been suggested that when Jansch first arrived at Luxford, he didn't actually know he was going to be recording there and it was only after one of Tony's brandy-fuelled, bon-vivant evenings that he awoke the following morning to find the trailer installed in the grounds and ready to go. In an interview for *NME*, Jansch told Fred Dellar: "I did about six tracks at Tony's place – two were done in the garden with the birds singing and everything – but then Mike [Nesmith] had to go back to the States, which meant that I had to go over and finish it there, otherwise it could have been months and months before we got together again. I'm glad we went over though, because that really saved the album for me. Working with Red Rhodes was different – it was the first time I'd ever worked with a steel guitarist. Looking back I think a lot of it was great, but maybe we overplayed things and there was a little too much steel – maybe we could have been a little more discreet."

As with several of Tony's projects, he had also arranged for part of the sessions to be filmed and footage exists of at least four tracks, interspersed with shots of the Luxford gardens, the musicians relaxing around the house, and at one point, the camera follows them on a visit to a local pub, The Wheatsheaf, where Red Rhodes is taught the intricacies of the traditional English game of bar billiards. As well as new material like 'Fresh As A Sweet Sunday Morning' and 'Travelling Man', the album contained a fresh recording of 'Needle Of Death', one of Jansch's most powerful songs and apparently included at Tony's request. As Jansch later recalled: "I never did like the original version, but Tony asked if I would do it, and since he was the head of the company I thought I'd better. It's one of the songs that has simply stuck with people down the years, but this version with Red is a little different, more earthy."

The resulting album, titled *L.A. Turnaround*, was released in September 1974 and is widely regarded as a high point of Jansch's recording career. *Melody Maker* claimed it to be "not far off being the perfect album", while Tony himself enthused, "This is probably one of the five best albums Charisma has ever released. An album to feel for; an album to love." Unfortunately, as is so often the case with classic albums, it sold poorly on its initial release.

Tony was extremely happy with his new signing and was equally pleased to hear that Bert Jansch had been booked into a studio by his manager Bruce May, no doubt with one eye on a Christmas hit single, to record his own unique arrangement of 'In The Bleak Midwinter', a Christmas carol based on a poem by Christina Rossetti. With May picking up the studio bill for the session, it was produced by Ralph McTell, a long-term friend of Jansch, who in turn enlisted Lindisfarne bassist Rod Clements and the vocal group Prelude to help out on the song. The session went very well and did produce a seasonal hit, but to Tony's dismay it wasn't one for Bert Jansch. In the spare studio time left at the end of the day, McTell used the assembled musicians to rerecord his own song 'Streets Of London' and it was this new version, released on the Warner Bros. Reprise label, that rocketed to number two in the charts that December.

Bert Jansch went on to complete four albums for Charisma, following up with the even-more American *Santa Barbara Honeymoon* in 1975 and *A Rare Conundrum* in 1977. If *Honeymoon* took Bert's American adventure a step too far, *Conundrum* was a return to classic Jansch and a British folk rock sound. *Avocet* was the final Bert Jansch record to appear on Tony's label and although widely felt to be one of his finest works, once again it was largely overlooked. Meanwhile Transatlantic Records were releasing compilations of old Jansch material to cash in on the new work that appeared on Charisma and this may also account for why, when *Avocet* was eventually released, it was part of Charisma's budget-priced CLASS series.

The photograph of Jansch on the front cover of *L.A. Turnaround* was taken by Mike van der Vord, a friend of B&C art director Frank Sansom, who was commissioned to work on a number of assignments for B&C and Charisma. For this assignment he drove down to Luxford, where Jansch stayed while recording tracks for the 'English' part of the album. "I remember being surprised to see Mike Nesmith when I arrived and there was this mobile studio that looked like a spaceship parked outside," says van der Vord. "Whenever there was a break in recording they would all go and sit outside because the weather was so good, and I'd just wander around and take shots."

Working for Frank Sansom and the B&C/Charisma group could never be described as dull. One day van der Vord might be back in his Glebe

Place studio, posing Peter Hammill for the striking portraits that graced the cover of the *In Camera* album, complete with swirling dark blue cape and glinting metal clasp, while on another he was producing the deliberately less-glamorous shots of Judge Dread for his Trojan album *Working Class 'Ero*. During 1975, van der Vord booked some location work in a department store in Oxford Street to photograph a reluctant Clifford T. Ward riding up and down their twin escalators (no prizes for guessing which album that was for) and two years later Mike found himself on an escalator once again, shooting stills during the video recording for Peter Gabriel's single 'Modern Love', which were subsequently used in the press advertising.

* * *

Signing Jansch was yet another example of Tony's eclecticism. Charisma was like a box of Liquorice Allsorts. It extended in all directions, to reggae, to comedians, to space rockers and even to siblings of artists already signed to Charisma.

In the spring of 1973, a white group playing authentic reggae long before UB40 caused a stir on the pub and club scene around London. G.T. Moore & The Reggae Guitars was the brainchild of Gerald Moore, a folk and blues guitarist from Reading who had previously worked with the folk rock group Heron. The Reggae Guitars were promptly snapped up by Charisma and they recorded two albums for the label, the first of which included a version of Bob Dylan's 'Knocking On Heaven's Door', several years before Eric Clapton took his own reggae version into the charts.

With several record labels hot on the band's tail, Gerald Moore pinpoints why he chose to sign with Tony and Charisma. "Strat was a unique figure and in all my years in show business I've never met anyone remotely like him," he says. "I was getting a bit of a name with my band, and because we played reggae the gigs were not only full of people but also musicians and music business people. It all came to a head one night at a gig in The Kensington pub on Holland Road. I think every record company in town was there, not only the big ones, but also people like the head of Trojan and Tyrone Downie. Strat wasn't actually there that night, but there were people from Charisma's A&R department. The atmosphere was incredible. Record companies were sending messages to and from each other, and passing offers of a deal to the band's dressing room. During the set someone even grabbed hold of the piano player's arm, so momentarily he couldn't play, saying, 'Are you signed to anyone?'"

Gerald's manager Peter Eden advised him to go with Charisma, largely because of Tony. "'He's like a big uncle, and with the other companies if your first record doesn't move they might drop you, but he will stick with you', he told me. So we went with Charisma and it wasn't long before I met Strat in a Soho restaurant. From the first moment, I had an uncanny feeling. It was partly that I'd never met anyone like him before, but as the meal progressed I realised that he wanted to have a good look over what he'd just bought. It was quite a strange feeling. I was to learn later that there was more or less a direct parallel with a racehorse being led around the paddock. I could tell from the start that he wanted to get to know me and in a short time I felt that I had a good friend who was committed to me and would help me get on in show business. A rare thing.

"Of course, the parallel between rock music and horse racing wasn't accidental. I came to the conclusion that in some ways Strat looked at his bands the same way he looked at his horses. He prided himself in having the best thoroughbreds and he looked at gigs a bit like race meetings, where he went to see his stable beat the competition. Over the next two or three years I got to know Strat quite well, we had dinner a few times and we often met in restaurants. I began to realise that he had a broad vision that encompassed culture, cuisine and fine wines, in fact, the 'dolce vita'. He signed me to a record label that believed in me and I thought he was a great guy. I still do."

In 1975 the diminutive comedian Charlie Drake recorded a very unusual single for Charisma, a novelty record with connections to the world of progressive rock. The singer-turned-comedian had a long and successful career as a stage and television performer in Britain, which already included a couple of novelty hit records, 'Mister Custer' and 'My Boomerang Won't Come Back', both of which made the UK top 20 at the start of the sixties.

The song he recorded was 'You Never Know', written by Peter Gabriel and Martin Hall, and it has since become much sought after by die-hard collectors of Genesis and Gabriel recordings. In response to a query on his website, Phil Collins offered the following recollection of the recording session. "The Charlie Drake session featured Robert Fripp, Percy Jones, Keith Tippett, me and Peter Gabriel. How he ended up with this line-up I have no idea. It seems the most obscure set of people to make a comedy record. On the day Charlie, who was quite small, turned up with a brand new denim outfit for his rock debut – it was quite touching to see him at it. Percy Jones and I were already in Brand X by then. The whole session was one of life's interesting snapshots."

Charlie Drake wasn't the only unusual signing that year, according to Colin Richardson. "We weren't really a singles company, but every now and again Strat would take a flyer and I remember one record we tried to put out with a guy called Pierre Cour, a French songwriter that Strat really liked because he was a very literary guy. It was a track he had written called 'Letter To A Teenage Bride'. We produced the single and I remember Gail Colson being absolutely incensed by it. In fact, nobody in the office liked it and I think that most of the promotion copies were put in the cupboard and quietly forgotten about. I couldn't see that it was that offensive, but Gail did. There was a bit of an old man and a young girl thing going on and to be honest, it was a bit cheesy, but then Strat sometimes delivered things to you which you worked on as best you could, whether you actually related to them or not."

Notting Hill space rockers Hawkwind reached a major crossroads in 1975 when their relationship with their record company United Artists came to a close, manager Doug Smith quit and bassist Lemmy was 'let go' after a drugs bust on the Canadian border. The remaining core of Dave Brock, Nik Turner, drummer Simon King and violinist Simon House added the extrovert Robert Calvert as their new frontman, along with a second drummer Alan Powell and bassist Paul Rudolph from the Pink Fairies. The Famous Charisma Label seemed, to them at least, to be the ideal place to make their new home.

This new line-up began by recording the *Astounding Sounds, Amazing Music* album in 1976, described as "a divisive blend of whimsical psychedelia and jazz-tinged instrumentals that impressed music journalists and alienated fans in equal measure." Founder-member Turner left, while Powell and Rudolph were removed during the sessions for their next release *Quark, Strangeness & Charm*. Although this album saw a return to their earlier science fiction themes, the band found themselves cited as an influence by the new punks in town, including Johnny Rotten and Joe Strummer. They changed their name to the Hawklords to release the *25 Years On* album, but none of their Charisma singles ever matched the chart success of 'Silver Machine' and their brief time with the label came to an end in 1978.

After leaving Hawkwind in 1977 (and not for the last time), Nik Turner took time out to holiday in Egypt and while visiting the Great Pyramid of Giza he was allowed three hours inside the King's Chamber to play and record some flute music. On his return to England, Turner assembled a new band that included Steve Hillage, Mike Howlett from Gong and Hawkwind's Alan Powell. While Hillage cleaned up the original tapes, Turner set about adapting lyrics from the *Egyptian Book Of The Dead*. When Turner took his ideas for an album to Charisma, Tony's love of horse racing helped sell the concept, as Turner later told Tommy Hash. "During my time in Egypt, I met a family who invited me to an engagement party at an upscale hacienda and there were all these fabulous horses there. Tony Stratton Smith was a real horse enthusiast and when I showed him my photographs and played tapes of my recordings in the pyramids he was completely sold on it, which was fantastic. Gail Colson was right behind me, too."

Tony gave Nik Turner's Sphynx the green light and the resulting album *Xitintoday* was released by Charisma in 1978, and the live Sphynx show was launched at the Roundhouse and then taken out on the road, complete with pyramid stage set designed by the inimitable Barney Bubbles, who would go on to design many covers for Stiff Records.

Genesis guitarist Steve wasn't the only member of the Hackett family to get the call from Tony. John Hackett, like his older brother, began his musical career as a guitarist, but took up the flute at the age of 15 after hearing Ian McDonald playing with King Crimson. The two brothers played together in the band Quiet World, releasing one single on Dawn Records and recording one album with the Heather Brothers in 1970. John later played on Steve's solo albums and, after leaving Sheffield University, recorded and toured with his brother, who had recently left Genesis. John recalls how he was summoned to the Charisma office. "I was asked to go and see Tony Stratton Smith," he says. "Apparently, he and his accountant, Brian Gibbon, had been on a flight discussing the possibility of my doing some kind of flute album. I cobbled together a few demo tracks with the help of Nick Magnus [Steve Hackett's keyboard player at the time] and presented myself at the Charisma offices.

"Tony seemed mildly irritated that I'd sent no covering letter with the demo. Then he was very complimentary about the music, which was mostly my own work. That's more promising, I thought. 'Stevie Winwood,' he said, 'that's who I thought you were, when I saw you up the corridor.' I really had no idea what he was talking about, but nodded politely, assuming Tony had taken an early lunch. 'The trouble is,' he continued, 'instrumental music is all very well, but people want songs. That's what they want – songs. Do you write songs?' I then made one of the biggest mistakes of my life. I should have said, 'Yes, I've got some tunes that would work really well with lyrics. Why don't I go away and record them and pop back to see you in a couple of weeks?' But no, instead I told him in no uncertain terms that I was a flute player, I'd spent my whole life concentrating on the flute and I had absolutely no intention of writing any songs. Smart move, eh?"

* * *

On October 18, 1976, Van der Graaf Generator made their American debut at the Beacon Theatre in New York City, and for many years this remained their one and only US concert. Tony always stated that he liked to accompany his artists on their first trip to the States and he kept his promise by flying into New York for the show, which followed a short tour of Canada. Although he'd left Charisma, Glen Colson was rehired as an advance man to drum up publicity for the show. He stayed in a Midtown hotel for a month and because he was new to the city sought the help of Chris Charlesworth, then *Melody Maker*'s US editor stationed in New York. "I put Glen in touch with New York writers and in return I ate for free in the hotel at Tony's expense," says Charlesworth.

In *MM* Charlesworth noted: "VdGG played their first US concert at the Beacon Theatre on Monday evening, drawing a surprisingly large and appreciative crowd for a band whose albums are sold mainly through import shops. Manager Tony Stratton Smith, obviously pleased at the outcome of what was an experimental gamble, plans to bring them back to the US early next year for a lengthy tour.

"It's just the same as with Genesis," he told Charlesworth. "We brought them over for one concert to test the land and look what happened. Van der Graaf will do the same." Following the show, Tony threw a party for the band at the Essex House hotel overlooking Central Park but was disappointed at the lack of support given to the band by Mercury, who handled Van der Graaf in the US.

According to Glen Colson, Mercury did no promotion whatsoever. "They said they didn't believe they could do a gig over there and said bluntly, 'No, we don't want them.' Strat said, 'You're having them!' Eventually the concert sold out and fans came from all over America to see Van der Graaf play. They went down a storm and played two encores. Strat threw a huge wobbler at the gig and grabbed hold of the top guy at Mercury, who had come backstage to congratulate the band. Strat said, 'I told you we would sell this gig out. Now piss off!' He would never give up on Van der Graaf because he loved the group so much."

The idea of Tony getting angry with anyone would appear to be totally out of character, but it could happen occasionally, as photographer Barrie Wentzell remembers. "Strat was from that old school of Bertie Wooster/P.G. Wodehouse types, he was totally different from the likes of Peter Grant and Don Arden. It was very rare that you'd ever see him get mad, but when he did it was like, 'Oh fuck, watch out'. It had that extra power."

* * *

Tony continued to explore the world of cinema when, in 1978, he acted as executive producer on *The Odd Job*, starring Monty Python's Graham Chapman, David Jason, Diana Quick, Simon Williams and Edward Hardwicke in a full-length feature adaptation of a TV production. Directed by Peter Medak, the film can best be described as a dark British comedy, in which a despondent businessman (Chapman) decides to end it all after his wife leaves him. Unable to commit suicide, he hires a professional assassin, the 'odd-job man', telling him to do the deed no matter what. However, as time passes and life quickly improves for the businessman, he decides he wants to stay alive. Unfortunately, nothing he says will convince his would-be killer to stop the pursuit.

Tony invited his friend Bush Telfer, then an apprentice jockey, along to the film première and afterwards to the launch party, which was held at a venue Telfer would come to know well. "Graham Chapman was quite eccentric – like Strat, because he did like that type of character, he liked that style," recalls Telfer. "I went to the première with a jockey called Paul D'Arcy, we travelled up to London and the party afterwards was held in The Marquee Club. The caterers moved in and it was all champagne and caviar. It was a massive do, so Paul D'Arcy and me were trying to sell a racehorse to David Jason, who was just as funny off-screen as he was on, he was a right character. But everybody mixed together well and that was always Strat's way, he liked to take on things that other people didn't believe could actually work. He was a real pioneer in that respect."

For his next major film project, Tony asked his old friend Vivian Stanshall whether he wanted to make a feature length film of *Sir Henry At Rawlinson End*, up to that point a cult radio play serialised during the John Peel radio show. Viv famously jumped at the opportunity, but the process was not without its problems. "What a project that was," recalls Neil Innes. "Written by a drunk, directed by a drunk, financed by a drunk, starred a drunk. What hope was there?"

Writing about Tony in the booklet that accompanied the Charisma box set in 1993, Stanshall summed up the *Sir Henry* project in his own inimitable style. "It was my birthday, March 21, 1980, and Strat thought it appropriate to pop a bottle of Tizer or three to celebrate. 'Would you care to make a film, dear boy?' Silly question! A joke? Three weeks later I was purred out at his country home near Lambourn village, bashing out the screenplay. Afternoons, bedizzened in sumptuous dressing gown, the gentlemanly beslippered Strat would appear, chuckle at my first drafts, smile encouragement, nod to his beastly collection of Bratbys, make a mysterious encoded 'phone call to his bookie and vanish, and leave me to it. He did never censure – I was utterly free. The film – *Sir Henry At Rawlinson End* – went into production that early summer. Strat had been quite serious and he backed the film with all the vigour and enthusiasm with which he backed his horses. We neither of us won really, but we won prizes and the fun of it – the doing of it!"

When Stanshall arrived at Coombe Lodge to work on the script, he found that Tony had not only entrusted him with his house, but also his butler, the butler's deaf wife and their two dogs. A daily routine developed whereby Stanshall would rise at eight in the morning and start on the vodka, encouraging the director, Steve Roberts, to join him. By midday the pair could barely talk, let alone write.

Nevertheless, Tony's country house proved conducive to the writing process, because against all odds, Stanshall and Roberts eventually emerged from Coombe Lodge with something approaching a workable script. Tony especially enjoyed the casting process, eagerly adopting the time-honoured 'let's have lunch' approach. As director Steve Roberts recalls: "Getting hold of Trevor Howard was the first step, which was Strat's function as producer. Trevor very generously said he would look at it, and we all had lunch, Viv, myself, Strat, Trevor and his agent. Breathing anywhere near Vivian was a remarkable experience and having lunch with him when there was drink flying about was something else altogether. Trevor just sat there, staring and chortling, and eventually he said to Strat, 'These people are entirely insane, I must do this.' It was that simple, there was no cajoling."

Cast and crew assembled at Knebworth House in Hertfordshire to commence filming, but the task of turning Vivian's dazzling wordplay into equally striking visual imagery proved problematical. What worked so beautifully on radio or on vinyl was not transferring quite so well onto film. A frustrated Steve Roberts turned to his producer Tony for advice. "What sort of approach do we want here?" asked the confused director. "Do we control the bugger or do we let him go?" Tony's response was typical. "I can't control him either, Steve. Why don't you just do something that you love?" With the ball lobbed firmly back into Robert's court, the problem seemed to be how to stop Stanshall from drinking long enough to get his role (as Sir Henry's brother, Hubert) in the can. Even Trevor Howard, no stranger to a drop himself, had spotted the problem with Vivian. Always professional and sober on set, the veteran actor simply told Steve Roberts, "You keep that bugger under control and I'll do my job."

Vivian's second wife, Ki Longfellow Stanshall – they married in September 1980, a month before the film was released – observed proceedings. "No one knew sweet FA about making a movie, not really – and certainly not Tony Stratton Smith, that all round soft-boiled egg and head of Charisma Records, which was at the time Vivian's record company," she says. "Loving trust, that's what it was. Strat trusted Vivian and Vivian trusted Strat... and they both trusted that Art was on their side. Which She was... but what does Art know about business? Oh, the picture got made – somehow. There was even a lot of Vivian in it, but it was far from what it could have been, very very far. Problem was, our choice for director knew as little as we did, and we, not knowing what he didn't know, trusted him. Which is why he and Vivian ended up with a script as long as the Bible, Old and New Testaments, one that would have needed twice Cecil B. DeMille's budget to shoot – and why it had to be cut back so severely, when someone who did know a thing or two got a look at it. Our director then had to 'save the picture' by demanding that Vivian write a narrative to go over the top to explain the damn thing. It is no wonder Vivian began behaving a bit silly on the set."

As well as the brilliant Trevor Howard, Vivian Stanshall's 72-minute 1980 film also starred Denise Coffey, J.G. Devlin, Harry Fowler, Patrick Magee and was directed by Steve Roberts. In the *All Movie Guide*, Hal Erickson describes the plot thus: "Trevor Howard is virtually the whole show in *Sir Henry At Rawlinson End*. He plays an eccentric-to-the-point-of-insanity nobleman, whose love affair with the bottle is a long-standing source of family embarrassment. When the family mansion is plagued by an unfriendly ghost, Howard finds himself the only one willing or able to exorcise the spirit. *Sir Henry At Rawlinson End* was based on a radio play by Vivian Stanshall and, as such, it is more satisfying for the ear than for the eye."

In commercial terms it was a recipe for disaster and had there been a 'straight-to-video' option in those days, that is where the finished product would probably have gone. Not for want of effort or funding on the part of Charisma however, as Glen Colson explains. "Tony wasted an awful lot of money on that film. He pumped in half a million quid of his own money and I don't think he made any of it back. It never made a dime. He didn't even know where to distribute it once it was finished. No one wanted it. It was an art-house film, so I had to go around trying to get people interested."

Given the unenviable task of trying to distribute the film, Colson called in Joseph D'Morais, an independent film distributor who had launched his own company, Blue Dolphin Film & Video, the year before. "Glen had organised a screening of *Sir Henry* at a little cinema in South Kensington called the Paris Pullman," recalls D'Morais, "and basically they didn't know what to do with it afterwards. I loved the film, I already knew the character anyway and I thought it could do well. I met with Tony and we hit it off straight away, so I got the film on release."

The pair got on famously, and Tony offered the film man a seat on the board of Charisma films. "I said, 'Yes, of course.' We put together our business plan and got a bank deal with NatWest, so it all dovetailed, Tony became a partner in Blue Dolphin and I became a director of Charisma Films.

"Tony was an incredible man, very generous, very warm, who very rarely got rattled, you know. I have seen him rattled, but he was usually in very good humour and not just because of the drink – that was his personality, he was very polite. A gentleman, in the proper sense of the word, that applied to him completely. But Tony was obviously a borderline alcoholic, you know, there was no denying that – although he could handle it far better than most.

"These were the Thatcher Years so the lunches were very long. When we first started, and before I knew about the drinking, the routine was that we would meet at The Ship in Wardour Street around 11 o'clock for two or three pints of Guinness. We then crossed the road to St Moritz, the Swiss place that was Tony's favourite place for lunch, arriving there around 12.30, after which I basically lost track of time. When I called the office just to check in, I thought it was maybe three or four o'clock – but there was no reply, where was everybody? So I went downstairs to check and it was seven o'clock in the evening! I walked back upstairs and asked Tony if this was normal and he laughed and said, Yes, pretty much.' It was all hugely enjoyable."

* * *

By 1976 Tony's relationship with his beloved record label was beginning to alter. The early hands-on approach had long been replaced by wholesale delegation to his trusted staff, who were becoming more and more frustrated by his apparent lack of interest in the changing music business. International manager Colin Richardson noticed the difference in his old boss: "After four years [at Charisma], I sensed that things were changing somewhat. Strat wasn't around quite as much and eventually he announced that he was bringing in someone to be 'him' on a daily basis, as he wanted to spend more time with his other love, horse racing."

That summer, Richardson was head-hunted by Bruce May, who was then running a small management company in Putney, handling his brother Ralph (McTell), John Martyn, Bert Jansch, Magna Carta and Jim Rafferty, brother of Gerry. When Charisma gave Bert Jansch a record deal, Bruce May regularly turned up at the office to keep tabs on what they were doing with Bert in Europe. Eventually May offered Richardson the chance to join him and run the European side of his business. "I went to talk over this job offer with Strat and this coincided with him saying that he wasn't going to be around as much anymore," recalls Richardson. "I told Tony that he was the only person I could relate to, he was the reason I came to work for Charisma in the first place and if he took himself out of the equation then I didn't have much to get fired up about. I told him that I was seriously thinking about leaving and that unless he could reassure me that I still reported to him and only him, then I would have to go. He totally understood and he said, 'No, absolutely dear boy, I can see that.'"

Gail Colson's considerable management skills had long been indispensable not only to Tony but to the company in general. With Tony moving 'upstairs' to take up his role as Chairman, Gail and Brian Gibbon were promoted to the position of joint Managing Director. Gail, of course, had arguably occupied that position since the label was first launched.

Not that her role was always plain sailing. Prominent positions for women in the music industry were still very scarce, as Gail was starkly reminded in an interview for the British edition of *Cosmopolitan* magazine. "A guy phoned me up and asked to interview me because I was the only female managing director of a record label," she recalls. "He came to interview me and the first thing he said was, 'What is your relationship with Tony Stratton Smith?' I said, 'What do you mean? I've worked with him for years and we started the company together.' And then he said, 'Do you sleep with him?' This was only his second question. I said, 'I beg your pardon?' And he said, 'Do you sleep with him?' So I said, 'No, I do not sleep with him,' and then he said, 'Is he gay, then?' I should have got up and just said, 'Fuck off!' But I didn't handle it properly, I went shy. Afterwards I couldn't believe it and from then on I decided that was it. Never again do I do an interview!"

At least the staff at Charisma knew the reality; you could stay out all night drinking with the bands, or taking a four-hour lunch listening to the boss's wondrous stories, but the bottom line was that there was still a business to run and someone had to say when enough was enough.

Chris Briggs is in no doubt who that person was – and it definitely wasn't Tony. "Gail was the only one keeping an eye on us, because we weren't nine to five types at all," he says. "Strat was still the owner, but Gail was the managing director or the general manager. If you took Gail away from that Charisma office, it would have collapsed in a heap. She was the grown-up, the one that pulled you up if you came in with one too many hangovers, she was the one that noticed if you bunked off for the afternoon to go and watch a film. Gail was the one that was wide awake, she was on everyone's case, including Strat's, and the fact that any work ever got done at all was largely down to her alertness and the manner in which she would pull you up in a way that was firm, but friendly."

In 1977, Lynda Wharton joined the staff at Charisma, initially to work for the Production Manager before moving across to be Tony's PA. Her recollections reinforce the general view of working for the most laid-back label in Britain. "I had no prior knowledge of the music industry, but liked music and just wanted to work in it," says Lynn (now Lynn Roskott). "My job was actually pretty cushy. A lot of the time Tony was out and about, and he was certainly the king of the long lunch, often reappearing at about 4 or 5pm. Although our office hours were officially 10am until 6pm, he was most definitely not a lark and would often turn up fairly late and then wander off to lunch a couple of hours later. I spent a lot of my time acting as a barricade between him and the people he didn't want to talk to. Being in the music business there were always people wanting to get to him and this happened again with the film people later on."

Lynn confirms that Tony was essentially a private man who rarely spoke about his early life. "The only thing I knew about his family was that he received cards and letters from his mother from time to time, but I don't really think there was any face to face contact. He was intensely private, and on occasion would completely disappear from view for a while, such as the year he went off to Rio for a couple of months.

"He was a wonderful boss and a pleasure to work for. He let me get on with my work in my own time. There was never a cross word spoken and he was a genuinely gentle and nice guy. I think everyone in the company liked him and respected him. Every Christmas Tony gave me a lovely piece of jewellery from Garrards, his favourite jewellers. I accompanied him to a couple of big, formal events where he needed to go with a female. I'm sure there were many women who would have liked to get their hands on his bank balance and status. For several years he held a big annual party at the house near Lambourn which was always a great occasion – with a band, a string quartet and a really interesting mix of people who had dealings with Tony in one or other of the different facets of his life."

Lynda Roskott's assertion that Tony was definitely 'not a lark' is echoed by Simon Christian, who had trouble rousing the sleeping Stratton Smith on more than one occasion. "I went away with Tony for a week in Paris. He was going to have a meeting over there, but we were also going to do all the museums and art galleries. He actually got somebody to open up part of the Catacombs for him. We certainly got to visit to somewhere that wasn't normally allowed.

"The only problem was that Tony would never get out of bed. I would arrange to meet him later in the morning and say we should set out around eleven or midday, but I'd get up and then have to go banging on his door. He'd just shout back 'Allez!' or go away, or something like that. Then we moved on to Versailles and once again I went banging on his door. I'm knocking on the door and eventually he shouts out, 'I'm English and I want to sleep, so bugger off!' He thought I was the maid."

Chapter 13

The Silver Tongues

"I don't know whether you would say it was a form of snobbery and I don't think this is being rude, but Strat was sort of upwardly mobile, to use that awful modern expression. In fact I think that half of the favouritism with Genesis was because they were all nice, bright boys and you could talk to them. The Monty Python team would fall into that category, too."

Peter Thompson, independent PR

It was a chilly morning on the streets of Soho, but Tony Stratton Smith was in particularly high spirits. Waiting expectantly in the narrow offices above 85 Brewer Street, he was about to sign a new act to his record label and the very thought made him chuckle out loud. A hot cup of tea appeared on his desk, but there would be plenty of time for something stronger later on – and the boys would be here soon. There were six of them in the group, five Englishmen and one American, and they were an exciting new prospect, totally unlike anything else on The Famous Charisma Label but, in Strat's opinion at least, they would be a perfect fit.

Strat! He smiled to himself again. It was a nickname that he was quite used to hearing by now, although a select few, Gail Colson among them, still referred to him as Tony. What would he do without her? She would be busy downstairs right now, putting the finishing touches to the all-important paperwork, a part of the business he happily left to others. The record label was ticking along very nicely, thank you. The first couple of years had worked out extremely well; plenty of hard work, of course and the cash flow was always a bit tight, but he had assembled a fine roster of artists and a good team of people to look after them. Now he was about to add another important name to that list.

These boys had already made one album, but their old label didn't have a clue how to market them properly and when the rumour circulated that their contract was up for grabs, Tony had no hesitation in making an offer.

Which had come as a surprise to some people in the company, certainly, but Tony was confident that the self-same people who were buying

229

Charisma albums were laughing themselves silly at a surreal comedy show first broadcast by the BBC in 1969.

Yes, he was absolutely sure it would work. Tony stood up, straightened his tie, brushed the cigarette ash from his trousers and had just started to cross the room when there was a knock on the door. Gail popped her head inside. "They're here," she said. "Graham Chapman and Michael Palin are in reception…"

* * *

The *Monty Python's Flying Circus* team had made their first record for the BBC in 1970, a selection of their best sketches in front of a live audience at Camden Town Hall. The Pythons – Chapman, Palin, John Cleese, Terry Jones, Eric Idle and Terry Gilliam – were less than happy with the outcome, not just in the lacklustre way it was produced but in its woefully poor promotion. A record company like Strat's Charisma, on the other hand, was tailor-made to handle this new phenomenon.

"The sort of people who buy Charisma albums are the sort of people who would also dig *Monty Python*," Tony told his friend, journalist Michel Wale. "The Python lads sensed that we were right for their image as we are slightly anarchic in the way we go about things. They didn't want to sign with an institution. They wanted the personal thing; a small label, where they could pop round for a drink and settle things in five minutes, rather than having to write letters and arrange appointments."

Tony was right. The first two Charisma Python albums – *Another Monty Python Record* (1971) and *Monty Python's Previous Record* (1972) – reached the LP charts. The third, *The Monty Python Matching Tie And Handkerchief* (1973), was cut with two parallel grooves on side two, so different sketches would be heard depending on where the needle happened to fall when it was played. It is therefore likely to be the world's only 'three-sided record', another first for Tony.

The success of Python on disc prompted the company to hire Ronnie Lane's mobile studio to record one of Python's shows during their 1974 run at the Theatre Royal, Drury Lane, watched by a dummy Princess Margaret in the Royal Box. This became *Monty Python Live at Drury Lane*, another collection of their favourite sketches, now adapted for the live stage.

So it was that Strat realised one of his great ambitions, to be written into a Python sketch, an honour they rarely bestowed. During Election Special, a sketch that parodied election night coverage with pinpoint precision, the improvised dialogue went like this:

John Cleese: *"Well there you have it, a Sensible gain at Harpenden with the Silly vote being split."*

Michael Palin: *"And we've just heard from Luton that Tony Stratton Smith has with him there the unsuccessful Slightly Silly candidate, Kevin Phillips Bong."*

Eric Idle: *"Kevin Phillips Bong. You polled no votes at all. Not a sausage. Bugger all. Are you at all disappointed with this performance?"*

Neil Innes: *"Not at all. As I always say: climb every mountain, ford every stream, follow every byway, 'till you find your dream..."*

Now Python-ed for posterity, no doubt Tony was tickled Charisma pink.

* * *

The spoken-word series of albums was another aspect of Charisma that set them apart from the norm. Two unusual LPs brilliantly captured the silver tongues of cricket commentator John Arlott and racing expert Peter O'Sullevan for posterity. First, though, came the poet Sir John Betjeman.

Of all the weird and wonderful recordings that Charisma released, the four LPs by poet laureate Betjeman must rank high on the list of Tony's vinyl eccentricities. In actual fact the recordings work surprisingly well, not just the quality of Betjeman's wordplay but the perfect musical settings of Jim Parker.

When Charisma came calling, Betjeman had only recently been made Poet Laureate, following proudly in the footsteps of Worsdworth, Tennyson and Masefield, taking over the post from Cecil Day-Lewis in October 1972. In the early days of the laureateship, the likes of John Dryden and Thomas Shadwell had received a salary plus 'a butt of Canary wine'. This practice was later discontinued, the fortified wine replaced with the monetary equivalent. When Betjeman was appointed, however, he revived the tradition and received 720 bottles of sherry in addition to his annual salary.

It isn't surprising that Tony would seek a close association with Britain's populist poet. Aside from Betjeman's standing in the literary world, he was a keen supporter of architectural conservation, campaigning tirelessly for the preservation of railway stations and churches right across the country. Tony, who was known to weep merely at the sight of a crumbling gothic bell tower, would have enjoyed conversations with the great man. Publicist Peter Thompson suggests that selling records was actually the last thing on Tony's mind when he signed the poet to the label.

"John Betjeman was really important to Strat, not to record sales necessarily, but important to Strat on a personal level," he says. "Strat revelled in knowing Betjeman, actually. I don't know whether you would say it was a form of snobbery and I don't think this is being rude, but Strat was sort of upwardly mobile, to use that awful modern expression. In fact

I think that half of the favouritism with Genesis was because they were all nice, bright boys and you could talk to them. The Monty Python team would fall into that category, too."

Betjeman was 67 when he launched his recording career with *Banana Blush* in 1974. The venerable poet read his work over 'sumptuous musical accompaniments' that veer between brass band, rock guitar, tea-dance jazz and big band swing. Producer Hugh Murphy played an integral part in getting Betjeman on record. Having worked on a collection of poems by the group Doggerel Bank (also for the Charisma label), he had expressed a desire to work with the poet laureate – and as luck would have it, a member of the group and former leader of The Barrow Poets, William Bealby-Wright, was an acquaintance of Betjeman and passed on Murphy's request. Bealby-Wright also suggested that Doggerel Bank's Jim Parker would be the ideal man to write and arrange the music.

"Tony was a unique character, even in the popular music era of the seventies which was full of people who, shall we say, were frequently verging on the eccentric," says Parker. "The Barrow Poets were a little unorthodox. We were in the process of making a record using Hugh Murphy as our producer and he said that he would like to make an LP with Sir John Betjeman. It happened that one of our group, William Bealby-Wright, had already made a record with Betjeman featuring the poetry of the Manx poet T. E. Brown and William was prevailed upon to approach J.B. about making an LP of his own poems set to music by me. John seemed bemused by this, 'I thought poetry was its own music,' he said. He was particularly taken with the harmonium, which was portable and reminded him of the ones he remembered from Sunday afternoon services on the beach, so he agreed, I suspect with some trepidation, to give it a try. Hugh was introduced to Betjeman, who was fascinated by Hugh's long hair and single earring, and we all went to see Tony Stratton Smith."

Sales of poetry recordings were miniscule but this never bothered Tony. "He was extremely keen to have Betjeman," continues Parker. "Tony was on the plump side with a quiet, cultured voice and impeccable manners, very unlike some of the tearaways he had to deal with. His first words to me were, 'Hello, I'm Tony but I'm usually known as Fat Strat.' He never interfered with the creative side of things and never tried to claim any credit or publicity for himself. I don't recall any occasion when he came to the recording or mixing sessions. He was thrilled at the reception accorded to our debut LP, *Banana Blush*, and had ideas to launch it in New York with a concert at Carnegie Hall."

This never happened. "Although Betjeman was more than happy to work in the studio, a live performance was quite a different matter and he demurred. Another probable reason was that John loved all of Great Britain and was very fond of Australia, but he really did not like America."

Paul Conroy recalls one impromptu visit to The Gay Hussar, the celebrated Hungarian restaurant in Greek Street, beloved of literary figures and Labour politicians and run by Victor Sassie. "Strat came into my office one lunchtime, when the agency was in Soho Square, and he called out, 'Connors, we're going to lunch... with John Betjeman' and I was totally unprepared, jeaned up, and with no idea this was going to happen. Apparently, Strat wanted John Betjeman to go out and do a live show. He was trying to convince him to go on the road with The Barrow Poets."

Betjeman may have enjoyed aspects of the studio process, but the idea of a tour and commercial promotion was definitely not for him. In a letter to a friend, Betjeman wrote, "The publicity of the pop world is so appalling that I was not prepared for it. They called the pop record *Betjeman's Banana Blush* and they've had a T-shirt made for me to wear, which I refuse to do. It had on it in white letters this frightful title."

Betjeman was constantly worried that his alliance with the music business was a mistake. Referring again to *Banana Blush*, he wrote to Sir Rennie Maudslay: "I committed a lapse of taste last month, and I will not be surprised if I am dismissed from my honourable office" (the laureateship). Fortunately for Betjeman and Charisma, a great many disagreed, including his biographer A.N. Wilson, who wrote, "If he felt in that moment that he was 'just' a pop poet, his self-reproach could not have been more misplaced. For these records are among the very best things he ever did. No one who has heard Parker's records can ever forget them. For ever afterwards, when you read Betjeman's lyrics on the page, the music starts."

Despite the poet's own misgivings, *Banana Blush* was well received by the critics and Charisma even released 'A Shropshire Lad' as a single, which was promptly voted single of the week in *NME*. Betjeman may have felt unsure about the world of pop promotion, but he did try to throw himself into it; when an *NME* journalist arrived for an interview at Betjeman's Chelsea flat, the poet greeted him with "It's awfully nice of you to visit me, I've bought some splendid cakes for the occasion. Would you like tea or whisky?" And then, over the course of the afternoon, while Betjeman waxed lyrical about the recording sessions, the reporter slowly but surely slid under the table.

Tony was keen to release a further collection to tie in with the Queen's Silver Jubilee in 1977. Musical director Jim Parker was at the lunchtime meeting when the idea was proposed: "Tony took John and myself to The Gay Hussar. This, by the way, was when the word gay meant happy and did not have its present implications. We spent a long time on drinks and a fulsome meal and eventually the idea was mooted and accepted. John said to me afterwards, 'Did you notice how he kept the conversation moving along until he finally popped the question?' Betjeman was a delightful man and could give the impression of being a poet with artistic things on his mind, but he was no fool."

The Charisma albums have subsequently proved to be an inspiration for the likes of Nick Cave and Suggs, with the Madness frontman even going as far as to select one Betjeman track, 'On A Portrait Of A Deaf Man', as one of his Desert Island Discs. Talking to *The Guardian* ahead of Betjeman's centenary in 2006, Suggs told the paper, "You have these lovely images of somewhere like Hampshire, but you also have this darker undercurrent and this fantastic music. That was what we were trying to do with Madness; to show English life, but say that it's not always jolly and, hopefully, have a few good tunes."

* * *

During the evening of October 30, 1938, listeners all across America turned on their wireless sets and radiograms to listen to the music of Ramon Raquello & His Orchestra, broadcast live from the Meridian Room at the Park Plaza in New York City. A few minutes in, the broadcast was interrupted with the disturbing announcement that astronomers had spotted 'enormous blue flames shooting up from the surface of Mars'. Moments later, the music was cut short again with news of a meteor crashing on farmland near Grovers Mill, New Jersey, where a reporter stood by the deep crater describing the scene.

What followed has gone down in radio history. The now-familiar tale has Martians invading the US from a three-legged craft, death rays and toxic black gas sending panic across the country, the press reporting on Americans packing their bags to flee the city or hiding in cellars until the deadly gas blew away. In reality, the programme was the Halloween episode of Orson Welles' popular *Mercury Theatre On The Air* radio show, an adaptation of *The War Of The Worlds* by H.G. Wells especially scripted by Howard Koch. Although the show included disclaimers stating it was pure fiction, many missed the one at the beginning and by the time the next statement was read out the dramatic events had sent people screaming into the night. The nationwide panic was nowhere near as widespread as reported – in fact it is thought that the American newspaper industry used it as a blunt instrument to beat down the rival upstart that was radio – but in this instance the myth is more delicious than the reality and the story has grown with each retelling. Thirty years later, the complete radio broadcast was made available as a double LP in America and Tony jumped at the chance to license the UK release on his label as part of the Charisma Perspective series in August 1973.

Charisma Records may have released the recording of *War Of The*

Worlds – "The original broadcast that panicked the nation" – but, sadly, it failed to put out an even more strange and startling album, this time by comedian Eric Morecambe, provisionally titled *Eric Calls The Birds*. In an internal memo dated July 1, 1983, Glen Colson wrote: "Dear Tony. So sorry I missed your ad hoc meeting yesterday. I have now the pleasure of presenting my next two projects, two more albums. First album: *Eric Calls The Birds*. Will feature Eric Morecambe waking up to the dawn chorus, brushing his teeth at the open window, a walk in the country, home for tea in the garden and a walk through the woods in the evening. I have already spent the day with Ralph Steadman, who is doing a book on vultures, and he loves the above idea. Can't wait to get started."

It was a bizarre enough idea, certainly, and totally in keeping with the general Charisma ethos, but once you find out that the second album in Glen's presentation was entitled *A.J.P. Taylor Talks Wars*, you could be forgiven for thinking this was simply Colson trying to tickle the boss's funny bone and keep the music press on their toes. Especially when the postscript to the memo has the mischievous publicist asking for money to cover the printing costs for a John Arlott poster. Not so. Colson had discovered that the taller half of Britain's favourite comedy duo was, in fact, a keen twitcher, who had spent much of his childhood birdwatching on the mudflats around Morecambe, the hometown that gave him his stage name. Only a combination of a lack of funding needed to start the ball rolling, followed by Eric Morecambe's untimely death in May 1984, prevented this peculiar addition to Charisma's spoken-word catalogue from hitting the shelves. Two years later, the RSPB nature reserve at Morecambe Bay named a birdwatchers hide after Eric, a tribute to his life-long love of wildlife.

If the idea of recording Eric Morecambe sounds more like the product of his press officer's fevered imagination, Tony did manage to secure the services of an Australian comedian whose alter-ego would go on to become a household name. The major breakthrough for Barry Humphries in Britain came with the stage show *Housewife-Superstar!* in 1976. Produced by impresario Michael White, it was a one-man show with Humphries taking the persona of Dame Edna Everage, with a preamble from a relatively new character, the equally loud if less-glamorous Australian 'cultural attaché' Sir Les Patterson. The show was a huge hit, largely because Humphries had already appeared on every available television talk show, where Dame Edna teased and terrified Michael Parkinson and Russell Harty. After an initial run at the Apollo Theatre, the show moved to the Globe Theatre in Shaftesbury Avenue where Barry/Edna quickly adapted the dialogue to fit the new venue: "This is the Globe, darlings, isn't it wonderful? It's oozing, ravaged by pageant and pomp. Little Shakespeare himself used to jump around this stage, dressed up as a woman most of the time, not that it proves a thing these days."

Humphries' persona as Edna Everage was to become his most popular and enduring stage character, and Simon Christian remembers seeing the flower-tossing Antipodean Dame in full flight. "Tony would take Noel Bennett, myself and Jack Barrie to the theatre. On one occasion, when Tony took us to see Barry Humphries in London, we were sitting up in the box and it was slightly embarrassing – if you can be embarrassed when you're young – because Barry was throwing all the gladioli towards us and tailoring the jokes to the racing industry, all for Tony's benefit."

Charisma promptly hired Ronnie Lane's mobile studio and captured Barry Humphries' live performance at the Globe Theatre on Thursday on July 8, 1976, for posterity. Tony sweet-talked John Betjeman into writing the sleeve notes and the album, under the cumbersome title of *Barry Humphries – By Permission Of Dame Edna Everage, Proudly Presents Housewife-Superstar*, was released later the same year.

Art director Frank Sansom worked on the sleeve and subsequent promotional material. "It was like the Mad Hatter's tea party every day and you never knew what was coming in from one minute to the next," he says. "I remember Strat telling me when he'd actually signed Barry Humphries, that he was flying in and could we get the *Housewife-Superstar* album out by a certain date, because he was coming in to do some shows. The first time I ever met Barry he was in the hairdressers. I was told to rush down because he'd just flown in and there he was having his hair cut. I had planned a series of radio commercials to launch the album and I got the agency to prepare all the press ads – and then of course, Barry immediately took over and completely rewrote it in his own inimitable style. That was typical of working with Strat – but it didn't matter if you were going for tea with Sir John Betjeman or whether you were catching up with Barry Humphries, there was a challenge every day – which was great and it was all down to Strat. And that's why I loved it."

Spurred on by the show's success, the following year Barry Humphries took it to America where it opened at New York's Theater Four, off-Broadway. Unfortunately, he was almost unknown there and the character of Dame Edna was seen as 'just another drag act'. As with almost every New York opening, success or failure lay with newspaper critics and after a poor review from the influential *New York Times*, the show closed after a couple of weeks.

Nancy Lewis was working in Charisma's New York office when Humphries tried his hand in the States and remembers the less-than enthusiastic reaction. "His off-Broadway show was a total disaster, because no one really understood what he was doing back then," she recalls. "Arthur Cantor was the man who brought him over. Oh God, he was a horrible producer and did no promotion whatsoever for the show. Then he threw Barry on some TV talk show for a morning and of course Barry went on dressed as Edna, so the people were just very confused, they had no idea what was going on."

Nancy Lewis saw the show die a death and how badly Barry Humphries was treated. "We talked about recording another album," she says, "and Barry was really keen. He said, 'I could even get Elton John to sing on it', and so I talked the London office into funding it. Strat agreed and Barry came back to London to record it. I thought the album was a brilliant idea, although I know that Barry originally wanted to have *The Scream* as the cover."

Humphries returned to London and went into the studio to record his second album for Charisma, *The Sound Of Edna*, released in 1978. Featuring classic Everage material such as 'Every Mother Wants A Boy Like Elton' and 'The Night We Burnt My Mother's Things'. The UK album sleeve is a clever spoof on *The Sound Of Music* film poster with Edna as Julie Andrews, running with her guitar in hand, chased by her Australian 'children' – namely the Bee Gees, Rolf Harris, Olivia Newton-John and a kangaroo. Humphries replaces Christopher Plummer, who looks on disapprovingly, arms folded. In the US and Australia, Humphries also got his original wish. The cover was changed to show Dame Edna echoing the tortured character in Munch's painting *The Scream*.

* * *

It was only natural that Tony used Charisma's spoken-word series to release an album that featured one of his all-consuming passions, horseracing. After many years spent around stables and on racetracks, he convinced one of his more famous associates to record *Peter O'Sullevan Talks Turf*, a fascinating piece of racing history, especially as it captured the best known voice in horse racing commentary. O'Sullevan's love of the sport, and his meticulous preparation for every race, led to a wonderful quote from the noted sports journalist Hugh McIlvanney: "Had he been on the rails at Balaclava, he would have kept pace with the Charge of the Light Brigade, listing the fallers in precise order and describing the riders' injuries before they hit the ground."

Released on the Charisma label in January 1983, the front cover featured a cartoon of Sir Peter as a horse's head, illustrated by Ralph Steadman, while the back cover photograph features Prince Monolulu, the colourful, larger than life racing tipster who was to be found shouting "I gotta horse..." at almost every major race meeting of the sixties. "It is like having a special guest sitting down at your dinner table," Tony told the *Daily Express*, who ran a special discounted offer on the album in the racing section of their newspaper.

237

The record had O'Sullevan answering such dinner-party questions as 'Which is the best horse he had ever seen? Who is the best jockey? What were his personal memories of life as an owner?' Racing correspondent Christopher Poole pronounced, "If quality and professionalism set records, then *Peter O'Sullevan Talks Turf* should be a chart-topper." Sadly, in terms of actual record sales it probably wasn't a racing certainty and even Tony felt a follow-up was unlikely. In a letter to John Webster at Virgin Records, he wrote, "You seemed to be interested in our doing another Peter O'Sullevan album, possibly in 1984. Were you serious?"

A second sports LP featured John Arlott, the great cricket commentator and wine expert. "Strat composed a letter offering Arlott a deal, which he accepted," says Glen Colson, who again commissioned Ralph Steadman to create an illustration for the cover, this time with Arlott's face as a cricket ball. "One day me and my friend Chris Charlesworth went to the Oval to watch a Surrey game and I went into the shop there to ask them to stock some Arlott LPs. The bloke behind the counter was a bit non-committal, so about half an hour later I got Chris to go into the shop and ask for one. An hour after that I went back to the shop and asked whether he'd thought about it. 'Yes,' he said. 'Someone was only asking about that record earlier today. I'll take half a dozen.'"

In 1983 Colson came up with the idea for another spoken-word album with Arlott and cricket on one side, and Peter O'Sullevan and horse racing on the other. Viv Stanshall suggested the perfect title: *Neck & Neck & Never Caught*. Colson asked Barney Bubbles to come up with designs for the album sleeve, but with money exceptionally tight at Charisma this was yet another spoken-word project that never came to fruition.

* * *

The Monty Python team had been a wonderful signing for Charisma and, for the most part, a constant delight. However all good things must come to an end, and with their contract nearing completion even the genial Pythons were becoming a problem, as lawyer Tony Seddon remembers: "They tried to get out of that contract and we ended up in litigation for about a year. They didn't play very fair and it's no coincidence that the last in the series of Monty Python discs is called *Contractual Obligation*."

The original contract with Charisma was for seven albums, to include one live album and a 'best of' compilation. The Python team hoped to complete their obligations with two film soundtracks, *Holy Grail* and *Life Of Brian*. By now they also owed albums to Arista Records in the USA with whom they had signed a five-album deal, originally hoping to give them the first five Charisma albums. Various legalities confounded this plan. Arista were disallowed from manufacturing and distributing the first three albums in North America and initially turned down *Live At Drury Lane*, preferring to hold out for another studio album. By the time they relented, the distribution rights to *Drury Lane* had been sold to another company.

To keep Arista happy the Pythons agreed to record an American show and, to keep Charisma happy, they released *Monty Python's Instant Record Collection*, the proposed 'best of' that was originally supposed to be the final album of their contract. Yet even this was not without its problems. Terry Gilliam came up with a brilliant, albeit complicated, design for the sleeve that folded out into a cube that looked like a large pile of records with silly names on the spines. In practice, and particularly in transit, so many of the sleeves became damaged that Charisma scrapped the fold-out sleeve and put it in a regular jacket instead. Meanwhile, financial problems in funding *Life Of Brian* were delaying the release of the film and the new soundtrack record, leaving both Charisma and Arista one album short. Charisma demanded the group head back to the studio to complete their contractual obligation, thus providing the Pythons with the title for their final album. "Yes, we had to do it," agreed Michael Palin. "There was no real problem with Charisma. Strat had been brilliant for us, but we were quite forcefully told that we had a commitment to record one last album with them. None of us really wanted to do it, if I were to be completely honest. I felt like it was stepping back a bit."

Having used up every available sketch from their television shows, Eric Idle supplied a batch of politically-incorrect songs, while the other members hastily recycled sketches from other productions they had worked on as individuals, with John Cleese throwing in two sketches from *At Last The 1948 Show* and Idle adding a piece from *Rutland Weekend Television*. *The Monty Python Contractual Obligation Album* did exactly what it said on the sleeve and wound up their largely successful time on the Charisma label.

Relationships between Tony and the Python team had certainly cooled by this time, but as Simon White rightly points out, it does seem strange that having put so much time, effort and money into *Holy Grail*, Tony was not involved at all in the next Python film, *The Life Of Brian*. Up until the eleventh hour, financial help had been promised from EMI Films but after their promise evaporated, producer John Goldstone turned to George Harrison. A great fan of the Python team, Harrison put up approximately £3 million, setting up the HandMade Films company in the process. The former Beatle put his hand in his pocket purely because he "wanted to see the film", leading Terry Jones to famously comment that it was "the world's most expensive cinema ticket".

Perhaps this time around, the Pythons wanted one single backer and Tony, or rather Charisma, was unable to stump up the whole amount. Either way, privately Tony was extremely disappointed – to say the least.

"He was very, very pissed off and felt completely let down," says White. "Tony told me he was incredibly hurt, having been so involved with the first one, that he wasn't allowed to roll it over to a second film. Normally on these things, if you get in once, especially if it's successful, you at least get a chance at the next film. But he didn't get an opportunity with the second film, because they went with George Harrison, who was a huge fan of Monty Python. The indication was that they were somewhat overwhelmed by George Harrison."

EMI had pulled out over what it regarded as controversial subject matter with their chief executive Bernard Delfont especially worried about a potential religious backlash. Consequently, having got the funding from Harrison and made the film exactly as they wanted to, the Pythons took small, but sweet revenge. A massive box-office success, *Life Of Brian* was the fourth highest grossing film in the UK in 1979, and the highest grossing British film in the US. To rub salt into the wound, as the credits are about to roll, the last words heard in the film are, "I said to him, Bernie, they'll never make their money back on this one."

Anthony Mills Smith, circa 1950.
Having just left Sparkhill Commercial School,
Tony joins the Birmingham Gazette as a cub
reporter.
Note the two sharpened pencils in his top pocket
and the ever-present cigarette.

Photograph courtesy Mike Norris

Read all about it

Stratton Smith.

Right: Read all about it. Stratton Smith, the
established and much-read sports journalist with
the Daily Sketch, 1958.

Photograph courtesy British Library

Tony proudly gets his sister June to the church on time. The marriage of June Smith to Albert M. Norris at Christ Church, Yardley Wood, 1953.

Photograph courtesy Mike Norris

The young 'jornalista' and his typewriter – circa 1957.

Photograph courtesy Mike Norris

Tony's South American adventure. Tea and chess as Edward M. Gilbert plots his next move. Rio de Janeiro, 1962.

Photo courtesy Edward M Gilbert

With The Nice - Brian Davison, Keith Emerson and Lee Jackson at the Bath Festival, June 1969.

With Ben Bunders, A&R manager for Phonogram International Head Office in Baarn Holland. Circa 1969.

The empire grows – as does the hairstyle.
Tony outside his flat/office in Dean Street, 1971.

Photograph © Barrie Wentzell

Tony goes furniture shopping and comes back with JRR Tolkein's desk. November 1972.

Photograph courtesy Oxford Mail & Times/Newsquest

Glen Colson listens to the Boss; Tony holds court in the colourful Brewer Street office, December 1972.

Photograph © Barrie Wentzell

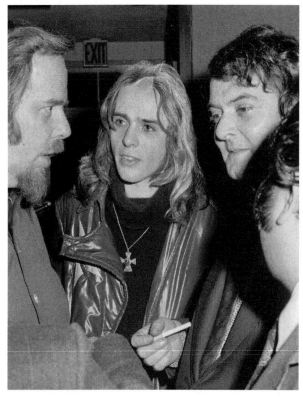

Peter Gabriel and Tony attend an after-show party for Genesis in New York, 1972.

Photograph © Bob Gruen

A quiet little place in the country. Tony takes tea outside Luxford House, Crowborough, Sussex circa 1973.

Photograph courtesy Charisma archive

Tony in celebratory mood with Lindisfarne's Alan Hull and some of the B&C team. Left to right: Lloyd Beiny, TSS, Alan Hull, Fred Parsons and Jim Flynn.

Photograph courtesy Lloyd Beiny

Corporate success at the track. Tony proudly presents the Charisma Records Gold Challenge Cup during a sponsored meeting at Kempton Park.

Photograph courtesy Kim Smith

Personal success at the track. Tony receives the Virginia Gold Cup for his horse Tower-Bird, winning the two-mile steeplechase at Stratford Upon Avon, September 1979.

Photograph © Bernard Parkin, Cheltenham

Over a cognac, the deal is done. Sealing the distribution deal with Phonogram boss Aart Dalhuisen at Chez les Anges restaurant in Frith Street, December 1980.

Photograph courtesy Holly Fogg

Pete Townshend, Chrysalis boss Chris Wright and Tony enjoy a joke with Peter Smith (right). Diana, Princess of Wales, looks most amused. The first Prince's Trust concert, Dominion Theatre, Tottenham Court Road, 1982.

Photograph courtesy Chris Wright

Rubbing shoulders with Royalty; a personal thank-you from Prince Philip, Duke of Edinburgh for Tony's fund-raising work with the Sports Aid Foundation.

Photograph courtesy Charisma archive

Drink in one hand, smoke in the other, Tony hosts a party at The Marquee. Wardour Street, London, 5th April 1984.

Photograph © Neil Mackenzie Matthews

The elder statesman and his young pretender. Tony relaxes with Richard Branson on the deck of 'Duende', Branson's houseboat in Little Venice, London. August 3rd, 1983.

Photograph © Neil Mackenzie Matthews

Not quite so relaxing; Tony gamely joins Richard Branson in a spot of 'double dutch'. Little Venice, 3rd August 1983.

Photograph © Neil Mackenzie Matthews

Steve Weltman (second left), Richard Branson and Tony get down with the Rock Steady Crew. Gold discs all round. Somewhere in Soho, November 1983.

Photograph courtesy Steve Weltman

Chapter 14

The Shock Of The New

"He could be amused by calamity."
Martin Lewis, music publicist

By the end of 1976 and on into 1977 the British music scene was undergoing its biggest transformation since the arrival of The Beatles in 1963. A new generation of fans had come of age needing heroes of their own to worship. Rejecting the superstars of the day, some of them formed bands that played the thriving pub and club circuit around London and the suburbs, their mission to take their music to audiences who could reach out and touch them, not watch them from a distant seat in an arena.

Dr Feelgood, Kokomo, Ducks Deluxe and Graham Parker pared down their sound to tight, raw-edged, raucous rock'n'roll for a crowd that preferred to hear their live music with a pint in their hand. For about 60p on the door, the back rooms and basements in pubs all over town became regular rock venues; the Hope & Anchor in Islington, the Fulham Greyhound, the Golden Lion in the Kings Road and the Clarendon in Hammersmith all played host to emerging stars – Elvis Costello, Nick Lowe and the rest. This back to basics approach took a further turn with the advent of what became known as punk rock, which often took the three chord 'do-it-yourself' mantra to its extreme. Suburban kids in Bromley and Croydon were forming bands left right and centre. Malcolm McLaren returned from a trip to New York inspired by the energy, passion and fashion sense of the New York Dolls, The Ramones and Television and set about putting together a UK version. Cue The Clash, The Damned and McLaren's Sex Pistols.

Not surprisingly these developments and much of this new music passed by Tony completely. He was spending far more time with the racing crowd than with his staff in the Charisma office. Gail and the rest were used to covering for their errant boss, but far more worrying was the drain on company resources caused by Tony's horse racing habit. "Once he got into racing financially, I knew where he was spending the money," says Gail. "The trouble was that it was the artists' money and so there were lots of arguments."

Paul Conroy is in complete agreement. "Because he'd got the cash flow from his books, seemingly there was money there for him to fritter away on the horses. We were working all the hours that God sends, trying to make sense out of the record label, and it was just heart-breaking," he says. "It costs so much money to look after horses and it was just something that we were not part of. And then on top of that, all these bloodstock people would come in and try to sell you half a leg and a fetlock."

The changing trends of the late seventies must have come as something of a shock to a label like Charisma, with its roots in the underground movement of the late sixties and the progressive rock groups that emerged later. The spikey-haired and safety-pinned punks were trampling all over the very sounds that Tony's label had lovingly nurtured. It was now time to move on. In an interview with David Dalton for *Music Week*, Tony said, "We have made profound changes here, and at a time when the rest of the industry is pulling in its horns and laying off staff, we've been actively seeking staff in line with the way we see Charisma going. We realised about a year ago that those who had been at Charisma from the start perhaps had rather fixed attitudes. The first thing to do was to make the label more accommodating to new talent."

Tony's attitude to business was nicely summed up later in the same interview, when he told Dalton: "With success comes responsibility and we received a sharp reminder of that in 1975, at the time of the liquidation of our distributor, B&C. Between them, Gail Colson and Brian Gibbon taught me that good housekeeping was the best launch pad for adventure."

Despite his pronouncements to *Music Week* on corporate positioning, consolidation and maximising potential, Tony's mind was often elsewhere, most often uncorking the bubbly and studying form for the afternoon's racing. Is there enough money in the account to hire the studio and book the restaurant? Then, dear boy, balancing the books can wait until Monday.

With Tony now settled into his 'upstairs' role as company Chairman (or company President, according to one letter heading), the key position of Managing Director at Charisma became fairly fluid for a while. Tony's first choice to replace him was Gail Colson who had known Tony for just about as long as anyone else in the music industry and had been right there beside him at Charisma since day one. Gail hesitated to take the job on her own, worried about her lack of financial experience, so the decision was made for Gail and finance director Brian Gibbon to share the role between them.

Bringing old friends and associates together to see if sparks would fly had long been a favourite pastime for Tony, but now that he was spending more and more time away from the music business, the projects became ever more bizarre. The illusionist Simon Drake, another left-field character in whom Tony took an interest, remembers one particularly strange idea. "Strat put me on at the Marquee and I did a few shows there. Then he came up with this strange project called Charlie Pinocchio. It was a musical and Phil

Collins was going to be in it, I was to be one of the stars and Viv Stanshall was to write for it, with a guy called Abb Dickson doing the magic. And that's about as far as it got. Strat flew me out to Atlanta, Georgia to work with Abb Dickson, a well-known magician whose family owned a funeral directors. So there we were, sitting among all these coffins, talking about the show and I spent a week just going out for hamburgers and talking about magic tricks, trying to write stuff. Then I flew on to meet Viv Stanshall in New York, where we stayed with my dad's friend Terry. Viv met me at Terry's apartment and drank all his alcohol and did nothing. Well he may have written something, but at that time he was a hopeless drunk, really dreadful. At that stage I had no conception of how to put a show like that together, but it was so typical of Strat to send you off, let you tread water and try to work out how the hell do we do this?"

Publicist Martin Lewis also found himself on the receiving end of a seemingly impossible mission from Tony. "He wanted me to come and work at Charisma, but I just didn't want to do that, I wanted to be independent and I wanted to be a producer. Strat hired me to work with Adrian Wagner, a synthesizer composer and keyboards player in the Mike Oldfield/Rick Wakeman style and supposedly the great, great grandson of Richard Wagner, the famous 19th-century composer. Adrian made this album about the Incas and how they were all from Mars. Now this would have been fine in 1974, but this was 1977/78 and you couldn't be doing grand concept albums in the face of the Sex Pistols. But Strat had Wagner and *The Last Inca* album and he hired me to promote it – and I needed the money, so I took the job. We were flying in the face of punk rock; phoning up journalists in the midst of the Sex Pistols and The Clash and trying to persuade them to give time to an album about Incas coming from Mars. It was never going to happen. I did what little I could, and Strat was still amused by it all, even though it was a dreadful campaign. He could be amused by calamity."

In 1977 the 'other' Tony Smith, unhappy with publishing opportunities offered elsewhere, formed Hit & Run Music Publishing, initially to handle the music of Genesis. Having been handed the management of the band on the proverbial plate, he then acquired their lucrative publishing rights for a proverbial song – all down to Strat's generous nature, as financial guru Andrew MacHutchon remembers: "When it came round to the publishing rights, Strat said, 'I have a great deal of regard for Tony and for the band and yes, I wouldn't really want to sell it to anybody else.' So we were left to negotiate with Tony Smith and Monty Wynn, who was their financial man at Hit & Run. He was an elderly guy with a very, very bright brain, a real gentleman, and we sat down and discussed the deal between us, back and forth, back and forth, until eventually we reached a settlement that Tony was happy to take. I would have kept pushing for more, but Strat said enough is enough. So we got there, we settled the deal and got it done – but of course in the background, Strat also had the up and coming artists like Julian Lennon and Malcolm McLaren."

Tony Smith outlines the circumstances in acquiring the Genesis publishing. "What happened was that the publishing became free when their agreement ran out with Carlin Music. First of all there was Stratsongs, Strat had signed them for music publishing for the first couple of records. He then did a licensing deal with Carlin and then they extended the deal. Genesis really didn't have a good deal; in fact I spent most of the first 15 to 20 years of my career undoing their deals. It was after *Lamb* that their music publishing became free and I said to them, 'Look, I can do this, you know, we can do this ourselves.' I suggested that instead of me taking my commission as a manager, I would do a straightforward deal for the same percentage, but then just do the publishing. So that's how Hit & Run started in publishing."

In the eighties, Hit & Run acquired Charisma Music and Jon Crawley moved across to become managing director at 'Hidden Pun', as Peter Gabriel nicknamed the company. "When he subsequently bought the Charisma publishing outright we merged the two, because Charisma had many more artists and writers, so we put the two together and Smithy brought me in as joint managing director. Eventually I became manager and shareholder."

By now, Genesis had started to enjoy a regular run of hit singles, and most of the individual members were making successful solo records. Stratton Smith's early patience and persistence was paying dividends, and not only for The Famous Charisma Label. The people over at Hit & Run must have rubbed their collective hands with glee.

Tony's views on singles were fairly relaxed to say the least and it's safe to say he considered them at best to be a necessary evil and at worst a waste of time. He had always seen Charisma as primarily an album label and they were certainly selling plenty of those. "Singles," he told *Rolling Stone*'s David Fricke, "were never Charisma's strong point simply because I saw no need for them. The use of B-sides that weren't otherwise available was really a ploy in the early days, especially with Genesis. Genesis never had any real acceptance as a singles band, so the use of an unreleased or live track on the B-side was simply to get the Genesis following to support the single in its early days."

Genesis' *Spot The Pigeon* EP consisted of three tracks left over from the sessions that produced their *Wind & Wuthering* album. This was the last Genesis release to include guitarist Steve Hackett, who was frustrated that more of his songs weren't recorded. The final straw came when his song 'Inside And Out', which Hackett believed strong enough for the album, was released only on the EP.

Under the management of 'the other' Tony Smith, and with Phil

Collins starting to call the shots in the band, Genesis were changing tack. Collins' more commercial songs were finding favour in the singles market, although in February 1978 it was Mike Rutherford's 'Follow You Follow Me' that became the band's best-selling single, reaching number seven in the UK and entering the top 30 in America.

While Charisma enjoyed the kudos and the cash flow, it is hard to believe that Tony wholeheartedly approved of the direction his boys were taking. Helping 'Follow You Follow Me' into the charts was record plugger Judd Lander. When the record broke into the top ten, a spot on the influential *Top Of The Pops* was up for grabs. Unfortunately for Lander, a precedent had already been set with 'I Know What I Like' and, as they had done before, Genesis didn't want to do it. Lander found himself under pressure from both sides, as he recalls: "*Top Of The Pops* were desperate for them to appear. Strat was also desperate for the guys to do the show, but Tony Smith told me to bugger off. I was getting grief from the television producer, I think it was Robin Nash at the time, because nobody turned down *TOTP* – but Smithy turned it down and the group turned it down. A pain in the arse they were, but I loved them for it."

Genesis eventually agreed to make an appearance on the show when 'Turn It On Again' reached the top ten two years later. Taken from the album *Duke*, Mike Rutherford's tale of one man's total obsession with watching television peaked at number eight in the UK charts in March 1980.

* * *

In the July of 1978, US music industry magazine *Billboard* announced that Charisma was planning a major expansion and were about to sign their first American artist, the relatively unknown singer-songwriter Chuck Brunicardi. Other new signings were to include Steve Joseph, the former-Bonzo frontman Viv Stanshall and two new bands, Razar and Blue Max. Apart from Tony's old mate Vivian, you could be forgiven for thinking that these new signings were unlikely to set the music world alight. In fact Brunicardi didn't even stay the course. He continued to dabble in songwriting but became better known as Dr F. Charles Brunicardi, a gastrointestinal surgeon-scientist and Professor and Chief of the Santa Monica UCLA General Surgery Group.

By now, Gail Colson was having major misgivings about Tony's decision making. After so many years of trying to keep the company on an even keel, joint managing director Colson finally decided to jump ship. It was a heartbreaking but necessary decision for Gail and it was those seemingly random signings, coupled with Tony's regular non-appearance in the office, which proved the final straw.

"Tony hadn't been around for about a year and I had tried to sign

Elvis Costello to Charisma, but he didn't like him," recalls Colson. "Then somebody sent me 'Satisfaction' by Devo, but once again Tony didn't like it. I went to America for a week to try and find a producer for a guy called Kim Beacon who was the singer in the final line-up of String Driven Thing and when I came back, Tony was waiting in the office. He said to me, 'Oh we've signed two bands.' I said, 'We've what?'

"This was someone who hadn't been involved in the music business for a year and he suddenly announced that we've signed two bands – one was called Razar and they were managed by Kit Lambert, The Who's old manager, who was on his uppers at the time. The other one was called Blue Max, and they were both awful, so I said to Tony, 'What are you playing at, just give Kit Lambert some money, don't sign these bands, what am I going to do with them?' And he just poo-poo'd it, so I said, 'Look, I'll tell you what, I'm giving you three months' notice and then I'm leaving.' Brian Gibbon was so surprised when I told him that he actually asked me if I had my period! So Tony and I made our peace, but I said to him, 'I suggest that you come back and run the company, because I've had enough.'"

Gail left on June 30, 1978. "I can remember the date clearly because that was when Genesis played the Milton Keynes Bowl and I always used to say that it was my leaving party!"

Gail Colson wasn't out of work for long. Within a matter of weeks she had joined Hit & Run and launched a separate company of her own, Gailforce Management, initially to manage Peter Gabriel and later Peter Hammill. She would also later apply her experience and no-nonsense approach to the management of Jesus Jones, The Pretenders, Chrissie Hynde, Morrissey and The Subways. Her involvement with Hynde was particularly rewarding, though Morrissey was, as she puts it, "interesting but difficult". The former Smiths frontman would disappear for months on end, refusing to answer his telephone and then, seemingly in a fit of pique, sack his manager, his accountant and his lawyer all on the same day. Morrissey would later ask Gail to return but, quite understandably, she refused.

Losing Gail Colson was a huge blow for Tony, but he put on a brave face, at least in print, when he gave the corporate line to *Billboard* magazine. "Charisma's new look means a total rethink in all areas, which may even lead to our launching another label. Because of our recent successes with Genesis, Peter Gabriel and Monty Python, I consider this an ideal time to expand. We are currently 40% over our sales target for the year and we expect to release around 10 albums in the autumn. As a preliminary to a substantial A&R expansion, we are fattening out our marketing and promotion activities and I myself shall be taking a much more active part in A&R. All product releases will be accompanied by national promotion and we expect to renew our distribution deal with Phonogram in September."

Such positive company statements may have blindsided the press, but several people, including financial advisor Andrew MacHutchon, saw Tony's deep personal hurt at Gail's departure. "Tony looked on Gail as a daughter," says MacHutchon, "and when they finally parted company, it was a massive loss to him – emotionally, as well as professionally."

If life at the record company was getting on top of him, Tony could always find a friend to console him over a drink or two. One of his many drinking partners around the pubs and clubs of Soho was Jeffrey Bernard, the journalist and celebrated alcoholic who perched on his regular barstool in the Coach & Horses at the lower end of Greek Street. An integral part of the bohemian Soho circle that at various times included Francis Bacon, Dylan Thomas and Daniel Farson, Bernard had written about horse racing for *Queen* magazine and *Sporting Life*. In 1975 he became a regular contributor to the Low Life column in *The Spectator*, largely documenting the people with whom he drank. Tony occasionally found himself mentioned, as in October 1979. "There are those people who simply can't help making money. Take my kind host of last Saturday at Kempton Park, Tony Stratton Smith, the boss of Charisma Records," wrote Bernard. "He only has to raise an eyebrow and you can hear cash tills ringing all over England. Can you imagine being able to make money out of something so appallingly wretched and banal as what is called 'pop' music? It's incredible, but I suppose it must be a marvellous investment."

In another article, from May 1981, Bernard submitted his copy from a holiday in Greece, where he was purported to be working on a film script for Tony, an unlikely scenario. "Tomorrow I'm going to a small fishing village in Evia where, under the shade of walnut and olive trees, I shall start work on a treatment for one of the greatest films to be made since the Marx Bros' *A Day At The Races*. *Seven Days At The Races*, simply a working title, has been commissioned by my friend Tony Stratton Smith, and if you're reading this Tony, don't worry that the job won't get done. There's nothing else to do here but work. After all, who the hell wants to lie around in the sun all day, taking the odd dip in the Mediterranean, sipping ouzo, eating roast kid, prawns the size of whales and strawberries as big as footballs?"

Jack Barrie has good reason to remember the stage play. "Jeffrey was one of Strat's great drinking companions. When I went to see the play *Jeffrey Bernard Is Unwell* I recognised half of the stories and anecdotes because Strat and I were party to them. One tale I recognised came from when we had been out racing one day and we all went back to Richard Hannon's place, Jeffrey Bernard and Gay Kindersley were there, Tony and me and one or two others. Richard Hannon's wife had recently given birth to triplets, two boys and a girl. All of a sudden Richard said, 'Hold on a minute' and he rushed upstairs and brought down these three babies, put them down on the sofa and said, 'Let's play a game – find the lady!'"

Another great Soho character was Noel Botham, an old school, hard-drinking Fleet Street journalist who had served his apprenticeship with the *Croydon Advertiser* before joining the *Daily Sketch*, where he became foreign editor at the age of 21. Undoubtedly, Tony first met Botham through his connection with the newspaper but a lasting bond was forged in the pubs and bars around Old Compton Street. Botham and his wife Lesley Lewis later took over the ownership of The French House in Dean Street, where Botham famously set up the AAA, or Anti-Alcoholics Anonymous, whereby anyone considering giving up the demon drink could call him up and be talked round. Tony never needed to make that call.

Charisma art director Frank Sansom recalls how different the area was in that period. "Soho was more like a village in those days, often really quiet with an almost village-like atmosphere, which was really good. You got to meet the whole cross section of people that would come in, from the bands and their managers, to writers, like all the people from *Private Eye*, to the pimps who ran the prostitutes. And Strat was always right in the middle of the whole damn thing."

The very centre, as least as far as rock music was concerned, was still the Marquee in Wardour Street and in March 1977 Charisma moved their offices into vacant space above the club. Each move that Charisma made brought its own favourite local. "First we were in Old Compton Street and the Swiss was across the road," recalls Sansom. The Swiss Tavern was renamed Compton's in 1986. "Then we moved up to Soho Square and we had the Nellie Dean near by. When we moved into Wardour Street our local became The Ship. As soon as they started sound checking the drums for the gig in the club that evening you couldn't work through it, so you just had to come down to the bar and then the evening kicked off from there. If you had any work left over, you knew you still had a quiet hour down in the bar to discuss things. It was a slightly unusual way to work, but everybody has their methods and it worked. And it worked in a very human way, which was always the most important thing to Strat."

The tenth anniversary of The Famous Charisma Label was fast approaching and whatever the current state of affairs at Wardour Street, surviving ten years in the music business was a cause for great celebration for any record company. Gail Colson, soon to leave, came up with a way to commemorate the event and provide Tony with the perfect birthday present, commissioning Pete Frame to draw one of the iconic family trees he generally created to illustrate the genealogy of rock groups. The framed original of 'The Charisma Story' was presented to Tony on his birthday in August 1979 and he adored it.

Over at Gailforce Management, Gail was now busy handling the two Peters, Hammill and Gabriel, both of whom were still recording for The Famous Charisma Label. Peter Gabriel, in typical idiosyncratic style, refused to give his early solo albums a name. The first four were either referred to by number, or – by fans – after the striking cover photography by sleeve designers Hipgnosis – *Car*, *Scratch* and *Melt*, while *Security* (Gabriel 4) was so nicknamed after the sticker that the Americans attached to the top corner of their record sleeves. Naturally, Charisma took such eccentricity in their stride, but the American distributors were losing patience. Atlantic Records had handled the first two, but it was *Melt*, the third album from Gabriel, that caused Colson the biggest headache.

"Atlantic said they wanted to pass on the album," she says. "Their A&R man asked if Peter could sound more like The Doobie Brothers! I went ape shit and said absolutely no way, you either have Peter Gabriel or you don't. So Atlantic dropped him."

The fact that Atlantic Records should adopt, in Peter Gabriel's words, such a "short-sighted and bigoted attitude" was of particular disappointment to Tony, who had always enjoyed a close working relationship with Ahmet Ertegun. Tony switched to Mercury Records whose president, Bob Sherwood, had impressed him. "I had extraordinary admiration towards Strat," he says in return. "If he found anyone from a wandering minstrel to a talking sheep, he would sign them in a heartbeat. He just signed what he felt was interesting and had this enormous passion for music. The team at Mercury did a terrific job. Not only did we take a very non-top 40 single a long way ('Games Without Frontiers'), but Peter also got a top 20 US album out of it, which was amazing because no one else could see anything barely resembling a hit on the album. We got enough airplay, did a lot of promotion, supported him on the road like he was still with Genesis and so to get top 20 with his first album for us, it was a great success. Strat was thrilled about this and we were obviously doing well."

Despite the success of Peter Gabriel's third album on Mercury, there was still the matter of his contract with Atlantic, so Gail Colson called in lawyer Marty Machat, now working with his son Steven, to represent Gabriel. Gail knew Machat senior well, having worked with him during her time with both Shel Talmy and Tony. "After the *Melt* album, Peter was out of his contract, so I went to Marty and said, 'I need you to help, I've got to find another deal,'" recalls Colson. "Now that third album sold as well as all the others, about a quarter of a million copies in America and it got great reviews. I think that when Atlantic dropped Peter, the advance was about $75,000, but now they wanted to sign him back for a million dollars. Every time I refused to take a phone call from someone like Clive Davis the advance would go up by $100,000! Of course, dear old Marty Machat was having the time of his life with all of this."

Eventually, Gail and Peter settled on a different record label, with a little help from their friends. "Marty helped out with the contractual move to Geffen Records. His son Steven was friendly with David Geffen. We went with David for half a million, which was about half of what Atlantic were offering. But the people at Geffen understood Peter, particularly the president, Eddie Rosenblatt. We just delivered their album as and when. There was no block from the A&R department."

Tony no doubt had misgivings at the way certain old friends were slipping away from his world. What some people saw as anger and resentment was more likely to have been disappointment and regret over the way things had turned out at Charisma. The company he had so lovingly nurtured for so long was now a totally different animal. Gail was gone. Brian Gibbon had left and would be superseded as managing director by Steve Weltman. The label had clung on to Genesis as their biggest asset, but their management and publishing were handled elsewhere.

More than anything else, it was the people that Tony missed the most, the day to day contact with creative minds – a pint with Peter Hammill, a literary lunch with John Betjeman, whisky and cigarettes with Graham Chapman. Steve Weltman would do his level best, bringing in new artists like Malcolm McLaren, Julian Lennon and the Rock Steady Crew, which was good news for the label and the company bank balance, but the music itself didn't set Tony's heart a-flutter as it had done in the early days of Charisma. Gradually, almost imperceptibly, an air of depression was settling in over the once cheerful and optimistic Stratton Smith.

* * *

Among the more outlandish rumours that hovered around Tony was that he was – or had been – some sort of government agent, working on special assignments for either MI5 or MI6. About as far removed from the smooth, athletic, skirt-chasing James Bond as it was possible to be, Tony was the least likely candidate to strap on a Walther PPK under his tailored jacket. Nevertheless, more than one close associate has reported instances whereby Tony blew his own cover after one strong drink too many, and while it is a tantalising thought, it is one that is likely to remain just that – after all, some secrets are actually meant to be kept that way.

In an interview with *Rock World* magazine, Glen Colson put forward the case for the prosecution. "Strat was quite a private person. When he left the Speakeasy club at 4am nobody knew what he did before reappearing later the next afternoon. Whether he was an MI5 agent, which he once said he was, I don't know. But he said he'd once been searching for Nazi war criminals in South America during the sixties. He was in the RAF and knew people in government and royalty. He had a very good 'cover' and he was always travelling, he actually disappeared for six months during the seventies and no one knew where he'd gone. He made a film about Ronnie Biggs, the Great Train Robber, and had a lot of connections in South America. He seemed to have a lot of private responsibilities on his shoulders. It was strange – he knew such a wide variety of people, and was very well connected. If he really was in MI5, it would not surprise me."

One evening, and it must be said that refreshment had been taken, a bleary-eyed Tony told both Glen and Gail Colson that he was once stabbed while working for the secret services. He claimed he had been tracking a Nazi war criminal in the sixties, possibly through Argentina, and was attacked by one of the Nazi's henchmen. Gail, not one to invent stories, is in no doubt about what Tony said and even recalls where the revelation was made – a restaurant just off Shaftesbury Avenue. "Tony was drunk and in a tearful mood, but when I brought up the subject again shortly after, this time Tony's lips were firmly sealed," she says.

Her brother suggests that Tony had spent time 'undercover' in South America and of all the Nazi war criminals, Martin Bormann and Adolf Eichmann are the two most likely fugitives he was tracking down. Even if Tony was there, and genuinely believed that he was following a trail, it certainly wasn't Bormann's. In 1998 a body was found in Berlin, where dental records and DNA both confirmed it to be that of the high-ranking Nazi – who had most likely died within a few hours of the Führer himself, as the Russian army closed in on Berlin in May 1945. Eichmann, on the other hand, is slightly more of a possibility. At the end of the Second World War, Eichmann fled to Austria where he stayed under the radar until 1950, when he moved to Argentina using false documentation. Israel's intelligence agency, Mossad, confirmed Eichmann's whereabouts and in early 1960 a team of Mossad and Shin Bet agents captured the former Nazi and hauled him back to Israel to stand trial. Eichmann was sentenced to death and executed on June 1, 1962.

Asked to comment in 2015, the British Security Services confirmed that Tony Stratton Smith was not a member of the Security Service prior to 1965. Enforcing their 50 years of silence rule, they declined to comment on whether Tony had been involved with them after that year. All perfectly reasonable, of course, although conspiracy theorists may wish to adopt the train of thought that argues, to paraphrase Mandy Rice Davies during the Profumo affair court case: "Well, they would say that, wouldn't they?"

* * *

Working in the Wardour Street offices during this period of change was

251

Holly Fogg, who joined in August 1980 and two years later became Tony's personal secretary. She recalls the shifting balance of power at the company. "Brian Gibbon was still the financial controller there and there was also Peter Mills, who did more of the actual figure work. Brian did a lot more contract work and Peter was in charge of the accounts department. Not too long after I joined, Brian left the company and I started working for Tony, which seemed to work out pretty well. Steve Weltman and Peter Jenner[24]* also came in around about the same time, although Peter and Steve weren't exactly the dream team, they worked completely differently."

Holly also worked for David Gideon Thomson, who had been brought in as a director, and later the chairman, of Charisma Holdings, an umbrella company that embraced the record side, the publishing and the films. "Tony was great" she says. "He and David Gideon Thompson were the best bosses I've ever had, they were just so human. I learned so much from Tony. There was such a broad spectrum of work; it covered so much ground, not just for the record label, but also the Tote Board work, all his horse racing ownership, all his charity concerns – all so very different. He would often be writing long letters to newspapers and because he had such a wonderful way with words, he did it in his own inimitable style. So everything I'd learned at college, you know, correct this, correct that – well, with Tony you just didn't do that, because he wanted it exactly the way he'd written it. This also meant that he did an awful lot of his own correspondence and script writing on his portable typewriter, a hangover from his journalist days."

By taking more of a back seat at the record label, Tony was able to spend much more time in the racing world. The horseracing crowd now occupied the lion's share of his social life and some of his most enjoyable evenings were spent in their company. Towards the end of the seventies he moved to a property just outside Lambourn village in Berkshire, a parish rumoured to have more racing stables than pubs. Having identified a suitable property – and Luxford House was an almost impossible act to follow – Tony turned once again to his friend Perry Press to arrange the purchase. Press began the process to buy in the autumn of 1976 and contracts were exchanged early in 1977 – with a mortgage from the Bradford & Bingley Building Society and this time in Tony's own name, rather than Charisma's. Perry Press then spent the first half of that year organising refurbishment of the property – a 'tiresome service' that he would not usually have undertaken for most clients – but this was Strat, after all.

In the summer of 1977 Tony finally moved in to Coombe Lodge in Farnborough, West Berkshire, only about ten miles from the stables in Lambourn. He brought this property from a French princess, partly on the

---

24   * Pete Jenner, with his partner Andrew King, managed Pink Floyd during the Syd Barrett era and their company Blackhill Enterprises managed other acts and promoted free concerts in London's Hyde Park.

recommendation of Ian Campbell. "Tony was looking for a place in the country, somewhere close to Lambourn so that he could enjoy the horses," says Campbell, "and I introduced him to Claire de Croÿ – who was a friend of my uncle who happened to be selling her house. I drove Tony's Bristol and took him over to view it. He liked the property and brought the house from her – and Claire became a good friend. So that gave him a base in the country, but Tony only ever went down at weekends or when he was going racing. He took on a couple to look after it during the week, Richard and Phyllis Parker. The husband acted as a sort of butler and actually drank his way through half the wine cellar and left the empty bottles behind. The wife was the cook and Tony would refer to her as Lady Macbeth."

According to Bush Telfer, a friend and associate from the Lambourn racing community, butler Parker's taste in drinks included whisky too. "One day Strat was expecting company and I heard him shout, 'Where has all the whisky gone?' Cracky was desperately trying to figure out where all the bottles had gone. Now, those rolling grounds running down towards the swimming pool were covered in mole hills so much so, that they had to employ someone to dig them out or blow them up, or whatever it is you do with moles. Of course, when the mole catcher hit the first one there was glass everywhere, because Richard Parker had been hiding the empty whisky bottles in the mole hills. They started digging around and there were all the missing, and now empty, bottles of whisky."

It has been suggested that Tony's move to Berkshire was not just to be closer to the racing stables, but also an attempt to get away from the drinking culture in London. Jack Barrie has reservations about this decision. "I would say the drinking in and around the racing people was far heavier than with the rock crowd," he says. "Of course Tony liked being the centre of attention and he would be buying the rounds, so all the stable lads would be in there and that would go on well after hours, drinking until one o'clock in the morning. What with the lock-ins and then those long Sunday lunches, I mean, they would go and have Sunday lunch in one of the pubs with people like Gay Kindersley, or one of Tony's trainers, and if they were having dinner in the pub it wouldn't finish until midnight, it would just go on and on. I went on a few occasions and I couldn't keep pace with any of them. So moving to the country may not have been such a good move after all."

Tony soon had a favourite pub in the village of Lambourn and one where, as a close friend of the landlord, he often found it hard to leave the premises, according to the trainer Simon Christian. "Tony used to go down to Lambourn to see Noel Bennett at The George. Before he got his house at Coombe Lodge, he would never leave the place. Tony would put on his suit on a Monday morning, intending to leave at mid-day and travel back to London, and then stop for just one more drink. Once, this went on for nearly two weeks before he actually left the pub. The same performance each day, getting ready to go back up to London, coming down to the bar… and then he would bump into somebody else and the drinking would start over again. I think there was a touch of sadness somewhere along the line too, but it must have driven Gail and everyone absolutely crazy."

For a number of reasons, Tony was never able to form a long-term romantic relationship with any one person. However, during the late seventies a combination of loneliness and convenience saw him consider the possibility of a female companion. He had taken a shine to a young barmaid, Mary Grover, who worked in The Swan at Great Shefford, near Hungerford. This was another regular haunt of the racing crowd and Tony would often arrive with Noel Bennett in tow, plus out-of-town guests such as Jeffrey Bernard, or Graham Lord, who was writing for the *Sunday Express* and *The Times* and lived in nearby Lambourn.

Despite the age gap – Tony was mid-forties, Mary in her early twenties – the pair got on famously. On several occasions Tony invited Mary to dinner at Coombe Lodge and even got to meet her parents, at a party to celebrate their wedding anniversary. "I was so pleased he came," said Mary, "because we often made these plans and then after a few drinks I'm sure some people wondered if Tony was actually real or not. Tony arrived in that big car of his with the most enormous bouquet of flowers for my mother. Cracky must have been driving that night and Mum asked if she could give the driver some food or something to drink, but Tony said, 'No, he'll be alright.'"

During the daytime Mary worked at a children's home and with his usual generosity, Tony paid for all the kids to see *Annie* in the West End. One day, Tony surprised Mary again – and everyone else in their circle of friends – with a proposal of marriage. And Mary said yes. Although not immediately, as she argues, "I thought about it for a long time, and I had started to wonder if it was just the alcohol talking, but then he asked me again." Mary insists that Tony's sexuality was never an issue and that his proposal was completely genuine. Either way, his matrimonial plans never came to fruition.

Tony's celebrated Coombe Lodge garden parties began in July 1978 and the following year guests can recall fireworks exploding into the evening sky while the exotic cast of *Brasil Tropical*, hot from their new stage extravaganza at the Theatre Royal in Drury Lane, performed on the manicured lawn. Tony was clearly in his element: "You had people like Genesis, a couple of Boomtown Rats, Peter Gabriel and a few Monty Pythons coming together with what somebody once called the 'Cotswold Chinless'. I've always enjoyed being at the centre of some social cross-pollination and it was a hysterical success to say the least."

Everyone loved the garden parties and Tony's hotly anticipated social gatherings could be likened to the 'Salons' of the 17th and 18th centuries – where the creative writers, artists and musicians of the day would assemble at the home of an inspired host, to talk and drink and broaden the minds of all involved. Where once the French philosopher might converse the night away with the struggling painter, at Coombe Lodge one could find a Genesis roadie deep in conversation with a Government politician, a *Melody Maker* journalist dancing with a Lord of the Realm, a jockey chatting to a Python. Quite often seen flying overhead was an enormous Charisma flag, a racing tricolour of purple, green and red, with the Charisma name reversed out in white and the old Mad Hatter symbol waving from the green centre section. The company flag more commonly used at corporate horse racing events, Tony also liked to fly it at his own garden parties and on days like these there was absolutely no mistaking who lived in this particular house.

Simon Christian attended many of the gatherings at Coombe Lodge and was intrigued at the way Tony mixed and matched his guests, not just at the house but in the local pubs too. "It wasn't so common to have such a mix of lifestyles in those days. You had all the big guys from the music industry and then there were stable lads and a smattering of Labour MP's like Denis Howell, although I don't think people were quite so much in awe of celebrity in those days as they are now. Tony introduced Monty Python's Graham Chapman to the valley at Lambourn and he would often surprise locals with the people he brought in to The George. I remember one afternoon when he arrived with Harry Nilsson. There was hardly anybody in the pub and in fact, Tony didn't really want to introduce him, because Nilsson definitely didn't want to be recognised. He could be a bit of a hell-raiser and used to end up fighting with people. I remember he had quite an aggressive game of pool. But he had a good few scoops and played pool with the people around him and to be honest, most of the people didn't even know who he was."

His weekends may have been spent carousing in racing country, but Tony still needed somewhere to stay in central London during the week and Perry Press again lent a helping hand in finding the property, Flat 56, 22 Park Crescent, London W1. Park Crescent is the sweep of elegant white-stuccoed terraced houses designed by the architect John Nash that form a semi-circle at the north end of Portland Place, just south of the Marylebone Road. Many of the houses were converted into expensive flats, and number 56 was occupied by Tony whenever he was in town.

"I have a clear recollection of inspecting it with Strat before he took on the tenancy," says Press. "Actually, he was much more impressed by the entrance lobby than the flat itself, which he saw as merely somewhere to crash. My less than confident recollection is that it was initially rented and only subsequently purchased."

Tony used his elegant Regency apartment purely as a place to lay his head during the working week and by all accounts it was the archetypal bachelor pad. Ian Campbell visited a few times: "Whenever I went to see Strat at Park Crescent, all the ashtrays were full with fag butts and the carpets were covered with cigarette burns as far as you could see, but then his flat was a typical single man's flat, nothing in it, just a few tea bags in the cupboard and that was about it."

Tony did employ a regular cleaner for the flat, a lady from Islington – but she obviously hadn't been in whenever Ian Campbell visited. According to Holly Fogg, Tony's personal secretary at Charisma, the overriding impression of the flat at Park Crescent was that it was full of papers – piles of documents, newspapers and magazines. It was comfortable, yet fairly basic. "I remember a conversation with Tony when the bathroom was being refurbished," says Fogg "and he was mulling over whether to do away with the bath and just have a shower installed. I can't remember the outcome but Tony did enjoy a bath, as I understand, so he probably kept it."

Country life at Coombe Lodge, although undoubtedly fun, was relatively short-lived. According to Perry Press, in December 1978 accountant Andrew Warburg asked for a valuation and the following March he received a message from Tony confirming that he wanted to sell. After some delay, by August 1980 an offer from a prospective buyer was on the table. Perry Press takes up the story: "Inconclusive negotiations with this party continued to the end of the year, by which time Strat agreed with my recommendation to take the property off the market and re-offer it the following spring. Perhaps significantly, he decided that in order 'to help with the tax position I have here, I want to park Coombe Lodge until the spring as an asset of Charisma'. Shortly after that, solicitors Woolf Seddon (whose partner Tony Seddon became a director of Charisma around this time) asked for information to assist in negotiations with the Inland Revenue. All then went rather quiet on the subject."

In the summer of 1982 Strat told Press he had sold Coombe Lodge, letting slip that the buyer was the same party with whom he had been negotiating in the second half of 1980. "Strat was clearly embarrassed at the revelation," says Press, "and hastened to assure me that he had not been involved with the transaction, which had been handled by Brian Gibbon – who by this time was styled as Charisma's managing director." Fortunately Tony still had the Regency apartment in Park Crescent in which to rest his head.

* * *

When Phil Collins released his first solo album in February 1981, he became the first member of Genesis to leave the Charisma family. Since *Trespass* in

1970, every record by the band had been a Charisma release, as well as solo work by Peter Gabriel, Tony Banks, Mike Rutherford and Steve Hackett, plus five albums by Collins' occasional jazz-rock outfit, Brand X. Throughout much of 1980 Collins was at home alone, writing and recording demos of songs that were both highly personal, based largely on the break-up of his marriage to his first wife Andrea and their subsequent divorce in 1979, and far more commercial than much of Genesis' output. He had also been working with his friend John Martyn on the album *Grace & Danger*, a collection of songs in a similar vein that related to Martyn's failed relationship with his wife Beverley.

Collins felt that the material on *Face Value* should be aimed at a far wider audience and that a new record label was required to reach this different demographic. Up to that point Charisma and Genesis had been intrinsically linked but Collins took the decision to join Virgin Records in the UK, unknowingly predicting the wholesale move that would occur only a few years later. 'Peelip', as Tony always called him, was the member of Genesis he had known the longest and was now the first man to jump ship. Collins faced an onerous task in telling Tony he couldn't have it on Charisma, noting in his autobiography he was adamant that he had to change label, "even if that meant letting down our Charisma label boss and my old pal Tony Stratton Smith, the man who, a decade earlier, pointed me in the direction of the Genesis gig in the first place. I have a sad liquid meeting with him in his room at L'Hermitage to break the bad news. He is in LA because the Monty Python crew are performing at the Hollywood Bowl, and John Cleese stops by to say hello to Strat. It's a very Fawlty Towers scene, with Cleese dressed in a Pittsburgh Penguins hockey shirt. 'Sorry, sorry – didn't know you were busy – not to worry, I'll come back later,' splutters Cleese. The whisky of our meeting does not mix well with the tequila of our Mexican lunch. A Strat cigar finishes me off. I'm as sick as a Norwegian parrot on the pavement. Maybe it's appropriate penance for ditching my old benefactor."

Tony was understandably upset by the move, but this time there was nothing he could do. In an interview with *Mojo* magazine, Collins admitted, "It broke his heart, but he understood. I just wanted to reinvent myself."

Charisma MD Brian Gibbon was understandably worried where this might leave Genesis and the label that made their name. "We had something of a love/hate relationship, as you do between managing director and artist, but we were a good label for them because we were able to give them the right amount of attention," he says. "When Peter left, that was a very traumatic period for us, even to the extent that Polygram and Phonogram all thought, 'Well hang on, this is the end of Charisma' so to speak, because the band probably represented 60% of our worldwide sales at the time. When Phil Collins went solo, the deal I offered Phil was better than the deal that he eventually took with Richard Branson, but I think Tony Smith was right, he just wanted to move him to another label. It wasn't like he was scraping around for a deal. I said, 'Well, you know it opens the door for Genesis to go somewhere else – and I don't know whether I can deal with that.' So we had a long talk about it and they didn't move."

Charisma's loss was definitely Virgin's gain, and Collins was proved right. *Face Value* was an enormous success, giving him (and Richard Branson) a number one album in Britain and three hit singles including 'In The Air Tonight' and 'I Missed Again'.

Returning to work with the band that made his name, in 1980 Genesis released *Duke*, featuring several songs written around the same time as *Face Value*, which in turn pushed the band towards a much more commercial sound. Their tenth album, *Duke* was the first to make number one in the UK, spawning three hit singles including 'Turn It On Again' which made the top ten. Inspired by this and the success of his solo work, Collins later told the press, "I'd love Genesis to get a different record label. I don't want to upset Charisma, but there are people who should have heard *Duke* and would have liked it, but they weren't really given a chance."

In fact, Collins' manager was in agreement. The other Tony Smith's focus was concentrated on getting the best deal for the band he now managed, even if it meant leaving the label they loved. "With Gail gone, Brian Gibbon was now sole Charisma MD and I was looking to extract the band from Charisma as much as I could. A bit later on down the line I renegotiated things and got Genesis a direct deal with Phonogram and I said to Charisma, you know, step aside."

In the event, Phonogram failed to exercise an option on Genesis by the required date, which enabled Smith to sign Genesis to Virgin. "Of course, Branson being Branson, he jumped straight in and made a huge offer. So I called Phonogram back and said, 'I'm sorry guys, we're out of contract.'"

After the fallout with Atlantic Records over Peter Gabriel's innovative third album, Gail Colson and Marty Machat had brokered a deal with the newly formed Warner-Geffen label. Gabriel still had a penchant for leaving his albums untitled, so when his fourth solo album was issued in America on the Geffen imprint it was suggested that the title be printed only on the shrink wrapper. It remained titled in the shops but, as Gabriel intended, untitled once the buyer had torn off the cellophane wrap.

Sometime around the release of Gabriel's fourth solo album, Steve Weltman remembers a lunchtime meeting in 'Strat's Cafe' – Armin Loetscher's St Moritz restaurant in Wardour Street. "Peter Gabriel, Strat and I were having lunch and during the meal, Peter told us that he was thinking of separating from Jill, his first wife. Strat burst out with 'Oh no, just like Philip...' By this time Phil Collins had embarked on a successful solo career and he had also been through a divorce and was now remarried to his second wife. It's fairly public knowledge that pretty much all the songs on Phil's first solo album were written about his separation from Andrea. So Peter turned to Strat, with a completely straight face and said, 'Well, maybe that's the key to having a hit record.' That was very much Peter's dry sense of humour."

Back home in Bath, Peter Gabriel was listening to different musical styles, beats and rhythms by musicians from Africa, India and China and felt the need to give these relatively unknown artists a platform. Tony Smith and Gail Colson would have preferred Gabriel to concentrate on promoting his fourth studio album but his interest in World Music led to the launch of WOMAD – the World of Music, Arts and Dance – that has since helped to spread the popularity of artists from across the globe. It was a perfect example of the cultural cross-pollination that Tony loved to explore. The WOMAD festival would blend major headline artists from the West with musicians from around the world, Echo & The Bunnymen sharing a stage with the Drummers of Burundi, or Gabriel himself performing with the Ekome Dance Company.

The first WOMAD festival in the summer of 1982 was a financial disaster, the crowd too low, the costs too high and the organisation haphazard. Gabriel, as the figurehead, took most of the ensuing flak. Gail Colson had not been keen on the idea from the outset. "When I arrived, there were more people walking around with backstage passes around their necks than there were punters. We went under for something like a quarter of a million and of course, the only director who had any money was Peter."

Gabriel's predicament was resolved when Genesis agreed to play a fundraising concert later that year at the Milton Keynes Bowl, with their former singer back in the line-up for this one-off special. There was some consternation about playing some of their older material but despite atrocious weather the gig proved to be a huge success, and the takings enabled Gabriel to pay his debts and keep his WOMAD dream afloat. Steve Weltman also suggested that such a landmark concert should be recorded for posterity, but no one at the label seemed interested. Predictably, within two weeks a gatefold sleeve, triple bootleg entitled *GABACABRIEL* was selling under the counter in record shops worldwide.

Tony certainly enjoyed seeing his old boys back together again on a stage. "The reunion was a happy success, and the members of the band revealed more emotion than one thought them to possess," he told *Music Week*. "This was a party spirit, effervescing earlier from 60,000 people enduring six hours of incessant rain; only a Genesis audience can make a Pacamac look like a kaftan."

Having proved his fund-raising abilities with the Sports Aid Foundation, it was inevitable that Tony would also get involved with The

Prince's Trust, established on the initiative of the Prince of Wales. In 1981, Tony and the Trust's Peter Smith came up with the idea of a compilation album of comedy sketches and songs, conscious that Prince Charles had a great love of classic British comedy – Tony Hancock, The Goons and Spike Milligan in particular. Royally paraphrasing Queen Victoria under the title of *We Are Most Amused*, the collection quickly turned into a double album, a joint venture between Charisma Records and Ronco[25]*, with all proceeds going towards the Trust.

Charisma were in the perfect position to kick off the compilation by supplying existing material from their own catalogue – three tracks from Monty Python and two from Barry Humphries, under the guise of Les Patterson and Dame Edna Everage, "representing the Commonwealth" as it said on the sleeve notes. The double album retailed for the price of a single LP, costing only £5.49p, and the bargain price, coupled with Ronco's pre-Christmas advertising campaign, ensured that the package went gold, with sales of more than 100,000 copies. To Tony's great delight, the Prince of Wales was undoubtedly most amused.

As with any venture that he felt was important, Tony was quick to bring friends and associates on board and when the idea of a Rock Gala Performance was raised he turned to Chris Wright of Chrysalis Records. "The Trust was still in its very early days," says Wright, "and he told me that Charles and Diana wanted to go to a concert, a pop music concert, and I said, 'Well, haven't they already got The Royal Variety Show?' Strat said no, that's too stuffy, they want something a bit more contemporary and so forth."

Tony and Wright were members of a committee that included George Martin and The Who's Pete Townshend, who chose the acts that would appear at the Dominion Theatre in London's Tottenham Court Road. "I suspect it was Diana who wanted the rock concert more than Charles," says Wright, "although Charles was trying to help young kids from ethnic minorities all around the country. While one might be sceptical about what the Trust actually does, Charles wanted to put on a show and he wanted an unknown group of young kids to be a part of that show. It was very important for the Prince of Wales to sit around with Pete Townshend and George Martin and me and Strat. We played all of this music and decided which group it should be. We had to sit around listening to the tapes from all these various bands that he'd given money to, most of whom were complete rubbish, but we eventually found one who were the best of the bunch. To put the show together we pulled in all of our contacts and friends. Diana was much more interested in the pop bands, you know, she knew Duran Duran and Supertramp and people like that. I don't think Charles knew much about them at all. So Diana was more engaged with the music side and for Charles

25   * Ronco specialised in TV-advertised compilation LPs of past hits.

it was a major opportunity to support some of the underprivileged kids that he was trying to help out."

Wright certainly put together a star-studded cast, adding Kate Bush, Joan Armatrading, Jethro Tull, Madness and Robert Plant to the bill, with a house band that featured Pete Townshend and Midge Ure on guitars, Gary Brooker on keyboards, Mick Karn on bass and Phil Collins on drums. The Rock Galas would go on to become a popular event in the Prince's Trust fund-raising calendar, with Tony always part of the supportive cast.

Chapter 15

The Turf

"Win or lose, we'll have some booze."
Tony Stratton Smith

The deafening roar around Kempton Park almost drowned out the rumble of horses' hooves, but from his vantage point in the grandstand Tony Stratton Smith could feel the vibrations as they thundered past. It was a photo finish at the line, but the flash of purple, green and red through his binoculars told him his horse was in with a fighting chance. Tony mopped his brow and shivered with anticipation as he awaited the result. He once told a reporter that a win at the track was better than a hit record, but then his involvement with the 'Sport of Kings' long preceded his life in the music business.

Tony's racing passion could be traced right back to those early days growing up in the back roads of Yardley Wood, days when his grandmother employed the younger members of her family to act as bookies' runners. The Smith children ran helter-skelter up the road to the neighbourhood betting shop and back, laughing and clutching grandma's betting slips in their grubby hands. When he was old enough, Tony spent more of his time and money at the racetrack and soon he was having a flutter of his own. Throughout his life, he would always love a gamble, the excitement that came with the risk, the sheer joy of a win, but also the ability to shrug off losses with a cheerful 'c'est la vie'. In Tony's opinion, life itself was one big gamble – so why not smile, place your bets and make the best of it.

This genuine interest in the horses, coupled with a degree of bluster and luck, had led Birmingham sports papers to publish his racing tips when he was barely 17 – albeit safely hidden behind the pseudonym 'Fieldmouse'. From that point on, he was never too far from a racetrack or a betting shop and by the early seventies, with the success of the Charisma label putting a few extra pounds in his pocket, Tony was ready to take his love of racing one important step further. It was time to own his own horse.

It was towards the end of 1973 when off he went to Lambourn Valley in Berkshire, a horseracing stronghold, to seek out a suitable trainer, taking the advice of Richard Pitman, who pointed him in the direction of Gay Kindersley. Tony was bowled over by the bon vivant Irishman and his wife

Magsie, the former actress Margaret Wakefield, and asked him to buy him two or three horses.

Kindersley was a colourful character with a family background in the peerage, the son of Philip Leyland Kindersely and Oonagh Guinness and therefore part heir to the Guinness brewing family fortune. On his 25th birthday in 1955, Kindersley inherited £750,000 from the estate of his grandfather Ernest Guinness and invested wisely in property at Beare Green, near Dorking, and a horse training establishment at Epsom in Surrey.

Tony and his new trainer made a good match and their partnership got off to a dream start when his horse Fighting Chance won on his first outing at Doncaster in January 1974. The six-year-old went on to take four races during that season, including the Midlands Grand National at Uttoxeter, with jockey Bill Shoemark in the saddle each time. As Robin Rhoderick-Jones wrote in his biography of Gay Kindersley, "The enthusiastic Stratton Smith, his huge bulk quivering with delight at each new success, became increasingly thrilled with his new venture. 'Better than having a record in the top 20,' he declared."

Still a relative newcomer to the training game, Kindersley was constantly trying to attract other serious owners, but apart from Tony, and the author Evelyn Anthony, there were few other takers at first. By Christmas 1974, however, he had accumulated about 24 winners and the racing press were including him in the cream of National Hunt trainers.

The same January that Fighting Chance gave Tony his first taste of the winners' enclosure, Gay bumped into Philippa Harper at a race meeting at Plumpton. Although Philippa was in the midst of an affair with the actor Oliver Reed, this failed to stop him pursuing her and an acrimonious divorce from Magsie took his attention away from training horses. Despite being a good friend of Gay's, and probably his most generous owner, Tony parted company with his trainer during the 1975-76 season, almost exactly the same time as Gay's final rift with Magsie.

As with many of the key people in Tony's life, the falling out did not last for very long. He had made his point and by the early part of 1978 Tony returned to the Kindersley stable, striking up the same easy friendship with Philippa, now the new Mrs Kindersley, that he had enjoyed with Magsie. Back in harness with his trainer, Tony took a half share in a horse called Carraig Dubh with Mrs Nikki Bennett, the wife of a publican who ran the Saracen's Head Hotel in Highworth, near Swindon. Unfortunately, "the horse was really not up to much", according to trainer Simon Christian.

Further success for the Kindersley/Stratton Smith combination continued with Boreen Daw, a horse bought specifically for Tony, who won a number of races over the next two years and finished a notable second in the Arkle Chase at Cheltenham. That particular race and the subsequent after-race party, has stayed long in the memory of racing man, and fellow owner, John O'Neill. "One of my fondest memories," says O'Neill, "was Boreen Daw coming second at Cheltenham in the early eighties. I shared ownership with Tony and the party that evening finally finished at dawn with Gay Kindersley at his best, singing Irish songs and telling riotous stories. As Gay always liked a flutter, we had a good each-way punt at the starting price of 33-1, much of which was spent that night. Had we won, we would probably still be at Cheltenham."

Sadly, Fighting Chance, one of Tony's favourite horses, came to an untimely end by accidentally getting its neck caught in the tack, the tangle of halters, reins and bridles left dangling from the stable wall. The news left Tony inconsolable and Gail Colson picked up the pieces at the Charisma office. "I remember that we came into the office one day and Tony was sitting there crying his eyes out," she says. "So he's crying and howling and I couldn't get anything out of him – and I was thinking, oh my God, his mother must have died. Eventually he told me that Fighting Chance was dead. I said, 'Oh, for God's sake Tony, it's a fucking horse, I thought it was your mother.' In previous conversations, Tony always maintained to Gail that the main reason he liked horses so much was that "They don't answer back and they don't break your heart." In this instance, Tony was proved wrong.

Once he was immersed in the world of horseracing, Tony was keen to introduce the delights of the turf to his friends and colleagues at The Famous Charisma Label. Many companies spend a corporate day at the races on Derby Day, bussing their staff to Epsom racecourse, and with Tony at the helm, Charisma were no exception. Steve Weltman recalls making the trip on several occasions. "We would all meet at Leicester Square on Derby Day, get on an open-top double-decker bus, with these big urns full of coffee and brandy. The artists would come, the media would come and the Charisma staff would all go along. We would arrive at Epsom and a catering company van would pull up alongside the bus, where Tony had reserved his space on the last furlong. We always had a fantastic day out. Later on, Tony ended up with his own box in the old grandstand, although I think it was only big enough for about eight people."

For his next step, Tony thought it only logical that he should hold his own race day, creating a rare opportunity to bring together friends from the disparate worlds of rock music and racing. He organised the Charisma Records Day, approved by the Jockey Club, which he established at Kempton Park in October 1974. Writing in the *Daily Mirror* on September 30, their columnist William Wolfe announced the event. Under the heading 'Rocking Horses', Wolfe wrote: "The latest venture of pop king Tony Stratton Smith is to marry the two passions in his life, sport and music. So with the backing of his £6 million-a-year Charisma Records company he is taking over Kempton Park racecourse for one day next month, putting up £6,000 in extra prize money and taking along rock groups to play live. Only in between the races, so that they don't scare the horses. If the music is a hit, Stratton Smith, 40, means to plug the gaps at other national hunt meetings, and at cricket and football matches. "Hard rock for football and horses," he says, "but something less harsh for cricket, like folk rock with swinging fiddles."

Tony fixed the distance of the Charisma Chase for his Midlands Grand National winner Fighting Chance and for many years, this race remained the first long-distance chase of the season and one with extremely good prize money. To celebrate the fifth birthday of the record label, the company sponsored four races at Kempton Park: the Charisma Records Steeplechase, the Genesis Handicap Hurdle, the Charisma Artists Opportunity Handicap and Monty Python's Holy Grail – A Very Silly Race For Amateur Riders. "This is the first time there has been a joke in the Racing Calendar in 200 years," chuckled Tony. Denis Howell, the Minister for Sport, happily agreed to present the race prizes, which also included an award for the best dressed bookie and gifts of albums to all the stable lads, while five Charisma artists played "very softly, so as not to frighten the horses".

It wasn't just the horses that risked being frightened by the antics of the lively Charisma entourage. Speakeasy boss Roy Flynn remembers one particularly eventful visit to the Derby in their company. Thanks in no small part to Tony's usual hospitality the majority of the day was spent drinking, with plenty of coffee and brandy on offer, and with most of the guests keeping only the occasional eye on the racing. "Every now and then a horse would run past," chuckled Flynn.

After a long but enjoyable day at the races, the Charisma double-decker left the racecourse at Epsom for the drive back into London, but it wasn't long before nature called and the bus was forced to pull in to a large roadside pub to let passengers use the facilities. While several trooped off to find the toilets, Tony led everyone else into the main bar to have 'just one more for the road'. After a while, one of the roadies burst into the bar and shouted, "Everyone get back on the bus, NOW!" It turned out there was a wedding reception taking place in the function suite next door and a female among the Charisma party had taken a shine to the bride. Much to everyone's surprise, especially the groom, she was starting to reciprocate. Fortunately, Tony and his guests scrambled back on board in double-quick time and the Charisma bus just managed to pull out of the car park before the wedding party turned nasty.

Tony's success with the horses didn't come as a complete surprise to Jack Barrie. "Well, he had an eye for a horse didn't he? It's all very well being a good owner, but you've got to be a lucky owner too," he says. "During my first year's involvement with him, Tony told me I was even luckier than he was, because we had a phenomenal first year. With half shares in Chukaroo and Ginnie's Boy, followed by a leg in Baronial, we managed an amazing 9 wins out of only 12 races with those three horses. Tony gave Jenny Pitman the responsibility of looking after a few horses and her success was probably all down to him saying, 'If you take up a traineeship, I will bring horses to you and give you the chance to do it.' He started Jenny off as a trainer and there may have been only one other female trainer around in that particular period. It was the same with jockeys, obviously he liked to use Lester Piggott whenever he could, but he was always willing to give the younger lads a chance."

Jenny Pitman's long and successful career as a trainer owes much to the unerring faith placed in her by Tony. The main turning point came when she was asked to work with a 'big grey gelding' called Biretta, who was, according to Pitman, "probably the best-bred horse I'd ever trained", coming from a pair who between them had won The Oaks and The Derby. Crucially for Pitman, Biretta was owned by Tony Stratton Smith. Up to that point, the horse had been under-performing and Tony suggested that a spot of hunting might freshen him up. It did the trick and Pitman asked if she could enter him in a hunter-chase, a race ranked somewhere between amateur point-to-point and professional National Hunt racing. Biretta came a credible third in his first race, fell in his second, but won the third at Fakenham, albeit after a stewards' enquiry.

Tony was so delighted with this success that after the obligatory celebration drinks he suggested that Pitman take out a professional licence and train Biretta under National Hunt rules. Initially she thought he was either joking or had imbibed one too many vodkas, but after six weeks' consideration and Tony's assurance that she would receive other horses to work with alongside Biretta, Pitman successfully sat her interview at the Jockey Club in the summer of 1975.

Pitman was also starting to work wonders with Gylippus, once regarded as too clumsy to make a decent racehorse. "He really was an ugly duckling," said Tony, smiling, "but like a living sculpture he has acquired shape and Jenny has moulded him into one of the best young chasing prospects in this country. I forecast a great future for this girl. I love her directness."

The Stratton Smith/Pitman success story really began when Gylippus won his first two races with relative ease, prompting Pitman to enter him into the Welsh Grand National at Chepstow, a bold move for a trainer in her first season. As a warm-up, Gylippus was entered into a race at Leicester and on the morning of the race Pitman rang Tony at his London office with the message, "If you want to back Gylippus in the Welsh National, then back him now. I promise you he won't be the same price after he's run at Leicester today."

Tony promptly gave his driver Cracky a large wad of notes and sent him off round various betting shops, but by the time he reached the third shop, the manager was waiting for him and asked, "Are you with this gang that's going round London backing Gylippus?" Cracky, of course, was the gang.

Pitman's prediction proved to be absolutely correct. Gylippus romped home at Leicester and his odds for the National shortened dramatically. A triumphant Tony decided to organise a party at the Red Lion in Lambourn the night before the Welsh National, but the race itself didn't quite go to plan the following day. As Jenny Pitman later recalled, "Maybe Tony had a premonition, because, sadly for him – and me – the great betting coup never came off. Looking every inch the winner, Gylippus met the last fence completely wrong. I knew what was going to happen three strides away, groaned and closed my eyes as he stood off too far in the very heavy ground and crashed to the floor, something I nearly did myself. Fortunately, Tony was there to catch me."

Former apprentice jockey Bush Telfer also remembers the occasion, more so for Tony's calm and considered reaction. "Brian Smart was the jockey. He went to jump the last fence – and this is after a three-mile slog in the wet and the mud – and he went to whip the horse one-handed over the last fence and it fell. Afterwards everybody was blaming Brian because this horse really should have won the Welsh National, but the trainer Jenny Pitman, who you think would have gone off the rails altogether, was actually quite okay with it. And Strat, bless him, who was having a good bet on this horse as well, just took it all in his stride and he said, 'No, what will be will be' and then came out with one of his favourite sayings, which was 'Win or lose, we'll have some booze'. I've heard him say that numerous times."

Tony also offered his star trainer a lifeline when Jenny Pitman separated from her husband Richard and their Parva Stud stable was put up for sale. The ideal move would have been to the village of Lambourn, home to most of the Berkshire trainers, but property there was well out of her price range. Tony's suggestion was to buy a vacant yard in the smaller hamlet of Upper Lambourn, where Jenny could live rent-free and work as his private trainer. However, as good as the offer was, the independent Mrs Pitman had her reservations.

"I thanked Tony for his offer and went out and bought a property myself instead," she says. "It was totally derelict. So derelict, in fact, that when my solicitor was looking round the place the stairs were so rotten that he fell straight through them. I bought bits of it at a time and we quickly tidied up the yard, because obviously I needed the horses there to pay my electricity bills. Hard going at the time, but it worked out fine in the end. We had some lovely winners for Tony and if you look at Weathercock House now, Richard Hughes is training there and it's just been sold for over £3 million."

Jenny Pitman remembers that Tony's generosity could manifest itself in smaller, but equally vital ways. "There was an incident when we were at Worcester one day and we were down at the start and Tony and I were just walking up the steps when I dropped my binoculars. I put the binoculars up to my eyes and I can now see two separate pictures. Tony could hear me moaning away and asked what was the matter, to which I said, 'I've just bust my binoculars, and now I've got two separate pictures which is absolutely bloody useless.' I'm looking at my broken binoculars and I say to him, 'What price is your horse anyway' and he told me it was 8/1 or something. We watch the race together, his horse duly wins and he never says a dickie bird. On the following Sunday, Tony's car pulls up outside with Cracky driving it – and Tony had sent down these very expensive, very smart binoculars which he'd bought with some of the winnings from Worcester. That's the kind of bloke he was. I've still got those binoculars, they are treasured by me and they have been everywhere, to every Grand National you can mention, every Cheltenham Gold Cup. They've been my lifeline."

Tony was indirectly involved when Jenny Pitman worked with the horse that would deliver her greatest triumph. He introduced her to Jeremy Norman, an owner who took her along to see an unnamed two-year-old he was thinking of buying. Mrs Pitman advised Norman to buy him but when he turned up at her yard, the horse had put on so much bulk he looked like a carthorse. Since buying the horse, Norman had sold a half share of the horse to his cousin Alan Burroughs in Jersey, who suggested the name Corbiere, after the Channel Islands lighthouse, although he quickly became known as Corky around Pitman's racing yard.

Corbiere narrowly won the Welsh National in December 1982. A further win at Doncaster and a decent performance finishing second at the Cheltenham Festival encouraged Pitman that this horse could compete around the tough Aintree course and Corbiere was good value for his 13/1 starting price in the 1983 Grand National, which he won by three quarters of a length. In her autobiography Jenny wrote: "The fact that I was the first woman to do it did matter, but that wasn't the most important thing. What mattered most was the joy on the faces of the people close to me. As I drove along the deserted motorway I thought about the people who had supported me through the bad times, people like Lord Cadogan, Tony Stratton Smith and Peter Callander. 'Well I hope that's given a bit back to you all,' I thought."

When Jenny Pitman appeared on *This Is Your Life* in March 1984, Tony was there to congratulate her, along with various family members, assorted childhood friends, champion jockeys and even her primary school headmistress. Running through her life story, genial Irish host Eamonn Andrews said: "You had first started to make your mark as a trainer in point-to-point meetings which were for amateurs, but you had a horse at your stables you reckoned was good enough for professional National Hunt meetings. You take it to Fakenham in Norfolk and it wins. The owner of the horse is delighted, he telephones with an offer that will change the course of your life." A beaming Jenny Pitman nods in recognition, as Tony's disembodied dulcet tones play out in reply: "Jenny this is an ultimatum. I'm giving you just two weeks to make up your mind to go professional."

Andrews then brought Tony onto the set with the words, "Just flown in from Germany, the owner who set you off on a winning streak, Tony Stratton Smith. Tony, how did Jenny react to that challenge?" Tony responds in typical fashion, saying: "Jenny's understanding of horses is very similar to a poet's understanding of life. She is wonderful. And I sent her two or three horses, among them a horse called Gylippus. All the male experts had told me that this horse was too slow ever to win a race. I have to tell you that Jenny won five races in the next 20 months or so with that horse and we came within one fence of winning the Welsh National."

Roz Bea joined Charisma in May 1975 as an assistant in the accounts department and recalls that she always knew exactly where to find her old boss – at one of the three stools at the end of the Marquee bar. "One night Strat showed me a letter that he had just received from the Queen Mother, thanking him for his gift to her of a VCR... obviously something to do with their shared horse racing passion and this would have been way before video recorders were common place." Only Tony would contemplate sending the Queen Mum the present of a video player, so that the racing enthusiasts in the royal household could relive the excitement of watching their horses romp home at Aintree and Epsom.

The Queen Mother was a dedicated supporter of National Hunt racing and owned many successful horses, racking up over 400 winners during her 'career' as an owner. Many of her horses were stabled at Lambourn and it is fun to imagine Tony and the Queen Mum sipping gin and tonics while discussing form for the weekend racing. According to Jack Barrie this is not too far from the truth. "Occasionally the trainers would have an 'Inspect Sunday' when the owners could come round and inspect their horses and look around the stables – and we would sometimes stay for lunch," he says. "I remember Tony told me afterwards, as he was not allowed to speak about it beforehand, that he was invited over one particular Sunday and was presented to the Queen Mother. As everybody is aware, he used to be a big gin and tonic drinker and he had a large G&T sitting down by his side. The Queen Mum must have knocked it over and it spilt everywhere and she said, 'Oh I'm so terribly sorry' and she's down on her knees mopping up with a hanky and everybody is rushing around. Later in the conversation, Strat discovered that she either wasn't aware of, or didn't have the ability to watch, video tapes. So the following day he arranged to send her a video recorder, at his expense, so that she could record and watch her races. And of course he later came in to the Marquee with this lovely letter of thanks, personally signed by her."

Following the temporary falling-out with Gay Kindersley, in 1978 Tony bought the Eastbury Stables in Lambourn, again using the bespoke services of Perry Press, and then took on Ray Laing as his main trainer. The son of a former flat-race jockey, Laing was a racing man through and through, who had been caring for horses for 40 years. Jack Barrie recalls the situation. "Tony was socialising and drinking in The George in Lambourn, which was owned by his friend Noel Bennett, and he met all the head lads in there. Ray Laing was a head lad with Peter Walwyn. He was in his mid-fifties. Tony said if Ray wanted to take up training, he'd give him the horses and start him off, which he did. Then he introduced him to a few show business types who brought in more money and subsequently a better class of horse and they had the successes. Chris Wright and Terry Ellis from Chrysalis came in purely through an introduction from Tony Stratton Smith. Wright, in particular, went on to far greater things as a successful racehorse owner, with some very good horses."

Four years later, Laing moved to the Delamere Stables where, alongside Tony, he was backed by a group of music industry people, among them Chris Wright, Dave Robinson from Stiff Records and Billy Gaff, the former manager of Rod Stewart & The Faces. According to one report in *Sporting Life*, "Laing's Delamere House yard became Berkshire's answer to Annabel's", with visitors including The Beatles' producer George Martin, actress Liza Goddard, pop star Alvin Stardust and the English character actor Robert Morley. "It was a lot of fun," Laing recalls. "I even had a horse called Ultravox, and the members of the group all came down."

Chrysalis boss Chris Wright was more than happy with Crime Of Passion, a mare he bought from that first involvement in racing. "We went to the sales at Newmarket and Tony recommended that she would be an ideal filly to buy, race and breed from." In the longer term Tony was proved right, as Crime Of Passion's daughter, Licence To Thrill, went on to produce eight winners from as many foals. Patience and foresight are obviously virtues in the racing world, qualities that Tony had in abundance.

"Win or lose, we'll have some booze" was Stratton Smith's general attitude to a day at the races and one of his more notable successes on the track came with a horse named Tower-Bird, which romped home to win the Virginia Gold Cup at Stratford-on-Avon in September 1979. Ridden by Paul Webber and trained by his father John, Tower-Bird flew first past the post in this handicap steeplechase over two miles (and a few yards, according to the official race card) where Tony scooped the owner's prize money of £966 and 50 pence. The American version of the Virginia Gold Cup is a huge race in their own racing calendar and Tony was presented with the trophy by a representative of the famous racecourse in Warrington, Virginia, USA, with whom Stratford was twinned.

The colours for Tony's racing silks were specifically chosen to reflect the diverse areas of his working life; the red cap to represent Manchester United, the green sleeves for his love of Brazil, both the country and their football team, and a purple/mauve body to represent Charisma. Among his other better-known horses were the handicappers Chukaroo, Beggar's Bridge and Tug Of Love. In 1980, Beggar's Bridge won the Falmouth Handicap at York ridden by the great Lester Piggott, one of six winners the master jockey notched up at the same meeting.

Clive Crawley was another keen racing enthusiast from among the Charisma staff. Originally the record plugger for Trojan Records when they shared the Neasden offices with B&C, Island Records and Charisma, Crawley moved across to work full time for Tony, becoming head of promotions.

Clive's son, Jon Crawley, remembers one particular racing story involving the great Lester Piggott. "My dad adored Strat, because they had so much in common: horse racing and gambling, because they both loved having a bet on the horses. They both shared a love of music, which was obviously what drew them together. On this particular day, Strat had a horse running at York. Dad said, 'We should go and watch your horse run' and Strat says, 'My dear boy, the race is in York, I'm not schlepping up to York' until my dad adds, 'Yeah, but our jockey has withdrawn and we've got Lester riding for us.' Now that was it, they were like two little boys rubbing their hands together with glee, they've got Lester Piggott riding their horse and so dad says, 'Come on, let's jump in the car and drive to York.'

"They arrive at York just in time, they are introduced to Lester in the owners' enclosure and they're both really made up, they're absolutely thrilled. The race starts and Lester comes storming out of the stalls and he leads from start to finish. He's never troubled at any point in the race, he just gets on the rounds and he pushes and he wins the race. The two of them are now in their heaven, standing in the winners' enclosure eagerly waiting for Lester to come in and give them his pearls of wisdom. Eventually England's top jockey wanders over and Strat says to him, 'So Lester, what did you think?' and Piggott just says, in his trademark lisp, 'Well, that was pith eathy' and walks off!"

Tony also moved into flat racing with trainer Bill Payne, and his horse Chukaroo won several races for the team. He became an active member of the Tote Board and defended the organisation to the last, believing not only in its right to compete, but the absolute necessity for the Tote to keep pace with the larger bookmaking chains, in much the same way that Charisma had done when taking on the corporate record labels. "Tony served with distinction for many years on the Horserace Totalisator Board and the Sports Aid Foundation," says Jack Barrie. "These responsibilities led to some curious social cross-pollination. After some board meetings, sitting with peers of the realm one minute, taking drinks at their private club the next, he'd mischievously invite them for drinks at 'his private club'. I can recall many a Lordship's hand shaking a little as he sipped his warm gin and tonic at the Marquee bar, surrounded by pink and green hair, lots of leather and the odd swastika or two."

A regular figure at the Epsom Derby, Tony eventually moved up from hiring his double-decker bus to the comfort of a corporate box in the old grandstand. Reporting from the racecourse in June 1977, the acid-tongued *Express* columnist 'William Hickey' wrote "Incidentally, boxes, at £400 each, are losing their cachet. Blue-bloodied racing figures like the Aga Khan, French owner Daniel Wildenstein and the Royal Family had to rub shoulders this year with such lacklustre companions as Blue Star Garages, pop manager Tony Stratton Smith and a certain fish and chip national newspaper. What is the world coming to?" Of course, William Hickey was simply a pseudonym under which several *Daily Express* journalists were able to gossip with complete anonymity.

* * *

In the autumn of 1975 Walter Winterbottom set up the Sports Aid Foundation, a fundraising organisation based on the similar Deutsche Sporthilfe (Sport-help) scheme in Germany. Initially, it was designed to raise money for British athletes training to compete in the 1976 Summer Olympic games in Montreal and the ever-enthusiastic Tony soon found himself on the board. Tony had contributed to the original 1957 Wolfenden Report, which recommended that the Government should provide money for sports development and facilities, but it was only when Labour came to power in 1964 and Denis Howell was appointed Junior Minister for Sport, that the Wolfenden Report recommendations were acted on, and an independent Sports Council was launched with Winterbottom as Director.

Denis Howell, now Labour Minister for Sport, fully embraced the idea of the Sports Aid Foundation and put together a crack team of six Governors under the Chairmanship of Peter Cadbury, made up from successful businessmen with connections to the commercial, professional and show business worlds – all of whom were prepared to give up their time thanks to their shared passion for sport.

Howell's chosen few consisted of Lord Rupert Nevill, Sir Robin Brook, Mrs Mary Glen Haig, Paul Zetter, David Nations and Tony. Their first formal gathering of the SAF on November 27, 1975, almost proved to be their last, however. In his autobiography *Bow Jest*, Paul Zetter describes the tense atmosphere and fraught discussions that took place, after which Cadbury expressed his distaste for the team that had been "foisted upon him", telling Zetter in no uncertain terms, "The three quango bosses, Nevill, Brook and the Glen Haig woman are a total waste of time as far as fund-raising goes. Nations might be useful if he ever stops talking, although I doubt it. Stratton Smith is a total nonentity and I shall lose him with some rapidity – and that leaves you." He added that he wanted Zetter to be his Vice-Chairman.

The next two meetings were equally frosty, leading Cadbury to telephone Denis Howell to try to rid himself of his Governors, with Tony apparently top of his hit list. Howell called an emergency meeting at his office. Cadbury waltzed in late and stated his case, that unless he was given free rein to form his own board of Governors, he would be forced to resign and the SAF would be over before it had begun. Fortunately the wise old Howell would have none of it. He told Cadbury that he had neither the power nor the inclination to make such changes and asked him to reconsider his position. Cadbury refused, Howell accepted his resignation and Cadbury walked out.

After a few moments of stunned silence, Howell addressed the shell-shocked team, encouraging them to go on with Paul Zetter as acting Chairman and asked for their decision the following morning. David Nations, a wealthy businessman and former water-ski coach, was first to voice a reaction. "It's worth doing, isn't it?" he argued. "Naturally we go on." With the room in total agreement Zetter proposed that he would take up the new role, at least until the following Easter.

Cadbury's reservations about Tony and the rest of the board proved totally unfounded and, as principal fund-raisers, Tony and David Nations set about bringing in the cash. In John F. Coghlan's book, *Sport And British Politics*, Stratton Smith and Nations would later be singled out as "gifted, generous and tireless workers".

Tony found himself working closely alongside Paul Zetter CBE, the founder of Zetters Pools. "Tony was, without doubt, one of the most charming people I have ever known," he says. "He was invaluable. Everybody loved TSS and his association with the music industry enabled him to arrange an Elton John concert at Earl's Court, wholly in aid of SAF. It was an outstanding success, both financially and in the considerable benefit that SAF gained in public recognition. The Sports Aid Foundation played a major role in advancing British sporting success which happily continues today and Tony was a key figure in this role."

Another example of Tony's musical fund-raising was the 1977 compilation album *Supertracks*, released on the Vertigo/Polygram label and including tracks by two Charisma artists, Genesis and Monty Python, as well as heavyweight contributions from The Rolling Stones, Yes, Pink Floyd and Led Zeppelin. It bore the unique catalogue number Sport 1.

* * *

While Tony appeared to know the racing world inside out and almost certainly had a keen eye for a horse, when it came to buying a new nag he was always prepared to hand over the reins to his trainers, placing his trust in their expertise. As with the staff at Charisma, Tony's instinct for putting together a winning team led to him working with trainers such as Fulke Walwyn, Ray Laing, Jenny Pitman, Bill Payne, David Arbuthnot and Simon Christian. The hub of Tony's social life in Lambourn village revolved around The George, owned by his friend Noel Bennett. Among the many racing regulars, from owners and trainers to jockeys and stable lads, it was here that Tony first met Simon Christian, at that time the assistant trainer to Fulke Walwyn.

"It must have been around October 1975," recalls Christian "I was about 20 years old and I'd gone to work for Fulke Walwyn, a leading trainer in the village. Noel was a larger-than-life Irishman and Tony was always there at The George, propped up at the bar. I spent a lot of time in there after work and I noticed that people always spoke to Tony and it wasn't long before I began talking to him too. He was just the most engaging character who loved racing and liked talking to young people. He was a good conversationalist in a very quiet way and he enjoyed talking about absolutely anything, whether it was horse racing, music, Catholicism, Manchester United – we found that we had a lot in common. I don't think he was actually Catholic, but he had this great interest in religion and he was fascinated by Catholicism, haunted by it, like most of us are.

"Tony already had a few horses and trained them with Jenny Pitman. Eventually he had a horse with my boss, Fulke Walwyn, who was a very established trainer and trained for the Queen Mother. Tony always desperately wanted to have a horse with Fulke. He seemed to admire the tradition of someone who was so successful and yet at the same time he supported so many young people when they were starting out. He seemed to be able to respect tradition on the one hand, while pretending that he wasn't actually interested in all that and that he preferred new ideas and bringing young, fresh people to the sport."

Fulke Thomas Tyndall Walwyn began his racing career as a jockey before becoming one of Britain's finest trainers and particularly successful in National Hunt racing. He was part of a racing dynasty that includes his twin sister, Helen Johnson Houghton, a racehorse owner and trainer who was one of the first women elected as a member of the Jockey Club, and his cousin, Peter Walwyn, also a notable racehorse trainer. Walwyn could count the 'notoriously difficult' Dorothy Paget and the Queen Mother among his more celebrated owners. It was little wonder that Tony would aspire to work with Walwyn and take his place alongside such exalted company.

"Fulke and his wife Cath liked Tony enormously but sometimes found him a little bit trying," continues Simon Christian. "They'd ask him up at midday for a drink because they wanted their lunch at one or one thirty – and Tony would appear about a quarter past twelve, not to eat lunch but just for a drink or two. They loved the way that Tony was always buying Cath champagne at the races and how he could treat every little occasion, whether the horse he owned finished second or third, he could enjoy it just as much as if it was the winner. He was never demanding and a very easy owner to train for, so they enjoyed working for him."

Tony bought a horse called Baronial from Fulke Walwyn. "It was a straightforward £5,000 which was fair money in those days," says Christian. "It wasn't a huge amount and Tony said, 'Well, I'm off to the airport this afternoon but I will pay for it when I get back.' Fulke was happy with that and Tony kept to his word. I think Jack [Barrie] came in as well and the horse must have won about 14 races, a whole stack of races. Tony got a good young jockey called Kevin Mooney and in those days there were a lot of early meetings at Cheltenham in September and October and Baronial was a real front-runner. I spoke with Kevin recently and he said, 'All I can tell you is that Tony helped me enormously, unlike most owners where if a horse gets beat first time out they want a more fashionable jockey, but Tony kept me going.' Kevin continued riding for Tony and he was a Lambourn guy too, so we had some wonderful parties whenever he turned up on a winner."

Tony worked with four or five trainers on a regular basis, all with very different personalities, as Simon Christian explains. "Ray Laing was different to the others, in that he didn't get a licence until he was into his fifties and Tony was certainly the leading light behind that. Ray was a fine horseman, he was head lad to Peter Walwyn, Fulke's cousin, and they were having a lot of success in the seventies. So this was Tony giving somebody a chance to train, who had never been in a position financially to start training, and it worked out very well. He bought the stable at Eastbury Cottage and Tony knew the yard because he'd trained with a lovely old couple Bill and Patsy Payne and then he went on to train with David Arbuthnot. Bill Payne was an old-time trainer, his horses always looked nice and well and both he and his wife were very hospitable. He was quite a shrewd operator too; he didn't have the big numbers like the Walwyn's, but he was a lovely guy and Chukaroo won some good races, including the Brighton Mile a couple of times. Tony loved the thought of winning the Brighton Mile, somewhere which had a bit of history and a sense of place, although it's lost some of its prestige now."

Another horse Tony bought was called Beggars Bridge, which on one occasion was ridden by Lester Piggott. "One day I saw Tony shuffling around and he told me he was going to have a big bet on Beggars Bridge," says Christian. "He wasn't normally a heavy gambler by any means, but this time he was going to have a proper bet, about £2,000 or something like that, and he half-jokingly said to Lester Piggott, 'Just make sure that you win, because I'm having a proper go at this one.' Apparently, as Lester got up on the horse, he just looked down at Tony and said, 'Whatever you've put on, double it.' Both Jack and Tony rushed off to double their bet and, of course, Beggars Bridge romped home. So the horse worked out very well for him in the end."

Racehorse trainer David Arbuthnot had held a trainer's licence since January 1981 and produced hundreds of racing winners under both codes, on the flat and over the jumps, including runners at the prestigious Cheltenham Festival and Royal Ascot. "I first met Tony through Simon Christian, when Tony had his house just outside Chaddleworth," he says. "We were both locals there, and Tony used to hold these incredible parties up at Coombe Lodge, that's basically how I got to meet him. He also owned Eastbury stables where Ray Laing was training for him and then I got to know him much better when I bought Eastbury stables from him in 1980. I think Tony kept a small share, but having sold it to me he was determined to still have a horse there, so I started training for him as well.

"Tony would say how much he wanted to spend on a horse, I would go and buy it and then he paid me training fees for that horse, so I wasn't a contracted trainer as Ray Laing had been. We started working together and that's how I first met Tony's friend George Thompson – that was the thing about Tony, he kept bringing new people in. Phil Banfield who was also in music, he had horses for a long time. Dave Robinson from Stiff Records, Billy Gaff, Chris Blackwell from Island Records, Tony brought them all in."

Despite his long love affair with the 'Sport of Kings', dressed for the big occasion, the thrill of the moment as your horse edges its nose in front down the final furlong, especially when the odds are good and you've had a cheeky flutter at the Tote, Tony's racing expertise probably owed a little more to luck than most people thought. The man who once happily offered racing tips for the *Birmingham Gazette* used more than his fair share of bluff and bluster alongside any real knowledge of racing form. "I think he was led by the trainers. He was always happy to let the professionals do their thing and didn't interfere too much," says Simon Christian. "Tony certainly liked the whole occasion of racing and the beauty of horses and all the stories behind the scenes, but I don't think he was a particular expert and I don't believe his racing ever had any real plan to it. If you are going to invest a certain amount of money, you don't sit up all night in the bar and buy a horse for £500. There was no real plan and I think it occasionally all got a bit too much."

David Arbuthnot also believes that Tony's decisions could be a bit hit and miss, but more often than not, they were based on altruistic reasons rather than a hard-nosed business sense. "Generally, Tony would leave all the buying to his trainer, you know, but there was another horse that we bought at Newmarket, and we called it Crown & Horns after Noel Bennett's pub[26*]. As well as Tony, George Thompson was involved and I had little share, too," says Arbuthnot. "We'd all been sitting having a drink and Paul Webber said, 'Oh you must come and look at this horse'. Tony used to have horses with the Webbers as well, you know. Well, it was pitch black when we go in to look at this horse, and it was lying down, but we end up buying it anyway. Paul said that he really must sell it, so Tony paid about twenty grand – and it was absolutely useless. I think it only ever ran twice, it was so slow. But that was Tony.

"Sergeant Smoke was a good horse and Love Legend was another, because Love Legend ended up winning in the end. When we bought him, Tony was determined he was going to be a Derby horse, because that was the way he was bred. That's why we bought him and we bought him privately, but he turned out never to get further than seven furlongs. After Tony died, George Thompson and my father-in-law and a couple of others came in and took him over and he went on to win 14 races, but all over sprint distances. Even Love Legend was brought privately from another man that Tony had only just met and we had to go down and look at it before Tony decided that he was going to do the deal. For whatever reason that deal had to be done, whether it was because he simply wanted to help this person, I don't know, because I don't think he particularly liked the horse. He could look at a horse, but then he would leave it up to his trainer to say either 'That's alright' or 'Don't touch it' – and even if you said don't touch it, he would often go ahead and buy it anyway. Tony could be very impetuous. And it always seemed to be while we were having lunch, he'd come over and say, 'Oh by the way, so and so wants to buy that filly, and I said that he could.' And this is the first you hear about it, over lunch, but anyway it's already sold and gone. He could be like that."

During the last year or two of his life, Tony completely threw himself into his racing ownership. After the sale of Charisma, money was burning a hole in his pocket and he went on a bit of a buying spree. David Arbuthnot was one of the trainers who felt both the additional benefits and the pressures.

---

26   * Bennett had moved from The George in Lambourn to the Crown & Horns in East Ilsley.

"That was an extraordinary time, because Tony had just sold Charisma and he was about to move out to Gran Canaria," muses Arbuthnot. "He went a bit crazy buying horses that year, he really did go crazy. I remember driving him up to the Newmarket sales and we stayed in a hotel there. After two days he said he'd bought enough and asked if I could run him to the station. Which I did, drove him to the station and then I went back to the sales, because I still had other business to do. About five hours later I see Tony sitting on a bench back at the sales – he had made his way back and bought another horse.

"Tony definitely had too many horses. He always paid you, but he was never the quickest payer and it came in occasional batches rather than regular month on month payments. The year he died Tony probably bought about 14 or 15 horses, which was way above what he normally had. I don't know whether it was some sort of premonition – Tony didn't appear to be ill at that time, he complained quite a lot about indigestion, but other than that he seemed his normal self.

"My wife Diane and I went out to stay with Tony just before Christmas, 1986," continues Arbuthnot. "He invited us out for a week in Gran Canaria and the drinking over there was horrific. Basically the waiter was pouring a bottle of whisky and just topping it up with water, and I'm sure that didn't help his health in any form. Tony had always drunk, but he was always a steady drinker. Once he started he drank steadily but he never became an angry drunk or even a gay drunk. He was always a complete gentleman and whatever stage of intoxication he reached, you would never have known he was gay. I think I only ever saw Tony overdo it once, when he'd drunk far too much and he just passed out and fell off his stool in the Crown & Horns."

The question of Tony's health and whether or not he understood exactly what his lifestyle was doing to him was never discussed. Tony was on the books of Dr Oscar Drexler, but by all accounts his visits to the consulting rooms at 31 Weymouth Street, London were few and far between. Those missed appointments, whether by accident or design, may well have contributed to his early demise. Simon Christian, who shared the same physician, also wonders whether Tony knew he was ill and possibly chose to ignore the fact.

"I know David Arbuthnot very well and while we've never really had that discussion, I know that David was as fond of Tony as I was," says Christian. "So perhaps he did know that he had certain problems – and most likely it was his liver. Oscar Drexler was a marvellous doctor and treated quite a few of the racing people. We always went to see Drexler up in London, one of those fancy practices in Weymouth Street. Whenever I saw him, he would always ask how Tony was and then invariably say, 'Tony was due to come and see me – he's a very naughty boy, but he was due to come in and see me the other day and he never turned up.'"

Chapter 16

The Last Hurrah

"I always knew when he'd had a skinful the night before, because if he was not in by midday I could guarantee that between 12.00 and 12.30 there would be a phone call saying, 'My dear boy, I think we should have a meeting in The Ship' and it was always a pint of Guinness first, that was his hangover cure, that was his Bloody Mary."

Steve Weltman, Charisma MD

Interviewed by James Johnson of London's *Evening Standard*, Tony confided that his two principal ambitions were to entice John Lennon back into the recording studio and to train a Classic racing winner. Not necessarily in that order. "My interest in rock never wanes because my other interests bring me back refreshed," he said. "A change of scene is always interesting and it's a marvellous life to be talking to Genesis one day about their next record, drinking with an assistant trainer the next in a local pub or sitting alongside the Duke of Devonshire and Nigel Broackes on the Tote Board. An old newspaper friend also asked the other day whether I'd like to come back and do a bit of sports writing. I was flattered and tempted for a moment, but sanity prevailed."

Sadly, John Lennon never became a Charisma act but Tony did find himself working with a younger member of the Lennon family. After the death of his father at the hands of a gun-toting lunatic, Julian Lennon, born in 1963 just as Beatlemania was about to explode, could be excused for going off the rails. He dropped out of school as a teenager, and the following year moved to London to stay with Elton John's percussionist, Ray Cooper. The six-month period living with Ray helped him discover some direction and in September 1983 an anonymous tape found its way onto Tony's desk at Charisma. Tony was suitably impressed, as was new Charisma MD Steve Weltman who quickly signed Lennon junior to a record and publishing deal, simultaneously signing with Atlantic Records in the USA. Julian Lennon would prove yet another key signing for the label, although Tony and Julian did not get off to the most promising of starts, as Tony later explained.

"Julian dropped into my office unannounced one day with a mutual friend, Kim Kindersley, the son of a racing associate Gay Kindersley, oddly enough. I went down and said, 'What the hell have you come in for, wrecking my day, can't you see I've got work to do?' but it was all a joke. I saw this curious lad with half-rimmed glasses. I thought he looked a bit familiar and, of course, I had known John, his father. I threw them both out, but in a nice way, 'Sorry, I'm busy'. I actually threw Julian Lennon out of my office, not knowing who he was."

The next time Tony saw Kim Kindersley he enquired who he'd been with that day and learned it was Julian Lennon. "I had read bits and pieces about Julian spending too much time in nightclubs and having rows with the family, so I obviously expressed an interest and said I'd like to meet him again. When we did meet, sometime later, I said, 'Look Julian, the name can be as big a disadvantage as it can be an advantage – and I don't think there's much point in talking until you've really got some songs, if you really want to write.' I didn't want to be the guy perceived as just launching 'Julian the name'. The material had to be good."

Julian took Tony's fatherly advice to heart and came back with a handful of promising songs, as Tony recalled: "He acquired a young manager Dean Gordon, much the same age as himself, who seemed to have got him working rather well. One night Dean called and said, 'Julian remembered what you said and he would like me to play some tapes for you', so I told him to come in after the office was closed, because I would be here on my own and I didn't want anybody chit-chatting about this. But I forgot that it was a Thursday night and *Top Of The Pops* was on. So half the office were hanging behind to listen to *Top Of The Pops* because we had an artist on. Tony Smith, whose office was only 100 yards up the road, also came round to watch *TOTP* on our television and he heard me listening to these tapes. Of course I refused to tell him who it was. There were half a dozen songs on the tape and they were excellent. Oddly enough only three of them made the first album, but they were cracking songs. The voice was so like the old man's, but deservedly so, because as I've often said, John's greatest gift to Julian, apart from talent, was leaving him behind in Liverpool. If he hadn't done that, Julian wouldn't have that genuine Lennon quality which he has, from continuing his education in Liverpool."

In an interview with Jody Denberg for KGSR Radio Austin, Julian offered a slightly different version of the signing: "Tony Stratton Smith was apparently walking by the studio one day and heard some of the tracks being played in the studio by their A&R guy. And he said, 'Who's that?' And the A&R guy said he didn't know. So Tony said, 'Well find out and sign him up.' And that's how it began."

Either way, the deal was done to everyone's satisfaction. Tony promptly packed Julian and his band off to the remote Chateau near Nevers in France, owned by the De Croÿ family. A firm family friend after purchasing

Tony's house Coombe Lodge, Claire de Croÿ and her older sister, Marie-Dorothée de Croÿ, better known as Princess Mimi, had converted some old stable buildings into a rehearsal and studio space.

Tony liked to keep a fatherly eye on his artists, and a few days with the always-entertaining Mimi and Claire de Croÿ at their remote French home made the task more enjoyable. Jon Crawley accompanied him on this particular trip. "I got to Heathrow and Strat is already in the bar when I meet him there," he recalls. "He's having a good old drink and he's drunk all the way through the flight and when we land I have to collect his luggage, because he's gone to the bar in Paris airport for another one. It's about eight o'clock on a Friday evening in Paris and we've still got a three-hour drive ahead of us, but he keeps getting me to stop at all these different little bars. We got so lost, and we were far out in the countryside in the pouring rain. I just kept driving. I had no idea where I was going, but somehow I found the place. Mimi had arranged for dinner for us, but of course by this time it was about 11 o'clock at night. The chef she had working for her was as drunk as a skunk, Strat was pissed as a fart and the chef hadn't started to cook anything, so there was no food for us. Mimi starts hitting the chef. It was pure madness. In the end, Julian cooked us some food and off we went to bed."

By the time they reached him, Julian had written 'Too Late For Goodbyes', and recorded about 90% of the album. They spent several days horse riding and fishing in a small lake. "Strat was drinking cognac and smoking cigarettes at eight o'clock in the morning," says Crawley. "Mimi told us some great stories. She had delivered most of the children in the village. On one occasion there was a woman who already had about 12 children, all by different fathers. Princess Mimi gets the call, the baby is coming and she goes out to deliver it, but the baby's not breathing. It's the middle of winter so she takes the baby out to a frozen water butt outside the house, breaks the ice and ducks it in the icy water. With the shock of the cold water the baby starts screaming and happily is alright. Unfortunately the story went round the village that Princess Mimi tried to drown the child because the mother had so many children by so many different fathers. Consequently, and very unfairly, many of the villagers turned against her."

Three months later, with the album ready to record, Steve Weltman travelled to New York to meet Phil Ramone and finalise an agreement for him to produce it. Weltman also arranged a licensing agreement with Ahmet Ertegun – a $1million advance co-signed by Tony. Lennon and the musicians, including guitarist Justin Clayton who had known Julian since their schooldays together, flew out to the Big Apple to record under the guidance of Ramone. Either by coincidence or design, the album was mixed at New York's Hit Factory, where four years earlier John Lennon had recorded the *Double Fantasy* album with Yoko. When Phil Ramone asked

Julian if he felt "the ghosts", he replied, "Yes, but they feel good for me. The vibes feel good and I want to be here."

The studio ghosts certainly worked their magic. The finished album, *Valotte*, named after the Manor de Valotte where it was conceived, was released in October 1984 and gave Charisma another huge chart success, notching up platinum sales (over 1,000,000 units) within six months, the biggest-selling debut album in the history of the label. Tony would later joke that it was in part recompense for Lennon senior's misdemeanours back in the days of the Pickwick Club. "Many a time I was stuck with John Lennon's wine bill," said Tony. "Not that John was mean, he was just very forgetful. He had this wonderful habit, where he'd go for a bottle of this or that and then suddenly he'd decide he was going and that was it, you'd be left with it. I told Julian I had to sign him just to get the old wine bills back!"

Tony asked Martin Lewis to produce a documentary that would aid the promotion and marketing of Lennon's album. "Strat was no fool," he says. "He knew that there would be suspicion [around the Lennon name] and he was seeking my opinion about how to deal with it. He saw it as a marketing challenge. Strat asked me to develop ideas. I asked to hear some more of the music and it was just as engaging as I thought it might be. I loved John Lennon and I looked on it as a duty of honour to do something for Julian."

Lewis sought the advice of Pete Townshend whose younger brother Simon had grown up in Pete's shadow. "It wasn't quite the same situation, but it's not wildly different," he says. "Pete said, 'If you take on this project, your job will be to make sure that Julian doesn't become a teddy bear for the John Lennon fans.' And that resonated with me deeply. I went back to Strat and I said it has to be a film, a documentary or something like that in which Julian speaks for himself and in which his talent can be seen and heard. Yes, there will still be questions, but you'll have set the tone. That way the conversation will have been started by us and not by tabloid journalists. Don't let other people dictate the story. Strat had a lot of confidence that I knew what I was doing film-wise, so he commissioned me. I was put in charge of the project and, as it happened, Julian was spending time in New York, recording his album with Phil Ramone. So I went back to New York and was introduced to Phil and Julian and the good news was that we immediately had a great rapport and I got on famously with Phil Ramone."

While Lewis had his doubts about the abilities of Julian's manager Dean Gordon, he set about making the documentary film and opted to approach Sam Peckinpah, then on a career low and virtually unemployable, to direct it. In the event, Peckinpah directed two videos for tracks from Julian's album. "'Valotte' in particular was a masterpiece of a music video," says Lewis.

With a successful record riding high in the charts on both sides of the Atlantic, Julian Lennon embarked on his debut concert tour of America, which sold out almost immediately. The set list featured most of the *Valotte* album, plus a sprinkling of rock'n'roll standards like 'Stand By Me', 'Slippin' And Slidin'', both of which his father had covered on his 1975 *Rock'n'Roll* LP, and the obligatory Beatles cover, 'Day Tripper'. The tour kicked off on March 29, 1985, at the Louisiana State University in Baton Rouge and wound up 28 gigs later on May 10 in Honolulu, Hawaii.

Lennon's connection to Charisma also enabled illusionist Simon Drake to cross paths with Tony again. He was booked as a somewhat surprising support act for the American tour, bewildering US audiences by opening the show with a set of strange tricks and situations featuring his diminutive assistant Kiran Shah, who appeared variously dressed as a circus strong man, a suitcase and ET. "Julian's tour, believe it or not, was bigger than all of them because it was like every Beatles maniac came out of the woodwork," says Drake. "Julian is such a sweet-natured guy, but the Lennon name is a huge curse. I think it's slightly different for Sean, but it's a curse for Julian. Julian was very good on stage, musically sound with terrific musicians. I was heckled to shit – 'We want Julian' – because he had a big teeny-bopper following, all these young girls were totally in love with him. Strat came out to see the show in New York and that was the last time I saw him. Unfortunately, for some reason he was incredibly drunk and bitter and not at all happy... but he really wasn't well."

Lennon's next release for Charisma suffered from the textbook 'difficult second album' syndrome. The new material was written in pretty short order on the back of the draining US tour and a hectic schedule of additional dates in Australia and Japan. Released in March 1986, *The Secret Value Of Daydreaming* was largely panned by the press and barely scraped into the *Billboard* top 40, although it did produce a further hit single, 'Stick Around'. Although Lennon released four albums between the years 1984 and 1991, amassing combined sales of five and a half million, he felt he was losing control over his career when Charisma was absorbed by Virgin, and left the music business for a while. He returned with the *Photograph Smile* album in 1997, bringing in Steve Weltman once more to oversee the project.

* * *

Charisma was among several labels vying to sign the Aylesbury-based Marillion in their early days but, like Queen, they slipped through Tony's fingers. Having pushed the likes of Genesis and VdGG towards success, it was perhaps understandable that Tony would be a fan of prog-minded Fish and co. and he apparently gave orders for them to be signed at all costs.

The group's singer Derek Dick (aka Fish) remembers meeting Tony at the Marquee. "The club had become my drinking hole and I was able to rub shoulders with journalists and record company A&R guys all scouting for the next big thing," he says. "One figure who had his permanent place at the bar was Tony Stratton Smith. He sat with his horse racing buddies in the dark corner at the entrance to the door to the backstage. He never moved into the club itself, which was separated from the bar by a wall with Perspex windows."

Fish admits to picking Tony's brain for ideas and revelling in the Genesis stories he told and, for Tony, signing Marillion became something of a personal crusade since few others at Charisma shared his enthusiasm. One was a new member of staff, Jon Crawley, the son of B&C's record plugger Clive Crawley, and the other was Steve Weltman, who arranged a seven-figure deal with Warner/Chappell publishing and hired Jon from RAK to help resurrect Charisma's own publishing company.

"Charisma had a small publishing company, and the biggest songs they had were 'Arc Of A Diver', which Steve Winwood wrote with Viv Stanshall, and 'Night Nurse' by Gregory Isaacs, and a couple of other things like 'Fog On The Tyne' but it wasn't an active company. Tony asked my dad if I'd be interested in coming to work for him. Considering the record company was really successful, Charisma just weren't leapfrogging on the back of it with the publishing, they weren't exploiting it at all."

Jon Crawley was asked by Tony to acquire Marillion's song publishing and to this end he went to watch them at a pub in Milton Keynes. "I thought to myself, well I can understand why the label don't want to sign them because they were similar to Genesis. In those days Fish even wore paint on his face just like Peter Gabriel."

Jon started work on a Monday and was introduced to the staff. "Strat came in and said, 'This is Jon Crawley, he is joining us and he's going to run the publishing company with Rob Gold.' Then he said, 'Jon wants to sign Marillion for publishing and I will not have anybody making life difficult for him, because I know there is opposition to sign them to the label, but he has got my full support.' He also sent a letter round to that effect, because there was a lot of hostility towards signing Marillion. So within weeks of working at Charisma, my first signing was Marillion."

During 1982 Marillion played a series of sold-out shows at the Marquee that proved crucial to breaking their career. Fish continues the story: "It was during the July shows that something memorable occurred. Tony Stratton Smith got off his stool and came into the main club to watch us. No one had ever seen this before. Days later he sent two of his cohorts up to Retford, where we were playing, with orders to sign us to Charisma Records. We felt they were not the real deal and, in fact, found out later that they had tried to pull a fast one on us and had disobeyed Strat's orders to sign us to an album deal. They were only offering a singles deal. We knew we were an album band."

Jon Crawley is adamant that Marillion wanted to sign to Charisma. "That's why it was so important that I got Steve and Strat's support early on, because being the new boy I would probably have had to roll with the tide. Nobody else at Charisma wanted to sign them – just Strat. So I had meetings with John and Fish and I got on really well with all the boys in the band. I used to go and see every gig and I'd just hang out with them."

Marillion subsequently signed to EMI, breaking the news to a "seriously disappointed" Tony at the Reading Festival in August that year. Thanks to the persistence of Tony and Jon Crawley, Charisma retained their lucrative music publishing and the group later dedicated their 1987 album *Clutching At Straws* to Tony. "In fairness, looking back on it, I think EMI probably did a better job than we could have done," admits Crawley, who was well rewarded for his work in Charisma's publishing arm.

"We had the Julian Lennon album and we had the publishing on Marillion's album and they both came out in the same year," he recalls. "We made an absolute fortune and Strat had never seen so much money go through the books. So one day I'm in the toilets at Charisma in Wardour Street and Strat comes in and calls out 'Crawley, are you in there?' 'Yes Strat, what do you want?' He said, 'I've got something for you. I'll slide it under the door.' He slides this big brown envelope underneath the door and there was about five grand in there. It was his thank you for helping to turn the company around. We went from turning over about 30 grand a year to something like a million quid. Strat was a very generous man."

It wasn't all sweetness and light for Crawley. Sometimes he was called upon to help with the dirty work at the record label. As other staff members had discovered, not all of Tony's signings were as successful as Marillion and Julian Lennon. "Strat loved going to see bands, but getting him out of trouble afterwards was part of the duty for all of us – and we were all very protective. He would go to the Marquee, get completely pissed and by the next morning he'd signed a new band – so by the following evening, we would have to un-sign them."

* * *

Regardless of the success that Julian Lennon and publishing coups like Marillion brought to Charisma, life at London's most laid-back label was not as enjoyable as it once was and record industry vultures, led by Dutch giant Polygram, were circling Wardour Street. Newly appointed Charisma A&R man Peter Jenner was a little more forthright: "Charisma was in a real mess.

Constant cash flow problems – we were haemorrhaging money. Charisma's golden era was pre-punk, they had never really got hold of post-punk. I was there to fire everybody, but I was a real fucking softy. I just let bands make another record. I was really unsuccessful at that job."

As the cash flow slowed to a trickle and Tony found himself under mounting pressure from Polygram, his reaction to the crisis was admirably predictable, as Jenner recalls. "He would still come into work at twelve, go to lunch at one, come back at four and then go out all night," laughs Jenner. "Great geezer. Old-school. Very sharp."

Working alongside this 'old-school geezer' gave Peter Jenner a first-hand insight into Tony's no-nonsense approach to Artists and Repertoire. "I spent one year working at Charisma, which is where I met Billy [Bragg] and I asked Tony Stratton Smith for his advice. Every day he used to go out to the pub. At 5.50pm he would leave the office and go to the pub and one day I said to him, 'Strat, how do you decide who to sign?', because I was supposed to be doing their A&R. 'How do you make that decision?' I asked, and he said, 'Oh, it's simple. I go out of the office, walk past the Marquee and if there's a queue around the block and I've never heard of the band, then I'll check them out. Simple.' I just thought that was absolutely fantastic, what a summary of what A&R is all about."

It was thanks largely to Peter Jenner that Billy Bragg, the 'Bard of Brentford', was briefly a Charisma artist. He had been gigging tirelessly, sometimes busking around London, performing solo with an electric guitar, but his demo tape was not getting through to the right people. Pretending to be a television repairman, he blagged his way into Jenner's office. Peter liked the tape, but the company was near bankruptcy and he had no budget to sign new artists. Bragg already had an offer to record more demos for a music publisher, so Jenner agreed to put them out as a record with Bragg's industrious gigging as the sole promotion.

Life's A Riot With Spy Vs. Spy initially came out on Charisma's new Utility imprint in July 1983 and Bragg was widely hailed as a promising new talent. Never one to miss an opportunity, one evening he heard DJ John Peel mention on-air that he was hungry. Bragg rushed round to the BBC with a mushroom biryani and was rewarded when Peel played a track from *Life's A Riot*, albeit at the wrong speed. Peel insisted he would have played the tape anyway, even without the biryani, and later played it again, this time at the correct number of revs per minute. Billy Bragg's time at the label was short-lived, as within months Charisma would be purchased by Virgin Records and Peter Jenner left to became Bragg's manager. A copy of *Life's A Riot* fell into the hands of former Stiff Records press officer Andy Macdonald, who was setting up his own record label, Go! Discs. He made Virgin an offer and the album was re-released on Go! Discs in November 1983.

Whatever the label's precarious financial circumstances it was still game for the odd quirky idea. Ever since he jumped on the Geno Washington tour bus with 'Cracky' Jones back in 1969, Keith Allen had been making a nuisance of himself; on the alternative comedy circuit and gruelling stand-up nights at the Comedy Store, supporting The Clash on tour and presenting a couple of 'youth TV' shows on the recently launched Channel 4. Whether or not it was his connection with Cracky that led him to the door of Tony's record label no one knows, but Charisma's Wardour Street office is exactly where Allen found himself in 1983.

In his autobiography *Grow Up*, Allen explains how he and his friend Glen Colson walked into Pete Jenner's office asking for money to fund a pirate radio station. "I thought an album of a recorded gig was a bit boring really, so I hit on the idea of doing an album as a pirate radio broadcast," wrote Allen. "It would give me the chance to present my gay characters to a wider audience. I thought Peter Jenner had misunderstood me. 'So why do you want us to buy equipment? Just go in the studio and record?' 'No, I don't want to pretend it is a pirate radio station. I want to set up a real pirate radio station.' Pete stared at me. 'What a great idea,' he said. And so, Breakfast Pirate Radio was born."

The Breakfast Pirate Radio format allowed Allen to vent his comedic spleen across the airwaves, taking pot-shots at celebrities, the police, the Tory government and spreading rumours about, among others, his new Charisma label-mate Malcolm McLaren, generally using the disguise of various gay characters, including the 'Northern Industrial Gay' Gerry Arkwright and a Rastafarian singer named Boots Sex Dread.

With Glen Colson's help, BPR managed one Sunday broadcast from a church in Islington that was recorded for the album. Pete Jenner set up its release on the Charisma subsidiary label Utility, Barney Bubbles designed the sleeve and *Programme 1* very nearly found its way into the record racks. Unfortunately for Allen, this all happened during the sale of Charisma to Virgin Records – and the debut album by BPR wasn't exactly what the Virgin executives had in mind when they purchased Tony's already esoteric label. The BPR recording eventually found its way into the marketplace in the form of a three-cassette package put out by Rough Trade Records.

Still, the future of Tony's beloved Charisma was still very much in the balance when in June 1981 *Music Week* reported a dramatic turn in the bidding war. "The financial haggling over the purchase of Charisma Records reached a point of high drama when Virgin's Richard Branson put in a new, last-minute bid – topping Chrysalis which thought it had clinched the deal, having agreed a price earlier in the week. Assuming Branson is able to raise the necessary cash, it appears Virgin will be the winner, unless Chrysalis chooses to make a further bid."

The story went on to state that Tony had indicated he would prefer the company to go to a UK independent, ruling out Phonogram, which had a matching bid clause in its current contract with Charisma. "Virgin is believed to be favoured by certain members of Charisma's staff because it has promised autonomous control for the label," the story added.

Billboard in the US was also keeping a close eye on events and in August 1981 they reported that, despite having offers on the table from Chrysalis, Virgin and RCA, Tony had taken the decision to ignore all the buyout bids, preferring instead to increase the pressing and distribution deal that was already in place with Phonogram. As a result, Charisma retained their all-important independence, added to a much-needed injection of cash from Phonogram. Although this move proved to be problematic for Steve Weltman and Brian Gibbon, it gave Tony the financial means to pursue his interests in other areas, in particular filmmaking and his beloved horse racing.

Fondness for the turf was largely restricted to music entrepreneurs but among the musicians who at one time owned racehorses was keyboard wizard Rick Wakeman, who knew Tony and found himself stymied by the imminent sale of Charisma. "In the early eighties, progressive rock and orchestral rock had reached a low ebb," he says, "but Strat very much felt that there was still a place on the shelf for the music." As a result, Wakeman recorded the album *1984* with a full orchestra and choir, with Chaka Khan, Steve Harley and Jon Anderson singing Tim Rice's lyrics. Plans for a rock musical based on this music were scuppered by the George Orwell Estate, as had happened when David Bowie tried something similar with the album that became *Diamond Dogs*.

A press launch for Wakeman's album was held in the disused underground station at Aldwych, one of the 'ghost' stations on the London Underground, originally named Strand. Charisma deemed it the ideal space in which to launch an album based on George Orwell's dystopian vision of the future.

Wakeman recalls that Tony told him he was thinking about selling Charisma in order to finance a film about the Manchester United Munich disaster. "He also told me that the downside, for me at least, was that *1984* was likely to go to Virgin, which at that time was very much a punk and new wave label. Sure enough, I was summoned to the Virgin offices to be told quite succinctly that I was not the kind of person they wanted on the Virgin label. Strat was very upset about this, as he cared for all the acts he had signed over the years. We remained in touch up until the day he died, but rarely discussing music – it was mostly about the horse racing."

* * *

As with most aspects of his private life, Tony kept his political cards fairly close to his chest. On circumstantial evidence it was probably assumed that his educated background, adopted home-counties accent and double-barrelled surname equated with the mindset of a privileged Tory businessman. Others may have taken the view that his liberal attitudes to life in general would naturally roll over into his politics, although most of his allies in Parliament tended to be died-in-the-wool Labour men. Denis Howell in particular was someone that Tony had known since their early days in Birmingham. More often than not, when the time came, Tony's political affiliations proved to be as red as his trademark braces.

In 1981, following a disastrous Labour Party conference that saw 13 MPs resign or defect to the newly formed Social Democrats, a 'stay in and fight back' campaign was initiated by Labour leader Michael Foot. His 'fight back' letter was signed by about 150 members of Parliament and on Tuesday, February 17, a meeting was held in the Grand Committee Room of the House of Commons, attracting 102 of the original 'gang of 150' whose aim was to form a new organisation entitled the Labour Solidarity Campaign.

Within days of the meeting, Denis Howell contacted Tony to ask for his help with the campaign. Without hesitation, Tony wrote back to his old friend, agreeing to fund certain advertising and print costs to the tune of £6,000 – and although he asked to be re-invoiced "as costs arise", Tony enclosed a cheque for £2,500 to get the campaign ball rolling. Three days later, Austin Mitchell wrote back in his capacity as treasurer of the campaign to thank Tony for his cheque and his "timely, welcome and generous support".

A further upset for the Solidarity campaign came in April 1981, when Tony Benn suddenly announced his decision to stand against deputy leader Denis Healey – hardly a show of party unity, let alone good timing. Solidarity campaign chairman Peter Shore was less than happy with the left-wing ambitions of Benn and the other 'wreckers' in the party.

Politics aside, back at the record company Charisma were about to appoint a new Managing Director. Brian Gibbon's time had run its course and he left the business in 1982, initially with the idea of retiring completely, before becoming Steve Hackett's personal manager. During his long service with both B&C and Charisma, Gibbon had sometimes found himself painted as the company bad guy, a situation he found difficult on more than one occasion.

"Sometimes it was just somebody Tony might have met in the pub who had a good idea and then they'd be handed over to either Gail and myself to try and sort out," recalls Gibbon. "Is this a good idea or is this not a good idea? And then Tony would say, 'Well, I gave him my word that we were going to do this and Brian, now you'll have to tell him that we are not.' It became that good guy and bad guy sort of thing. So I had this horrible reputation of being the one that always said 'no'. Which wasn't very endearing to some of his friends, even some of his closest friends. Of course, somebody had to tell them and that person often turned out to be me."

Tony considered picking up the reins again himself but turned instead to long-term associate Steve Weltman as Gibbon's replacement. Following a spell as International Manager at RCA Records, where among others he worked on the 'Berlin Trilogy' of *Low*, *Heroes* and *Lodger* with David Bowie, and the Elvis Presley catalogue, Weltman returned to the Charisma fold in 1981 and barely a year later, succeeded Brian Gibbon to become Charisma's Managing Director. Among his earliest decisions was to ditch the old accounts department and take the books away for an intense three-day scrutiny with a new accountant. Suffice to say there were certain inconsistencies.

Steve Weltman had always got on well with Tony; he already knew the company inside out, both its history and its structure, and he certainly wasn't afraid to broaden the horizons by bringing in new artists. His first was Malcolm McLaren, the colourful – some would say notorious – manager of the Sex Pistols who now had more projects up his sleeve.

Weltman first ran into McLaren in New York, where McLaren was on tour as manager of Bow Wow Wow. At the time Weltman was considering using Bow Wow Wow on some Japanese jingles. "I was coming to the end of my tenure at RCA, but we'd just signed Bow Wow Wow and we were launching them in America," recalls Weltman. "Malcolm and I were in New York and we'd worked right through until about 10pm, gone out for something to eat and then we went to a club for a drink. This record came on the turntable and it was like somebody putting their hands round your neck and saying 'Listen to this'. It was like nothing I'd ever heard before."

What they heard was 'Planet Rock' by Afrika Bambaataa and the Zulu Nation. Weltman and McLaren were the band were doing a gig that night in the South Bronx at three o'clock in the morning. "We jumped straight into a cab and went out there. What Malcolm and I saw that night was complete chaos. There were kids spraying things on the walls, there were Double Dutch dancers, the Rock Steady Crew were breakdancing, there were people playing, DJs, rappers and MCs – I mean, it was just extraordinary."

Back in London, Weltman told Tony he would accept the managing director job if he could sign McLaren. "I told him, 'Let's be honest, nothing has happened at Charisma since the late seventies. For whatever reason it has become a cosmetic label where Genesis and Peter Gabriel put their records out.' I said, 'Strat, if we get it right, doing this record will bring us right back.'"

A surprised Tony spluttered "What? That Sex Pistols man? He can't sing, can he?" Two days later, when Weltman met up again with McLaren and mentioned Charisma, McLaren's reaction was almost as extreme as Tony's had been. "Charisma? That's the hippie label with that big fat bloke Tony…!" Steve Weltman convinced him that it was not who was at the label, it was the commitment and belief in good product that mattered. All of which, largely thanks to Tony, Charisma had in abundance. The deal was done.

So it was that in 1982, Charisma released a single that at first glance seemed a most unlikely marriage of minds – punk Svengali McLaren and a pair of hip hop DJs from New York. Few outside of the American club scene had even heard of hip hop and the technique of 'scratching' – and it's fair to say that had Tony still been in sole charge of A&R, then Charisma might never have got involved. But new MD Steve Weltman had other ideas – and the single 'Buffalo Gals' and the subsequent album *Duck Rock* both became huge sellers for the label, undoubtedly introducing hip hop to a wider audience in the UK.

McLaren brought the 'World's Famous Supreme Team' back to England to work with producer Trevor Horn. According to Weltman, when he first approached Horn to produce McLaren with what would become the *Duck Rock* album, Horn laughed and said, "He's a manager, he doesn't write or play."

At that time, the Supreme Team consisted of two New York radio disc jockeys, Se' Devine and Jazzy Just, who hosted a hip hop and classic R&B show on WHBI and were among the first exponents of the dubious art of scratching. In the sleeve notes to the album, McLaren described it thus: "Suffice to say they have developed a technique using record players like instruments, replacing the power chord of the guitar with the needle of a gramophone, moving it manually backwards and forwards across the surface of a record."

Although some at Charisma Records were reluctant to release 'Buffalo Gals', after positive reaction to early radio plays on both sides of the Atlantic, and strong encouragement from Weltman, the label relented. In fact, when Weltman played the final single version of 'Buffalo Gals' to Phonogram MD Brian Shepherd, it absolutely blew him away. Shepherd then called for his head of promotion Julian Spear, they played the track to him and Spear said it was amazing and he had never, ever heard anything like it.

"It paid off handsomely," says Weltman. "*Duck Rock* was one of *NME*'s best albums of the eighties and we had three huge singles from it. Vivienne Westwood had designed the Buffalo Girl look and she was the first British designer to show in Paris. When her models came down the catwalk, they walked down to *Duck Rock* – it was like having an extra advertising campaign that we didn't have to pay for. Every time you saw a Buffalo Girl, or a model, or a hat on an artist, it was also plugging our record."

According to Weltman, Tony loved the success of the record and, more importantly, the kudos it brought back to the label. He was also mightily impressed that Peter Gabriel loved the album. "Strat loved what *Duck Rock* was all about, i.e. moving the goalposts, which is why I wanted it for Charisma," he says. "He enjoyed Malcolm's intellect and wit but sometimes he found him a little draining, although he was not alone in that. In all businesses there are very strong characters and Malcolm was certainly another one of those. So yes, there were times when Malcolm rubbed Strat up the wrong way, but he loved to pit his wits against him. Regardless of what anybody says, Malcolm was a very intelligent guy and I remember several times when they were together where their intellects were just off the charts. They were very understanding of each other and Strat loved the adventure in what Malcolm was doing."

As an example of just how comfortable Tony was with Steve Weltman's new signings, on August 3, 1983, he spent the day with Richard Branson at his houseboat home in Little Venice on the Regent's Canal. Photographer Neil Mackenzie Matthews captured the event for posterity and while most of the shots show Branson and Stratton Smith relaxing on deck in the warm sunshine, they also include the more bizarre sight of Tony wearing tight shorts and a promotional T-shirt, skipping. The elder statesman and his young pretender appear comfortable in each other's company, but while Branson was prepared for the promotional stunt, happily bounding barefoot down the towpath, Tony looks as though the photo opportunity was sprung on him at the last minute. Nevertheless, the Charisma boss gamely pulled the T-shirt over the top of his casual clothes, but did at least insist on keeping his shoes and socks on – some decorum, dear boy, please!

The reason for the merriment was the release of 'Double Dutch', the latest single by Malcolm McLaren, a hip hop song based on the old skipping game and taken from the album *Duck Rock*. After a number nine hit with his debut single 'Buffalo Gals', McLaren's 'Double Dutch' would eventually reach number three in the UK.

Once again, Tony had taken a huge gamble, placing his faith in the musical savvy of his new managing director. Fortunately, just as Steve Weltman had hoped, delving into exciting and uncharted musical waters helped to ease the Charisma bank balance back into the black. "I can't remember the exact numbers," said Weltman, "but when I became MD of the company we were well in the red and then through the whole McLaren period, the Rock Steady Crew, the Supreme Team, Julian Lennon, alongside Genesis and Gabriel, we gradually turned the company and the profitability right back around."

Among the final acts to be signed to the Charisma label was a young

American singer, Mercy Ray. Steve Weltman snapped her up, but the deal was done with half an eye on getting her producer Stephen Hague into the bargain. Hague and Mercy were an item at that point, as well as being songwriting partners and later husband and wife. Hague cut his teeth playing keyboards in US pop band Jules & The Polar Bears and quickly made a name for himself as a producer with Gleaming Spires, a Sparks offshoot. "Mercy was absolutely one of mine," said Weltman. "I also signed Stephen to Charisma as a producer to do 'x' amount of tracks for the company – and he produced 'Madam Butterfly' with Malcolm McLaren after 'Duck Rock' was exhausted."

Hague also co-produced the first single for the Rock Steady Crew, working with Soldier to give Charisma a top six chart hit with '(Hey You) The Rock Steady Crew' in 1983. Soldier's sister Blue was their manager. Originally a group of breakdancers who got together in the New York Bronx during 1977, the Rock Steady Crew competed with other NYC boroughs in energetic dance styles known as 'b-boying', but at this point they were still largely unknown outside of the city. Among the most influential dancers was Richard 'Crazy Legs' Colón, who helped to bring the style to the hip hop scene in Manhattan, and it was his 'chapter' of the RSC that Weltman and McLaren added to the bill at the Ritz nightclub, performing alongside Bow Wow Wow and Afrika Bambaataa in 1982.

In November 1983, the annual Royal Variety Show had opted for a dance theme and Steve Weltman made sure the Rock Steady Crew were on the bill. In an evening hosted by Gene Kelly, Her Majesty the Queen and the smartly-dressed audience at the Theatre Royal, Drury Lane found themselves grooving to the young breakdancers from the Bronx, who performed their hit single '(Hey You) The Rock Steady Crew'. Afterwards the group retired to a restaurant in Soho, in the company of Tony and Steve Weltman, to celebrate in style. "Somewhere there is a photograph of Strat, Richard Branson and myself – and Branson is wearing a tuxedo, which is a rare thing in itself," says Weltman. "We are presenting the Rock Steady Crew with gold records that hadn't even come out the cellophane, because they'd literally just come from playing the Royal Variety Show."

By the autumn of 1983, McLaren was angry that *Duck Rock* had failed to be a worldwide hit and wanted out of his contract with Charisma. He blamed Weltman for its failure and wanted him sacked. Storming into Tony's office, he told him: "You fire Steve Weltman and I'll stay."

Tony flatly refused – in fact, the normally placid Strat told McLaren in no uncertain terms to fulfil his contract with one more album before he could leave. McLaren responded by sending in two lawyers to see if they could succeed where he had failed, with first Howard Jones, and then Irving David attempting to convince Charisma to let their client go. One poorly thought-out plan was to offer the out-takes from the *Duck Rock* sessions as the outstanding album, although as Steve Weltman pointed out, Charisma already owned any existing recordings so it would make little sense to accept those as contract fulfilment.

Despite the often-litigious nature of the music industry, Charisma lawyer Anthony Seddon rarely found himself forced to represent the company in court. McLaren, however, proved an exception, perhaps predictably in the light of his provocative business style.

"Surprisingly, when you think of how things were in the music business generally, Charisma pretty much managed to keep out of all that," acknowledges Seddon. "We had our differences in business over the years, but we managed more or less to resolve any potential problems, largely because Strat was always the most amenable guy. We did end up taking Malcolm McLaren to court and he did have to appear in front of a judge, because of the outrageous way he decided to break his contract."

McLaren found himself legally stuck between *Duck Rock* and a hard place. Eventually the Charisma team came up with an interesting compromise – to add a third album to the contract, but to allow one of those records to include the existing out-takes. A fuming McLaren signed the new papers and promptly moved back to New York to start work and knock out the extra material. His 1984 album *Fans* contained six tracks that married opera – *Madame Butterfly*, *Carmen* – with contemporary R&B with varying degrees of success, followed in 1985 by *Swamp Thing*, McLaren's contractual obligation album that contained whatever scraps were left over from the *Duck Rock* sessions. Proving that you can never fool the record-buying public, *Swamp Thing* made absolutely no impression on the charts on either side of the Atlantic.

It was around this time that Steve Weltman noticed a change in Tony's general demeanour and daily working regime, along with a marked increase in his drinking habits. Tony had always enjoyed a long lie-in of a morning but now, often still hung-over from the excesses of the night before, he wasn't even bothering to drop by the office first, but heading straight for the pub.

"I always knew when he'd had a skinful the night before," says Weltman, "because if he was not in by midday I could guarantee that between 12.00 and 12.30 there would be a phone call saying, 'My dear boy, I think we should have a meeting in The Ship' and it was always a pint of Guinness first, that was his hangover cure, that was his Bloody Mary. One particular day in 1984 I met Tony at mid-day in the pub, he was totally hung-over and we were talking about The Opposition."

Formed in 1979, The Opposition were a three-piece band from South London who combined new wave and reggae with a post-punk image

– plenty of eyeliner and attitude. They had already recorded a debut album for Ariola Records, before being headhunted by Steve Weltman and signed to Charisma. They recorded three albums for Charisma, *Intimacy* in 1983, *Promises* the following year and *Empire Days* in 1985, all with producer Kenny Jones. "The Opposition were on their first trip to America as support to Thomas Dolby," recalls Weltman. "Tony thought one of us should really be there on their first night. I said, 'Okay, what if one of us just gets on Concorde and goes out there?' Tony was adamant that I go, but I said, 'No you go, I'm busy.' The argument went on. Eventually Tony simply said, 'Let's toss a coin' and took a coin out of his wallet. I said Strat that was too quick, show me that coin – because I thought it was a double header, but it wasn't. So Tony got the girl behind the bar to flip the coin and I lost, so I got to take the last-minute trip on Concorde."

In January 1984, the music world lost an influential figure whom Tony held in particularly high regard. Within months, Charisma proudly released the posthumous album *Juvenile Delinquent* featuring the final recordings of blues pioneer Alexis Korner. Tony himself wrote sleeve notes that reflect his obvious affection for Korner, one of the godfathers of British blues. They concluded: "I was in Cyprus when I heard Alexis's uniquely abrasive voice had been silenced by lung cancer. The fierce sunset that day was itself a powerful blues. I raised a glass to the Hoochie Coochie Man; only 55, and with much left to teach us."

On top of everything else, Tony's world took yet another, far more personal blow in 1984 with the death of his mother, Mollie. Of all the members of his immediate family, Tony had stayed close to his mother, who by this time had moved down to Devon to be nearer to her daughter, June. June's husband, Mike Norris, remembers that when Mollie first moved to Torquay she lived with the couple at their flat and stayed with them until about 1983, when Tony bought her a cottage in Princes Street, close to the coastline in Babbacombe.

As is so often the case with families that grow apart, the funeral at Torquay Crematorium offered a rare opportunity for Tony to catch up with other members of the Smith clan. His cousin Patricia Widdows recalls: "After Tony moved to London his visits back home were few. He was successful, he had new friends and the family understood that most of the time. We were always very proud of his achievements, but sadly did not get to see him."

Acknowledging that the only family gathering in the eighties was for his mother's funeral in 1984, Patricia added: "Tony always wanted a get-together – it was discussed often, but sadly never came to pass."

* * *

STRAT!

At the end of an eventful and emotionally taxing year, Tony was in need of a change of scenery to recharge his batteries. His old friend George Thompson came up with the perfect solution. "Zoe and I decided to go for a winter holiday in 1984 to find some sun, to Barbados. We were going with friends and were very happy when Strat decided to join us – along with David Gideon Thomson. It was a wonderful time, full of stories, laughter and the inevitable drink, mostly at one of the little beach bars, where all the local characters hung-out. One day Stratton decided to have a hat made by a strolling beach salesman using palm leaves and it was fascinating to watch the measuring of the head, then with a few quick movements of his hands and wrists – hey presto – it was ready. The result was perfect and it suited Stratton so well."

The party watched cricket in Bridgetown for several days, experiencing the noise, the colour, the buzz, the wonderful music and the mouth-watering smells of food being cooked all around the outside of the stadium. "Apart from the atmosphere outside, the noise inside was deafening," recalls Thompson, "topped by a trumpeter who played all day long, supported intermittently by a drummer. Strat loved the whole jamboree."

Chapter 17

The Sale

"I remember him getting very weepy. He was obviously very depressed.
He felt that everybody was leaving him and I didn't know what to do.
He was very sad about something. Perhaps he felt that he wasn't
appreciated by Phil or by Peter, and that night he was
feeling lonely and low. I felt so helpless.
There was nothing I could say that would assuage whatever
fears he had."

Martin Lewis, music publicist

All good things must come to an end, dear boy. Even though he had known for some time that the day was fast approaching, it must have been with a very heavy heart that Tony Stratton Smith finally decided to sell his shares in his beloved Charisma to Richard Branson's fast-growing Virgin Group. In a personal letter to Gail Colson, dated June 27, 1985, Tony outlined his plans, describing the move as taking the "route of least disturbance".

"You will appreciate that I am not getting any younger," he wrote, "and with the working years still available to me I am anxious to develop my interest in writing and in the development of films. My first screenplay, *The Last Enemy,* is being filmed for Yorkshire Television in August and September, starring Anthony Andrews and Patrick McGoohan. This development has given me great pleasure and there is more in the pipeline, for which, of course, I need to devote more time. I have therefore decided to reduce my day-to-day involvement in music, and towards that end, I am selling my shares in Charisma Records to Richard Branson of the Virgin Group. Virgin have been very supportive towards Charisma since taking over our distribution in August 1983 and the Charisma management team has been delighted with the association. I hasten to add that this is the route of least disturbance, as Virgin intend to maintain Charisma Records as a separate entity, under the continued management of Steve Weltman and his team."

It was Steve Weltman's decision to take Charisma's distribution away from Phonogram and place it with Virgin. A little while later, Weltman was asked to present Charisma's future releases to Virgin's directors in Amsterdam and after the meeting, Virgin boss Richard Branson took Weltman to one side and broached the question of whether he thought Tony would consider selling the company. When Weltman later related Branson's interest to Tony, the Charisma boss' reaction was priceless. Tony smiled, sighed theatrically and said: "Ohhh, if you have to, Steve – and to be honest, these days I don't feel quite so comfortable in a room full of teenagers."

Virgin weren't the only horse in the race, as Chris Wright and Chrysalis had made some of the early running. "When Strat eventually sold Charisma in 1985, he came to see me," says Wright. "At the time, Chrysalis and Virgin were the hottest independent companies in the country and he was in negotiations with both of us, but Virgin offered him more money. I made him what I thought was a very good offer before he went to see Richard Branson. Strat then called me from Richard's office, with Richard listening to the call, to tell me he had a bigger offer, and asked me to increase mine. I was tempted to figure out how I could rescue the deal, but I knew that Richard, having got him in his office, would not let him leave without an agreement. So, just to muddy the waters, I said, 'Whatever Richard offers you, I will double it.' I imagine Strat extracted a little more from Richard and that was that."

Wright was disappointed at the outcome as he felt that buying Charisma would have been the perfect solution to resolve issues that were developing between him and his partner Terry Ellis. "One of us could have had Charisma and the other one could have had Chrysalis. I would have been equally happy with either. We should really have broken the bank to buy Charisma."

Richard Branson wasn't the only one who was disturbed at the prospect of Chrysalis profiting in the Charisma sale. Gail Colson was also against selling to them. "Tony phoned me when he was in real trouble and told me he was going to sell the company – and at that point he was planning to sell it to Terry Ellis, who worked with Chrysalis," she recalls. "I said, no Tony, you can't sell it to Chrysalis, anyone but them. So he agreed not to sell it to Chrysalis. Then he said to me, 'I'm going to sell it to Virgin.' So I spoke to Richard Branson and I said, 'Just do me one favour, don't give the money to him all in one go, because otherwise if you give it to Tony in one go, he'll just spend the lot.'"

By all accounts, Tony did his best to lead Richard Branson a merry dance before making Virgin his final choice. "It will make Virgin a force to be reckoned with in the industry," he told anyone who would listen, somewhat mischievously.

"I thought he was being rather cheeky at first," recalls Branson, "but when I looked over his list of new young artists, I thought, what the hell, let's go with the flow, and I made him an offer. Tony Stratton Smith was, I suspect, the most delightful person ever to be in the music business and everyone who dealt with him loved him. He collected together a band of artists, which, as far as Virgin was concerned, were keys to its future success – people like Phil Collins and Genesis, Monty Python, and a host of others. He would have wonderful long lunches, normally starting at twelve and finishing at seven in the evening, if at all. Anyone who had dealings with him, I'm sure, found him to be an extremely special person. He could have passed what he'd built on to any number of people – so, as well as all the work that Simon [Draper] and everyone had done, we were still very lucky really, that he chose to hand Charisma over to us."

As Virgin's Simon Draper readily admits, his label had been eyeing up Charisma for quite a while. "Our association with Tony Smith and Charisma Records had really begun with Phil Collins, but in 1983 we looked at buying Charisma. By '84 they'd got into more and more financial difficulties so we ended up buying the company then."

The crown jewels in the Charisma catalogue, of course, were the contracts for Genesis and Peter Gabriel, which Virgin were obliged to renegotiate. The crux of the matter is that Branson was fortunate in that his approach to Tony came at a time when Charisma's boss had become disillusioned with the music business and was keen to move on. Shortly after selling the label to Virgin, he reluctantly admitted "I still loved the label, I still loved the bands. I just wasn't too impressed by the music anymore."

The terms of the sale were undisclosed and because both Charisma and Virgin were privately owned at the time there was no legal requirement for the sale price to be revealed, in the music trade press or elsewhere. Although Branson complied with Gail Colson's suggestion that the payments be staggered to prevent Tony from squandering the proceeds, some past and present staff members felt that Charisma was undervalued and that Branson came away the winner.

According to Steve Weltman, the quality and size of the Charisma catalogue was only a part of the thinking behind Virgin's offer. After all, Charisma's future was starting to look good again. "To me, Charisma had been in a deep hole because although it had Genesis and Gabriel, it didn't have anything hip," he says. "Then when *Duck Rock* came out we were hip again. The number of acts phoning us up to ask if we would be interested in them was just astounding. Of course it wasn't too long afterwards that Branson made the final approach to Strat – and I could write a book about the stupidity of that deal, because Strat seemed to be the only person on the planet who didn't realise that Richard Branson wasn't buying Charisma because of the great records or the great bands – Branson was buying the catalogue to add to his Virgin portfolio, ready to go public."

Weltman urged Tony to demand stock in Virgin as part of the deal – or walk away if it wasn't forthcoming. "I tried to negotiate shares for Strat in that flotation, I did a fair amount on the commercial side and tried to insist on that in the deal, but Branson and his people refused to give in. To me it was a deal breaker, but Strat eventually caved in and gave it all up – and he could have made more money in the week that Virgin floated than he ever made in the record business. But, you know, that was Strat."

Glen Colson believes that while the Charisma sale may have come at the right time for Tony, it was for nowhere near the right price. "I think Strat was highly relieved, as he'd been trying to sell it for years and was waiting for the right bid, but he got into such financial straits, he had to sell it for less than he might have got. Virgin got the entire Charisma catalogue and one of the biggest bands in the world [Genesis] and one of the biggest acts, Peter Gabriel."

Tony could never let go completely, as this letter to Richard Branson, dated August 28, 1985, shows. He still held the company interests (and his interest in the company) very close to his heart.

"I am dismayed," he wrote, "and so is Tony Smith, with whom I had dinner last week, about an emerging business plan for Charisma which in my view, if implemented, could cause serious problems for the label. You may find some of this subjective but most, I assure you, is highly practical. When giving up the ownership of Charisma, the issue which caused me most loss of sleep was the ongoing development and relationships vis a vis artists. The strength of Steve Weltman was crucial in this, and I so assured the artists in a personal letter from myself. I repeat unto boredom my old teaching that artists are about material; performance; and ability to get it on with an audience. You juggle the balls of creativity until they (or it!) fit; essentially that meant artists able to build up a following on the road, and so achieve longevity. Sometimes it took relatively little time as with Julian (18 months), sometimes more, as with Genesis (three years).

"With Steve in place, I (and Tony Smith) felt comfortable that Charisma would retain its 'difference', that unique quality each successful label must have. It would have our continued support, and, certainly in my own case, it would be the first label to be offered our new signings. Now I cannot be sure. I would not pretend to question your right to cut back staff and overhead (not with the figures I've produced in recent years), but to cut the last important link with the 'Old Charisma' seems to me totally illogical. The label becomes merely a name and a serious gap is opened between it and the artists, which could well be reflected when one comes to discuss new contracts. Also, it implies a fundamental – possibly negative – change in the nature of the label, for no two managements think alike. This could seriously harm the development of one or two existing artists of very real potential, as well as making Charisma less attractive to the kind of artist for which it has had traditional appeal. The matter also, of course, concerns my pocket. I have a stake in the performance of Charisma through the next four years.

Solving Charisma's problems are one thing, reducing it to a ghost another. We should talk about it.

"Sorry 'Challenger' caused the wrong kind of splash. I admire your guts. Personally I get nervous on a cross-Channel ferry.

"Yours sincerely, TSS."

Even though Tony was showing his displeasure, there is a lightness of touch to his wording and he still manages to finish with a friendly quip. Only two weeks beforehand, Branson's speedboat the Virgin Atlantic Challenger had capsized in heavy seas while attempting the fastest Atlantic crossing from New York to the Isles of Scilly. Branson, the veteran sailor Chay Blyth and the rest of the crew were rescued by a passing ship and airlifted safely to hospital.

* * *

Meanwhile the work on the Julian Lennon documentary continued, straddling the sale of Charisma to Virgin. Martin Lewis now found himself dealing with a far more corporate group of people than when the project first started. One of these was Robert Devereux, the husband of Branson's sister Vanessa, who had been brought in to run Virgin's publishing arm and was now handling the film, television and radio side of the company.

"While I always had cordial conversations with him, there was an arrogance," recalls Lewis of Branson's brother-in-law. "There was an absence of care and an absence of art, an absence of interest in anything and I just thought, 'Oh fuck, what is this?' I got involved in this project because it was Strat, my dearly beloved Strat and Charisma and now I'm dealing with some oik, the kind of person who was in the sixth form of a minor public school that I was thrown out of, the kind of people I emigrated to get away from and now this is who is running the show. This was not worthy of Strat or Charisma, but you know, I had to deal with that."

Nevertheless, Lewis finished the film. "Strat was very complimentary when I saw him at the Marquee maybe about three months after the film was over. This would probably be around September or October 1985. I remember him getting very weepy. He was obviously very depressed. He felt that Phil Collins was slipping away from him. He felt that Peter Gabriel was slipping away from him. He felt that everybody was leaving him and I didn't know what to do.

"Tony was crying on my shoulder, not because I was any close buddy. There must have been lots of people much, much closer to him than I was but I just happened to be there that night. He'd found a familiar face, that's all. He was very sad about something. Perhaps he felt that he wasn't appreciated by Phil, or by Peter, and that night he was feeling lonely and low.

I felt so helpless. There was nothing I could say that would assuage whatever fears he had.

"I probably came out with platitudes. 'I'm sure they do appreciate you' but these were just platitudes, you know. I wanted to make him feel better but I didn't know how. There was a feeling of poignancy, some loss, something missing in his relationships with these other people that really meant something to him. Remember, by this time Phil Collins is huge, Peter Gabriel is huge, Genesis are huge and yet he is feeling this emptiness. How could he feel this way? Didn't he know what he'd achieved? And I do remember coming away that night just feeling that I loved Strat and yet I couldn't make him feel better, there was nothing I could say. I remember being struck by that feeling of helplessness, of wanting to help but just being clueless and ill equipped to make him feel better. And the worst thing is, I never saw Strat again after that."

There may have been another reason for Tony's apparently depressed state, unknown to Martin Lewis and most others at that time. The record company had always sailed a little too close to the wind as far as its finances were concerned and it would be only too easy to lay all the blame for Charisma's ailing bank balance at Tony's door. He was certainly guilty of taking his eye off the record company ball and of overspending elsewhere, especially on racehorses and film scripts. But there were rumours among those close to him that he had been swindled by a third party, an associate perhaps, possibly an insider – and we are not simply talking about someone flogging a few albums to a market stall as a perk of the job.

If the rumours were true, this was a cold, calculated case of fraud, a situation where huge amounts of company money were diverted away from the Charisma coffers. By the time the problem came to light, Tony was shocked and distraught – yet he felt so humiliated that he let the perpetrator get away with the crime. Tony refused to take the matter to the courts, choosing instead to take a hit of somewhere in excess of £1 million, rather than suffer the shame and humiliation of his peers should news of the scandal ever come to light.

Tony Stratton Smith was an old hand at hiding his innermost feelings – chin up, old boy, was always the English way. If these rumours are true he chose the stiff upper lip of convenience over the swift uppercut of revenge. Close friends had already begun to notice an increase in his already heavy drinking and that the black clouds were descending on his mood far more often than before. As Martin Lewis and others noticed, Strat was not the same happy-go-lucky, cock-eyed optimist of old.

Chapter 18

The Silver Screen

"When it came to the business side he would let his enthusiasm get in the way. That total enthusiasm and his emotions, he would often let them get in the way of his business decisions – and not just his business decisions, but also some of his personal decisions about what was good and what was not."

Tony Smith, manager of Genesis

With The Famous Charisma Label now part of Richard Branson's growing Virgin empire, what Tony needed was an exciting new project, a new venture into which he could throw himself wholeheartedly and get his creative juices flowing again, just as the journalism and the record label had done in the past. For the last few years he had spread himself thinly across his various interests, but perhaps now the time was right to concentrate on Charisma Films, the last division of Charisma Holdings actively using the famous name. He was only too aware of just how expensive filmmaking could be and now, without the safety net of the record label, he looked into ways of raising extra cash. One of the first companies he went to see was Centrespur Film Services, which is where he met an up and coming film financier, James Atherton.

Despite having trained and qualified as a chartered accountant with KPMG, Atherton hankered after the rock'n'roll lifestyle and had played in a couple of bands. Centrespur was a specialist UK film finance company and Atherton worked on independent films such as Derek Jarman's *The Tempest* and *Scum* by Alan Clarke. In the early eighties, he helped to raise funding for many big budget feature films including *Yentl*, *The Far Pavilions*, *Evil Under The Sun* and two in the Pink Panther series.

Tony and Atherton hit it off straight away. Tony asked Atherton to help run his recently formed film company but while the offer was tempting they never actually joined forces, although they did work together on a couple of projects, including a reworking of *Sir Henry At Rawlinson End*. By this time, Charisma Films was based in offices in Russell Chambers in Covent Garden, overlooking the piazza and sharing space with United British Artists, a production company founded by six British actors including

Peter Shaw and Richard Johnson.

Atherton believed that a strict work ethic was essential to success in business, and he was amazed by the 'lunch ethic' that ran through Charisma. Yet, despite the copious amounts of alcohol Tony consumed, Atherton always felt that he was at least one step ahead of everyone else involved in a business meeting.

Tony's initial partners on the board of Charisma Films included David Gideon Thomson, Roy Baird and Who manager Bill Curbishley, all of whom were involved in the making of *Quadrophenia*, based on The Who's rock opera, which subsequently brought money into Charisma Films. Gideon Thomson, who acted as Chairman on the board of both Charisma Records and Charisma Films, became one of Tony's closest friends and allies. Generally known as D.G.T. – not only an acronym of his name but of his favourite tipple, a double gin and tonic – he had tried his hand at acting, appearing uncredited in the 1953 wartime drama *The Cruel Sea,* but went on to pursue a long and successful career in the entertainment industry, starting at London Weekend Television before moving on to become a Director at Polygram Records. As well as overseeing their many subsidiary labels, which included Polydor, Mercury, Phonogram, MGM and Deutsche Grammophon, it also gave him a working interest in Chappell and the world of music publishing.

As if that wasn't enough work for one man, DGT also became Deputy Chairman of the Robert Stigwood Organisation, working on films such as *Saturday Night Fever* and *Grease* and consequently producing the soundtracks and publishing the music for both multi-selling productions. He also worked on the stage version of *Evita* and was executive producer on the film versions of *Quadrophenia* (1979) and *McVicar* (1980), which starred The Who's Roger Daltrey. Gideon Thomson proved to be a good man to have on your side. According to various sources, DGT was on hand to get Tony out of several extremely sticky, and potentially reputation-damaging, situations.

The other partner in Tony's film company, Joseph D'Morais, agrees that while working with him was never dull, it was not always orthodox. "He had some crazy ideas," recalls D'Morais. "When I had four short films at the 1984 London Film Festival, Tony's immediate reaction was, 'We must have a party.' Patrick McGoohan was going to fly over for the film and Robert Altman was here already, so we took a room, a space at the Royal Festival Hall from where we conducted the press for the festival and then held the Charisma Festival Party for our films. There is an amazing photograph somewhere of him with Julie Christie, and some of the Genesis boys came."

The star-studded extravaganza warranted a two-page photo feature in movie magazine *Screen International*, on December 8, 1984. Under the headline 'Blue Dolphin's Festival Party' it was noted that "Blue Dolphin's

Joe D'Morais and Charisma Films' Tony Stratton Smith jointly hosted a party at the Royal Festival Hall to celebrate Blue Dolphin's four entries in the London Film Festival." Guests of honour were the directors Robert Altman (*Secret Honor*) and Alexis Kanner (*Kings And Desperate Men, starring Patrick McGoohan*).

Featured were snapshots of Tony deep in conversation with Robert Altman and Tony Banks of Genesis, while in another shot, actor Alexis Kanner makes a point to Joe D'Morais and Robert Blay of Embassy Home Video. Unfortunately for Tony, Patrick McGoohan didn't make the party, but others caught on camera included Archie Tait (ICA Cinema), Derek Malcolm (festival director), Joe Steeples (*Daily Mail*), Penelope Houston (*Sight & Sound* editor), Mike Rutherford and his wife (Genesis), David Gideon Thomson (Charisma Films), Roy Baird (producer), Julie Christie (actress), Mr and Mrs Patrick Chaney (politician), Chris Rodley (writer), Nome White (Blue Dolphin), Roy Graham (Rank Organisation sales), Steve Roberts (director of *Rawlinson End*) and Ray Williams (Pollyanna Music).

"The social side was great, but that's all we ever seemed to be doing really, it was any opportunity to hold a party," says D'Morais. "Tony knew Labour Party Foreign Secretary Denis Healey very well, and he arranged for Altman's *Secret Honor* to be screened in the House of Commons. There was to be a party afterwards, with Robert Altman as guest of honour. I invited Julie Christie as she had already worked with Altman on *McCabe & Mrs Miller* and she duly turned up."

Unfortunately Robert Altman failed to show – some issue over a credit card – and the MPs were diverted by a vote on the miners' strike. The final guests numbered only 12. "With Tony, as you can imagine, these parties weren't just the standard wine, beer and orange juice – this was a full and generous bar and the cost was astronomical. So I think we all just got hammered that night and it worked out not too bad in the end. The thing with Tony was everything always seemed to work out."

Tony was guilty of vastly overspending on writers and scripts. During their five or six years, Charisma Films spent close to £1.5 million without actually making one major feature film, although Joseph D'Morais brought quite a few low-budget projects to Tony's attention, one of which was *Letter To Brezhnev* starring Alexandra Pigg and Margi Clarke, and written by her brother Frank Clarke. Set in the Liverpool docklands amid Thatcher-era high unemployment, two young women meet up with a couple of Russian sailors for a night on the town. The boys have to be back on the ship the next morning, but one of the girls, unable to forget her new Russian friend, writes her letter to Soviet Secretary Leonid Brezhnev in a bid to reunite the two lovers. Essentially a romantic comedy, the film was also an entertaining slice of British social realism and the perfect example of "how to make a film that is fast-moving, funny and poignant, with almost no money and unknown actors. In short, how to make a British film."

Despite the enthusiasm of Joseph D'Morais, Tony turned it down – and it went on to become one of the more successful British independent films of 1985. "They ran out of money and they got a recommendation to talk to me, as they needed someone to fund it," said D'Morais. "They sent me the script and some stuff on tape that they'd already done and it looked really good. So I said, 'Come on Tony, they only need something like £150 grand or whatever it was, I think this is a great film.' But as usual, some race meeting or something came up and Tony said, 'Oh no, I want to do bigger stuff.' So we passed it on to another company and of course it was a hit."

Charisma Films never achieved much commercial success, but Tony did take out film options on several books, one of which ought to have brought a better return than it actually did. *Fletch*, starring Chevy Chase, was based on the novels by Gregory Mcdonald about Irwin Fletcher, a newspaper journalist who goes undercover to investigate the Los Angeles drug trade, uncovering a far bigger story along the way. Tony sold his option to Universal Pictures and the film was released in May 1985. Unfortunately the small print in Tony's option failed to include the rights to any prequels, sequels or follow-ups – and Universal always insisted that it was the second film, *Fletch Lives!*, that took the big money at the box office. The actual figures may well suggest otherwise.

Charisma also made *The Optimist* for Channel 4. An experiment to bring back silent comedy for a modern audience, it starred Enn Reitel in the title role, as a cobbler who stumbles through life forever trying to look on the bright side, although events rarely go right during a series of bizarre events and dream sequences. First transmitted in 1983, the programme ran for two series and consisted of 13 episodes in total, with offbeat titles such as 'Turf Luck' and 'The Fall Of The House Of Esher'.

The lack of success was a constant source of frustration for D'Morais. "I just wish that we'd actually gone and made another major feature film, because it was all so frustrating, endless amounts of lunches and then these crazy schemes. One day Tony said, 'We're going to buy Thorn EMI.' Now we are talking about one of the biggest entertainment companies in Europe at the time, they owned ABC Cinemas, Elstree Studios, some of the biggest electronics companies… and Tony simply announces that, 'We're going to buy it all, and you're going to run the film division – then we're going to do this and that.' And I just said, 'So where are you getting the money from?' And of course, Tony never worried about the money, he hadn't even given it a thought."

Genesis' manager Tony Smith has a theory as to why Tony was so obsessed with the move into the film business. "I think it was mainly driven by the fact that he really wanted to be a writer. He had been a good journalist, but he really wanted to be a proper writer and obviously the film production side appealed to him, because getting a script done was what it's all about," he says. "But it's tough as well, I mean I've produced movies and believe me, producing independent movies is tough. And Strat wasn't really equipped to do it, when it came to the business side he would let his enthusiasm get in the way. That total enthusiasm and his emotions, he would often let them get in the way of his business decisions – and not just his business decisions, but also some of his personal decisions about what was good and what was not."

* * *

During 1978/79, Charisma Films produced yet another oddity. Excited by the relatively new concept of pairing music and the visual arts – MTV was still a few years away – Tony returned to one of his early musical inspirations to produce *A Samba School*. Scripted by Tony and set in Rio de Janeiro, it was ostensibly a documentary about the Mangueira School of Samba, one of the many Brazilian dance schools that could be found preparing for Carnival each year. The production crew was almost entirely South American, apart from one interesting 'on-screen participant', that well-known Brazilian resident and former Great Train Robber in exile, Ronnie Biggs. The director was an odd choice too. Tony enlisted Zygmunt Sulistrowski, a Polish-born film producer and director who had worked in the film industry in London before moving out to Brazil. Not particularly known as a documentary maker, the rest of Sulistrowski's cinematic output appears to have been early soft-porn films with titles such as *Naked Amazon*, *The Awakening Of Annie* and *Africa Erotica*.

Of course, Tony never required too much of an excuse to fly down to Rio for a few weeks – his love of the country and its music stemmed back to his exciting times there in 1962. But it does beg the question as to whether Tony's real aim was to produce a programme about Biggs himself. Following the robbery in 1963, Biggs had fled to France, then on to Australia and Panama, before finally settling in Rio de Janeiro where he fully embraced the Brazilian culture. It took four years for the authorities to track him down and even then they famously missed their chance to bring him back to England. When Detective Chief Inspector Jack Slipper and his police sergeant flew out to arrest Biggs in February 1974, they overlooked two things; first, there was no extradition treaty between Britain and Brazil, and second, Biggs had set up home with a samba dancer called Raimunda, who was carrying his child. By the time the South American court came to a judgement it was decided that Biggs, as the father-to-be of a Brazilian citizen, could not be deported. A dejected Slipper flew home without his man and Biggs continued to relax in the wealthy district of Santa Tereza and play his tambourine to a samba beat at Carnival for many years afterwards. Feeling untouchable, at least for the time being, Biggs enjoyed his title as Rio's most infamous resident – in fact, during one particular Carnival a float was even decked out as a replica of a British postal train.

The same year that *A Samba School* was in production, Biggs hooked up with Malcolm McLaren and two of the Sex Pistols, recording 'No One Is Innocent' with Steve Jones and Paul Cook and appearing as 'the exile' in Julien Temples' film *The Great Rock 'n' Roll Swindle*. Originally conceived as a TV documentary, the appearance of Ronnie Biggs in *A Samba School* may well have accounted for the non-appearance of the programme on British television. It was never commercially released.

Eternally fascinated by the Second World War, it was inevitable that Tony should turn his attention to this as subject matter for a film. *Eye Of The Dictator*, alternatively titled *The Men Who Filmed For Hitler*, was made in 1983, but did not become generally available until 1994. Directed by Hans-Günther Stark and written and produced by Tony himself, this interesting oddity examined the work of German cameramen from the early thirties right through to the end of the Second World War. It included interviews with Walter Frentz, Hitler's personal cameraman, and filmmaker Fritz Hippler, and looked at how Joseph Goebbels, the Nazi Minister of Propaganda, controlled their work, manipulating it to maximum effect both as propaganda and art. Incorporating original newsreel footage, the film also pointed to the fact that of the 1,200 cameramen sent out to cover the war, more than one third were killed on the front line.

Tony chose a director who had first-hand knowledge of the battlefield. Hans Günther Stark had served as an officer in the Wehrmacht and took part in 'Operation Barbarossa', the German invasion of the Soviet Union in June 1941. A member of the regular army, there is reason to believe that Stark and three of his men disarmed an SS officer and actively prevented the execution of Jewish civilians, a humanitarian gesture in the midst of a brutal war that would have endeared him to Tony. Nevertheless, if it can be considered an art form, and Tony certainly thought so, it was a dangerous art indeed.

Perhaps understandably, the film proved to be impossible to promote and provoked something of a hostile reaction, according to Joseph D'Morais. "I tried to put him off, but he was so keen on doing it that nothing could put him off, because he was a journalist and he had this fascination with the war and in particular, with the Holocaust. You know that he was actually accused of being a Nazi sympathiser? In the film it's all about the cameraman who worked under Goebbels to produce the Nazi propaganda – and there are interviews with about six or seven of the surviving cameramen."

Tony could certainly see the contradictions here, but in his view, and that of the cameramen, they were more interested in the art of movie making than in promoting Hitler's evil regime. The end results were completely controlled by Joseph Goebbels, who manipulated their work to maximum effect. Only when Goebbels was happy was the final film shown to Der Führer for his personal approval. Tony was intrigued that such a potentially beautiful art form as cinema could be misused, altered and twisted to further the ambitions of people hell-bent on the ultimate horror. Surely everyone else could see that?

Apparently not, according to Joseph D'Morais. "What Tony couldn't understand was that in some ways it seemed he was condoning it. They shot all this footage, but Tony never asks the difficult questions, he just talks about the films themselves. He is certainly not objecting to their work or their involvement in it. And there are no accusations... they're not being put on the spot about their part in helping the Nazi cause, there is no, 'Didn't you feel bad about what happened?' I showed it to some film critics and Derek Malcolm from *The Guardian* said, 'It's true, it does appear to be pro-Nazi.' When I told Tony this, he was really upset about it, he thought that he was just being objective. I told him there are certain things that you can't be objective about, and that this film had to have a point of view. Tony was so stubborn, he said, 'I didn't want the film to have a viewpoint. It's called *Eye Of The Dictator* for a reason and I wanted the camera-work to speak for itself.' Consequently, it was never shown anywhere at all."

Charisma Films eventually released the documentary on video and DVD in 1994 and it can be found in museum and university libraries right across the world, now fully appreciated as a unique and important piece of historic reference material. Another example of Tony's interest in heroic characters from the Second World War, and probably the last screenplay that Tony ever worked on, was *The Last Enemy* based on the book by Spitfire pilot Richard Hillary. Sadly the film was never completed, but the Richard Hillary story was later made into a television drama.

* * *

The one project that was always uppermost in Tony's mind, yet strangely never came to fruition, was a dramatic retelling of the Munich air crash. Ever since his days as Northern sports editor, working out of a small flat in the centre of Manchester, Tony had been close to the team and its manager Sir Matt Busby. His friendship with several of the Busby Babes, and the last-minute decision not to travel with them to Belgrade, would have made the events of February 1958 seem all the more visceral to him.

Tony had started to write the screenplay, lined up Steve Roberts for the director's role and had already put out feelers for the music, with former Genesis guitarist Steve Hackett getting the call. His instrumental track 'Concert For Munich' was originally commissioned for part of the film soundtrack, but after Tony's death and with any likelihood of the film ever appearing fast diminishing, Hackett added it to his 1988 album *Momentum*. In dedicating the track to Tony, Hackett wrote: "Tony was a man governed by his passions, but was able to inspire many musicians during his lifetime – a true patron of the arts. It would take a book to cover all his activities as author, journalist, record company boss and friend. God bless you, Tony!"

Tony also enlisted Glen Colson to assist on the ill-fated project. "I was very excited about that," he says. "I thought it could have been the greatest movie ever, but he never really got that one off the ground. I don't know why – because they had already made the plane, they built a mock-up of the plane in a hanger somewhere. I was working on music for the movie. I was going through the charts from that era and finding tracks that we could have put into the film. But then I think he just got a bit bored with all that."

The film was to have been called *Extra Time* and was within a whisker of getting the funding it needed to go into full production but, sadly, Tony was a contributory factor in its downfall. Joseph D'Morais recalls what happened. "I sent *Extra Time* to Rank Film Distributors and they loved it. They said, 'We can do this, how much do you want?' I told them the budget was about £2.5 million. It wasn't going to be a problem. I arranged the meeting with Tony, but why he brought David Gideon Thomson along, I don't know. The meeting was booked for after lunch, which in hindsight was a major mistake. Unfortunately I didn't go to lunch with him that day, I arranged to meet them in the reception at Rank in Wardour Street, but the minute I saw them I could tell they'd overdone the drinking.

"The Rank Organisation were a fairly puritanical company, their founder Joseph Arthur Rank was a very religious man. Their managing director Fred Turner had carried that on, and I thought to myself, 'Oh God, this is not going to be good.' Tony handled himself reasonably well, but David could barely speak. So we are in front of Rank's board of directors and they don't put on a good show, they don't make a good impression, and within 20 minutes of leaving that meeting I knew the deal was off. I called Fred Turner the next day and said, 'Look, I'll be producing the film, they're not going to have that much to do with it', but he said, 'No, I'm sorry, I simply can't deal with people like that.' And that was that."

In July 1982 an 'exclusive' article by Nick Ferrari appeared in the *Sunday Mirror* suggesting that there was a backlash against the proposed film from some players and the families of those who had died. Under the heading 'BUSBY BABES FILM ANGERS FANS' Ferrari wrote: "A major row has erupted over plans to make a film of the Manchester United air disaster. Fans and relatives of the dead footballers have launched a campaign to stop the £3 million project. Star Albert Finney has been asked to play the team's manager Matt Busby, in the film *The Day The Team Died*. Sir Matt, who was on the airliner when it crashed in Munich twenty four years ago, has been sent the controversial script. He said: 'I understand a lot of people are worried, and I was certainly not in favour of the idea when it was first proposed. But I cannot make a final judgement until I have read the script.'"

Another survivor, Bobby Charlton, was strongly against the film. Speaking from the World Cup finals in Spain, he said: "There is no way I want to see this go ahead. It is obviously going to cause great unhappiness to the relatives." And Mrs Joy Worth, widow of United star Roger Byrne, said: "It's the height of bad taste."

Tony was quoted as saying: "I don't want to upset anyone, but the suggestion that it is too recent an event is unfair. We will do this in good taste."

D'Morais denies that there was ever a problem. "No, that wasn't the case at all. Tony was very good friends with Sir Matt and also with Jean Busby and Matt's son Sandy. We had players like Bill Foulkes and goalkeeper Harry Gregg on board. Gregg's story in particular – I mean he was the quiet hero, he went back in to the wreckage two or three times to drag people out, you know, and he is such a lovely, humble man. It is true that Bobby Charlton wouldn't get involved, but if anything, we always got a positive reaction."

D'Morais held the option on the film after Tony died but although there were numerous attempts at getting it into production, it never happened. The BBC produced a dramatised documentary about the Munich air disaster in 2008, after which those involved with the Charisma film felt there was little point in pursuing it. The rights are still held by Charisma Films.

While looking for finance for *Extra Time*, Tony connected with Andrew MacHutchon, a venture capital specialist. They met for lunch at the St Moritz restaurant in Wardour Street, an episode that MacHutchon recalls with some dismay for all the obvious reasons. His next appointment was with George Walker, the controversial businessman behind the Brent Walker empire and after a typical Stratton Smith lunch he hailed a taxi from which he emerged to fall flat on his face.

"George Walker's secretary said, 'Mr MacHutchon, I think you need a cup of coffee!' She put me in George Walker's office with a strong cup of coffee and when George walked in he said, 'Andrew, you're drunk.' Then he said, 'Actually, so am I, let's have some more coffee.' When I told George that I'd just had lunch with Tony Stratton Smith, he laughed and said, 'Oh yes, I should have warned you about him.'"

MacHutchon admits that Tony led him into bad ways. "That lunching thing did for me for the rest of my life, because I liked to lunch and he was a man who gave you one or two pleasant, but potentially bad habits. He was a whisky and Guinness man. Strat would break up a board meeting and say, 'Right, I think it's time for a jolly old drink', and so we'd go across the road to the pub for a couple of drinks and that's when he introduced me to Guinness. David Gideon Thomson would always have his double gin and tonic, that's why we called him DGT and there would be producers or directors from various film companies that we were dealing with. We would have lunch in some restaurant around Covent Garden, and there were plenty to choose from, get back to the office and carry on for another three hours, and then Strat would head off again to the Coach & Horses so that he could have his Bell's whisky. Guinness and Bell's whisky featured heavily in his life. He even wrote to the chairman of Guinness complaining about the situation with Distillers because they'd merged the two companies together. He would certainly have a glass of wine with his meal and the occasional gin and tonic, but for most of the time I knew him, he was a whisky and Guinness man."

Chapter 19

The Island Years

"I remember Vera saying that she thought he had been out of sorts because he hadn't been boozing. In fact he'd been drinking a lot of water, which made her think something was not quite what it ought to be. But I have always believed that Tony knew he was living with cancer but he just got on with it, until that day he felt really ill and that was it, end of story."
Ian Campbell, vintner

Although he was increasingly involved with his films and racing interests, in 1985 Tony moved temporarily to Las Palmas, the largest city on the Spanish island of Gran Canaria which, with its consistently warm temperatures all year round, is said to enjoy the 'best climate in the world'. James Atherton has suggested that Tony went out there to write, as it was a place in the sun, well away from the stresses and demands of central London, where he could relax and work on film scripts or possibly another book or two.

Taking sound legal advice, in June of that year Tony registered a new company, TSS Management Services Limited, its purpose 'Artistic creation – business consultancy and television and film production'. As his lawyer Tony Seddon remembers, "That was set up to be his personal service company. The idea was that with anything he did, they were all services that could be routed through his management company, rather than be in his own name and thus expose him to liabilities. There were obvious tax advantages to that because, let's face it, Strat often had some fairly crazy ideas."

According to Jack Barrie and Andrew MacHutchon, Tony took his year out in Las Palmas purely for tax purposes, staying in a property owned by nightclub owner Archie Dunlop. "Tony was doing a tax year out," says Barrie. "He was still in the transition of selling Charisma and it would delay monies for tax reasons. He needed to take some tax time out."

Andrew MacHutchon thinks this was not just a necessary business move, but one that also suited Tony. "Prior to the first disposal, I sat down with Tony Seddon and said, 'Look, before we do this deal, I think it's time Strat went offshore.' We knew that he liked the sunshine. He liked areas where he could be creative. So he picked the Canary Islands – although I think Archie Dunlop, who owned property out there, also had an influence in deciding or introducing Strat to the islands."

Simon White confirms that Dunlop was involved in Tony's decision making. "Archie actively helped Strat to get his final house in the Canary Islands. He was very, very fond of Strat. Strat kept on asking me to go out to visit him in Las Palmas, but it didn't work out at the time. He was always saying, 'When are you going to come down?' and trying to persuade me to buy a flat in the Canaries. He even told me that I could stay with him until I found a place."

Tony's impressive-sounding Spanish address was Edificio Alberbao Apartment, 3B Portal 1 Calle Eduardo Benot 5 35007, Las Palmas de Gran Canaria, and by all accounts the apartment was the height of luxury. Unfortunately, no matter how fine the accommodation, Tony's final year in Las Palmas was not always the idyllic holiday in the sun that one might have expected. Away from the driving passions that had previously made up his working day, Tony slid further into unhappy bouts of heavy drinking, often egged on by a new raft of sycophants who no doubt saw him as an easy touch.

Ian Campbell did not visit Tony in Spain, but concurs with the opinion that he was under a bad influence. "I didn't go there, but I've spoken to one or two who were there and they said it was almost pathetic to see the amount that Tony was drinking. He would drink every lunchtime, crawl back to his beautiful apartment in the afternoon, then back to the bar in the evening and of course all these ex-pat Brits would latch onto him for a free beer."

Tony may also have found that the Las Palmas gay scene, to which he was introduced by Archie Dunlop, was a little too overt for his tastes. Having endured the homophobic attitudes rife in the fifties and sixties, not everyone wanted to throw themselves out of the closet with such abandon, as the other Tony Smith points out: "Strat had always been quite a private man from that point of view. I think his sexuality was a problem for him, in that he really tried to keep that under the radar – and in those days it was incredibly tricky. So while he was very private, there were lots of nice young men hanging around. It was a funny old time, but he certainly had his demons. Strat was such a lovely, warm guy, very, very social, but he did have quite a few problems and it was a shame towards the end, when his drinking really became a problem."

In the opinion of Simon White, Tony was feeling more than a little lost and in dire need of a new direction. "The real point is that Strat never quite replaced the idea of running a record label with anything that he really wanted to do. He was trying to do his two years out for tax reasons and he couldn't come back here, that was the problem. If he had returned to the UK and not tried to save himself a bit of tax, maybe he would have found that elusive thing that he really wanted to do, but just rolling around the Canaries, drinking... I think it was a bad mistake to go out there. I understand why he did it, but it wasn't the right decision for him."

In what must have been one of his last major interviews, recorded on October 24, 1986, with the American record executive and former broadcaster Joe Smith, Tony was asked to isolate one period in time that he felt encapsulated the best of his career in the music business. He replied: "I think the time of discovery is the most exciting, in a sense it requires a bit of creativity and judgment. The period that excited me most would be from 1964 to 1973; from learning to love the records of Sam Cooke, through to the time when I knew that America was going to take Genesis to its heart. That was when I was beginning to perceive heroes. You did everything for fun, you didn't care, you really didn't look at the bottom line. That was never the driving thing because you didn't know where the bottom line was. So the mid-sixties, mid-seventies period was it, for me. Particularly because I love instrumentalists as well, that period when the guy who could play his instrument had at last won his battle and come to the front. Keith Emerson, Eric Clapton, Jimmy Page, Ian Anderson – all these guys who in one form or another put certain instruments right there in front and put musicianship back in front, rather than just an arrangement, a song and a pretty face."

* * *

Among the racing crowd at Lambourn was Ronald Charles Bampton who had moved to the Channel Islands in 1969, purchasing Keswick House, formerly known as the Chateau Rocquebrune, a prime property overlooking the bay of St Aubin on the island of Jersey. He met his wife, Vera McCullough, when she was working as a cocktail waitress in a Covent Garden hotel, and by October 1972, Veronica Frances Bampton had moved into Keswick House. A short, feisty Irish woman with a colourful turn of phrase, she quickly became known on the island as 'Effing Vera' and by all accounts her parties were legendary.

Tony met Vera Bampton through their mutual friend Noel Bennett, the publican of The George in Lambourn, as Noel and Vera had grown up together in Ireland. "Ron had made his money in the city and he had been married before and was divorced," says their friend Ian Campbell. "He did not totally approve of Vera's drinking or indeed some of her friends. Often, if she had friends round he used to walk down to a nearby hotel for lunch. And then she would ring up her friends and say, 'If you're coming up to see me, can you bring a loaf of white and a loaf of brown', which meant a bottle of whiskey and a bottle of gin. They say that Vera had to tip the dustmen to be very quiet when they emptied the bins. Vera was friends with absolutely everybody, every taxi driver, every restaurateur. She was a great character and I was very fond of her."

Ronald Bampton's death in March 1979 – in tragic circumstances – may have inadvertently served to bring Tony and Vera closer together. Ronald was the victim of an accident that occurred while he was working beneath one of his cars. "He didn't realise the car was in drive and not in neutral," says Campbell. "He pulled a belt or something and the car just rolled onto him. A terrible shame, he was a very nice man."

"Tony was very fond of Vera and Vera was fond of him," he adds. "They were a real pair. They loved to sit in her Jersey house and smoke and drink and reminisce. I can still picture him sitting there with Vera at breakfast, both in their dressing gowns, going through all the runners and riders. Then he would get out his book with all the breed info, working out which horse to back, what its breeding was and whether he thought it was going to be alright – and then they would place their bets and of course they'd win more than a few."

Tony became a regular visitor to Keswick House, not just to see Vera but because it was handily placed for business meetings, as Andrew MacHutchon remembers. "With him being offshore, as and when required Tony would get a flight to Paris and from there he'd get a flight over to Jersey and I would meet him [at Vera's house] to go through all the current financial and management issues. Sometimes DGT would come along too. The business was always conducted on Jersey, there were plenty of flights back and forth and I could easily do it in a day or occasionally stay over."

"Strat still needed to talk business and meet with his accountants and lawyers," says Jack Barrie, "so they decided that they would meet up in Jersey because that way he would still be out of the country, but at least they'd have the television where he could watch the racing, so he could still be involved in the Cheltenham meeting."

Tony's stewardship of his finances was as haphazard as ever, no matter where he lived. MacHutchon recalls one visit to Keswick House when Tony contradicted him over the amount in an account. "I said, 'Right, this is the situation, we've got so much in this account and so much in that account...' and he said, 'No'. I said, 'What do you mean, no?' and Strat said, 'No, that's wrong.' I said, 'It can't be wrong, Tony, here are the figures.' He just laughed and said, 'Ah, well what you don't know is that I bought another filly the other day, so I plundered the account.' But that was Tony. He just went right ahead and bought himself another filly."

Despite her great love of racing, Vera only dabbled in ownership, co-owning a couple of horses with Tony, including one called Very Adjacent. Much to Vera's great dismay the horse went on to do very well in Italy – but only after it had been sold on, largely without her knowledge.

Vera Bampton continued to host her grand bashes and welcome old friends to Keswick House. One such occasion took place in October 1985, and Tony was invited. The Jersey branch of the Royal Air Force Association was celebrating their diamond jubilee and Vera's latest excuse to throw a party was arranged as a fund-raiser for RAFA. Tony flew over to the Channel Islands with Lambourn publican Noel Bennett, Ian Campbell and his wife Jacqueline, and John Karaiossifoglou, who owned a delicatessen in East Ilsley, opposite Noel's pub the Crown & Horns. Vera had asked John along to handle the catering for her 'Fly-Past' party, always a big event in the Jersey calendar. Mingling in the autumn sunshine alongside Vera's social set from the island, Tony and his friends watched the air display from the elevated terrace of Keswick House, the highlight of which must surely have been the dramatic sight of Concorde circling low over Elizabeth Castle in St Aubin's Bay.

Tragically, it was during just such a visit to Jersey in March 1987 that Tony fell ill. As usual, he'd flown there via Paris and it was pure chance that saw Andrew MacHutchon with Tony, on what turned out to be his last business trip.

"The last occasion coincided with the Cheltenham Gold Cup and as it happened, it was also Paddy Week when the Irish celebrate St Patrick's Day, and so I flew in," recalls MacHutchon. "I went loaded down, because I'd come over with Christmas presents and various things that had been left behind for him in London. There were presents for this and that, and a load of video tapes of all the races that he'd asked to have. Tony met me at the door and he looked a lot thinner. I said, 'My god, you've lost some weight' and he said, 'Yes, I've been doing a lot of walking. Yesterday I spent all day walking around Paris. In fact I'm really tired, my legs ache.' So I gave him all the mail I'd brought for him, plus the videos and the presents, and he said, 'Oh by the way, Vera, you and I have been invited to a St Patrick's dinner tonight.' Vera was pottering about in the background and he said to her, 'I'm a bit tired, so what I would rather do, if you don't mind, I'd rather stay in and review the videos of all those races.'

"Anyway we agreed that I would go with Vera, and she knew all the people of course, so we had a lovely evening at the St Patrick's do with all her Irish friends. When we came back, Strat had obviously gone to bed a lot earlier than usual, which surprised us a little. But we had booked a meeting with our bankers down in St Helier the next morning for about 9.30am – and Strat was not an early riser."

The following morning MacHutchon got up, showered, dressed and went downstairs where Vera was preparing breakfast. "After a while Tony still hadn't come down," continues MacHutchon. "So I went upstairs and knocked on his door and he asked me to come in. He was sitting on the edge of the bed. He said, 'I hope I haven't upset you or disturbed you during the night.' Between our two bedrooms, there was a bathroom that we both had access to. I said, 'No, why?' Strat said, 'Well, I spent a great deal of time in the toilet last night.'

"Tony came down the stairs and said, 'Oh, I feel bad...' and he rushed over to the sink and just vomited blood everywhere. He said, 'I've been having this problem all night.' I said, 'Why didn't you say so?' and Vera immediately rang for an ambulance. He said, 'But we've got an appointment, Andrew', even though by now we'd gone past the bank time, so I rang them to say, 'I'm sorry, but we're not going to be able to make it today, Mr Stratton Smith is not too well.' We'd got to know the lady at the bank quite well and she said, 'OK, just let me know when is convenient, I'm here all day.' When I got back to Strat, he told me, 'I've also got this journalist coming to interview me about Peter Gabriel.' He said, 'Can you meet him? He's coming here.' I said, 'Tony, just settle down.'"

MacHutchon helped Tony back up the stairs. "We found a basin for him to vomit the blood into, because he was still doing that, and I said, 'Look, I think you've got an ulcer in your stomach, Strat, you need to get that looked at, we'll get you to the hospital and get you seen to.' He was more worried about the missed appointments and the journalist that was due any minute. He was a very private person and said, 'I don't want this chap knowing that I'm going to hospital.' So this chap arrived in a taxi and I met him at the door, took him through to the lounge and asked if he would like a coffee. I could see the ambulance coming up the drive and going round to the back entrance, the kitchen entrance. Anyway they got Strat out on a wheelchair and into the ambulance and meanwhile I just kept talking to the journalist, who was completely oblivious to the fact. I said, 'Look, Strat's sorry he can't keep this appointment, but he's asked me to take you into town, give you lunch and see you back to the airport and he will reimburse you for your fare and pay for you to come over for the interview another time at his expense.' We went and had a quick lunch and I packed the journalist off to the airport."

According to Ian Campbell, when Tony was collected by the hospital Vera Bampton walked out with him by the side of the wheelchair and when they lifted him into the back of the ambulance, Tony, who was still in his pyjamas, called out, "Oh Vera, please make sure I've got a packet of fags and a lighter with me."

Vera's home, situated just off La Route de St Aubin, was actually quite close to the capital and Tony was driven straight to the General Hospital in St Helier, a distance of less than four miles. Even allowing for traffic around the busy town centre, it was a ten-minute journey at most.

Andrew MacHutchon continues the story: "Afterwards I went round St Helier to pick up some bits and pieces for Strat and then rushed to the hospital. He was sitting on the edge of the bed and two nurses were wiping the floor, it looked like he'd been sick again and I put his stuff on the bed and sat down. I said, 'What's happened? What have they done?' Strat said, 'Well they've tried to put a balloon in, to try and put pressure on the stomach to close the wound. But it's not worked.' I said, 'So what are they going to do next?' He told me they wanted to operate and then he turned to me. Completely out of the blue, he sat there on the bed and said to me, 'Look, Andrew, if this turns out to be a Smith's gamble... I don't want any fuss, I want you to deal with it all over here.' I said, 'Strat, you've lost me, what gamble?' He said, 'Well, there was a horse at Cheltenham called Smith's Gamble – and it lost.' So I said, 'Don't be stupid, the guys will just open you up, they'll probably have to stitch you up, it's probably no more than a normal ulcer, you'll be alright.'"

It was agreed that an operation would take place that evening. MacHutchon returned to Vera's house where they awaited a call from the hospital. "It got to about half past 10 or 11 o'clock and the phone rang. It was one of the hospital staff. She said, 'The team have operated on Mr Stratton Smith and unfortunately there is nothing more they can do.' I said, 'What do you mean, nothing they can do?' The lady said, 'I'm afraid they found a cancer in the liver and the pancreas. Frankly Mr MacHutchon, he is bleeding to death.' She added, 'I would suggest you come down right now.'

"Vera was in her nightdress, as she'd already gone to bed. I said, 'Vera, from what they've said, there's not a lot of time.' She told me to go down straightaway. I got a taxi down to the hospital and they showed me into a side ward where he was on a ventilator. The nurse said to Tony, 'Mr Smith, your friend has arrived' and his eyes flickered open and I sat down next to him and held his hand. I talked to him, you know, I just sat there talking, talking, talking and his arm was getting colder and colder. Eventually a nurse came in and took his pulse and she said, 'I'm sorry, he's gone now' and that was about 2.30 in the morning, maybe a little later. So anyway I went back up to see Vera, bless her, still sitting there in her dressing gown and we had a wee dram for Strat and went to bed."

Early the next morning MacHutchon phoned Tony Seddon and David Gideon Thomson, and discovered the whereabouts of Tony's sister. "I contacted his sister and told her that her brother had passed on and would she like to come to Jersey. I contacted everyone at Charisma, to say that he wanted everything dealt with over here. Genesis were on tour but they cancelled, they all made the service."

Jack Barrie was among the first to get the bad news. "I knew that Tony had gone in to hospital, that he was very ill and I had been told they would keep in touch. I remember it was about a quarter to three in the morning on the Thursday, Gold Cup Day, that I got the 'phone call from the accountants

[MacHutchon]. When they rang, it was to say that unfortunately they had operated but he had not recovered, which was absolutely terrible. I waited until the more civilised time of about 8.30 in the morning and then started ringing around. Gail Colson was the first person I called and then I started to ring round the trainers and racing people, some of whom were already on their way to Cheltenham for the Gold Cup. It was a terrible, terrible time."

When Gail heard that Tony had died, she telephoned *Music Week* to get them to run an announcement. To her amazement, instead of being met with shock and sadness, she encountered a wall of ignorance – the first two or three people that she spoke to had absolutely no idea who Tony was. Still raw from the news and outraged by the response of the *Music Week* staff, Gail gave up in frustration and called Jon Webster, the managing director of Virgin Records, who agreed to speak to the magazine on her behalf. *Music Week* apologised unreservedly and promised that Tony's death would be treated with the due respect it deserved. The resulting obituary stated that it was 'the end of an era'.

Ian Campbell adds: "Obviously, Vera was very shocked by it all. I remember Vera saying that she thought he had been out of sorts because he hadn't been boozing. In fact he'd been drinking a lot of water, which made her think something was not quite what it ought to be. But I have always believed that Tony knew he was living with cancer but he just got on with it, until that day he felt really ill and that was it, end of story. All a bit strange."

Charisma lawyer Tony Seddon remembers receiving an urgent telephone call from Jersey. It was David Gideon Thomson on the line, who told him: "Strat really needs to make a will." Over the years, Seddon had overseen the drafting of several versions of a will, none of which had ever been finalised or signed. "Yes, that's true, he should," sighed Seddon. "When shall we arrange to meet?"

"No, you don't understand," replied an anxious Gideon Thomson. "He REALLY needs to make a will. How soon can you get there?"

Realising exactly how ill Stratton Smith was, Seddon took the first available flight out to the Channel Islands, but by the time he landed on Jersey it was too late, Tony had died.

* * *

Anthony Mills Stratton Smith died in the early hours of Thursday, March 19, 1987, at the General Hospital in St Helier. On his death certificate, the cause was recorded as a gastrointestinal haemorrhage due to ulcerating carcinoma of the pancreas. Pancreatic cancer is notoriously hard to diagnose, as the symptoms often present themselves late, and consequently survival rates are low. The most common causes are heavy smoking, high alcohol consumption and obesity – and Tony ticked every box on the danger list. Tony Stratton Smith certainly knew how to live the good life but his excesses had finally caught up with him.

The funeral was organised by local undertakers Pitcher and Le Quesne. An entourage of friends and business associates flew over to the Channel Islands for a service and cremation, among them Tony's sister June and her husband, along with Jack Barrie, George Thompson, Gail and Glen Colson, Steve Weltman, Jenny Pitman, James Atherton and members of the 'classic' Genesis with their manager Tony Smith.

Organising the service once again raised the issue of Tony's religious affiliations. Andrew MacHutchon hedged his bets. "At the hospital they didn't know what faith Tony was, so they hadn't given him the last rites," he says. "The nurse said that he had a rosary on him. I told her that although he carried a rosary, he wasn't strictly Catholic, if anything he was more Anglican, but he really was betwixt and between. So I arranged for the local Anglican Minister and the Catholic Minister to conduct the service at the committal. Each one did a little part of the service."

While Tony almost certainly came from a strict Catholic family, his own religious beliefs were not always evident. Even his closest friends could not agree on whether a Catholic service would be appropriate for his funeral, as Jack Barrie recalls: "We had the discussion with Gail Colson when she was arranging the London memorial. Should it be a Catholic service, or a non-religious service, because nobody could ever decide – and in the end I think it was his own sister who said, 'No he was never a Catholic.'"

Genesis and their manager Tony Smith chartered a private jet. Hit & Run's Jon Crawley was on the same flight and recalls that the light aircraft containing Tony Smith, Mike Rutherford, Peter Gabriel, Phil Collins, and Margaret and Tony Banks almost didn't make it. "Either Peter or Phil turned up late. Tony Banks, who doesn't normally drink, turned round and said, 'I think we should have a glass of whisky to toast Strat.' This was about eight o'clock in the morning. I'd had no breakfast and now we're having a whisky, so I felt really heady after that. It turns out that Tony Banks doesn't like flying, so it was a good way to calm his nerves, which is partly why Margaret was with him.

"We got to the church and we're the last ones to arrive, even though we busted a gut to get there. We entered in single file and I am between Peter and Phil. Of course they start the hymns and you've got to sing, haven't you? So you've got Gabriel singing in a very low register and you've got Collins in his high register and there's me fluctuating somewhere between the two of them."

Andrew MacHutchon remained in Jersey for about ten days, staying with Vera and organising, arranging the undertakers, picking people up, ordering taxis and everything. "DGT came over. Tony Seddon came over and he had to try and sort out where everything was, what the position was with regards to the will and so on."

George Thompson simply had to make the trip over to say farewell to his old friend. "I went to the funeral in Jersey with Jenny Pitman and David Arbuthnot. I asked Phil Collins how much of an effect Strat had on his life, he replied, 'If it hadn't been for Strat I would not have been so successful, so I am here today to say thank you to him and to remember him.'"

James Atherton had only known Tony for a couple of years, mainly through people from the film industry. He recalls feeling like a bit of an outsider at the service, in among some of Tony's oldest friends from the music business. After the service everyone went back to Keswick House where Vera Bampton had insisted on holding the wake. "Fortunately she had a large house," said MacHutchon, "with a huge lounge looking down to the beach at St Aubin. Everybody was there for the wake and then afterwards we all went to the airport to get the same flight back."

The trip to Jersey proved a trying occasion for trainer Jenny Pitman, in more ways than one. "One of the final things that Tony did, indirectly, was to actually make me get into a light aircraft," she recalls. "On the day of the funeral in Jersey, I went down to the airport with trainers Eric Wheeler and Ray Laing, and we congregated there thinking that we were all going out on a scheduled flight, but as we are all marching down onto the tarmac, I'm beginning to get a little apprehensive, because I'm terrified of flying. I mean I can just about cope with it if it's a big plane. Anyway we're walking out and I'm thinking, 'I don't like the feel of this' and there is this tiny light aircraft parked on the runway. It takes all my courage to start going up to the steps and when I get to the top of the steps I turned round in a panic and said, 'I can't go in there…' and Eric Wheeler just got hold of me and gave me a massive shove and said, 'Get in' – and they sat me right next to the window.

"On the way back, we've now had Tony's funeral and a bit of a wake afterwards, and of course they were all well-oiled. We clamber back on board our little plane and there are these little cardboard boxes under the seats with drinks in them, miniature bottles of vodka and cans of tonic. They were all calling from the back of the plane to the front saying, 'Steward, can I have a vodka and tonic?' and then flinging these things down the length of the plane. And I am terrified, I am sat there thinking this is completely mental and I was so scared and it was completely nuts. I keep thinking, what if one of those cans hits the bloody pilot? And then I started laughing at the complete and utter madness of the situation. It was completely mad, but then it was Tony's farewell do – and that's exactly how it would have been if he had been able to take part in it. Then it made perfect sense."

Andrew MacHutchon collected Strat's ashes from the funeral

director and took them back to the UK. "I kept them at my home in Yorkshire until I took them to the services in Newbury and London and then on to the Marquee afterwards."

* * *

The racing community, and in particular those based around the Lambourn valley, were hugely affected by Tony's sudden death, so it was no surprise that they wanted to hold their own local memorial service. The great and the good of the racing world gathered at St Andrew's Church, Chaddleworth on Tuesday, April 28 to celebrate the life of a fellow racing man. The service was taken by the Rev. Robert Greaves and there were readings by trainer Gay Kindersley and Monty Court, the editor of *Sporting Life*. Simon Christian read the poem *Upper Lambourn* by Sir John Betjeman and the prayers were led by David Arbuthnot, Ray Laing, Jenny Pitman, John Webber and Eric Wheeler.

The choice of churchman was especially apt, as Ian Campbell remembers. "There was a vicar that Tony particularly liked called Bob Greaves, a traditional sort of gentleman vicar who was also into horses and racing, so it was very logical that he would take the service for the racing people. I don't think Tony was a churchgoer particularly, but this vicar amused him and he liked him. Bob was into racing, he was a bit of a lad and he liked a drink, which fitted in with Tony's social ideal of what it was all about."

According to Campbell, the well-liked cleric was given an expensive and well-bred former racehorse that he used as a hack to ride around the village. In one report in the sporting press, Ray Laing said, "We are all very sad. It is a blow to us, since Tony was the man who set me on the road to training. His death is a great shock, since less than three weeks ago my wife and I enjoyed a holiday at his house in Las Palmas. A trainer could not wish for a better owner or friend."

In the same piece, trainer Simon Christian added, "I had known Tony for about 12 years. He was always a marvellous help and encouragement, not only to me but to everyone else in racing. Scores of people in Lambourn owe Tony the kind of debt it is difficult to repay. I have never heard anyone having anything bad to say about him."

Tony was not only loved and respected by his trainers, he was also extremely popular with the stable lads who looked after his horses. It was noted that many winning races were followed by a large party at Coombe Lodge near Farnborough, where Tony lived for about five years.

"He was a very kind person was Tony, that's what he was," added Jenny Pitman. "Kind and caring – and what's interesting is that the most fundamental word you can use, the most important word you can use of the four lettered variety, is 'care' – because if we don't care about what we're doing, then we shouldn't be doing it."

* * *

After the services at Jersey and Chaddleworth, a final Service of Thanksgiving was held at St Martin-in-the Fields in London on Wednesday, May 6. The largest gathering of the three, it attracted friends, family and a veritable *Who's Who* of the music business. Tony would certainly have approved of the venue, a landmark church of beautiful Georgian architecture, situated on the northeast corner of Trafalgar Square.

During the service, Keith Emerson played his 'Lament To Stratton Smith', especially composed for the event. Two of the Monty Python team, Michael Palin and Graham Chapman, were in attendance, with Chapman introducing 'Always Look On The Bright Side Of Life' from the Python film *Life Of Brian*, which has since become a popular choice at funerals and was sung at Chapman's own memorial service in 1989. This jaunty little ditty was played in its entirety, including the verses about life being a piece of shit and always looking on the bright side of death. "Strat," thought Palin, "would definitely have approved."

Journalist Michael Wale spoke about Strat's fondness for public houses, although, as Palin also noted, no one mentioned the fact that it was most probably "the lotion that did him in". Lee Jackson and Peter Hammill both spoke fondly about their old manager and the service featured three proper 'old-fashioned' hymns, known to be firm favourites of Stratton Smith, especially 'Jerusalem' and 'To Be A Pilgrim'. As mourners left the church, a retiring collection was taken on behalf of the Mother Teresa Mission of Calcutta.

Afterwards most attendees repaired to the Marquee in nearby Wardour Street, where a suitably lavish spread had been laid on. Walking into the Marquee during daytime took *Melody Maker*'s Chris Welch a little by surprise. "The strange thing was that it was in the afternoon and while we were all talking about Strat this light came in and lit up the Marquee. It was daylight and I suddenly realised that there were actually windows in the Marquee. I never knew that. You only ever saw the club late at night and I had always assumed it was some subterranean hole in the ground, but actually it was on ground level and they had windows."

Bazz Ward roadied for his old mate Tony right to the very end. "I was even the stage manager at the memorial service," he says. "I was going anyway, but Gail Colson called me up on the morning and said, 'We are going to need a microphone and stand, and something for the guitar, and a CD player', so I ended up being the bloody roadie for the service. Of course, when it was all over I was left there to pack all the bits and pieces up again. I went to The Ship because that is where Tony would be, and that's where I first met him. Gradually everyone else came in too. And nobody had even bothered to tell Sid and Delia, the two old dears who ran the pub, who were wondering what everyone was doing there. Which was strange really, because Tony was always cashing cheques behind their bar, and occasionally some of them would bounce."

Later that year Jack Barrie, who once acknowledged Tony as "my first real friend in the city", organised the scattering of his ashes over the final hurdle at Newbury racecourse. "We had always known where he wanted to be," he says. "During one of our late-night drinking sessions, Strat said, 'When I go, I want my ashes sprinkled over the last jump at Newbury and then I'll always be able to watch the winners get home.' So we arranged it. There was a meeting coming up at Newbury and we asked the course for permission, but they wouldn't give it so we did it totally illegally. We were getting quite paralytic in the bar at Newbury, because we'd had a big win. The horse in question was called Sergeant Smoke, which was quite apt considering that this was the horse we chose to run on the day that we were going to scatter the ashes, and lo and behold he walloped home at 20/1. So Simon Christian and I went out there and the ashes were blowing all over us, but Tony is definitely sprinkled at the final fence. He's squatting, quite illegally!"

Jack Barrie went on to say this about his old friend. "Many words have been used to describe him. Bon viveur, raconteur, delightful host, ardent patriot are a few that spring to my mind. However, I'll best remember him as a generous romantic. A romantic because he made dreams come true – and generous because they were always other people's."

* * *

Tony's will, or rather the lack of one, would become a major bone of contention. Several individuals claimed to have been promised something from the estate and were surprised, and not a little disappointed, to find themselves left out. It is not difficult to imagine an emotional Tony, whisky in hand, gesturing at a painting, or a framed music memento with a cheery, "After I'm gone, dear boy, this will be yours."

It fell to Stratton Smith's legal team, led by accountant Andrew MacHutchon and lawyer Tony Seddon, to sort out his complex financial affairs. It no doubt came as a complete surprise to everyone involved to discover that Tony had died intestate, not least his older sister June Norris, his closest surviving relative and therefore his sole heir. As Jack Barrie remembers: "He never left a valid will, at least this is what everyone was told. Even though the accountant told me at a late stage that Strat obviously thought a lot of Noel Bennett and myself, because he had left almost everything to us 50/50. But that will was invalid on the basis that it had only been signed by one witness and that witness was also a beneficiary – and of course you can't be both. So everything went to his sister."

There is a certain irony in that after he'd drifted apart from his own relatives and assembled a surrogate family of friends from Charisma and elsewhere, his nearest living blood relation inherited everything. Or at least what was left of everything. Tony may have adopted the lifestyle of a wealthy man, but almost all his capital was tied up in companies and their various divisions. Without any warning, his sister June found herself introduced to people from totally different worlds to her own, dealing with business issues about which she knew absolutely nothing, and probably cared even less. Much like Tony, June was a very private person, so the attention and intrusion from people from the worlds of rock'n'roll and racing must have been difficult for her as she coped with the sudden loss of her brother.

Tony Seddon remembers the problems involved in sorting out Tony's estate, particularly with regard to the will. "By dying intestate Strat inadvertently helped his sister quite considerably towards the end of her life," he says. "He did get me to make a number of draft wills with bequests of a kind that were more appropriate to somebody with liquid wealth, but because Strat lived the lifestyle of a wealthy man, there was not so much in terms of actual hard cash at the end of the day, as can be seen from the public documents. He did arrange a number of draft wills and clearly, if he'd been happy with any of those he would have signed one, but unfortunately I couldn't get there to deal with his instructions or whatever it was he wanted to tell me on his death bed."

Andrew MacHutchon agrees. "There was a draft will and it would be a problem for me to say what was in it – in fact, I have seen two draft wills. Strat had this thing where if he signed a will it was an acknowledgment that he was dying – some people are like that. He understood that he needed to do it, but then he'd waiver about it and think, 'Well, I'm not ready to go yet, so I'll leave it until later.'"

In the aftermath of the memorial services, MacHutchon became involved in the lengthy unravelling of Tony's estate. He visited the near empty flat in Park Crescent looking for clues to any personal or business affairs that needed to be tidied up. Tony was notoriously bad at keeping paperwork, everything was either scribbled on scraps of paper or jotted down randomly in notebooks. MacHutchon remembers that Tony always carried a notebook with him and would regularly take it out in the middle of a meeting, or a meal, in order to record something that took his fancy. Which could be anything and everything; notes on business transactions, the opening sequence to a film, an idea for a new book and lines of poetry – whether his own or other people's – and in one instance, MacHutchon recalls seeing a long soliloquy to Genesis.

Holly Fogg was part of the entourage that visited the Park Crescent flat to help with the clearing out, along with Mark Richards, another loyal staffer known as 'The Chief' who was Charisma's despatch and post room manager. Richards was an elderly man who shared Tony's passion for horse racing and carried out many errands for Tony personally. Patrick Doyle, the accountant for Charisma Films, completed the clear-up team.

It could be argued that one of Tony's finest business attributes (or his worst, depending on your side of the transaction) was his preference for the gentleman's agreement – the business deal struck on the shake of a hand and the raising of a glass. It may have driven his legal team to distraction, but it often worked in favour of the working man, as the graphic artist Paul Whitehead found out.

"Strat's method certainly worked to my advantage, because I had some problems with copyrights in the late nineties when the Genesis management were using my stuff all over the place and not paying me," says Whitehead. "So I put them on notice and I said this is not right, you know, and [the other] Tony Smith said, 'You don't own the copyright, we own everything.' He basically told me to go screw myself, but I said, 'No, this is not right, I still own the copyright.'

"Fortunately it turned out that because I had done business the Stratton Smith way, there was no written assignment of copyright, it had all been done on a handshake. Strat had simply said to me, 'You do your illustration, we'll use it for the cover and you keep the artwork' and that was it, there was no real business deal. So consequently I do still own the copyrights, which came as a real surprise to 'the other' Tony Smith. He was completely shocked. All the other record company guys could be pretty mercenary, but Strat was never like that."

By December 1990, Tony's sister June Norris was added as a director to the board of TSS Management Holdings Limited and the following year she became a company director of both Charisma Holdings Limited and Charisma Films Limited. This token directorship barely lasted for five years before she resigned all three posts in November 1995. James Atherton, who had been talking to Tony about running the film side of the business, subsequently brought the Charisma Films catalogue from her, but then spent the next couple of years unravelling the "chaotic" company accounts.

Andrew MacHutchon remembers the reaction of Tony's sister when they met at the first funeral service on Jersey. "We arranged that June would fly out and stay at Vera's house and both her and her husband were absolutely stunned. They had no idea about Tony's life or his business interests and when I asked if she was interested in horse racing, she said no. I said, well I've got some news for you... you've got a string of 20 racehorses. Ah bless her, she had absolutely no idea."

Suddenly finding herself in possession of about 20 horses was another problem for June, and through her solicitor she approached Jack Barrie for advice on what to do with them. Rather than sell them off immediately, Barrie's solution was to keep them running under Tony's name. It was near the start of the racing season and Barrie knew that to dispose of the horses at that point could have proved disastrous for Tony's two main trainers, Ray Laing and David Arbuthnot. He offered to run them on June's behalf, as executors of the Stratton Smith estate, and worked out a business plan estimated at £110,000 over a set period of time, at the end of which she would easily get the money back on the sale of the horses, having further enhanced their reputation, their value and earned a little bit of prize money on the way.

Jack Barrie named the syndicate Keep the Colours Flying and was joined by George Thompson, June Norris, Simon White, Phil Banfield, Neil Warnock, Adrian Hopkins, Noel Cronin, Vera Bampton and another lady friend from Jersey, Irene Corbin. Their first horse, Strat's Legacy, was a gift from Tony's sister June as it was Tony's first-born colt from his recently formed breeding campaign. Strat's Legacy won more than ten races and led to the syndicate acquiring Strat's Quest who won a further ten. The syndicate continued to keep Tony's colours flying for some 16 years after his death.

Only too pleased to help in keeping Tony's memory alive, George Thompson was happy to become part of a successful racing syndicate alongside some newfound friends. "This time we were in the winners' enclosure," says George, who has a greater claim than anyone to be called Tony Stratton Smith's oldest friend. "It was September 1990 and during the next four weeks I had four winners, including Strat's Legacy, as part owner in Prenonamos, Appliance Of Science and Love Legend, who won the Portland. Love Legend was, of course, at one time, Strat's horse. It gave us all so much pleasure, especially sharing it with Pam Yeomans, Di Arbuthnot's mother and with trainer David Arbuthnot. Wouldn't Strat have been pleased."

Chapter 20

The Legacy

"The world is a richer place because of him. Many words have been used to describe him. Bon viveur, raconteur, delightful host, ardent patriot are a few that spring to mind. However, I'll best remember him as a generous romantic. A romantic because he made dreams come true – generous because they were all other people's."

Jack Barrie, comrade

Strat's Legacy was an appropriate name for the racehorse in which George Thompson had a share but the enduring legacy of Tony Stratton Smith isn't confined to the name of a horse. There was a major race, too. Traditionally, the Marlborough Stakes was an ungraded conditions race for three-year-olds held over five furlongs at Newbury racecourse, but in 1992 it was renamed in Tony's memory and for the next five years, the Tony Stratton Smith Memorial Stakes became a regular event in the September racing calendar. It was expanded in 1993 to include thoroughbreds aged three years or older and the name of the race was eventually changed to the World Trophy in 1997 when Dubai Airport took over the sponsorship, after which the event held Listed status and in 2002 was promoted to Group 3 level.

In 1993, Virgin Records released a magnificent four-CD box set featuring the best of Tony's artists on The Famous Charisma Label. It was the brainchild of former staffer Paul Conroy who, after spells at Stiff Records, WEA and Chrysalis had taken over the role of President at Virgin Records UK in 1992. "Virgin had obviously bought the Charisma rights some years earlier and as part of my remit as the incoming overseer of the label, I needed to maximise the sales where I could," he recalls. "Having worked for Strat and Gail as almost my first main job in the music biz, I always had more than a soft spot for the label, my time with it and of course its eclectic set of artists."

Timed to coincide roughly with the 25th anniversary of his old company, Conroy knew exactly the man to bring the whole thing together and handed over the task to his old mate, Glen Colson. It must be said that Colson did a fabulous job, wading through piles of master tapes that hadn't seen the light of day for many years, collating memorabilia from the archive and commissioning some excellent montage photography from Adrian Boot.

331

"Glen was the obvious choice of person to pull everything together," says Conroy, "and by crossing his palm with a reasonable amount of silver, he did a splendid job. It's a brilliant collection of Charisma music over the years and while it didn't break any sales records, it certainly got released or exported to all the various Virgin labels worldwide."

Nevertheless, *The Famous Charisma Box* sold out its limited run and reviewers noted how it was assembled as a fitting tribute to Tony's wide-ranging tastes, with journalist Fred Dellar opting for a racing analogy in his review: "Like some of Strat's horses, this release must rate at 500-1 in the chart stakes, but in terms of sheer fascination, it's a winner all the way."

Reviewing the compilation for *Record Collector* magazine, Patrick Humphries happily agreed that, "*The Charisma Box* is a beautiful potpourri. Spread over four CDs, it brilliantly captures the eclecticism of the label while reminding you that, along the way, Charisma produced some great pop records... The real joy in this box is to be found on the third CD, 'The Silver Tongued Years': 18 tracks which joyously celebrate Charisma's fondness for the spoken word... So great was the label's diversity that *The Charisma Box* shouldn't really work – and indeed there are some dud tracks spread over the discs. But as a testament to Tony Stratton Smith's idea of what a record label should be about – warts and all – it is a definitive record."

The cover of the box, and the lavish, album-sized book that came with it, both feature brilliant colour illustrations by Paul Slater, whose work is humorous, highly eccentric and populated with uniquely British characters. Who better, then, to conjure up Tony and his quirky roster of artists and friends? The box lid itself sees a beaming Strat as the Mad Hatter, holding court at the centre of the tea party from *Alice In Wonderland*; Peter Gabriel and Phil Collins appear as Tweedledum and Tweedledee, holding the record-shaped birthday cake, and Clifford T. Ward is Alice, while Dame Edna Everage becomes the grinning Cheshire cat. Dear old Viv Stanshall and Peter Hammill take their place at the table. Like a surreal snapshot of Tony's personal artistic vision, Monty Python's Eric Idle pours a cuppa for cricket commentator John Arlott, while Sir John Betjeman pokes his head, doormouse-like, out of the tea pot. More tea, vicar?

Inside, former *Melody Maker* writer Roy Hollingworth paints a loving portrait in words of the man at the centre of it all. "I see the big man cry 'Whoops!' and his dazzle brightens all around him for he is the Charisma King and magic touches all who follow him." Other contributors to the booklet included Peter Gabriel, Peter Hammill, 'Legs' Larry Smith, Jack Barrie, Cathy McKnight and Alan Hull, who wrote: "There was nobody quite like Strat in the music business. He was erudite and he was a gentleman. That was the difference. In a business largely noted for being cynical and uncaring, Strat cared."

The last word went to Jack Barrie: "My life has been enriched by knowing him", wrote Tony's greatest friend. "The world is a richer place because of him. Many words have been used to describe him. Bon viveur, raconteur, delightful host, ardent patriot are a few that spring to mind. However, I'll best remember him as a generous romantic. A romantic because he made dreams come true – generous because they were all other people's."

With the original vinyl albums becoming highly sought after, most of the Charisma artists now have their early work available on CD. A further compilation, *Refugees*, was released in 2003. Named after Tony's favourite Van der Graaf track, it is a handy three-CD set that concentrates mainly on the progressive rock pages of the Charisma catalogue.

Interest in the large and varied Charisma back catalogue has never diminished and there are a number of publications devoted to it, in which it is easy to get lost in the minutiae of matrix numbers, run-out groove messages and misprinted labels. These vary from the early pamphlets collated by Paul Pelletier to an enormous (and expensive) Russian limited edition tome by Yuri Grishin. Mark Jones' book *The Famous Charisma Discography* and Neil Priddey's collectors guide to the 'pink scroll' years are both highly recommended, as are the two colourful booklets by the Norwegian discographer Jørn R. Andersen – look for Parts 9 and 10 of his *Collectable UK Labels* series. On the internet, Mark J. Moerman has assembled an extremely comprehensive website devoted to the label and its history. The Famous Charisma Label lives on – both in print and online.

* * *

There is a general consensus that Tony should have been in line for some sort of official award or recognition. Even if he made an unlikely candidate to feel the weight of the Queen's sword on his shoulder, accompanied by the words 'Arise Sir Stratton Smith', then surely some sort of minor gong in the New Year Honours list would have been his, at the very least. Anthony Seddon is in total agreement: "He absolutely should, and had he not died so young, I think he would have had something by now. I believe there was a reason that nothing came his way earlier and I think that reason was to do with the debts – and that is a pity. The authorities could be quite small minded about these things. Okay, he did get into scrapes about his tax affairs, but having said that, he was also responsible for creating huge amounts of paid taxes, so you might have thought that would work in his favour, the number of his artists that generated royalties and from one or two other things. There definitely should have been some acknowledgement for his services to British music. Tony made a significant contribution that was not formally recognised in that way and that is a great pity."

While Tony may have gone largely unrecognised during his lifetime, one of the most pleasing, and thoroughly deserved, aspects of his legacy was the creation of 'The Strat' Award – and the growing number of top professionals who have been its proud recipient. Ever since Tony's death in March 1987 the industry broadsheet *Music Week* has included the prestigious 'Strat' at their annual awards ceremony, presenting it to those individuals considered to have made outstanding contributions to the UK music industry during their career.

In the months following his death, the *Music Week* editorial team of David Dalton, Jeff Clark-Meads and Dave Laing hatched the plan to honour the Charisma boss with this special award in his name. Throughout the build-up to the big day, the category was still billed as the 'Exemplary Service Award' but by the time of the next awards luncheon on February 22, 1988, the new name had been agreed and Island Records founder Chris Blackwell became the first recipient of 'The Strat'.

It stands as a fitting tribute to a true original, whose own outstanding contribution can be heard in the music of the many artists that started their career on his ground-breaking label. Long considered the highest honour at this annual event, its recipients include such music luminaries as Blackwell, Michael Eavis, Lucian Grainge, Paul McGuinness, Brian McLaughlin, Daniel Miller, Martin Mills, Maurice Oberstein, Rob Partridge, Jazz Summers, Tony Wadsworth, Pete Waterman and Muff Winwood. Of particular interest is that the Chrysalis team of Terry Ellis and Chris Wright, Tony's great rivals, jointly accepted the award in 1990; Richard Branson, the man who brought Tony's label, was the recipient in 1991; and Tony Smith, the man who inherited the good ship Genesis from his genial namesake, rightfully picked up the award in 1994.

On receiving the award in 2010, Lucian Grainge, chairman of the Universal Music Group declared: "Tony Stratton Smith and the label he founded, Charisma, typified the best in our business: understanding music, taking chances, and supporting those who are unique. I am honoured to receive this award in the name of a great music man."

Tony's charismatic life was brim-full of laughter, love and happiness. As the man himself once said, "One day such happiness should be celebrated with a book." So what would he have made of it all? He would, I imagine, have chuckled loudly, shaken his head in disbelief and wiped away a joyful tear. Then he'd buy everyone within earshot a large drink to toast such outrageous success.

"Anything good of its kind, dear boy," Tony Stratton Smith, this most avuncular of men, would have said as the glass touched his lips. "Anything good of its kind."

ACKNOWLEDGEMENTS

My sincere thanks go out to the following for their time and patience, assistance, encouragement and generous support. In a variety of ways, you have all helped enormously with this project:

Marcel Aeby, Steve Aldo, Robin Anders (Bob Anderson), Richard Anderson, John Anthony, David Arbuthnot, Kathleen Atkinson, James Atherton, Hugh Banton, Michael Barnes, Jack Barrie, Paul Barton, Roz Bea, Lloyd Beiny, Kenny Bell, Robert von Bernewitz, James Blake, Jerry Bloom, Scott Bomar, Tony Bramwell, Richard Branson, Chris Briggs, Steve Bunyan, Rodney Burbeck, Ian Campbell, Paolo Carnelli, Howie Casey, Chris Charlesworth, Barbara Charone, Andy Childs, Glen Christensen, Simon Christian, Jim Christopulos, Rod Clements, Gail Colson, Glen Colson, Paul Conroy, Simon Cowe, Jon Crawley, Joseph D'Morais, Martyn Day, Terence Dackombe, Steve Daggett, Simon Drake, Keith Emerson, Anthony Ferguson, Graham Field, Joe Flannery, Roy Flynn, Holly Fogg, Pete Frame, David Fricke, Peter Gabriel, Armando Gallo, Brian Gibbon, Paul Gibbon, Edward M. Gilbert, Michele Powers Glaze, Barry Glovsky, Brian Goff, Gillian Gould, Roger Greenaway, Jo Greenwood, Mary Grover, Bob Gruen, John Hackett, Steve Hackett, Peter Hammill, Charlie Harcourt, Colin Harper, Mike Heatley, Ernest Hecht, John Hedley, Dave Ian Hill, Roy Hollingworth, Patricia Hull, Angela Hyde-Courtney, Lee Jackson, Ray Jackson, Reina James, Derec Jones, Mark Jones, Fraser Kennedy, Terry King, Ray Laidlaw, Judd Lander, Anna Lawford, Don Lehnhoff, Roz Levy, Martin Lewis, Nancy Lewis-Jones, Armin Loetscher, Jude Lyons, Andrew MacHutchon, Neil Mackenzie Matthews, Richard Macphail, Beryl Marsden, Chris Mayfield, Cathy McKnight, Teddy Meier, Peter Mills, Billy Mitchell, Mark J. Moerman, Stuart Moody, Gerald T. Moore, Roy Morris, Justin Nash, Margaret and Reg Nend, Albert M Norris, Michael Palin, Jim Parker, Bernard Parkin, Annie Parsons, Don Paul, Adrian Paye, Jenny Pitman, Aubrey Powell, Perry Press, Sarah Radclyffe, Alan Reeves, Julia Revell, Colin Richardson, Ira Robbins, Lynda Roskott, Mark Rye, Frank Sansom, Brian Scovell, Adrian Sear, Anthony Seddon, Bob Sherwood, Eve Slater, Phil Smart, Kim Smith, Robin Smith, Tony Smith, Willy Spiller, Mark Sutherland, Shel Talmy, Bush Telfer, Jemma Tickner, George Thompson, Peter Thompson, John Tobler, Johnny Toogood, Mike van der Vord, Mark Ashton-Vey, Klaus Voormann, Rick Wakeman, Michael Wale, Barrington (Bazz) Ward, Chris Welch, Steve Weltman, Barry Wentzell, Howard Werth, Simon G. White, Paul Whitehead, Patricia Widdows, Trevor Williams, Dave Winslett, Chris Wright and Paul Zetter.

During the course of this project I personally interviewed well over 60 people and corresponded with a great many more, either via email or using good old-fashioned pen and paper. Consequently the majority of the quotes used in this book are from my own original sources. For those that came from an already published source I have endeavoured to mention the journalist or publication involved, and in most cases also tried to contact the authors for their permission. My apologies if there are any that I have missed.

I have used several quotes from the radio interview that Tony recorded with Joe Smith in 1986. These came from a transcript from the Joe Smith Collection at the Library of Congress, Washington, D.C. and I would like to thank Bryan Cornell, reference librarian at the Recorded Sound Reference Center, for his assistance.

Thanks also to my editor Chris Charlesworth, for his rigorous edit and structural engineering skills (he even agreed to take on the index), and to the eagle-eyed proofreader Lucy Beevor.

And finally, a huge thank you to my publisher, Jerry Bloom and the Wymer Publishing team for taking a Strat-like gamble and finally putting Tony's story into print.

BIBLIOGRAPHY

Cable, Michael. *The Pop Industry: Inside Out* (W.H. Allen, 1977)

Carruthers, Bob. *The Bonzo Dog Doo-Dah Band: Jollity Farm* (Angry Penguin, 2009)

Coleman, Ray. *Brian Epstein: The Man Who Made The Beatles* (Penguin Books, 1989)

Collins, Andrew. *Still Suitable For Miners: Billy Bragg* (Virgin Books, 1998)

Collins, Phil. *Not Dead Yet: The Autobiography* (Century, 2016)

Fricke, David. Tony Stratton Smith (*Trouser Press Collector's Magazine*, 1979)

Hanson, Martyn. *Hang On To A Dream: the Story of The Nice* (Foruli Classics, 2014)

Hedges, Dan. *Yes, The Authorised Biography* (Sidgwick & Jackson, 1981)

Hollingworth, Roy. Tony Stratton Smith interview (*Melody Maker*, 15 January 1972)

Judd, Neville. *Adventures Of A Folk Rock Troubadour* (Helter Skelter, 2001)

Machat, Steven. Gods, Gangsters And Honour (*Melody Maker*, 15 January 1972)

Mackenzie Matthews, Neil. *Snap: Music Photography* (Red Planet, 2020)

Pitman, Jenny. *Jenny Pitman: The Autobiography* (Bantam Books, 1999)

Southern, Terry. *A History Of Virgin Records* (Virgin Books, 1995)

Wale, Michael. Vox Pop: *Profiles Of The Pop Process* (Harrap, 1972)

Welch, Chris. *Close To The Edge: The Story Of Yes* (Omnibus Press, 1999

Welch, Chris. Tony Stratton Smith interview (*Melody Maker*, 23 February 1974)

Whittingham, Richard. *The Boy Wonder Of Wall Street* (Texere Publishing, 2003)

Wright, Chris. *One Way Or Another* (Omnibus Press, 2013)

Additionally, here are a number of print and online sources that I found extremely useful:

Chris Adams talks about Strat: The Famous Charisma Label website: www.charismalabel.com

String Driven Thing information – Dave Thompson: SDT website: www.stringdriventhing.com

Ray Jackson interview with Chris Kelly – Lindisfarne website: 2004

Beryl Marsden information – Mersey Beat website: www.triumphpc.com

Anthony Phillips interview – Genesis website: www.worldofgenesis.com

Ki Stanshall on the making of Sir Henry – Vivian Stanshall website:
www.gingergeezer.net

Richard Branson on Virgin's acquisition of Charisma – Virgin website:
www.virgin.com

Paul Whitehead interview with Jim Christopulos, 1977:
www.vandergraafgenerator.co.uk

Davey O'List quote from his 'Art Into Dust' online blog:
www.artintodust.blogspot.co.uk

Robert John Godfrey talking to Jon Berry for 'Progress', 1993: Progress
website: www.

Nik Turner talking to Tommy Hash for YTSEJAM, 1993: website:
www.YTSEJAM.com

Lloyd Beiny talking to Mark Rye about B&C: www.RockHistory.co.uk

National Youth Orchestra; interview with Bill Ashton from the Vinyl
Vulture website.

INDEX